For the fabulously narcissistic Moira.
I miss you every day.
You were the sharp edge of my blade
that dulled the day you died.

You can take your past with you,
but you can't go back.

LADY GAGA

What happens when life breaks down
When there is systemic contradiction?

RAVI ZACHARIAS

LIFELINE
TO MARIONETTE

A NOVEL

JENNIFER WAITTE

Published by Madim Larcy Literary
San Francisco, CA

Paperback ISBN: 978-1-7349322-0-1
eISBN: 978-1-7349322-1-8

Cover and Interior Design: GKS Creative
Project Management: The Cadence Group

1

From the top of the escalator, the airport terminal's wide corridor below looked like a swiftly flowing river of heads. As Michelle was lowered into its current, it became clear that she would be quickly swallowed up and carried away by the throng of people amassed into one giant, faceless centipede.

Michelle ducked into an alcove to save herself. She would not survive by trying to fight it, nor would she survive if she allowed it to swallow her up and become part of it. She couldn't even find the strength to remember how she had managed to get this far. But somehow, she had, and she reminded herself of that.

Her frail body shuddered as she fell back against a row of lockers, sinking slowly to the ground, shrinking further inside the heavy, baggy clothes that concealed her. She felt hot, cold, edgy, afraid. She pressed her palms to her temples and tried to squeeze out the deafening echo of a thousand feet moving across the dirty tile floor just a yard away from where she crouched. She lifted her face from its stifling hiding place between her chest and her knees. The locker rattled and vibrated as she knocked the back of her head against it. All she wanted was a single breath of fresh air to clear her mind enough to get herself together, get up, and continue on. But there was no fresh air in the alcove, or in the airport, or anywhere in the city on that day, and so her mind remained clouded.

Boarding the plane in Zurich was now only a vague memory, but she could recall with frightening clarity being huddled in the last seat, with her face pressed against the cool window, pleading as she always did for time to pass quickly and for the ordeal to be over. It wasn't over.

For as long as she could remember, her prayers had always included some wish to be catapulted forward in time. *Please, God, bring this day or this week or this event to an end. Please, God, let me skip the rest of this year. Please, God, make it tomorrow. I can't bear another minute of today.*

And yet, for all the days that dragged after one another in precise succession, so unyielding they made her question her belief in anything, the summation of her life to this point was like the history of the earth. Although in existence for what seemed to be an inconceivable eternity, her life was composed of large expanses of unaccountable, unexplainable gaps punctuated by instances so profound that each occurrence altered the course of her life with an impact such as were found in the forces of nature.

Everywhere she went, she felt the eyes on her, burning into her. Strangers stared. They followed her with their curious gazes. They frowned at her, and when she stiffened her back in resentment, they scowled deeper. *Let them stare. I don't care.* That was her chant, and she repeated it to herself until it became the rod rammed down her spine that kept her head up.

On the airplane, she could clearly remember looking down the runway, thinking how impossibly long it seemed, and yet wondering, despite its length, how anything as large as an airplane could lift off into the air before reaching the end. *How ironic. How bizarre. Run, run, down the way. Then fly or die. Reach for the stars that explode in your face. Michelle, Michelle, Michelle! Over here! Smile pretty so I can blind you.*

She worked her hand underneath the layers of her clothes to an inside pocket. It was there, somewhere. Just as her groping fingers closed around the tiny glass vial, a boarding pass fluttered to the ground in front of her, followed by a frantic passenger flinging himself into the alcove to retrieve it. The ticket landed inches from her feet, and the large, dark-haired hand that chased it passed so close to her face that she flinched. Their eyes met and Michelle's heart lurched to its place in her throat. Then he was gone. The eyes were gone. But once again, as if he had pointed a finger at her to flush her out, she could feel the anxiety creeping up on her. It slithered toward her, searching the crowded corridors of the airport for her. It would catch her if she stopped too long. She forced herself to her feet and fell back into a gap in the centipede's legs.

Outside the airport terminal, a cold, dirty, New York December wind attacked her. She hurried for a taxi.

"West Sixty-Fourth and CPW, please," she managed to say, avoiding the eyes in the rearview mirror.

As the car lurched away, she braced her feet to keep from sliding across the stained vinyl seat. The smell of the taxi nauseated her as she set herself up to endure yet another endless journey.

The doorman moved forward to open the glass door, nodding apprehensively in recognition, yet at the same time acknowledging that he did not recognize her. It was like a code. Those who did not wish to be seen weren't. Their eyes did not meet and his gaze did not follow her as she passed. If asked, he would not recall having seen her at all.

Her shoes made a familiar tap-tap sound across the marble floor, but the familiarity brought her no comfort. She clenched her fists as she waited for the elevator, wanting it to arrive more quickly than it could. When it finally did, its confines were unbearable, and its ascent gave her a sick, heavy feeling that pulled her stomach to her feet.

The elevator's digital counter stopped on twelve and the door opened to a long, carpeted hall so plush that, in it, no loud sound could retain its sharpness. She followed the cream-colored path to her door. For a moment she just stared blankly at the keypad on the wall beside the ornate doorknob. Then the numbers came to her. The lock clicked and she opened it.

As she closed her apartment door behind her, locking it, she felt relieved to be locked inside, as if the white door that stood between her and the world outside was a sufficient barricade. It wasn't, but the silence was. The bleak whiteness of the apartment was too bright for her. She had once loved its whiteness. Now, she wanted everything dark. She pushed her cap off her head, brushing her neglected hair away from her eyes. She felt hot again. Sinking down onto the white marble floor of the foyer, she pressed her cheek to the spotlessly polished stone. It was cool on her skin. The nausea returned and her stomach lurched, but the bile rose only as far as her throat before sinking back to her stomach. *I should call someone. Sasha? Rita? No.* They would be looking for her. They would find her. Eventually, yes, without calling anyone, she would be found. It was just a matter of time.

Time. It was eight o'clock in the morning, but she did not know that, nor did she know for certain what day it was. On crumpled receipts in her pocket were printed various dates; the only substantial evidence that she had actually passed from one point to another. But now those dates were just numbers that meant nothing to her. She hadn't looked at them when they were given to her and she didn't look at them now. She felt herself fading away.

Rita Herron paced her office frantically, throwing desperate glances at Sasha, who remained just inside the doorway, out of her way. He leaned casually against the wall, seemingly devoid of concern, looking past her and out the window. The window was closed, but the sounds from the rue du Faubourg Saint-Honoré still found their way in.

The Nouveaux Créateurs de Mode show was over now, and Sasha was relieved. What was supposed to have been a landmark event had been a disaster. And still scurrying up and down the halls outside Rita's Paris office was the whimpering aftermath of that disaster. The show should have been an enormous success. But, as it so often is in this city of haute couture, disaster could strike in any form at any time. Still, no one could have guessed that the disappearance of one small person would trigger such a monumental undermining of the American dream in Paris. The show was over, and there would be other shows. Michelle's whereabouts were still unknown, but this wasn't the first time. They'd been through this so many times before that Sasha could no longer even pretend to be worried, as Rita clearly was.

"Just find her!" She barked at him.

Sasha absorbed her anger, unaffected by it. He frowned sourly, but nodded in acknowledgment. His eyes wandered absently around the room as Rita repeated the fragments of evidence she had, her voice wavering. His mind pushed her voice as far into the background as he could. Certainly, he thought cynically, in the four days since Michelle's disappearance, Rita had already found plenty to cry about, not necessarily out of worry for Michelle.

Fortunately, Michelle was easily tracked, as long as she kept moving. It was when she no longer had the strength to continue on that finding her became difficult. And time was always a factor. They had last seen her at the couture show, where she was supposed to be, doing what she was supposed to be doing. Then she was gone. It was almost an afterthought by the time they had come to some sort of agreement that she was actually absent. The show concluded without her, but her absence destroyed it.

That was four days ago. Two days ago, she had flown to New York under her real name, charging her ticket. If she had gone to her apartment, no one could recall seeing her there. More than likely she was still in New York, which meant finding her could prove impossible. And, unfortunately, since Michelle was nose-diving into day five of her disappearance, she had to be dangerously close to the end of the line.

Sasha no longer looked at the photographs of Michelle on the wall when he came into Rita's office. He used to gloat over them, but now they made him sick. She was his best work, but only because he was so good at hiding the evidence.

"You'll have to go to New York. Can you go to New York? How soon can you leave?" Rita fired at him.

Sasha only nodded. Yes, he would go. Of course, he would go. He lived there. What Rita really meant was would he leave this minute and go search for Michelle? Of course, he would. Who else would take on such a task? Who else would know where to start looking for her? Annalise and Marc would be going back to New York soon—if they hadn't left already. Annalise would know where to look, and might even try to find her, but Marc would only want her found if it meant dredging the Hudson. She had killed his show, thus killing him. The only thing he'd ever dress Michelle in again would be a body bag. Rita would also be returning to New York. This had been her gig. Everyone else involved felt angry and defeated. Rita had failed. But that wasn't to be talked about.

"Is there any way that she could have found out about our plans?" Rita asked.

"No, I already told you," Sasha replied. "There's no way she could have known. Annalise and I didn't talk about it at the show, and I didn't say a word to anyone else. There's no way she could have found out."

"But that would have explained her leaving," Rita responded.

Sasha agreed. If she had discovered what they had conspired to confront her with after the show, she certainly would have fled Paris. But that would have been just another reason on top of the ones she already had.

Sasha shook his head. The show had been exhausting. He was physically tired from lack of sleep and mentally tired from supporting Michelle day in and day out. Supporting her meant covering for her and covering for her meant being on the constant lookout for that monster, Marc Montori. Sasha had become damn good at both hiding her and hiding from her at the same time. *I'm just a fucking makeup artist, for Christ's sake.*

But in spite of everything that had happened at the show, he couldn't blame Michelle for what she did. He was angry with her, but he didn't blame her. If he had her life to live, he would probably do the same thing.

Rita finally stopped pacing. "What if she ODs again? What about the mess that will cause?" Rita hovered before him. "She was shooting up at the show, wasn't she?"

He backed away from her and rubbed his eyes, trying to push the strain he felt in them back into the depths of his brain. He was growing more tired by the minute.

"I wouldn't be surprised," Sasha replied, neither confirming nor denying Rita's suspicion. "How in the hell do you think she gets through the insanity of it all?" He turned his back on Rita. He'd had enough. "I'll find her," he said, walking out.

2

Smoke swirled around the moving bodies, but the ricocheting neon lights cut through them, adding a jagged dimension to the maze. The girl was no older than twenty, and yet she looked aged beyond normal life; she looked dead, but alive. Heavy, dark eye makeup circled her already sunken eyes. Her hair was jet black and stringy. It was long, greasy, and unkempt, and smelled of her body and cigarette smoke: sour. She was an emaciated apparition that barely survived the days to live the nights. A heavy chain, with the letter *S* for Serena dangling from it, hung around her neck. But Serena wasn't her real name, just what she called herself. No one knew her real name; no one cared.

Serena forced her way around the perimeter of the crowded dance floor. "Sasha, come quick! She's here!" Serena screamed above the heavy, reverberating music. She grabbed his arm. "She's really sick. You gotta get her out of here!"

The bathroom was crowded, and the stench of cigarettes and perfume was soured by rifts of vomit, urine, and sweat. Serena and Sasha pushed through the crowd to a closed stall door.

"Michelle? It's Sasha. Open the door."

Sasha rapped on the warped, graffiti-covered plywood door. Hearing no response, he grabbed the top of the door and easily hoisted himself over it. Michelle was collapsed sideways across the floor of the stall, barely conscious. Sasha knelt down over her, propping her up against the wall. Her head wobbled as she tried to look up at him through glazed-over eyes. Her normally alabaster skin was now a ghostly gray.

"Why do you do this to yourself?" he muttered, shaking his head in disgust. He pulled his shirt over his head and, unlocking the door, handed it to Serena. "Get this wet."

Not bothering to be gentle with her, he wiped the vomit from Michelle's face and chest. He had to double her over to pull her matted hair away from her face and twist it down her back.

"Somebody get me a coat. And get everyone out of the bathroom!" Sasha yelled back to Serena, who still stood staring at Michelle from just over Sasha's shoulder.

"Jesus! She gonna be all right?" she asked, more out of curiosity than concern.

Sasha ignored the question. He wrapped Michelle in an overcoat, covering her face. He lifted her easily—she didn't weigh much—and carried her in his arms like a small child. Ahead of him, a bouncer pushed people away so they could make it to the rear exit of the club.

Sasha was almost to the door when a long, elegant hand grabbed his arm. He glanced quickly over his shoulder. It was Annalise. She let go, saying nothing, because there was nothing to say. Sure, they were all in on it. Rita, Annalise, Marc, himself, and even Aaron Perlman. But they left the dirty work to Sasha. Annalise, especially, knew how to take a step back before anything got on her hands. They were the horses and he was the only hound. But it didn't matter what any one of them thought as individuals, because they all thought the same thing. So Annalise surprised him when she offered her chauffeured car. He accepted quickly, since the alternative was a taxi. The bitter night air bit into Sasha's back as he ducked into the car.

"Where do you want to take her?" she asked. "To the hospital? We could put an end to this right now."

"No," Sasha replied. "She's not that bad off," he lied. "Let's just take her home."

When Michelle finally awoke from what, to her, was another gap of blackness, no one greeted her with relief. She rubbed her eyes, trying to ease the pain. The room was dark, but she could see daylight seeping around the edge of the drapes. She had no idea what time it was, nor did she care. With a groan, she rolled over to find Sasha sitting on the sofa near her bed. They regarded each other for a while, then Michelle closed her eyes.

"Are you mad at me?" she asked, whispering because her throat was so dry. She already knew he was.

"Why would I be mad at you, Michelle?" Sasha replied harshly. He forced his voice to be stern, although he could not have honestly said that he cared anymore. "How much did you do?" he asked.

Michelle pulled the covers over her head, not wanting to answer him. Sasha sat down on the bed beside her and pulled the quilt back.

"I'm not kidding. I want to know."

"None." Michelle coughed, unable to tolerate the taste in her mouth. Her skull felt like it was going to split open from the pressure of her pounding brain.

Sasha handed her a glass of water, then picked up her right hand, because Michelle was left-handed. The spaces between three of her fingers told him everything he needed to know. When Michelle was sober and not too stressed, she would not shoot up. It scared her too much. She could go day after day just snorting heroin, but as soon as something set her off, she was jamming needles between her fingers and toes. At that point, whatever it was that set her off—usually Marc—was more frightening to her than the needle. And once she made it past the first needle, neither it nor Marc mattered anymore.

He was tempted to tell her how close she had come to dying—again—elaborating on every detail, because doing so would spark panic in her. She would skyrocket into a state of hysteria, because she was more afraid of dying than of anything else. He could paint for her such a vivid portrait of her near-last moments on earth that she would be on her knees pleading with him to stop, swearing that she'd never do it again. He used to like to pretend he didn't believe her, because that always sent her even further over the edge. It was sick, but she deserved it.

But he backed off this time, because no one was pretending anymore. He thought she looked bad, really bad. He didn't ask her where she had been for the last five days or why she had left the show. Those questions would come later.

"Annalise saw you last night," he said, not bothering to hide the spitefulness in his voice. Wanting, in fact, to be spiteful.

Michelle groaned. Closing her eyes, she turned away from him.

"When I was carrying you out," he continued, "after you had thrown up all over yourself."

Pulling a pillow over her head, she started to cry. Sasha pulled the pillow away.

"You should get yourself together and go see Rita," he said. "Otherwise I'm going to call her and tell her to come over here." He left Michelle's bedside and opened the drapes, filling the room with the blinding white daylight that she hated.

3
_____

Annalise L'Heurus entered Rita's New York office. Dressed in a cream-colored tailored suit and wearing only two-inch heels, she still stood well over six feet tall. Kissing Rita on the cheek, she took a seat across from Rita's desk.

"Bonjour. Marc is coming," Annalise said with a heavy French accent.

Rita studied her proudly. Annalise always conducted herself in a professional manner, even more so now that she was married. *It so suited her,* Rita thought. Annalise had taken her modeling career and turned it into a highly successful enterprise. Annalise L'Heurus was a wise, wealthy, beautiful woman, and it showed. She didn't work as much now; she didn't need to. With a multimillion-dollar, multi-year cosmetic contract and her recent marriage to one of New York's top up-and-coming designers, Annalise did not need to work at all.

Marc came briskly into the office, greeting Rita as Annalise had, with a kiss on her cheek. It was almost as if, having all fled the barrage in Paris to put as much distance between themselves and the ugly rumors that were circulating the European fashion scene, with every French designer wondering where their precious Michelle was and wanting her back, and with Michelle's reappearance in New York, the crisis was over. Marc gave the impression, now that he was back in his city, he didn't give a shit what the Europeans were saying. That wasn't true and Rita knew it, so his casual and cordial attitude toward her made her cautious.

"You must be excited about your holiday," Rita said.

Annalise only nodded, suspicious. It would have been appropriate for Rita to say something like "Well, at least we found her," or "Thank God she didn't OD," or "You should have committed her while you had the chance," or "What in the hell do we do now?" But not "You must be excited about your holiday." Rita wanted something, something that had to do with their trip to Colorado, the trip they almost canceled, but now couldn't wait for.

"Well!" Rita crossed her hands on her desk, leaning toward them. "I know how busy you are, Marc, so I won't waste your time. I want you to drop this nonsense about Michelle."

Marc laughed dryly. He said what Rita expected him to say. "No." He had already thought long and hard about this. He could sue Michelle for walking out in the middle of the biggest show of his career, but that wouldn't hurt her enough. Probably wouldn't hurt her at all. He wanted to do something that would hurt her intensely, and he knew what that was. Michelle was under contract with him. He had originally agreed to go along with their planned hiatus for Michelle, which meant that after the Paris show he would release her from her obligations to him. But now, after walking out on his show, she was going to work out the rest of her contract if it killed her.

"I don't care how sick she is," Marc said.

He didn't have to say more, because, even though they could sit across from one another and be civil about it, he would, and could, sue both Michelle and Rita for every job with him that she missed. That would hurt Rita. So, if Rita still wanted to have Michelle committed to rehab, then she would have to do it without interfering with Marc's schedule, which included his New Year's Eve benefit in Aspen, Colorado. But the fact that he and Annalise were leaving for Aspen early to spend Christmas there was none of Rita's business.

Rita remained quiet for a moment, having received the response she expected. "Then I have a favor to ask," she finally said, sounding sincere. "If you won't take her out of your next show, then take her with you."

Marc and Annalise looked at each other, then back at Rita. "Take her where?" Annalise asked.

"To Aspen," Rita replied.

"But we're leaving tomorrow," Annalise said.

Rita nodded. "I know you're leaving tomorrow, and I'd like you to take Michelle with you."

Annalise looked back and forth between her husband and Rita, while the complications of what Rita was asking gradually set in.

"You want us to take her . . . tomorrow?" Already Annalise was shaking her head. "Rita, I saw her last night. She needs to go to a hospital, not to Aspen, and certainly not with us tomorrow."

"I know all about last night," Rita replied.

Marc snorted in disgust. "If you two are so determined to play out this scheme, then why in the hell didn't you commit her last night when you had the chance? Christ! She was practically comatose. How hard could it have been to drive her to a hospital, then let the doctors commit her?"

"Because she would have freaked," Rita replied. "You know that, Annalise knew that, and Sasha knew that."

"Yeah, so what?" Marc snapped. "You should have dumped her off and been done with it. There are a lot of things Michelle doesn't need right now, including a holiday in Aspen. She can fly out with everyone else. I don't care what you do with her between now and then; just make sure she's there when she's supposed to be."

Rita remained calm, taking her time to carefully prepare her explanation. "We've all already agreed that she needs to be committed to a drug program, but not in New York. Had everything gone as planned, she would have been in Grenoble by now, but she's not, and I can't get her on a plane back to France without her suspecting. But I can get her to Aspen, because you are going."

"So what's in Aspen?" Annalise asked.

"Aaron Perlman," replied Rita. "There's a hospital there, a reputable one. It's quiet and private. Aaron thinks that's where she needs to be. I'm just asking you to get her there. I want her to have some time off, get some fresh air. If you won't let her out of your show, then take her with you. Aaron thinks he can ease her into it."

"After my show," Marc said.

"She's in no condition to work right now," Rita replied, knowing she would have to do whatever she could to get Michelle together by New Year's Eve.

"Does Michelle know about this?" Annalise asked.

"Of course not," Rita replied. "I don't even know yet if I can get her on the plane with you. Sasha is bringing her in this afternoon."

Annalise was shaking her head. "Even if I wanted to take her tomorrow—which I don't—I think you are asking the wrong person. Michelle and I haven't exactly been on the best of terms lately." She looked at her husband. "Even if everything between the three of us was fine, you're also asking us to deal with something I don't know I can deal with."

Rita looked at Annalise, who had been Michelle's friend for so many years, and whose marriage to Marc was part of Michelle's dive into self-destruction. "Annalise, it's almost Christmas," Rita said. "What will she do? Spend the next two weeks here in New York? With Sasha?"

Annalise scowled. "And have another night like she did last night."

"And what if she does? And what if you or Sasha can't get to her in time?" Rita pleaded.

"Then we'd all be relieved of a huge headache," Marc said.

Rita just looked at him, knowing he was only being sarcastic. He needed Michelle in this show.

Annalise sighed. "I'm sorry Rita, but the last thing I want to do is take her with us. Please understand; I am so tired of her, the way she acts, the things she does. It's like she's saying, 'See Annalise? See what you've done to me?' She has a drug problem, Rita. We all know that. We've all tried to help her. She doesn't need to go to Aspen; she needs to go to rehab."

"I agree, but we all know she won't go," Rita replied. "I also know she doesn't want to do your show, but I think she'll go with you to Aspen if the two of you could make some sort of peace. That might be the first step toward getting her together."

"Rita, she will do the same things in Aspen that she does anywhere else," Annalise replied. "It's not going to make a difference. It's only going to make us miserable."

"There are drugs in Aspen, too, Rita," Marc said. "She can get them wherever she wants. You know that."

"I don't want her to stay at the hotel," Rita pressed. "She would be alone there. The other girls aren't flying in until the day before the show. I want her to stay with you or Aaron," Rita added, remaining calm.

Annalise owed her—a lot. Annalise just needed to convince Marc of that.

"I want you to take her." Rita got up from behind her desk. "I'll give you a minute to talk about it." She left her office, closing the door behind her.

Annalise didn't look at Marc. "I can't say no to Rita. You know that."

Marc threw his arms up. "I can't believe this. First, we wind up having to practically evacuate Paris because of the disaster she caused there. I don't even feel like I can show my face, much less my collections, anywhere in Europe after that debacle. And now we're supposed to pack her along on our Christmas vacation like it never happened? Think about it, Annalise. Do you think we'll have a quiet couple of weeks to ourselves? Or will the media be breathing down our backs like they were in Paris? Do you actually think it's possible to take her with us tomorrow to Keith's? Just like that?"

"How do you think Keith will feel about that?" Annalise asked.

"How will Keith feel?" Marc snapped back. "What about how I feel?"

"Marc, we have to take her. People are talking. And they aren't talking about her; they are talking about you." Annalise lowered her voice. "If we take her with us and make it look like everything is fine between you two, then maybe it will curb some of this bad press. If Aaron Perlman wants her once we get there, fine. But I think if people see us all together, it will be for the better."

Marc scowled. He hated the bad publicity that he was always getting because of Michelle. And Michelle was everywhere. She was the media darling. She could do no wrong. She could probably shoot up on national television and, somehow, he would be blamed. He let Annalise's words stew for a moment. She had a point. Some happy holiday photos of them together in Aspen might be just the thing to get him off the Paris blacklist. "But she stays with Aaron," he finally said. "I won't share a house with her."

"Yes, but let's be tactful about that," Annalise said. "We have a lot we need to gain back and . . ." She pointed a finger at her husband. "Rita is probably thinking the same thing."

"But if she goes on another binge, this could really blow up in our faces," Marc warned.

"We'll have to make sure that she doesn't," Annalise replied

"Easier said." Marc glared at his wife.

"Just be civil to her or stay away from her," she said. "She'll stay clean so long as she's not freaked out about something."

Marc nodded as a plan slowly came together in his mind. He would agree to this, but he also had his own agenda.

Rita looked up at the framed poster of Michelle that hung behind her desk. Little Michelle, bigger than life, bigger than anything or anyone. A multimedia megastar. That was what the fashion world called her. To the rest of the world, she was an enigma, and the world was fascinated with her. Rita removed her glasses, rubbing her eyes. Michelle was number one, and had been for almost four years. She reigned as the highest-paid model in the world. She was an international celebrity whose face bankrolled anyone who used it, and she was very, very wealthy. Even with twenty years in the business, Rita was still astounded by the amount of money people were willing to pay to have Michelle Seko. And yet the Michelle Seko that the world saw had become further and further removed from the Michelle who lived within the body of this incredible image. The conflict was enormous. Michelle was no longer this person. She was in trouble, serious trouble.

It amazed Rita that Michelle had held up as long as she had. Michelle was not a strong person to begin with, and she seemed to be constantly facing a bombarding influx of immeasurable personal obstacles. But somehow, she managed to hold herself together for what Rita considered to be a very long time. It wasn't until Annalise's engagement that Michelle started to crack, and Rita realized it had been Annalise who had held Michelle together for so long. And now, with Annalise removed from her life, they were all watching Michelle fall to pieces before their very eyes.

The biggest problem with the whole situation was its delicacy. Michelle was not a strong, independent individual. She needed to be with someone who cared about her. But those people were numbered. Annalise had always been that person, but Annalise had found Marc and a whole new life that didn't include Michelle. Annalise had certainly done nothing wrong. It was Michelle, if anyone, who had made the situation so complicated.

Rita looked back up at the poster. She hoped by sending her to Aspen she was doing the right thing. Annalise was being tolerant far beyond fair. And Marc, too. But the whole situation was a land mine. All it would take would be one incident, like the one at the Paris couture show, and their careers would be blown apart. Rita hoped Annalise understood the situation would not cure itself by simply sending Michelle to drug rehab, because drugs were not the root of Michelle's problems. Rather, drugs had become what Michelle thought to be her only solution—the only way to escape in her mind what she could not escape otherwise. Michelle needed to be free of the reasons she did drugs. Rita knew that a few weeks in Aspen would not solve them all, but perhaps it would lift her spirits enough that some real progress could then be made. Unfortunately, saving Michelle was going to be a full-time job for someone, and that someone was neither Rita nor Annalise. She looked down at the envelope on her desk. Maybe that someone was Aaron Perlman.

Michelle entered the office without making a sound. Rita looked up and suddenly she was there—a pale, frail little girl folded up into one of her chairs. Rita smiled at her. Michelle smiled back, but she did not look well. She looked sick and tired. Wearing old tattered jeans, a faded, baggy sweater and a floppy cashmere beret that concealed only part of her face but all of her long, blonde hair. She looked sixteen. She was twenty-two. Rita's eyes moved to another photograph of Michelle, one of her favorites that hung on the wall behind her. It was hard to believe this frail, eggshell of a human being sitting in her office was the same person. The sad part about it *was* that it was the same person.

Rita studied Michelle, noticing her trembling hands. Little Michelle, barely five feet six, barely one hundred pounds, was the biggest phenomenon in the industry. Everyone loved her; everyone wanted her. And when they got her, or even got near her, she left them speechless. She was this tiny person with the face and aura of an angel, always so soft-spoken, always smiling, who could not help but soften any harshness in those around her. She was a freak, and being a freak automatically made her an outsider. And not only did Michelle want desperately not to be an outsider, the contradiction between the image she projected and the turmoil inside her was killing her.

"I know about last night," Rita said, mentioning nothing about Michelle's disappearance from the show.

Michelle made no reply, but only plucked absent-mindedly at the frayed hole in the knee of her jeans.

"Michelle, honey, we all care about you." Rita knew to be careful of what she said and how she said it. Michelle did not mean to do the damage that she did to herself. Her body simply couldn't take what her mind craved. "It's only going to take that one time that Sasha can't get there for you . . . just one time that he might not be there for you. Do you know how awful he would feel?"

Michelle just sat there, plucking, saying nothing.

"I talked to Annalise and Marc this morning," Rita continued. "They're leaving for Aspen tomorrow. They want you to go with them."

Michelle tilted her head back, exposing her finely sculpted throat. She closed her eyes. "I find that hard to believe," she said with her quiet, delicate French accent.

"We all think it's a good idea," Rita said. "Take some time off and have some fun. Get some fresh air and exercise. It will be good for you."

"Where will I stay?" Michelle asked.

"With Annalise, if you'd like," Rita replied. "They're staying with a friend. Apparently, it's a very large house. Aaron will be there. If something doesn't work out, then you can stay with him, okay?" She handed Michelle the heavy, brown envelope. "He sent this for you."

Rita didn't mention that the envelope had originally been sent to Paris, and Rita was to have given it to her there. After Michelle disappeared, Rita had carried it around with her while they all waited for Michelle to resurface. "He wants you to call him as soon as you get there," Rita said.

Michelle took the envelope, but did not open it. She knew what it was.

"Is Sasha going?" Michelle asked.

"Right now, he's booked, but I can try and change his schedule if you want him there," Rita replied.

"It would be nice," Michelle said.

Rita made a notation, already thinking that having Sasha there might not be the best thing for Michelle. He was her stylist, and no doubt being Michelle's stylist had elevated his career. But since Annalise's marriage, he had also become her chauffeur, bodyguard, babysitter, night watchman, nurse, and closest friend. At this point, Michelle was lucky to have him. He was always there to help her, but his help was not necessarily the kind of help she needed. Too keen to the damages of scandal, he sometimes protected her more from the press than he did from herself. But that was not necessarily the problem. Just that morning, Sasha had admitted he needed a break from her. Her dependency on him was wearing him out. Rita was afraid that if she sent Sasha to Aspen for the show, Michelle would want to come back to New York with him. Rita needed to make sure she stayed in Aspen.

"One more thing, Michelle." Rita's tone became solemn. "No drugs. I don't want you to take any with you and I don't want you to do any when you get there. Nothing. And try not to drink." She handed Michelle another folder. "Promise?" she asked, although knowing how pointless her request actually was.

Michelle nodded.

"Now go home and stay home," Rita said. "I'll send a car to pick you up in the morning."

It was as if the incident in Paris had never happened.

Michelle and Sasha sat across from each other. She only picked at her salad, taking small, uninterested bites of it. People in the restaurant were watching her, although she seemed not to notice.

"So, after all that's happened, you're really going to go?" Sasha asked.

Michelle nodded, almost not believing it herself. "Tomorrow morning," she replied. "At least it's someplace I've never been." She didn't mention Aaron Perlman.

"I'll help you pack," Sasha offered. "Then you'll be all ready to go." He wanted her on that plane tomorrow as much as Rita did. Offering to help her pack would keep her home. Why, though, he wondered, was she so neutrally agreeing to this? He might accept her agreeing to go, but with Marc and Annalise? Why would she voluntarily commit herself to such a situation? He was dying to know, but he didn't ask. There was never any point in asking Michelle questions. Her answers were always ambiguous—if she answered at all.

Later, they sat on her living room floor, listening to a compilation of Mozart's piano concertos, among Michelle's favorites. Surrounding them were piles of down-filled jackets and ski pants that he had pulled from one of the back bedrooms. Michelle's apartment was a stockpile of clothing samples from many of her hundreds of photo shoots, few of which she ever actually wore.

Sasha took a quick inventory and packed several suitcases. Michelle made only a small effort to help with his selections. She didn't think about clothes; she was too accustomed to having someone else do that for her. Clothes were work, and Michelle didn't want to think about work.

They talked lightly, but Sasha was careful not to mention Paris, Marc, or the upcoming New Year's Eve show. He didn't want to say or do anything that would jeopardize Michelle's departure. After a while, after spurts of scattered, fragmented conversation, they had nothing left to talk about at all, and so Sasha went home. It was no longer like the old days, when they would stay up all night, talking about *everything*. Sasha no longer knew what to say, and Michelle never felt like talking. He contemplated staying, just to keep her from going out, but the need to get out was too great.

"I'll be back in the morning," he said as he walked to the door. "I'll take you to breakfast." He paused. "Promise me you won't go anywhere tonight."

Michelle nodded. She was tired.

"Michelle?" Sasha wanted more than a nonverbal acknowledgement.

She knew what he meant. *Don't go out and don't check out, either.* She shrugged him off. She had what she needed to get out of bed in the morning, to get through the day, and to sleep at night, but she denied this to Sasha. After he left, Michelle curled up in her bed. She had promised not to go out, and she kept her promise, but only because there was nothing drawing her out or trying to flush her out.

Under the soft light of her reading lamp, she opened the envelope from Aaron Perlman and removed the script. *The Ballerina* was typed on the cover, and below it a handwritten note from Aaron, telling her to take her time reading the script. Michelle gazed at the title for a long while. Memories of her child-hood—painful, buried memories—came to the surface of her thoughts. She closed her eyes, fighting the sadness. She had known this would happen. She had known the script was coming, and she had anticipated that reading it would bring back memories she'd tried for so long to forget. They returned before she'd even read a word of it.

It was December in Aspen and all the kings had come down from their mountains. Keith Bennett surveyed his dining room. The big boys had come out to play and it was a full house. They were all here, the movie stars, multimillionaires, models, and rock stars, many of whom owned vacation homes there. It would be hard to imagine the combined worth of the people dining at Andiamo at that very moment, but the thought made Keith smile to himself. He supervised the dining room with the skillful eye of someone with many years in the restaurant business and many years in this town. He knew the people who came here and what they expected. It was his job to see that their expectations were met.

There was something unique about Aspen. This jaded town had the best of everything to offer its guests—the best food, wine, shopping, and, of course, skiing, all incorporated into the most pretentious atmosphere possible. People who were bigger than life came here because they could be themselves, be left alone to enjoy themselves yet still be treated with the respect and sense of priority they'd come to expect from life. Aspen was certainly accommodating to the rich and famous. And, even to them, Aspen was a dearly appreciated luxury.

"Looks like you've got everything under control," Keith commented to Ruben, his assistant manager. "I'll be upstairs if you need me." Keith pushed through the double doors at the end of the bar and went upstairs.

Last year, the offices over the restaurant had vacated and Keith jumped at the chance to expand. He had remodeled the entire space, adding a larger office for himself and a private bar at the request of some of his closer friends. The main bar, situated in the center of the dining room and all its activity, sometimes got too crowded and too loud for some of his patrons. At first, Keith thought the upstairs lounge would breed some resentment, as it was open only to certain people at certain times. But, so far, it hadn't been a problem. His friends had been primarily taking advantage of its privacy for late-night parties. Movie producer Aaron Perlman had reserved the lounge for himself and his friends on both Christmas Eve and New Year's Eve. Keith had no problem making that kind of arrangement.

"Jason Henrey's on line two for you," Ruben said over the intercom as Keith entered his office.

Keith punched the flashing button on the phone. "Hey, buddy, where the hell are you?" Keith asked, leaning back in his chair.

"I've just been busy," Jason replied. "Been trying to get there for a week."

Jason Henrey was one of Keith's closest friends. Andiamo was the most successful restaurant in Aspen thanks to Jason. He had helped Keith out financially years ago, and it had paid off for both of them. Backing Keith had been pocket change to Jason; he was one of the wealthiest men Keith knew, and certainly one of Aspen's wealthiest residents. Even though time and ambition had pulled Jason away from Aspen, and he spent less time here than he used to, they were still close.

"So, are you going to make it?" Keith asked.

"Hopefully tomorrow," Jason replied. "Is everything good there?"

"The place is a madhouse," Keith said.

"That's good," Jason replied. "I'll see you tomorrow."

After hanging up the phone, Keith sat at his desk for a minute, thinking. The holidays were going to be exceptional this year. The ski areas had opened early for the season, and the restaurant was doing well. But that wasn't what Keith was thinking about, nor was it Jason's arrival. No, tomorrow he had houseguests coming, and it was his houseguests—one in particular—who were going to make the holidays so exceptional.

5

The drone of the Falcon's engines seemed to have a numbing effect on everyone but Michelle. Annalise was napping quietly, her slender body stretched down the length of the lounge and her head in Marc's lap, who was solemnly engrossed in reading. Michelle did not know what he was reading, nor did she ask. Sitting across the narrow aisle from them, she kept her eyes fixed out the window at the Rocky Mountains below.

It was just the three of them traveling directly to Aspen, and the tension surrounding them was suffocating Michelle. No one mentioned the Paris couture show. No one had much to say at all. Occasionally, Annalise and Marc chatted between themselves, in soft, hushed tones, smiling and laughing with each other, as if they were sharing some private secret. After a while, Michelle found it easy to pretend she wasn't even there. If they talked about Marc's upcoming show, it was just between the two of them. They said nothing about it to Michelle. She couldn't focus her mind enough to read a book, even though she loved to read, so she slept as much as possible, curbing the obviousness of their exclusion. Now, she just couldn't sleep anymore.

Marc closed his eyes, leaning his head back against the seat, and Michelle took the opportunity to study him. Even with his eyes closed, he had an icy appearance. Although Michelle had worked under contract for him for two years, she did not know him on a personal level. Few people did, with the exception of Annalise, of course. He was difficult to get to know and he intimidated her.

Not once in the past two years had they ever had a casual conversation between them. Not once had he ever so much as asked her how she was or how a weekend or a trip had been. Not once had he so much as said good morning to her in a pleasant tone. Even when he offered her the contract two years ago, he had done so with as few words as possible, letting his attorney spell out the details to Rita. It was an odd arrangement in that it was not an entirely exclusive contract. Michelle could and did work for other designers, but only their runway shows and only in Europe. He had a North American exclusive with her. Having built an entire campaign around that and around her had made him the most popular designer in the US.

Why had he gone to Paris? Michelle couldn't come up with an answer. The European designers resented the hell out of his cavalier New York attitude—not to mention their ill feelings over his contract with their Michelle. The European fashion scene was a closed camp made up of easily irritated people who had little time and little patience for newcomers. They much preferred that he stayed on his side of the ocean. What had he hoped to accomplish by trying to present something that was so American in a city that was so European, with Michelle, of course, caught in the middle? Whatever his plan had been, it had backfired smartly in his face, and no one within earshot of her was talking about it. Michelle certainly wasn't going to bring it up.

Michelle studied him. Even with his eyes closed, he looked angry. He always looked angry, with a dark scowl permanently engraved across his forehead, further accentuated by his dark, slicked-back hair. In his midthirties, Marc Montori was heir to his family's textile fortune. His interest in fashion design had begun as a hobby, but he was at the epicenter of the New York fashion industry. Michelle thought him incredibly arrogant, in a chilling way. But so did a lot of people.

Marc disliked Michelle—adamantly disliked her. She knew this. Everyone knew this. It was common knowledge in the business, and it made headlines because, although he could not tolerate her personally, she was his star. She was his spokesmodel. As much as he disliked her, it was because of her that his last two seasons had been so successful. And the fashion critics loved to remind him that the reason his designs sold so well was because Michelle Seko promoted them. This infuriated Marc, who claimed he had created the commercial sensation known as Michelle Seko, not vice versa. The bantering continued back and forth between the press and Marc, with Michelle silently suffering in the middle. And whenever the press harassed Marc, he took it out on her, behind the scenes. Witnesses were plenty, but they were silent. That was just how it was.

But there was so much more to it than that, she thought. She closed her eyes to these thoughts because they made her uncomfortable. Working for Marc was torture, physical and psychological torture that she endured silently. She had done nothing to him or against him, and so his dislike confused and upset her.

Michelle's gaze shifted to Annalise. Just looking at her made Michelle sad. She had always admired Annalise, who, it seemed, had helped Michelle grow up but then left her before she was finished. The truth was, Michelle needed Annalise. She longed to curl up next to her, just to be physically close to her. She needed Annalise's understanding and support; she needed guidance from Annalise. But Marc prevented Michelle from reaching out to her and prevented Annalise from accepting her.

Annalise was the part of the *elite*. She was already a top model when Michelle was just getting started, and, although it seemed an unlikely match, they had become friends. There had been a time when they had shared everything. Michelle and Annalise had been inseparable. They lived together in Paris, worked together, and were always seen together. They were as close as two friends could be, yet they were complete opposites. They had traveled around the world together, or rather, the world had traveled around them.

It was because of Annalise's support that Michelle had endured her first year working for Marc. But then Marc came into Annalise's life. As Michelle watched their romance unfold right in front of her, she could neither believe it nor comprehend it. The romance escalated quickly, and within a month they were living together. Michelle was left angry, confused, upset, and alone. Even though Michelle's life was nothing but one act of abandonment after another, this time had been different. They were two feet apart with a mile of misunderstanding between them. Now, Annalise seemed so much older than Michelle, and, in her presence, Michelle felt very much like a child.

Marc opened his eyes, blinking. He only glanced at Michelle and then looked out the window. "We're almost there," he said.

Annalise sat up, stretched, and ran her fingers through her short brunette hair.

The snow glittered on the mountains surrounding Aspen. As the jet coasted over Aspen Mountain in its descent toward Sardy Field, Michelle could see skiers gliding down the runs. They looked like bright flowers on the icing of a wedding cake.

From the gate, Keith watched the Falcon drop down onto the runway. He felt his adrenaline rise in anticipation. Keith was anxious to see Marc again. It had been a year. The thought of meeting Michelle Seko made him a little nervous, which was unusual for him; he met celebrities every day.

The jet came to a stop and Keith walked out to it. Michelle stepped out onto the top of the jet's stairway first, catching her breath as the crisp Aspen air snapped at her face. Taking a deep breath, she looked around. The sky was cobalt blue. Everything, right up to the edge of the runway, was covered with crystal white snow. The air smelled clean and clear, with just a hint of the aroma of a woodburning fireplace. The smell made her heart swell as it suddenly flooded her with long-forgotten memories of Swiss winters and happy times. Taking another deep breath, she descended the narrow set of steps.

Marc was right on her heels. As soon as she stepped away from the plane, he rushed past her. Marc and Keith embraced in a masculine hug.

"Good to see you, buddy!" Keith said.

"I thought we'd never get here," Marc replied. "Michelle, come here," he said, turning toward her. "Michelle, this is Keith Bennett." Marc turned to Keith, bringing them together.

Michelle held out a delicate hand to Keith, smiling. *"Enchanté,"* she said softly.

Her gaze caught Keith completely off guard. He was instantly astounded by her. Taking her hand, he somehow found the words to welcome her to Aspen. He smiled at her, still somewhat at loss for words. She was even more beautiful in person. She was ethereal.

Driving through town on busy, snow-lined streets, Keith talked enthusiastically about skiing, shopping, and Aspen's nightlife. "Aspen, at this time of year, is really something to see," he said to Michelle, looking at her in the back seat through his rearview mirror. "People get as excited about the parties as they do the skiing."

She smiled uncomfortably at him and then focused her gaze out the window. Aspen Mountain towered above them and the glittering town. Now midafternoon, skiers making their last run could be seen streaming down the mountain. Keith drove through town and started up a narrow mountain road. As Michelle took in as much as she could through the steamy window, an empty ache consumed her. The town reminded her of St. Moritz—so much so that coming here no longer felt like she was getting away.

Keith's home, perched on the lower bench of Red Mountain, had a magnificent view of town and Aspen Mountain. The two-story log home had a modern appeal, and equally modern were its amenities, yet its atmosphere and decor were that of a hunting lodge. A massive lodgepole deck circled the exterior. The interior was decorated with oversized, carved furniture, enormous fireplaces in every room, and Native American art that added a sense of Santa Fe to its style. The minute Michelle walked through the huge pine doors, she loved it.

After a quick tour of the house, Keith showed Michelle to her room. Thanking him politely, she closed the door behind him, relieved to finally have a moment to herself. The large room was rustically decorated, like the rest of the house, and a sitting area with an entertainment center and wet bar took up a good portion of its space. In the refrigerator, Michelle found an assortment of sodas, juice, bottled water, wine, and chocolate. There were flowers and fruit on the table. Michelle smiled to herself. Keith seemed to be so pleasant and considerate. On the plane, Marc had spoken highly of Keith to Annalise. She wondered how they had come to know each other.

Michelle opened a bottle of wine and poured a glass, taking it with her into the bathroom. It was lavishly appointed with floor-to-ceiling mirrors, a large walk-in closet, and a dressing area. In the center of the room was a large whirlpool bathtub. Multiple sets of French doors opened out onto a private deck that offered a view of the town.

She sat down at the vanity, avoiding the eyes of the monster in the mirror. Sorting through a small makeup bag, she found a fresh pack of cigarettes, which she opened immediately, a small mirror, and a lipstick case. Unscrewing the end of the lipstick, she started to tap a small amount of almost pure heroin onto the corner of the mirror. Her hands started to shake in anticipation. She stopped, closing her eyes and clenching her fists and her teeth.

No. No. No. No. This is how it all starts. One blast. One blast that leads to another, and then another and then another. No! Michelle threw the lipstick case into the sink, frustrated. She had promised—promised Sasha then lied to him, promised Rita then lied to her, and promised herself, which was always a lie. She closed her eyes. Silence rang in her ears. She could feel the monster in the mirror staring at her, but she refused to look. She wanted something. *Something!* Anything. She took a swallow of wine. More wine. More wine and a Valium. But no drugs. *No. No. No.* God! It was the one thing she really did want. But there was no saying no. She picked up the mirror and held its corner to her nose, quickly snorting up the white powder. Sniffling, she closed her eyes, waiting for it to rush through her body. When it came, it felt good. Like an electrical current, it lightened the dullness in her brain and heightened her senses. Replacing the mirror, she took a large gulp of wine.

Then her eyes caught those of the monster. She stared at the image in the mirror in front of her. She lit a cigarette, watching herself do so in the mirror. Inhaling, she let the smoke curl out of her mouth, up into her face and eyes, making them burn, making her grimace, making her ugly. She blew out the smoke and rubbed her eyes, unable to look at herself without wondering who in the hell she was and who the monster staring back at her was.

The knock on the door made her jump. Too quickly, she moved to answer it, and her head spun wildly as she moved across the room like seaweed in an ocean current.

It was Keith. "Aaron called for you," he said casually, handing her a piece of paper. She took it quickly, because a slow hand would shake.

"You know Aaron?" she asked.

"Of course," he replied. "I think everyone knows Aaron." He backed politely out of the doorway, leaving Michelle to wonder what else he knew.

Then Michelle remembered the script. Most likely, that was why Aaron was calling. Surveying her luggage by the door, she realized the suitcase that contained the script was missing. Reluctantly, she went out into the hall to locate it. As she neared the living room, she could hear Annalise's voice, then Marc's. Then Michelle heard her own name. This stopped her.

"Is something wrong?" Michelle heard Keith ask.

"Actually, there is something," Marc replied.

"Marc, please," Annalise said, trying to keep him from telling Keith.

Marc looked over his shoulder and down the hall, not wanting Michelle to hear him talking about her. He did not know she was standing just out of sight and that she could hear everything he said.

"There is something you should know," he said to Keith, "but it's very personal and you have to keep it that way. I'm only telling you because you're a good friend and we're guests in your house."

Annalise scowled at Marc, not approving of what he was doing. Why bring more people into the pit than were there already?

"We didn't want to bring Michelle with us," Marc said to Keith, "but certain circumstances gave us no choice. Her agent has been trying for months to maneuver her into a rehab clinic but, every time, she either disappears or ODs. Then there was this drama in Paris."

Annalise finally interrupted. She didn't want to talk about Paris. "We brought Michelle with us because she really needs to be away from all the crap and bullshit that's going on with her right now," Annalise said.

"Don't defend her!" Marc snapped at his wife. "That's the problem. Everyone is always defending her."

Michelle sank back against the wall, feeling every ounce of breath and blood spill from her body. Her stomach turned. She closed her eyes, trying to push out their voices, wavering under the sick feeling in the pit of her gut and in the bottom of her heart. Quietly, she made her way back to her room.

The pillow was soft, but she did not notice its softness as she buried her face in it. She hated herself. She hated her life. She hated the loneliness she was feeling—that she always felt. But most of all, she hated that they were right. What she lived was bullshit, that was what Annalise had said. She was right. Michelle pressed her face into the pillow. *Why? Why, why, why? How had it come to this?*

She rolled onto her back, staring up at the carved pine ceiling. If she could have one thing, just one thing, it would be someone who could say to her, "Michelle Seko, if you quit, quit everything, I would still be there for you. It would not matter."

There was no one like that. Even those closest to her—Rita and Sasha—had their vested interests in her. They wanted what was best for her, because it was what was best for them. But conspire to send her to a rehab? Why did they find it necessary to conspire? What was Rita going to do? She never said or indicated anything. And the show in Paris. What about it?

There was a sudden shattering of glass in Michelle's brain that sent her bolting upright, then back again, as if she had been electrocuted. Then it was gone. She could leave this house. She could go back to New York. This minute. Not even unpack. Why should she stay? Why should she leave? Why didn't she have anyone to help her find the right answers? She threw the pillow across the room. She sure as hell couldn't seem to come up with the right ones herself.

There was a knock on the door. "Michelle?" It was Annalise.

"It's open." Michelle answered softly.

Annalise opened the door, but stayed in its opening, looking at Michelle. "Are you okay?" she asked.

Michelle sat up, wiping her eyes. Annalise came in and sat beside her. Not close though, Michelle noticed. Not as close as she once might have.

"I heard you and Marc talking about me just now to Keith," Michelle said.

"I'm sorry," Annalise replied. But she wasn't sorry; she just did not know what else to say.

She took one of Michelle's cigarettes from the pack on the nightstand, lighting it. She took a drag then passed it to Michelle. They shared it, something they had not done in a long time. It was a trivial gesture on Annalise's part that meant something to Michelle, as if the last thing in the world they had to share with each other was a cigarette and, once it was burned out, as was everything else, there would be nothing else.

"I don't know what to do," Michelle said, wanting to talk, needing to talk.

Annalise sighed. She couldn't look at Michelle. "You've got to get yourself together."

Michelle only nodded. "And . . . "

"And we think it would be better if you stayed with Aaron," Annalise said.

A aron, of course, would have her. A taxi took her across town to his house. There had been halfhearted offers to drive her, and even a genuine one from Keith, but Michelle wanted to be transported without conversation or the strain of having to try to make conversation. Keith, Marc, and Annalise seemed to disappear when the driver arrived at the door to help Michelle with her bags. Although humiliated, she was relieved to be relocating. She wouldn't have to think about Marc or his show again until New Year's Eve, when he would push her out onto the catwalk.

She arrived at the Perlman house relieved to be greeted by members of the Perlman family, not a horde of Aaron's Los Angeles entourage, except for George and Julie Peters, who Michelle knew and liked. She arrived not knowing what to expect and found herself invited to a family gathering. And the Perlmans were a real family. Aaron was now almost sixty and his wife, Hannah, was in her forties, Michelle guessed. They had three children. The two young Perlman boys, ages nine and thirteen, were obnoxious and rambunctious, and Michelle ignored them. Sixteen-year-old Katrina was thrilled to see her.

Michelle had known Aaron and his family for four years and had spent a considerable amount of time with them. Hannah was courteous toward Michelle in her usual cool manner as she showed Michelle to a large, comfortable room in a quiet wing of the house. They did not say much to each other, but the silence was not uncomfortable. Hannah told her they were just sitting down to dinner, and so Michelle followed her back down to the dining room.

Throughout dinner, the conversation remained casual and comfortable. Only Katrina questioned her in her juvenile, curious way that Michelle did not mind. Aaron talked about Aspen, but did not mention Marc's upcoming show. Michelle suspected he had been briefed by Rita, as usual. How and when these briefings took place Michelle did not know, but Rita always got there ahead of Michelle. And as always, it wasn't what was said that left Michelle suspicious—it was what wasn't said. For the moment, this was okay with her. In due time, Aaron would tell.

Michelle could feel George studying her in a way that gave her a strong sense that he, like Aaron, knew something she did not. Occasionally, she would meet George's gaze and see in it the scheme of some picture unfolding in his mind. She suspected, although no one mentioned *The Ballerina*, that George would be directing the film.

"Come, Michelle. Let's talk," Aaron said after the plates had been cleared. He held his hand out to escort her to his study the same way someone might hold out an arm to shepherd a small animal a certain direction. Michelle quietly went where Aaron wanted her to go.

Once in the study, he motioned her ahead to a chair, closing the door behind him. Aaron was a formidable figure in the film industry. He had always been kind and fair to Michelle, but sometimes the strength with which he did things intimidated her, differently, though, than the way Marc intimidated her. Around Aaron, she felt very safe.

"We are all very excited about *The Ballerina*," Aaron said, taking a script from his desk drawer and handing it to Michelle. "It's already been rewritten since I sent your copy to Rita."

Michelle took the script, only glancing at the cover. She wondered how long Rita had held onto the first script before giving it to her. She looked questioningly at Aaron.

Aaron chose each word carefully. He wanted to coax Michelle out into the open without creating a confrontation. He was on her side. If she thought otherwise, even for a moment, she would run from him. And once she ran from something, it was hard to get her back.

"I understand you've had a rough couple of days," he said, testing the water.

Michelle did not reply. He was the first to comment about her disappearance. But Aaron did not know. He couldn't possibly know. No one did. Not yet, anyway. Eventually, it would all come out; something would leak, and it would suddenly have everyone's attention. The wave would start in Geneva, spread to France, then out across Europe and over the ocean to the United States. It was inevitable and she knew it. But here in Aspen, she felt that she had placed herself as far away from it as possible—for now. Michelle knew Rita, Marc, Annalise, and even Aaron all felt that they had succeeded at something because they had gotten her here. Privately, she was relieved. She didn't even care that much that they were conspiring to send her to a hospital, even though knowing that those closest to her would operate in such a way hurt Michelle. She wasn't all that surprised. It was the same sort of manipulation she was subjected to on a daily basis. There was always some reason behind it. Everything came from the same bag of tricks that they all pulled from—the one labeled "for Michelle's own good, but for my best interest." They all thought she followed blindly. Silently maybe, but not blindly.

Just as with everything else, she was here at Aaron's for a specific reason. But at least he would be honest with her. She trusted Aaron because he had once helped her, even though doing so had hurt him. No one else would do that. He had motives, but he would tell her what they were. For the time being, regardless of their plans, she felt safe. She took only a fragment of comfort in this, but her mind screamed to tell Aaron, to beg for a way to deal with something that she couldn't even begin to comprehend. Yet she said nothing. No one had asked her where she had been for the days between leaving the Paris show and somehow getting herself to New York. It was like Rita, Sasha, and even Marc had deleted those days from their minds and then squeezed the gap together. She wished she could do the same. But it wasn't like them, and their silence made her suspicious, so she remained quiet, as well.

Aaron was watching her carefully. "It's been some time since you and I first talked about this picture," Aaron said, once he decided it was safe to proceed. "A lot has happened since then." He walked the room casually, occasionally glancing over at her, still giving careful thought to his words. "Michelle, I promised you a part in this film. And, unless for some reason you are no longer interested, you can still have that part." Aaron sat down on the edge of his desk, took a pen from the canister, and tapped it on the desktop. "But what I really have in mind is for you to play the part of Anna Pavlova."

Michelle's eyes widened in surprise. The part of Anna Pavlova was the starring role in the film.

Suddenly, another memory filled her mind. As a child, ballet had been the most important thing in the world to her. Michelle's memory rewound to the day that had changed her life, the day that her own dream to be a ballerina had ended, along with her father's dream that she follow in his footsteps—a dream that had grossly contradicted hers. He had objected harshly to her wanting to study ballet, and she had silently resented his forceful demands that she study music. That disastrous day had marked her last as her father's daughter, as his musical muse and protégée, her last day in Geneva, and the last day of her childhood. By the next day, she was in Paris and her life was changed forever.

She forced herself back to the present. Although she tried desperately to forget, sometimes by using desperate measures, she had never forgotten her one and only childhood dream. Now, years later, Aaron Perlman had brought her dream alive again. But it wasn't like he was pulling forward something that had been set aside or set back; he had dug down into a dark, damp grave to retrieve an ugly, decomposed fragment of a youth that was just as decayed and probably better off left buried. Aaron's project was a movie, not a new life, but Michelle could still be the ballerina she had wanted to be as a child.

It was nearly a year ago when Aaron had first mentioned to her his plan to make a movie about the famed ballerina Anna Pavlova. When Aaron expressed his interest in having Michelle in the film, she hadn't cared how small the part might be, she had wanted it. Even though the mere mention of dancing again cleared painful trenches that time had filled in, she wanted the part. Now he was talking about the starring role.

"But what about Sophie?" Michelle asked, thinking that Sophie Catalano had already been cast as Anna Pavlova and, based on her experience and appearance, was the ideal choice for the role.

"Frankly, Michelle, she hopes you choke," Aaron responded.

Michelle swallowed hard.

"Michelle, I'm not offering you the part just yet. You have a long way to go before I am convinced that this is something you can handle. What I am going to require of you will seem like hell at times, but I am going to help you, too."

He took a seat behind his desk. This set Michelle a little at ease to no longer having him hovering over her.

"First, what would be expected of anyone who is the lead," he said. "Three months of preproduction training. For you that would mean three months of grueling work with an acting coach, a dialogue coach, and the film's choreographer, all before any film is shot. Then the next six months for filming. Basically, we're talking at minimum nine months of your life where nothing outside this project will exist or interfere. This role demands total focus and dedication. I will demand total focus and dedication. If you are cast as the lead, I will expect you to put your modeling career on hold, get your personal life in order, and clean yourself up."

Michelle only vaguely nodded. She knew what he meant.

"I will not tolerate drug use—or users—on my project," he said matter-of-factly, without spite. He said it as he meant it, as a conditional detail. That was how he was and Michelle appreciated that.

She looked away. She thought about what had happened on the set of *The Islanders*. That time, it had been Aaron himself who had saved her, not Sasha. And now, in spite of her having done serious damage to herself, to him, and to his picture, he was offering her another chance. He was forgiving her for something terrible and offering her an opportunity she wasn't sure she deserved. And even if she did, certainly someone else deserved it more. Certainly, someone else could handle it better than she, even doing her best, could. Aaron must have very strong reasons for wanting her to lead his picture.

Aaron leaned forward. "Michelle, if you want this role, you have to prove to me that you want it more than anything in the world, then you have to agree to give me nine months of your life, maybe more. My demands will seem impossible at times, but I will be there to help you if you need it."

Michelle just looked at Aaron. She was frightened and the look on her face told him so.

Patiently, like a father, he left his desk and sat down beside her, taking her hands. "I wish," he said, squeezing her hands lightly, "that you could step into my shoes and see through my eyes what I see in you. You are so special and so very talented. You know that I've taken a special interest in you. I've followed your career. I read articles about you and I don't always like what I read. I think sometimes that you are wasting your life. I can't help but want to involve myself. You probably think you have so much money and so much fun that you don't want me involved in your life. And you are probably thinking, who does this man think he is? But I will push you, Michelle. I am not going to let you go home and say, 'This is too much work. I don't want to work that hard.' I am going to make you realize how much you want this, and then I am going to make you work for it like you've never worked for anything in your life."

Michelle felt paralyzed.

Aaron sat back, giving what he had just said a moment to sink in. And, gradually, it did.

"What does Rita think about this?" Michelle finally asked.

"Truthfully, she thinks that you are so strung out that you are incapable of doing anything that requires you to function thoughtfully. I'm not trying to pit you against her, but she honestly doesn't think that you are up to it."

Too fucked up to do anything but model, for which Rita receives a percentage of my income. That was what Rita really thought. But even zombies could model. That was why Michelle did it. She let out a heavy sigh because now she did have to think coherently and make decisions. "I overheard Annalise say that Rita has been trying to get me into a rehab clinic. Do you know anything about this?"

Aaron nodded, making Michelle let out a small but exasperated laugh.

"Trying? How? No one has ever said anything to me. What did she think she was going to do?" Michelle asked.

"She had arranged an agreement with Marc that if she could get you to consent to going to Grenoble after the Paris show, Marc would let you out of your contract while you were there, including the New Year's Eve show, without suing either of you," Aaron said. "There were some strings, of course, but that was the basic plan. Rita and Sasha were going to approach you about it right after the show. They really did have your best interest in mind."

There it is again, my best interest in mind.

"But," Aaron continued, "you pulled a disappearing act. As soon as you turned up again, she put Plan B in motion."

"And what is Plan B?" Michelle asked.

"Aspen," he replied. "See, you've got to do Marc's show now. If you had stayed in Paris one more day, you'd likely be sitting in a plush hospital room at Grenoble, instead of here. Rita wanted you here because she figures that I can keep you together until then."

"Is that it?" Michelle asked. "It seems too simple."

Aaron nodded. "It's only as complicated as you make it."

Complicated. "But if Rita thinks I'm too much of a loss to be able to do your picture, then why has she pushed me in your direction?" Michelle asked.

"I told you," Aaron replied. "Because I can keep you together."

Had anyone else said that to her, she would have bristled in defense, but coming from Aaron, it was a comfort. She needed someone to help her. He meant what he said. Michelle went to the window, which offered another view of the town. Aaron followed her. They were both quiet for a moment, looking down at the twinkling lights of Aspen.

"Such a charming town . . . " Her voice trailed off.

This could be St. Moritz, a long time ago. Although, not so many years ago in the sense of time. She felt like she'd been through a century of changes since she last looked down on the lights of St. Moritz. Aaron couldn't know what it meant to her to be someplace she had never been before, yet which reminded her so much of her favorite place as a child, nor could she have explained it. But she felt it.

She told Aaron what had transpired earlier at Keith's. "It's okay, though," she said, trying to convince both her and Aaron at the same time.

Aaron smiled, understanding. Michelle was correct in knowing where she could and could not find reprieve. "Maybe tomorrow you and Katrina can ski," he said.

Michelle nodded only vaguely. "Or the day after."

He placed a fatherly hand on her shoulder. His voice was stern. "We are going to get your life back in order. You need to get some help, so I want you to start getting used to the thought of that. If we get you into a hospital, it will be a nice one, I promise. You won't be a prisoner. And I'll get you out of Marc's contract, too. I want you in this picture, so you have to do this first. This is not a patch-together job, like fixing a car just so it will get you to the next town. I am offering you an Academy Award–caliber picture. I want you to give me an Academy Award performance. Then I want you to walk back into your own life—intact."

Michelle nodded meekly. *Her own life? She didn't know what that was.*

Clutching the script to her chest, she retreated to her room. She knew she would not be able to sleep, so she didn't bother trying. Opening the French doors to the back of the house, she pulled on her coat and walked out onto the balcony. The night was quiet. Even the bitter cold seemed to be absolutely still. The mountains spread out before her, glimmering ice blue under the moon.

The cold drove her back inside, where she curled up into one of the chairs and started to cry. What exactly was it that Aaron had said that made her suddenly feel so lonely? He was offering her something that might never come again in her life. What if she couldn't do it? The thought of going through treatment was lonely and depressing. Was that what she was afraid of? Going through rehab? It seemed so stupid. But it wasn't just going through it that frightened her; it was going through it alone. She knew that committing to Aaron Perlman and all that it implied, even though he offered his support, would make Michelle a very lonely person. And more than anything, Michelle hated being alone.

She curled up on her bed under the light and began reading the script, this time seeing herself as Anna Pavlova. The intensity she felt in her connection with the character both moved her and frightened her to depths she had never felt before. As she lost herself in the tragic life of the ballerina, she found it impossible to remove that sense of tragedy from her own life. The reality of Pavlova's life made Michelle realize her own life lacked such reality. She felt she was no one outside the roles or clothes she was placed in. It spurred a painful awakening. She did not know who she was. She did not know if she could do the picture, if she could find an Anna Pavlova inside someone who was no one. She wanted to relieve herself of her eggshell existence, unable to accept the emptiness beneath the surface. She turned the last pages, closed her eyes, and fell asleep.

In her dream, she was fourteen again. It was opening night and she was dancing. She could hear voices behind her. They said terrible things. She looked out into the audience and saw only her father's face in every chair. She was dancing now, spinning, bowing, floating across the stage. She was leaping now, high into the air. Suddenly, her feet dangled limp and lifeless and she felt herself falling, falling, falling . . .

7

orning light penetrated Michelle's sleep. It poured over her through the open drapes, waking her. She buried her head, wanting darkness. She heard hushed voices in the hall and tried to shut them out, wanting to lie undisturbed in a void of darkness and silence. The voices disappeared. She heard laughter outside and car doors slam and engines start and then she knew she was alone.

She rose and stumbled over to the window to close the curtains. She had not thought about closing them the night before. She paused to look out the window, which faced the street, and saw a man leaning against a truck parked along the road across from Aaron's house. Around his neck hung a camera. He was writing something. Instinctively, Michelle stepped back from the window and pulled the drapes closed. She returned to bed, choosing sleep disturbed by unsettling dreams over waking thought.

When she woke again, it was three in the afternoon. She listened for any sounds in the house for a while but heard nothing. Everyone was still skiing. She pushed back the comforter and sat up on the edge of the bed. Her frail body felt heavy, sedated, and sweaty. A shower helped, and she stood under the pulsating stream, turning the water as cold as she could tolerate it. She returned to the corner of the bed, wrapped in a towel and shivering. She felt like she had wasted the day, but she had needed the sleep, she told herself. This was the first time in weeks that she had slept for more than a few hours at a time. Her eye caught the script on the bed beside her. *Anna Pavlova.* She had dreamed about Anna. She had fallen and failed. Michelle pushed the thought out of her head. That was no way to start the day, no matter how late it was. She tried to sort through everything that had happened the night before. So much. Too much.

From somewhere in the house, Michelle heard a door close, so she pulled on a robe and went downstairs.

Keith was standing in the entryway. He had let himself in, not wanting to leave her bag outside. When she saw him, she stopped, not knowing what to say.

Keith, too, stopped. He made a conscious effort not to stare at her. "We must have overlooked this," he said, nodding to one of her suitcases.

Michelle hadn't missed it, but she was now suspicious. What was it with her suitcases that one always seemed to be left behind?

"I just thought I'd drop it by," Keith said. "I have a key, if you were wondering. I look after the place when Aaron's not in town."

She smiled nervously, wanting to thank him, but the words wouldn't come.

"Is Aaron here?" he asked.

"I think everyone is skiing," she replied.

He nodded. "I made a couple of runs this morning with Marc and Annalise," he said, trying to make conversation. "But then I had to go in to work. I didn't see him." He paused, shifting his weight uneasily. "I'm putting together a small dinner party for some friends tonight. Would you like to go?"

The invitation caught Michelle off guard. "For whom?"

Keith laughed. "An old friend who used to live here. He's still got a house here, but he only comes a couple of times a year. The party isn't actually for him; I'm just using his house. It will be mostly people from the Aspen Music Festival and School. Won't be a big gathering, just a few friends. Aaron and Hannah are going." Keith stopped himself, realizing that he was almost babbling. "Anyway, it's only for a couple of hours."

Michelle smiled. "Sure, I'll go."

eith pulled out of Aaron's driveway and, rather than turning toward town, he drove up the narrow, winding road that ascended Smuggler Mountain. The SUV slowly made its way up the freshly plowed path cut into the snow. The road climbed continuously up the mountain, much higher than where any houses had been built. Aspen fell farther and farther below, nestled in its little valley. Michelle could see glimpses of the view out of the rear window. It was breathtaking.

They continued to climb, winding through bare aspens and snow-laden pines bowing under the weight of their load. Everywhere Michelle looked, pristine snow in endless billowing drifts like frozen, sparkling sand dunes shimmered blue in the last light of day. The snow-covered mountain was just as beautiful, if not more so, than the view of town below.

"We're almost there," Keith commented.

Michelle could not see from the passenger window but, just several yards from the SUV, the mountainside fell away forever. Although he had driven this road many times, even plowed it himself a few times, Keith never ceased being careful.

"What do you do if there is a car coming down?" Michelle asked.

Keith laughed. "Fortunately, that rarely happens. But there are turnouts . . . see?" He pointed to a spot along a curve that was barely wide enough for two cars. "The car coming down the hill always has the right-of-way. This is actually all Jason's driveway, so it's not exactly Main Street."

"Jason. Is that your friend?"

Keith nodded. "Yes. Jason Henrey."

"Jason Henrey," Michelle repeated. "I'd hate to be Jason and have to drive this every day."

Keith laughed. "He loves it."

The SUV slid slightly as it rounded the last corner. Michelle instinctively clenched the dash.

"Sorry," Keith said. "It's just been scraped and there's a lot of ice under the snow."

Michelle looked out her window again as they rounded the last corner. They were close to the top of the mountain now, and the view of the entire valley was spectacular. Michelle thought about mentioning what Marc had said about her, but realized there was really nothing much she could say. She could either defend herself or excuse herself, neither of which she wanted to do. And even if she did, what had transpired would not change. Marc had told Keith the truth. Michelle only wished he hadn't said anything. She decided it was best that she not say anything more. *Don't give them a reason to say anything more; that's all you can do.* Keith did not mention it either.

As they came around the last switchback, an enormous red stone castle burst majestically out of the snow ahead of them. Michelle caught her breath, not expecting what she saw before her. Three stories of massive red-rock block, spirals, turrets, stone-carved balconies, and stained-glass windows sat perched on the crest of the mountain, clutching it like a great eagle. It seemed to have risen from the snow, and on its every surface the snow still clung. Gallant, sword-like icicles hung from the eaves, like fringe.

"Incredible, isn't it?" Keith commented, stopping the SUV momentarily. "There is nothing else like it in the whole world. Jason made sure of that."

"I believe it," Michelle replied, her voice echoing her awe.

"In the summer, you can't even see it," Keith said. "It's so big, yet it blends perfectly into the native bedrock. You practically have to be on the inside looking out to know it's here. From town, you can only see it in the winter. It just doesn't get any better than this."

He drove forward through a short tunnel, which brought them out into a courtyard, with the castle towering in an arc around them. Michelle hurried to get out of the vehicle. As soon as she set foot on the stone of the courtyard, which was neatly cleared snow, she could feel that she was on top of the mountain. The air was thin enough that the slightest sound intensified. She could feel the wind trying to whip her, so she tucked herself deeper into her heavy coat, even though the stone wall surrounding the courtyard protected her from the full force of the mountaintop wind.

"How long has this been here?" she asked. Its solidity made her think it had been here forever.

"About ten years. It took Jason almost that long to build it."

"He built it himself?"

Keith nodded. "He did. His company did, actually. Every square inch of this place was his conception. Wait until you see the inside. It has secret passageways and hidden rooms and labyrinths. Jason collected pieces of the interior from all over the world—entire ceilings, even. It's fascinating. You won't want to leave."

Michelle followed Keith along the curved walkway and up the stone steps to the entryway, taking in everything around her: the carved, black granite lions at the base of the steps, seeming ready to leap off the edge of the cliff; the turrets towering above her; the thick, etched windows; and the massive doors that rose several times her height. The sense of strength and security was overwhelming.

She paused in the foyer as Keith closed the towering door behind her. The ceiling seemed miles above her. In the center of the foyer stood a handsome, twenty-foot Christmas tree, not yet decorated. An assortment of boxes was stacked at its base. Behind it curved a wide, ornately carved staircase that opened up to the foyer like a flowing river.

"We'll decorate the tree after dinner," Keith explained. "It's kind of a tradition around here."

Keith crossed the foyer and Michelle followed. "Every inch of this house is the result of Jason's craftsmanship," he explained, sounding like a tour guide.

It was not a brightly lit house, but rather dark, yet warm. A man's home. He led her into the large main room off the foyer. Most of the furnishings were sixteenth to eighteenth century, Michelle guessed. A fire burned in the fireplace and Keith added a few more logs to the open hearth. The new wood crackled and sparked, throwing light across the room.

"I've got to check on dinner, if you don't mind," Keith said. "You are welcome to look around—just don't get lost. When Jason gets here, I'll have him give you a formal tour. And help yourself to the bar."

He left Michelle alone in the vast room. She looked up at the ceiling, noting its carved ornamentation. The room was more than eighty feet in length, with a span of French doors opening onto a balcony at the opposite end. The doors were closed, but she could see the orange glow of gas lamps outside.

In one corner of the room, sitting stately on a fine Persian rug, was a vintage Steinway & Sons grand piano. It rendered Michelle motionless. "Bonjour, Madame B," she whispered. She knew immediately what model it was, and was tempted to play a few notes on it. It beckoned her, calling to her like an old friend. She resisted playing it. *Maybe later.*

Except for the crackling of the fire, the house was silent. *This is a house of strength, comfort, and security.* She could feel it. It was warm, inviting, and protective of its occupants. An assortment of spirits in heavy, leaded crystal decanters was arranged on a sideboard. She helped herself to a glass of vodka. Michelle wandered slowly around the large room. She added another log to the fire, liking the way it roared as if it could melt the mountain. *Fires built in hearths like this should roar*, she thought, remembering the fireplace in her father's house in Geneva. She remembered how, in the summer, when it wasn't used, she would stand inside it.

The rugs, art, artifacts, and antiques Michelle recognized as museum-quality pieces. Expensive, she thought—very, very expensive. But this was a house on which obviously no expense had been spared. Remembering what Keith had said about his friend, Michelle wondered what kind of man he was. She imagined a man like Aaron—eccentric, influential, strong, powerful. He would be an individual of magnitude. Older than Aaron, though, whose children were grown, perhaps even with children of their own. Michelle wanted to think he might be European, as it was hard for her to believe an American could conceptualize something as European as this house. She wanted to step out into the cold night air, look far down the mountain and see St. Moritz, not Aspen, Colorado. But, at the same time, there was something about this town and this house that belonged together. She had a very strong feeling this house was just like the man who owned it: private, secure, above the rest. She hoped so, at least. She was forever searching for examples of reality. She would be disappointed if it turned out to be nothing more than a rich man's showpiece.

She returned to the foyer and chose to explore the corridor that ran underneath the staircase. The double doors at the end stood open, and the light coming from within drew her. It was a library. She wanted to take in its every detail, but she heard the heavy front door open and shut behind her, so she retreated back to the foyer, which was empty.

She wandered up the wide staircase to the second floor. From somewhere in the house a woman's laughter rose up to meet her. The second-floor landing was open to the foyer below, with the furniture arranged in the sitting area to look down over the balcony. The top of the Christmas tree was now at eye level. Dimly lit corridors extended in opposite directions from the central sitting area. Michelle opened only a few doors, all of which opened into bedrooms. Unlike the rest of the house, they were cold and, Michelle assumed, not being used. She could see that several of the rooms were decorated with children in mind, and would be warm and cheerful if fires were started in their hearths. Looking down the halls, she realized that none of the rooms were open and warmed, as was the rest of the house. She wondered why.

Returning to the landing, she looked up at the wide flight of stairs leading to the third floor. She started up them, hearing the voices below drift further and further away. At the top of the stairs was an alcove with a small sitting area and, beyond it, large double doors. She opened one of the doors and went in, leaving it open behind her. She stood for a long time just inside the door, looking around the room, which was unmistakably a man's room, a man of privacy, wealth, and power. In the center of the room was a large, four-poster bed covered with a quilt of plush, chocolate velvet. Everything about the room was rich, deep, and dark, and entirely devoid of a woman's touch. The turrets at each end leant their curvatures to the room, creating a retreat at one end and, at the other, what was likely to be a bathroom and dressing area, although the door was closed. While there was a comforting feeling to the room, Michelle was overwhelmed by its sense of privacy, which she felt she was invading.

A fire burned in the fireplace, waiting. She went to the hearth, where a photograph on the mantle caught her eye. She picked it up. It was of two men in their early forties, she guessed, standing in the foreground of an erupting volcano. She could almost feel the hot wind that blew their hair. She wondered who they were. Brothers. Was Jason Henrey, whoever Jason Henrey was, their father? Michelle gazed at the photograph for a long time. Something about it, perhaps its degree of reality, disturbed her. It captured a real moment in someone's life. Whoever they were almost did not matter. They were real. The smiles were real, the wind in their hair was real, the volcano in the background, spewing yellow and orange, was very real.

It pained Michelle to look at the photograph, because it, like so many things lately, made her take note of how unrealistic her own life was. She could duplicate this picture with props and fans, but it would not be capturing a moment in her life the way the one in her hand had captured a moment in their lives. The difference was in the story. There was a story behind this picture, a story of adventure and excitement. Her pictures told no stories. They were just images with corresponding paychecks.

She traced her delicate finger around the man on the right, wondering what it would be like to have herself in the picture, to look at it and say, "I remember that day. What a great day that was."

Michelle did have a few treasured photographs that her father had taken of her when she younger, but the memories they brought back were painful, not happy. Scattered around the world were photographs representing literally every moment of Michelle's adult life. The public looked at these pictures of Michelle to be reality. Why then could she not do the same? She knew why. Because she knew that they were just images and she was just a prop, created and recreated to sell something. Michelle, like the apparel or the cosmetics or the jewelry or the perfume, was nothing more than a product. A young girl looking at Michelle's picture, wishing for what it promised, did not know what she was wishing for. Michelle did. Nothing. There was nothing those pictures were selling that was worth wanting, and Michelle hated knowing that. Michelle's life was a lie, a big, beautiful lie.

She studied the face of the man in the photograph, the one on the right. His features were rugged and tanned, yet soft. His smile was brilliant. The man on the left was gazing off at something; the one on the right was looking directly into the camera, and there was kindness in his eyes. Michelle's gaze lingered on him. His eyes were blue. She was momentarily consumed by the kind, passionate face in the photograph. What was it about this photograph? She knew the answer, but it was hard for her to accept. This man so obviously loved life, and the photograph had captured that love of life. This, too, pained her, and she replaced the photograph on the mantle.

Michelle curled up into one of the oversized, wingback chairs that faced the fireplace, thinking again of the photograph. *My life lacks everything that life should possess: quality, moments considered precious, family, friends, and time shared with those people. And, above all, my life lacks any purpose that is personal. I do nothing that is important to me.* This was a dangerous thought, she knew, because so often this lack of purpose could smother her with a lack of reason to live. She frightened herself when she began thinking that way—having no reason to live because nothing in her life was worthwhile. And yet, she was afraid of dying. It was wrong, and she knew that if she could find a way and reason out, it was also unnecessary. Her life did not have to be this way, but she did not know where to even begin to change it.

She thought back to Aaron and their conversation. The film was not the way out, but it was a project, a purpose. It certainly would bring her no closer to reality, and, if anything, might actually take her further from reality. But for the next nine months, it was something.

Keith said that Aaron would be here tonight, and for that she was glad. She wanted to talk to someone, and he was all she had. She knew one thing for certain—she wanted to get away from Marc Montori and the world of haute couture.

A creak outside the doorway startled her. A man entered the room and Michelle recognized him immediately as the man in the photograph. He did not see Michelle peeking out at him from behind the edge of the chair. He set a duffle bag on the bed and left again. Michelle watched every step he took. He looked exactly as he did in the photo. Then he was gone.

Michelle was about to get up to leave when he returned, this time carrying a crate of firewood. This time, he saw her. He stopped. When Michelle looked up at him, she found herself looking into the same warm blue eyes she had seen in the photograph.

He smiled. "Hello," he said pleasantly, putting the box down on the hearth. Michelle did not know what to say, nor did she know what to do. She stared at him, realizing she was staring. She was both frightened at being caught and overwhelmed by his nearness.

He looked at her casually, smiling, surprised to find that she did indeed look frightened.

"Did you start this fire?" he asked.

"No. I didn't." She could feel her face flushing. "I'm sorry if I've intruded." She started to get up.

"It's okay." His voice was quiet, comforting. "You don't have to leave."

Michelle smiled and sat down again. She wondered who he was, wanting desperately to know. She was afraid to ask for fear of further embarrassing herself. "It's not entirely my fault," she said. "It's this house. It drew me up here."

When he just looked at her, Michelle wondered if she had said something wrong.

"I'm Jason." He held out his hand.

Michelle could not have possibly hidden the surprise on her face. She managed to take his hand, which completely enveloped hers. Silently she wished he would never let go.

He did. "And you?"

His question caught her off guard. It was rare that she was asked her name. People knew her name. It felt strange to be saying it.

"I'm Michelle."

"Pleased to meet you, Michelle," he said, smiling. He turned his attention back to the fireplace, adding wood to it. "You have a lovely accent. Where are you from?"

Michelle pulled her knee to her chest, resting her chin on it, watching him. "Geneva," she replied.

He looked back at her, smiling. "Since I don't think you mean Geneva, Wisconsin, I'd say you are a long way from home."

He made her laugh, but inside something cracked. Even though she had said she was from Geneva, there was no place for her that felt like it was her home.

"Have you been there?" she asked.

"Wisconsin?" he replied, joking. "Yes."

Michelle smiled at him; she could not help it. "Well, I've never been there, to Wisconsin."

"No? How about Montana?"

Michelle shook her head. "Is that where you are from?"

Jason nodded. "The most beautiful place in the world," he said, rising. He walked away, opening the door to the other room, the one Michelle guessed was a bathroom, closing the door behind him. She saw a light come on from underneath the door. She took one last look at the photograph on the mantle, wanting to remember it, to preserve the feeling it evoked in her, and left.

Voices and laughter rose from the main room, with Aaron's voice rising above them all. As soon as she entered the room, she became the center of attention.

"Michelle!" Aaron came toward her. "I was beginning to wonder where you had gone." He led her to the center of the small group to introduce her to everyone. Catherine Orland, a striking, well-dressed woman in her midforties, and Jayne Brikelle, who was in her sixties, introduced themselves.

"Jayne owns Brikelle's in town," Aaron explained. "A beautiful boutique."

Michelle smiled graciously. However, while she was warmly received by Jayne, Catherine's instant iciness toward her was evident. *This happens every time. Every new person I meet is a gamble; they either love me or hate me, and whichever it is, they make it apparent.*

Next, Aaron introduced her to John and Melissa Garrison, who were openly fascinated by Michelle, and Melissa expressed her excited anticipation of the upcoming fashion show.

"She plans on spending all my money," John laughed sarcastically.

Aaron acknowledged them as members of the board of trustees of the Aspen Music Festival and School.

"Where is Hannah?" Michelle asked Aaron.

"She decided to stay home with Katrina and the boys," Aaron replied, giving no indication that Hannah's absence was anything out of the ordinary.

Michelle was sorry to hear that. She felt uncomfortable. This was a smaller group than she expected. These people were all close to each other. She was a stranger among old friends. *Here is just one more thing I am missing in my life.*

Jason reappeared, and Aaron steered Michelle forward to meet him, not knowing that she had already. Jason took the reintroduction courteously, smiling, but not telling.

"This is an incredible man, Michelle. You will love him," Aaron said, clapping Jason on the back. "And very talented, I might add. He built my house for me, you know, and Keith's."

"I'm impressed," Michelle said.

"Oh, but not as impressed as you should be by this house," Aaron said, turning to Jason. "I do wish you'd sell it to me."

Jason laughed, but there was a sense of modesty in his laugh that impressed Michelle far more than his accomplishments.

"I have this feeling this house was not built to impress people," Michelle commented. She was right, and Jason gave her a look that told her so.

Keith appeared and insisted they all be seated. The small group followed him to the dining room, where the heavy, ornately carved table had been set with the first course. The table was large enough to seat twenty, so the small dinner party was clustered at one end. Although seated in the center of the table, Michelle was actually at one end of the entourage, with Aaron at her right and John Garrison across from her. To her left stretched the unoccupied rest of the table like a long, heavy gangplank.

Jason took the seat at the head of the table. She looked around the room at Jason's friends, wondering how they knew each other. Her mother had once taught Michelle how to read a room at a dinner party so as to make the best choices for conversation. Trying hard to apply her mother's theories about people, Michelle could only guess that their gathering had something to do specifically with the Aspen Music Festival. But why was she here? Was Keith's invitation really meant to be as casual as it had been delivered? Michelle felt like she couldn't take anything at face value anymore. Her life made her too suspicious. She looked at Jason, hoping the source of the friendships—and the reason she was included—would come out in the conversation. Their eyes met occasionally, and he smiled at her casually. This embarrassed Michelle, because she felt like she was staring at him. But she couldn't help it; he fascinated her.

Catherine noticed the occasional exchange between Jason and Michelle. "So, Michelle, how do you like Aspen? I understand this is your first time here," she asked coolly.

"From what I've seen so far, which I admit is not very much, it's wonderful," Michelle replied. "But I just arrived last night. I've not been into town yet."

"We're all excited about Marc Montori's show," Catherine continued. "But I'm sure it's just another day's work for you."

Michelle cringed at the mention of Marc's show. She was sure Catherine's comment was meant to be insulting, and the insult stung. Not knowing what to say in response, she made no reply.

"You know," Catherine added, speaking to the group, "it amazes me how lucrative a modeling career can be, considering how little a model actually does. I mean, I used to model while I was in college. It was fun and easy, and I made some great extra money."

Michelle could feel the heat of humiliation rising in her face. This woman was attacking her. Why? She kept her eyes on her plate. She felt everyone was looking at her. Under the table, Aaron placed his hand on her thigh, giving it a light squeeze. It reassured her that someone was on her side.

"I happen to know that Michelle works very hard," Aaron said in her defense. "Certainly much harder than anyone in Aspen."

The Garrisons laughed. Keith voiced a jovial objection. The tension lifted slightly.

But Catherine was not yet finished. "I find Annalise L'Heurus to be fascinating. I look forward to meeting her."

At this, Michelle looked at Aaron. He knew what she was thinking. Meeting Annalise was like stepping into a den of rattlesnakes. You had to tread very, very carefully. One wrong move and she could lash out at you with deadly precision. If Catherine really was looking forward to meeting Annalise, she would have to change her attitude about the modeling industry. A look of higher understanding passed between Michelle and Aaron. Jason noticed it and wondered what it meant.

To Michelle's relief, Aaron took control of the conversation, questioning Jason about his project in Hawaii. Michelle learned a lot about Jason by listening to the conversation around the table. He was a real estate developer, an architect and an engineer. He owned two companies, a custom home-building company in Aspen that he started while in college, and a relatively new engineering technology company. His project on Maui was finished after four years of work.

"Is it a housing project?" Michelle asked.

Aaron laughed. "Houses, hell, it's the whole island!"

Jason smiled modestly. "It's not the whole island."

Catherine looked over at Michelle, intentionally interrupting the conversation. "You've hardly touched your dinner, Michelle. Don't you care for it?"

This brought everyone's attention to Michelle's practically untouched plate.

"I'm sorry," Catherine said. "I forget, in your line of work, you really don't eat. I've read about many models who develop eating disorders to stay thin, you know, like anorexia."

Michelle felt her face flush. It was true. Although Michelle did not eat, she did not consider herself anorexic, at least not in a clinical sense. Michelle was painfully aware that she was thin, but it was not something she strived for. She just couldn't eat. She felt humiliated. She was unprepared for such an attack. Even though she had experience in deflecting every imaginable insult, on this occasion, she was blindsided. So, too, were the other guests. An uncomfortable silence fell over the group.

Jason watched her with a gaze that, although soft, was as persistent and as searching as an eagle's. He took in what he saw critically. A young woman that was both ageless and exquisite in appearance, with finely sculpted, extreme features. She had the perfect skin of a child. Her eyes were deep and knowing. She exuded intelligence in a childlike way. She gave nothing away. She was dressed simply in an elegant black turtleneck dress that flowed to her ankles. She wore no makeup, and wore her hair pulled smoothly back to the nape of her neck, braided and rolled into a neat coil. He knew it was long, because he had seen pictures of her. Of course, he had known who she was. Everyone knew who she was. She was fascinating. He could think of no better word for her. His mind screamed an apology to her, wishing that she could read it. Her reaction at this moment was everything to him, as it would tell him so much about her—if she exhibited any reaction to Catherine. *Come on, Michelle, show me you are not made of stone. You cannot be; it would be too great a contradiction.* Never had he come across someone who, without a word or gesture, emitted such volatility. This tiny person, so reserved in so many ways, possessed such overwhelming presence as to fill this room, or any room. Aaron had once said something to that effect about her to him.

Jason let the uncomfortable silence linger a moment longer, although it was at her expense, while he waited for some sign that told him that she was indeed fragile and that people did affect her. He wanted a sign that she was human. He wanted to know that she did not live inside some plastic bubble, unaffected by what went on around her, unaffected by what people said and did to her. He wanted to know that if he showed her compassion, she would accept and understand it.

She never lifted her eyes, but let her gaze hang in her lap. He wished she would. There! Ever so delicately, she brushed a wisp of hair from her face, a wisp of hair that wasn't there. Her fingers lingered at her temple, her hand trembling ever so slightly. Her lashes closed down on her cheek only briefly. She sighed. From across the table he could see her breathe.

The uncomfortable silence persisted. It shrouded the guests, making every shift in posture, every cleared throat, every knife against the plates sound deafening. Only for one second did Jason avert his eyes from Michelle to have them meet Aaron's. *Aaron knows what I am thinking. Don't take her away, Aaron. Please, don't take her away. Not yet. She's far too fascinating to let go so soon.*

Jason leaned over to Catherine. "Could I speak to you in the kitchen for a minute, please?" He got up, excusing himself. Catherine had no choice but to follow.

Aaron leaned toward Michelle, whispering. "Don't let this woman get to you."

"I could really use a cigarette," she whispered back. "Do you mind?"

Aaron nodded. "I'll join you." He excused them both without explanation and went into the living room. "She's Jason's girlfriend, or, rather, ex-girlfriend,"

Aaron explained. "It's a long story. I'll spare you. She is insecure about you being here, around Jason. Don't let her get to you. There's no reason for it. But she is being rude, and I'm sorry."

This made her feel a little better. "I'm just so tired of people hating me, people who don't even know me. I don't think I'm better, so why do people feel compelled to prove that I'm worse?"

"Michelle, people react the way they do to you either out of jealousy or because they cannot put themselves in context with you. It's not your fault."

Michelle sighed, wanting to change the subject. "I'm glad you are here, though," she said. "I've given things a lot of thought," she paused. "I just need to get through this show," she said, already knowing that she couldn't.

"You can get through anything, Michelle, but, like I said before, I'm going to do everything I can to get you out of it."

Michelle nodded. It would be ugly, but, yes, she wanted out, because staying in would be worse. "I'd like to spend some time with Katrina, if that's okay with you," she said.

"Katrina would like that. Maybe you could talk to her."

"About what?"

"About herself," Aaron said. "I don't really know what's going on in her head, but she doesn't seem happy with herself. She's only sixteen, but she thinks she's overweight and ugly. She talks about plastic surgery. It's crazy." He looked at Michelle. "She wants to be like you."

Michelle understood all too well. Millions of young girls around the world wanted to be like her. It was models like Michelle who triggered image problems and eating disorders, all because models—Michelle in particular—put forth an image that was too unrealistic and ludicrous to attempt to duplicate.

"It's sick, isn't it, Aaron, what a profound effect someone like me can have on an entire generation?" Michelle said. "I'm as bad as the drug dealer who sells drugs to kids. I know exactly what's going on with her, and I'll talk to her. She shouldn't want to be like me."

Aaron said nothing more about his daughter. Michelle was both insightful and smart, and he appreciated her for both reasons. He looked over at the piano. "Would you do me the favor?" he asked.

She smiled, happy that he asked. "Do you have any special requests?"

"Only that you play with a smile on your face."

She went to the piano. Her first instinct was to lift the lid of the bench to see what scores were stored underneath. As a child, that long, narrow box had always been a favorite place of hers because it had always held music that she adored. An old, dog-eared book of Christmas carols caught her eye. Taking it, she sat down at the vintage Steinway, silently introducing herself. "Bonjour, Madame B," she said again. "You don't know me, but I know you." It was her own personal ritual whenever she played a new piano. She touched the keys softly, listening to their tune, which was almost perfect.

As a child, music and her father had been the two forces in her life. She had grown up studying classical music and had a deep appreciation for the masters. There had been a time, now seemingly long ago, when music was to have been her future, so much so that it had smothered her childhood. Her father, demanding that she give everything she had in order to be the pianist he expected her to be, had taken away everything else that a child should have. He had stuffed her down into such a narrow pipeline that eventually she could go no further. Even though it had changed her life—and ruined it in many ways—she still to this day did not regret standing up to her father and saying she had had enough. She had been passionate about music and still was. But as a young girl, she had longed to be passionate about other things as well, especially ballet. She still played, but she would never let her father know this. In his eyes, she had failed him, and so, at the time, he seemed determined to see that she failed at everything else she tried. He had won in all ways except one—she never played for him again.

Aaron seated himself on one of the couches behind her, listening. She began with Beethoven's "Moonlight Sonata," one of her favorites, and she played it perfectly. She had every note committed to memory. The music carried through the room and through the house. It filled the air, Aaron's mind, and Michelle's heart.

Michelle looked up from the keys to find that she had drawn the dinner guests around her. They joined her, quietly, so as not to disturb her. Catherine was not with them. Jason remained in the entryway, leaning against it casually.

Michelle paused and they begged her to continue. She obliged. She attempted several chords of "Silver Bells" but, laughing at herself, could not remember the music.

Melissa sat down on the bench beside her and paged through the book. "How about this?" Melissa asked, stopping at "White Christmas."

Michelle played it effortlessly, and Melissa, Jayne, and Aaron joined together to sing. Spirits lifted. Even Keith joined them, offering liqueurs and coffee. He seemed to enjoy playing the host, while Jason remained idle. The group gathered closer around the piano, standing behind Michelle to see the music. Melissa, turning the pages, sang beautifully.

Michelle played the closing notes of the carol, laughing again, which was something she rarely did. Melissa selected another carol, and Michelle began the opening chords of "God Rest Ye Merry Gentlemen" with fluid precision.

From across the room, Aaron and Jason's eyes met. Aaron wanted Jason to like Michelle, for the next few weeks at least. He knew Jason well, and knew also that Jason could help Michelle in ways she never knew.

"Can you play Handel's 'Hallelujah Chorus'?" Melissa asked.

Michelle nodded. "But it makes me cry every time." She began, opening with the impact it deserved, the way it was intended to be played. A hush fell over the room as the power of the music overwhelmed them. Only Melissa sang, trained in vocals as Michelle was in piano; she contributed to Michelle's power and emotion. Tears rolled down Michelle's face but she never missed a note. A drop fell on the keys and Jason saw this and was touched. She brought the final chorus to a slow, sweet close, pressing her hands to her eyes. Silence lingered in the room as the music faded away.

"Enough," Michelle said softly. "This music makes me sad." She looked at Melissa. They smiled at each other.

"We should recruit this young lady," John Garrison said.

Jason came toward her, placing a strong hand gently on her tiny shoulder. She looked up at him. "That was beautiful, Michelle," he said. "Thank you."

As the group moved to the entry to decorate the tree, Michelle went to the sideboard, needing some water.

"How about a drink?" Jason offered, lingering with her.

"I'd love something warm, if that's possible."

"Of course. Cognac? Coffee? Tea?"

"Cognac," she replied.

Jason beckoned her to follow him through the house to the kitchen. It was a marvelous kitchen, large and rustic. It was situated at a corner of the house, with large windows spanning two sides of it. The floor was thick plank board and brick that seemed to absorb the warmth from the fireplace. The ceiling was of heavy beam and white plaster. A butcher-block island surrounded by stools separated the cooking area from the rest of the room, which consisted of an eating area and a large sitting room. At the far end of the sitting room was another fireplace, surrounded by plush couches, thick fur rugs and heavy carved tables. An assortment of books was scattered across a heavy, plank-board coffee table.

"What a wonderful room," Michelle said.

"My favorite place in the whole house," Jason replied. "I love to sit here in the morning and read."

"I bet the view is spectacular," Michelle said, going to the window. She could not see out—only the reflection of the fireplace and Jason behind her.

Jason nodded. "Especially at dawn. I built it to face east, just so I could watch the sun rise."

She returned to the island and took a seat across from where Jason was standing. Michelle liked that the large table was between them. She was sensitive to how near she was to him, and was painfully aware of how frail she felt.

"Thank you for playing," he said. "You're very talented. Where did you learn?"

"My father," she replied. "I've been playing since I was very young. I still do all the time. It soothes me." She was not entirely truthful in answering him, but the answer she gave was sufficient.

"Then why did you say it makes you sad?" He asked.

"I'm not sure if it's really sadness or just a powerful emotion all its own," Michelle replied. "But Christmas music does make me a little sad when I hear it and suddenly realize that the holidays have crept up on me. It happens every year. Then they are over."

Jason nodded, agreeing with her. "I think it makes everyone a little sad in that same way, especially when you are away from your family."

Michelle only nodded, not wanting to talk about her family.

"Then you are staying for the holidays?" he asked.

Again, Michelle nodded. She had no place else to go.

"Alone?"

She looked up at him. "No," she replied, thinking of Aaron and his family. "Well, yes." She was here alone.

Jason smiled. "Me, too."

"Why?" Michelle asked, surprised. Over dinner he had mentioned his rather large family.

"I just need a break," he replied. "Cognac, right?"

Michelle nodded, watching him swirl the snifter of cognac over the blue flame of a tiny butane heater.

"My family is staying home this year," he continued. "My dad just had surgery, so he's not able to travel, and I was just there for Thanksgiving. They can be a pretty loud bunch."

"And it's so quiet up here," Michelle said.

Jason nodded. "That's why I'm here." He paused, but wanted to say more. "I'm sorry that Catherine was so rude to you this evening. She wasn't herself tonight."

"It's okay," Michelle replied. "I'm accustomed to it."

"But that doesn't make it right."

Michelle looked up at him.

"You certainly deserve the same courtesy that anyone else does," Jason said. "To tell you the truth, I was embarrassed that a friend of mine treated you so poorly, especially in my own house." He handed her the snifter.

"Thank you," she said, not for the brandy, but for his compassion. She wanted to tell him that for her to meet only one person a day who disliked her was pretty good. She followed him back to the foyer, feeling almost invisible beside him.

She sat down alone on the stairs, holding the snifter in both hands, to watch Aaron, Keith, Jayne, and the Garrisons decorate the tree. Jason joined them. She thought about what Jason had just said. It disturbed her, because it went against what she had always been expected to accept. Even Aaron had said so the night before. Everywhere, every day, she would face people who did not like her for whatever reason, be it envy or jealousy. What she had to do was face it, accept it, and be unaffected by it, but certainly not react or question it. And here Jason was saying that just because she was someone different, someone that others were jealous of, did not make being treated poorly by them fair and acceptable. In his eyes, it was not. She wondered what had happened to Catherine. Had Jason asked her to leave?

"Of course, you can ask her. I'm sure she'd be delighted to go," Aaron said to Melissa as they moved around the tree.

Michelle overheard them. Aaron looked over at her. "Every year the music school hosts a Christmas concert at the Wheeler Opera House," he explained. "It's a wonderful event."

"This year, we'll be performing Handel's *Messiah*," Melissa added.

Michelle's first thought was that Melissa might ask her to perform. She hoped not.

"I'd like to invite you to the performance, as our guest," Melissa said.

Michelle smiled. "Handel's *Messiah*? In its entirety?"

"Of course," Melissa responded.

"Then the school must have a choir."

"A beautiful choir," John replied.

"And you'll be going?" Michelle asked Aaron.

"Every year. I would have mentioned it to you, but Melissa is more efficient than I am." Aaron said, smiling at Melissa.

"It's a wonderful event," Melissa said. "We have a reception before and after the performance, and the money goes to support the school."

"Sounds lovely," Michelle said, wanting to go, but feeling a little apprehensive, as she was about so many things.

As the group continued to decorate the tree, and the boxes of ornaments were opened and sorted through, Aaron came to sit beside Michelle. "About the concert," he whispered, knowing when something needed to be clarified, "it really will be a nice event. It will have a prestigious turnout, it always does, but you'll enjoy it. And you can come with us."

Michelle smiled thankfully at him.

"Just one thing." She touched his arm. "Please don't tell Marc I'm going."

Aaron nodded in agreement, understanding. Michelle's gaze lingered on Aaron's back as he walked away. Then it grew vacant as she remembered sitting in her apartment a few nights before with Sasha, packing her clothes. She remembered the dresses Sasha had wanted to pack for her.

"Can't wear the same Prada twice," he had said. Michelle flinched. *Can't wear Prada at all, not without Marc blowing up about it.* Something as simple as choosing an evening dress could have so many implications. She hated the thought because she hated the fight.

Keith stopped beside her. "I've got to take off," he said. "I need to check in at the restaurant," he said. "Do you want to go back with me?"

She really did not want to leave. "I'll go with Aaron," she replied. "I'd really like to stay, if you don't mind."

"Not at all," Keith said. "I'm glad you are having a good time."

"Thank you," she said. *Thank you for not mentioning yesterday.*

Michelle went back into the main room, checking that no one followed her. She refilled her empty snifter with vodka and took her coat from the back of chair where she had left it. Making sure her cigarettes were still in her pocket, she went out onto the balcony, which was expansive and lined with gas heaters that glowed orange like the lava of the volcano in the photograph upstairs. She followed it around one of the turrets to an alcove. The light that poured from the room cast a yellow hue across the red stone but did not quite reach the alcove. Neatly cleared of any snow, it was sheltered from the wind and cold, but cantilevered out into the darkness, sharply contrasting the night-blue wonderland beyond it. She looked out over the edge and the mountain seemed to fall away beneath her.

The town of Aspen, twinkling far below, looked like a tiny picture postcard from where she stood. She saw it as some sort of magical kingdom. She felt so out of place. Now, after having met these people, she suddenly felt as though she was missing out on an entirely different element of life that she had never known existed. It made her heart ache but, already, she loved this place. She wanted to be a part of it. She loved the stunning cold, the stillness, the crispness, and the way sounds echoed in the air. She loved the way the cold air was laced with the aroma of burning wood. She was reminded of Switzerland, only now she had the chance to appreciate it. *I could just stay here forever,* she thought, *as still as the night.*

She heard doors open above her and a light illuminated the balcony overhead. As she looked up, Jason appeared at the railing above her. She watched him, fascinated. He stood gazing out at the same view that she did. There was a sense of strength in his aura that intrigued her and drew her to him. *Here is a man who knows about life and the quality that life can have.*

Jason ran his hand through his hair, and when he did, noticed Michelle on the balcony below him.

"What are you doing down there?" he asked, surprised.

"Enjoying the view," she replied, wondering if her voice could carry far enough to reach him.

"Stay there. I'll be right down," he said, disappearing from sight.

A few moments later, Jason reappeared on the balcony where she was. "What are you doing out here? Aren't you cold?"

"No, not at all," Michelle replied softly. Bundled in her full-length cashmere coat, she hadn't noticed the cold. "I just needed some air. I guess I lost track of time."

"That's easy to do," he replied, looking at her carefully, yet discreetly. Her skin was fair and glowing, but her eyes looked troubled. Yet she looked so serene he felt like an intruder for interrupting her, certain she had a very good reason for being out here alone.

Every time their eyes met, Michelle's heart stirred. She almost couldn't look at him without feeling something inside of her. Her mind swarmed with a million questions she wished she could ask him, things he must know— things she knew nothing about. There was something about just being near him. For a moment they regarded each other, saying nothing. His smile was understanding, as though he might know what she was thinking. She was curious about him; he could see that. Each to the other was unlike anyone they had ever met. They were from such different worlds and Jason was just as curious about her as she was about him.

"Come on." Jason motioned her to the door. "It's too cold to be out here."

Michelle followed him into the house. To her surprise, everyone but Aaron had left. At their encouragement, she returned to the piano. Aaron and Jason retreated to talk, but occasionally would stop to listen to her music. It changed now that everyone had gone. She no longer played Christmas music from the book, but music written into her memory that flowed from to her hands via her heart and soul.

"Amazing," Aaron said softly as he watched her. "It amazes me that she remembers music the way she does. This is good for her . . ." His voice trailed off, wanting Jason to offer to let her stay awhile. "It's sad," he continued softly when Jason made no reply. "As a child, she was remarkably talented. But her father pushed her and pushed her until she snapped." His voice was distant, as though he was reminding himself of Michelle's past, rather than telling it to Jason.

Jason studied Aaron, studied the way he looked at Michelle. He showed a deep concern for her that seemed to make him tired. *He knows her, knows her well.* Jason watched her, listening. She was fascinating.

"I suppose I should be going," Aaron said reluctantly. He looked at Jason. "I'm sure Michelle would like to stay awhile longer. This is good for her," he said again.

"If she wants to stay longer, I can bring her down," Jason offered, not minding.

Aaron smiled appreciatively. He went to Michelle while Jason lingered, watching them. He watched as Aaron approached her, placing a gentle hand on her shoulder. The music stopped and she looked up at him. They talked, too softly for Jason to hear. Michelle looked over her shoulder at Jason, smiling faintly at him, then looked back to Aaron, nodding. Aaron kissed her on the cheek, leaving her to return her attention to playing. He nodded cordially, thanked Jason, and left. Jason wondered, after Aaron had gone, what exactly he was being thanked for.

He returned to the balcony at the far end of the room. The doors were still open to the night and the city lights far below. The gas heaters hummed and kept the cold at bay. The silvery Rocky Mountains shimmered in the moonlight. He moved farther out onto the balcony, sinking back into one of the overstuffed leather chairs under one of the heaters and crossing the heels of his boots on the railing. He closed his eyes and listened to the music. Eventually it stopped, although he was not sure exactly when because it lingered, hanging, ringing in the room behind him. He looked back. Michelle still sat at the piano, but she had crossed her arms on its mantle, with her head resting on them and her eyes closed. She sat there awhile. Then, knowing where he was, she rose and came to him.

"Thank you for letting me stay," she said, taking a seat in the chair beside his. "It's been so long since I've been able to do something like this. Too long."

He smiled, not minding.

"If I'm keeping you . . ." she said, not sure if she was.

"I'll say so." His voice was soft and understanding.

He's at peace and is content, Michelle thought.

The view below drew her attention. She leaned forward, crossing her arms on the railing, just as she had on the piano, looking down at the tiny town, so small, so serene, and so complete, and the endless mountains that surrounded it, protecting it. This was a world in itself, she thought, a world apart, secluded, secure, and safe from the rest.

Jason studied her, unable to prevent himself from doing so. There was something about her, something precious and exquisite. What exactly it was, he had not yet identified, but he knew, if given the time, he could find its essence. She was beautiful, far beyond anyone he had ever seen, much less been this close to, but it was not her beauty that affected him, but something she emanated. She was like those precious things that were real, yet intangible, such as a rainbow, rain, or snow. His eyes fell on her delicate, porcelain hands. Those same hands, so small and perfectly formed, with the same delicacy with which they rested on the stone railing, had mastered Tchaikovsky and Mozart just moments earlier.

Occasionally, her eyes met his, only to fall again with a modest, blushing smile. Her eyes did not meet his long enough to tell what they could, and so he caught only glimpses of their story, of the truth behind them. Through them, if one could look into them long enough and carefully enough, it might be possible to tell when she was happy or sad, what aroused her, angered her, amused her, or pained her. She had the kind of eyes that could not lie, that might reveal anything their owner wished to hide. He thought about finding her in his room. He had startled her, not by his presence, but by being so unexpected. Then he had surprised her, to his amusement. Throughout dinner he had seen Catherine insult her, which she absorbed. He had seen Aaron console her, and she received his consolation in a way that told Jason their friendship was deep. Her eyes did not give away the content of what lay behind them, only the weight, and Jason could see that it was heavy. He wondered how old she was, as he realized it was impossible to guess her age. Her skin and mouth were that of a child's, but she carried herself with an air of maturity. Although she was silent now, her voice rang in his ears. She spoke softly and was perfectly articulated. Her accent was charming. He liked it. She spoke in such a way that reminded him how European she was and how American he was.

He reached into the pocket of his jeans for a penny and held it out to her on the palm of his hand.

She smiled curiously.

"For your thoughts," he said. "It's an old cliché."

For a moment, she just looked at him. She had the feeling that she could talk to him. He radiated a comfort that drew her. She had been thinking about people, about meeting them and meeting him.

She told him so, smiling. "I meet people every day. Many don't like me, for no apparent reason. It's funny—I think people feel obligated to react to me, favorably, unfavorably, curiously, whatever. There seems to be some prerequisite hanging over my head that requires people to react to me." Michelle shrugged. "I'm accustomed to it, but I've yet to understand it."

Jason rested his chin on his hand. "Did I do that?"

Michelle smiled. "Yes, but you surprised me."

"That I did."

Michelle laughed. "I did not expect you to be *le monsieur de la montagne*."

Jason smiled. She had paid him a dignified compliment. "So, are you French or Swiss?" He asked.

"Both."

"And where do you live now?"

Michelle did not answer right away. Nowhere. She lived in whatever room corresponded to the number on the hotel room key. "I have an apartment in Paris and one in New York, but I spend most of my time living in hotels."

"That must be hard," Jason replied. "Do you like New York?"

"I used to," she said. "But now I find living in New York to be dangerous. It's a strange feeling, having to think about my safety. I'd rather stay in Paris." Michelle lowered her eyes.

That was a lie.

"You must have a lot of friends in Paris," Jason said.

Michelle made no reply. A distant, troubled cloud seemed to pass over her eyes.

Friends, she thought. *Such a subjective word.* She had friends, depending on the definition. She had many, many friends in Paris, all over the world, in fact. She was the muse of many of the top designers in Europe. She was Rita's cream of the crop. She had made Sasha the top stylist in the business. She was Aaron's next great discovery. Were these her closest friends? Regretfully, they were.

"How about finishing the tree?" Jason asked.

Michelle smiled and followed him off the balcony.

Looking up at the tree, she touched a branch, bending to smell it, loving its smell. Jason picked an ornament out of one of the many boxes still scattered around the base of the tree. It was an antique blown-glass bulb. He turned it over in his hand, gazing at it as memories of past Christmases filled him. For many years, the ornament in his hand had been hung ceremoniously on a tree exactly where this one stood, and before this house had been built, it had hung on other trees in other houses. It was a constant part of Christmas.

Michelle was looking at him. She reached out, taking the ornament from his hand. "May I?" She hung it carefully on the tree. "It seems like such a long time since I decorated a Christmas tree." She touched the bulb to keep it moving, watching it catch the light.

Jason handed her another, thinking how, earlier, she had remained on the stairs, watching from a distance, while his friends had tossed tinsel on the tree. They didn't say much. Occasionally, Jason would choose an ornament from the box that would make him smile, remembering whether it was old or new and where it had come from. He handed Michelle hand-blown glass trinkets that had belonged to his mother when she was young, miniature horses and angels that his nieces had brought, and expensive, elaborate gold and crystal icicles that had been a gift from a friend. He found a box of starched, crocheted snowflakes that his grandmother had made many years ago. They were now slightly yellowed from age. She had given each of the Henrey grandchildren a box of snowflakes when Jason was very young. He wondered if his brothers still had theirs. With the ornaments hung, Jason and Michelle stood back to admire their work. It was good work.

"How about another drink?" Jason offered.

"That would be nice," Michelle replied.

They went back to the kitchen, and again, sitting opposite him, Michelle watched his hands as he carefully heated the cognac in giant snifters. He had beautiful, strong hands. He offered her a glass.

"Toast?" she asked.

Jason smiled. "To losing track of time."

She touched her glass to his then took a sip. It was warm and wonderful. Rich. *To losing track of time.* How many times in the last six months had she lost enormous chunks of time? How many times had she awakened wondering how big the gap was? She never thought she would be toasting to losing time. They each sipped their drink in silence, Michelle thinking and Jason wondering what she was thinking.

She blinked and came back to him, giving him a reluctant smile, then looked around the room again, as if she had been physically absent and needed to familiarize herself with the space. She saw the large photo album on an end table in the sitting room. "Do you mind?" she asked, nodding toward it.

No, he didn't mind.

She sat down on one of the plush couches, which seemed to swallow her up. She picked up the album as Jason sat down beside her, looking over her. She opened the album and the heavy cover crackled. The first photograph was of a large group, at least thirty people of all ages.

"Who are all these people?" Michelle asked.

"My family."

"There are so many!"

Jason laughed. "There's a lot of us, that's for sure."

"This is really your family?"

"Yes, it was taken last summer at my parent's fiftieth wedding anniversary. That's my mom and dad there," he said, pointing. "And my brothers, Dennis, Cole, and Law, and me. And this is Dennis's wife and his kids." He pointed to four people in the picture. Several of them looked older than Michelle. "And Cole's wife and his kids. And Law's wife and their two kids."

"Law?" Michelle asked.

"Short for Lawrence. The others are my mother's family."

"You call them kids, but they look older than me," Michelle commented.

"Some of them probably are older than you. But they're still my nieces and nephews. To me, they're kids."

"Is that what you think of me, a kid?" Michelle asked. It was such an American word. She never used it.

Her question, put so casually, caught him unexpectedly. She was asking him to make a judgment about her, and he had not yet clearly made that judgment for himself. But he shook his head. "Not at all." Jason looked back at the photo.

"I wish I had a big family like that," Michelle said, turning the page in the album. The next several pictures were of Jason, his brothers and two of his nephews rock climbing. Michelle glanced at all of the pictures, but her eyes kept returning to a picture of Jason, straining against the ropes on a granite wall of rock. It was an incredible picture of an incredible man. She thought about the photograph upstairs, the one with the volcano in the background. *Another moment in his life, captured,* Michelle thought.

"Tell me about your brothers," Michelle said, turning the page.

"My oldest brother runs the ranch. Cole owns a distribution company, and Law, he's a doctor, a cardiologist. Lives in Chicago."

The next set of pictures was of the Henreys' Bar H Ranch in Montana. "Is this the ranch?" Michelle asked.

Jason nodded. "It is."

"So you must love horses," Michelle said.

"Sure," he replied.

"I've never been on a horse," Michelle said. "I was going to ride one for a photo shoot once, on the beach, but the thing was so big, it frightened me. I wouldn't do it."

"Maybe someday I'll have the chance to teach you to ride. It's really a thrill."

Michelle flipped further through the album, looking at more pictures of Jason and his family rafting, kayaking, fishing, and riding across what seemed like endless fields. "Tell me about Montana," she said.

"Montana . . ." Jason smiled, "is the most beautiful place on earth."

"Prettier than here?" she asked.

"Not prettier, but bigger. It's a place where the sky and mountains go on forever and the wind comes down from the north to teach a rancher a thing or two about respecting the land. It's a place where a hayfield can stretch for a hundred miles and the rain can come along and flatten it in a matter of minutes. It's a place where the most important thing to a boy is becoming a man and the best day of a boy's life is the day his father calls him a man." He smiled, thinking how overly nostalgic he must sound, not knowing that Michelle had neither a sense nor a notion of nostalgia.

"Do you remember that day?" she asked, having taken his description in its absolute literal form. Its true form. And there was truth in what he had said, in all he had said.

"You bet I do," he replied. "I was fifteen. My horse—my favorite horse I ever had—got spooked in a storm and bolted over a cliff. She broke her back. My father pulled out his rifle and said one of us had to put her out of her misery. He said a boy would have his father do it for him, but a man would do it himself. He knew how much I loved that horse; that's why he wanted me to do it."

"Did you?" Michelle asked, alarmed.

Jason nodded.

"Must have been hard . . . to shoot an animal."

Jason winced. "An animal? That horse was my best friend."

Michelle remained silent for a moment, not sure what to say. She wished she could understand what he was saying in such a way that she could be honestly sympathetic, but she couldn't. She had no similar point of reference. Her own life was too far removed from what his was to be able to draw from it and offer condolence. And she regretted this.

"Tell me more about Montana," she said, genuinely interested.

Jason told her about the electrical storms in the summer and the snowstorms in the winter. He told her about the bald-faced calves that were born every year and the autumn harvest moon. He told her that Montana was a place where young men learned about life and love at an early age, and about hard work and honor at an even earlier age. He talked about concepts like heritage and tradition, and he talked about wild horses and family gatherings on Sundays. He told her about riding fences with his older brother on summer nights, when it would be getting dark and they still had ten miles to go. He told her about mountain lions and elk and bighorn sheep and eagles.

Michelle listened in awe. She didn't have to pretend to be interested in someone else's life because she genuinely was in his. *This is real. His life is so real.* And it was better than any book she had ever read, because she could question certain details. She marveled at his description. She wanted to go there. She wanted to be there. She wanted to smell the earth and the rain.

When she told him this, he laughed. Not at her, but at her honest enthusiasm. "You cannot experience Montana in a day," he said. "It takes a lifetime. Every time I go back, something new happens—something that always astounds me. Every time I think I've seen it all, it shows me something new."

A photo slipped out of the back of the book. Michelle picked it up. "Is this your project in Hawaii?" she asked, looking at what she thought was a resort.

Jason laughed. "That's my house on Maui."

"You're kidding! It's so big."

Jason nodded. "It is big."

"Do you like Hawaii?" she asked.

Jason shrugged. "Not really. I was only there because of my project. I don't plan on going back very often. Kind of burned out on island life. I need mountains and seasons. I'll probably sell the house." He looked at her.

"It's probably like your apartment in New York. I only built this house so I'd have someplace to call home while I was working there."

Michelle agreed, but doubted his reasons for not wanting to go back to Maui were anything like her reasons for not wanting to go back to New York. She replaced the album where she had found it. She saw Jason look at his watch.

"I told a friend I'd meet him at the Woody Creek Tavern," he said. "Want to go?"

His invitation surprised her. But also, the thought of going out to a night-club, or any nightspot, which she assumed the tavern was, sent an old familiar anxiety creeping up her spine. She shook it off, but not before Jason saw it pass across her face.

"If you're worried about people bothering you, I promise they won't." His voice was reassuring. "The tavern's just a little shack outside of town. There's a band, good beer, and a couple of pool tables. That's about it. If you don't like it, I promise I'll bring you right back."

"Can I go like this?" Michelle asked.

Jason eyed her attire, amused. "You're a little overdressed for the tavern, but, yes, you can."

The phone rang and Jason crossed the kitchen to answer it. It was Aaron calling. "She's right here," Jason said, looking back at Michelle, mouthing Aaron's name to her. "Do you want to talk to her?"

"No. Is everything okay?" Aaron asked.

"Everything's fine. We're just getting ready to go down to the tavern." He smiled at Michelle, but she looked worried.

"I don't think that's a good idea," Aaron said.

Jason did not respond at first, and so there was a momentary, strained silence.

"Why is that?" he finally asked Aaron.

"Just don't let her drink too much," Aaron said.

"I promise to take very good care of her and have her home by midnight." He winked at Michelle, who smiled.

Michelle looked at him as he set the receiver down. "He didn't want me going, did he?"

Jason thought carefully about how to respond. He was being handed a puzzle here, piece by piece. If he were attentive and careful, he'd be able to put it together. It was a delicate puzzle. Trying to force the wrong pieces together would damage something, most likely Michelle, he guessed. "He was just concerned about you."

9

They drove out across a snow-covered mesa that Jason called McClain Flats, heading away from town. Along the way, Jason told her stories about the Woody Creek Tavern and its famous customers who drank there. "I've been shooting pool at the tavern for twenty-two years," he said, laughing, "and I've lost more money playing there than I have in all my business ventures combined."

The Woody Creek Tavern came into sight at the end of a narrow, winding road. It was a small, shabby, snow-covered lodge, a shack, as Jason had described it, lit by strings of Christmas lights and headlights. The door was open to the ice- and mud-covered parking lot, and the bright light from within streamed out.

As they pulled into the lot, Michelle could hear a country band playing. She looked up at the roof of the building, on top of which was mounted a giant stuffed boar. She laughed. "This is the strangest place I've ever seen."

"Just wait until you see the people inside. You don't know what strange is, yet," he replied, laughing too.

They walked up the porch steps together and into the bar. Everyone inside, about thirty people, including the band and the bartender, looked at them. Half of them said Jason's name in greeting, the other half nodded to him. If anyone recognized Michelle, they didn't let on.

"About time, Henrey!" yelled a silver-haired cowboy leaning on a pool table. "Get yourself a beer and get the hell over here. I'm losin' my ass!"

Jason hung their coats on the wall and nodded toward the bar. "Couple of Coors, Mike," he said to the bartender.

He handed one to Michelle. *Colorado beer*, she thought, taking a swallow right out of the bottle, like everyone else in the tavern. She never drank beer. It was icy cold and smooth. It was good.

"This is my friend Tommy." Jason introduced her to the silver-haired man who handed Jason a pool stick. "And the only reason he wants to play pool with me is because he always beats me." He motioned Michelle to a stool by the table. "But he doesn't know I've been practicing."

Michelle hopped up onto the stool, swinging her feet and sipping her beer. She looked around and found she was the only one not wearing jeans. *This is so unlike any place I've ever been. This is so unusual.* Just as with Jason, she had no point of reference. This left her facing a situation that, although unfamiliar, was not uncomfortable. Just different. She didn't mind.

When she looked back at Jason, she found he was watching her from the other side of the table. "You don't mind if I play?" he asked, coming to lean against the wall beside her.

"Not at all." She had never watched a game of pool before. In Europe, or at least in the Europe she knew, there was no Woody Creek Tavern or bottled beer or country music or stuffed boars.

"Good, because I need you here for good luck."

She watched him play. She watched him break. She watched him plan his shots thoughtfully, carefully, and she watched him shoot skillfully. She listened to him jeer Tommy when he was winning and swear when he was losing. She had another beer and met his friends who came by to chat. He introduced her as his friend Michelle. That night, at the Woody Creek Tavern, that was who she was—Jason's friend Michelle. She was happy.

The band played one of Jason's favorite country songs, one he liked to dance to. Ignoring Tommy's protests, Jason shelved his cue stick.

"Can you two-step?" he asked Michelle.

She looked up at him slyly, yet smiling, as if his question had been a challenge. "I don't know," she replied.

"I'll show you." He took her hand and led her to the dance floor.

He turned her to face him, taking her hand in his. He showed her the steps, counting. That was all she needed to know. It came easily for her. She never missed a beat, never missed a spin or a turn. She didn't know the song, but that was all she didn't know. They started at half the tempo of the music then quickly caught up.

Then the music slowed. For a minute, they just stood there, looking at each other. A choice had presented itself. They could either dance close or leave the dance floor.

"Dance?" he asked, and she accepted.

He took her hand, pressing it to his chest, and wrapped his arm around her tiny waist. They swayed together to the music, barely touching.

"We'll make a country girl out of you yet," he said, smiling at her.

"And how is that?" she asked.

"Well, you've got the cowboy and the dancin' feet. You're halfway there."

She smiled. "What else do I need?"

He thought for a moment then laughed. "It would help if you weren't afraid of horses."

"What about my accent?"

"You can keep the accent."

When the band stopped playing, they returned to the pool table. It was getting late and the tavern was beginning to empty, but Jason gave no indication that he was interested in leaving. Instead, he offered to show her how to play pool. He taught her how to hold the cue and how to chalk it. He explained the strategy of the game and lined up easy shots for her to take. They played a game together, and he let her win, taking his loss with an exaggerated display of dignity, making her laugh. When the band packed up their equipment and left, he dropped quarters in the old jukebox and ordered two more bottles of beer. Time went by fast, but it was time passing that Michelle would remember.

Eventually, Jason did decide, reluctantly, that it was time to leave. She followed him out, and he took the steps down from the porch in one stride. She was amazed by his agility. She didn't know men like Jason Henrey, and there was an openness to her curiosity about him that conveyed that. He didn't mind.

They drove back across McClain Flats under a bright moon that lit the snowy meadows, bright enough to cast shadows on the blue-white landscape. She felt peaceful inside. The beer made her feel warm and full, and she liked the feeling. Jason pulled into Aaron's driveway, leaving the engine running.

"Thank you for taking me to the tavern," she said. "I've never done a lot of the things we did tonight." She spoke softly, but with perfect articulation. Her voice hinted at her intelligence. "And, until tonight, I've never heard of steer wrestling or a Chinook, and so I must thank you for introducing me to those things." She touched his hand as though she was thanking an old, dear friend, and then turned away, got out of his Range Rover, and walked toward Aaron's house.

He watched her go up into the house. She did not turn around to look back at him. He drove away. At the end of Aaron's driveway, he stopped, thinking about her and all that had happened that night. Why had Keith brought her to his house in the first place? Why did Aaron leave her with him? It had been a nice night, that was true, but he had seen many sides of her in such a short period of time, and everything he had seen was either on her surface, or just below it, peeking through. Her smile was honest, but he sensed she had scars that were deep. She intrigued him. He should have asked to see her again. No, he would see her again. He should have asked her to dinner, so he would know when he would see her again. *No. Don't get involved.* Talking himself out of her, he looked at his watch, then turned down the road, heading into town.

10

A persistent knock on the bedroom door woke Michelle. She opened her eyes to a room flooded with sunlight. "Michelle?" It was Katrina. Michelle looked over at the clock. It was almost nine. "You can come in," she said.

Hearing Michelle's reply, Katrina burst into the room, throwing herself across the bed, the top half of her ski suit dangling around her waist. "You're coming, aren't you?" Katrina asked, her voice excited, yet betraying how disappointed she would be if Michelle were to say no.

"Of course I am. You should have wakened me earlier," Michelle replied, not sure if she really wanted to ski.

"I want to see what you are going to wear!" Katrina cheered, jumping to her feet, a little too excited.

Michelle laughed. "I don't know; you pick something for me."

With Michelle's permission, Katrina began sorting through the suitcases that Michelle had brought, the ones Sasha had packed for her and that, although they were now all accounted for, she had not yet bothered to unpack. Michelle watched Katrina while she enthusiastically organized Michelle's clothes, holding each garment up in front of her, looking at herself in the mirror.

"That will fit you," Michelle said of an oversized Dolce & Gabbana sweater. "You can have it if you like." Michelle was more than happy to relinquish anything to Katrina. She rarely wore anything the designers gave her, nor did she really care for much of it. But she was careful not to say that Katrina could have something because it was too big for herself. That would touch a sensitive nerve.

Katrina pulled the sweater over her head then turned to see herself in the mirror. "Thanks," she replied, choosing to wear Michelle's sweater rather than her own. "You're lucky you get all this for nothing," Katrina said.

Oh, but it's not for nothing. "You can have whatever you want," Michelle replied, throwing back the heavy quilt. She reached for her robe, which was on the floor by her bed, but she sensed Katrina looking at her naked body.

"You are so thin, Michelle," Katrina said remorsefully.

"I'm too thin," she replied, covering herself up.

"I don't think so," Katrina rebutted. "It's very in to be so thin." Katrina let out a heavy, discontented sigh. "I feel rotund." She sat down on the edge of the bed; her enthusiasm suddenly gone.

Michelle sat down beside her. "It's not *in*, Katrina. It's unnatural. And you shouldn't want to be that way."

Katrina just shook her head the way any sixteen-year-old would, resisting having to accept what she knew was right. Michelle thought about what Aaron had said the night before. Katrina was sixteen, but she looked older. She wore makeup so she would look as old as she possibly could. She was taller and much larger boned than Michelle, making Michelle look diminutive next to her. She knew that Katrina agonized about this. She wanted to be like Michelle—thin, blonde, fair-skinned and blue-eyed, and she complained because she was none of these things. But Katrina was beautiful, and Michelle pointed this out to her. She was dark-haired with olive skin like her mother and had the strong features of her father. Katrina reflected her upbringing. She was the only daughter of a Hollywood producer. She attended high school in Beverly Hills, where, she told Michelle, she didn't learn much. She had her own car, an expense account, credit cards, and a cell phone. She attended luncheons and polo matches in the company of famous people. She was the daughter of a very influential man and she had friends who were sons and daughters of influential men. And because of all this, what would otherwise be a traumatic yet normal teenage identity crisis was, for Katrina, a crisis on a far grander scale. Every girl her age went through it. Even Michelle had gone through it. What was unusual were the stimuli associated with the crisis, which, in Katrina's case, were quite extreme. Michelle, too, could understand that. Katrina, although she smiled on the outside, was crying for help on the inside. She was unhappy with the way she looked, and when she saw how other people dealt with this type of unhappiness—with plastic surgery and dangerous eating disorders—how could she not want to do the same? How could she think it was anything but acceptable when she was surrounded by it on a daily basis? How could she possibly view herself objectively when the two women she admired most were her stone-faced, perfect mother and Michelle Seko? Michelle wondered if Katrina did any drugs.

Michelle loved Katrina. She loved her because she was sixteen and she took Michelle back to when she was sixteen. For that one year, even though she went through very much the same crisis that Katrina was going through now, Michelle's life had been as close to wonderful as it could possibly ever be—for a very, very short time.

Katrina and Michelle had met in Monte Carlo three years ago, when Michelle worked for Aaron for the first time. Katrina had pestered her father continuously about meeting Michelle. "Please, take her to lunch, so she'll leave me alone about you," had been Aaron's request. Michelle thought back to that summer in Monte Carlo. She had been nineteen at the time. It had been both a wonderful summer and a horrible one. Up until then, Michelle had spent as much time as she could in Monte Carlo and had even considered buying an apartment there. But after that summer, she never went back unless she had to for a job. What had made it so horrible, Katrina knew nothing about. Aaron had kept that from her, and for that Michelle was thankful. But Katrina positively idolized Michelle. Katrina, like so many young girls, wanted to be like Michelle. That was the underlying evil of Michelle's business. She sold the look that every young girl wanted, and that look was both unrealistic and unhealthy.

Katrina, if I told you the real reason I look like this, if I told you what my life was really like, would I frighten you into seeing how good your own life is, or would you adopt my lifestyle and ruin your life, as I have ruined mine?

Katrina wanted to talk about hair and makeup and clothes and other models who she thought were not as successful or as pretty as Michelle. Michelle did not like this. That was talking about work and Michelle did not like her work. She tried to discourage Katrina, but it was hard. But Michelle could relate to her. She had been sixteen when she started modeling, and, at the time, everything revolved around hair and makeup and clothes and other models who were not as pretty as she was. It was the first time in her life that she had ever been showered with flattery. The first person who ever told her she was beautiful was a stranger. Katrina did not model because her father forbade it. It was a battle they fought regularly, one that Aaron always won. And he would never change his mind. For that, too, Michelle was grateful. Even being the daughter of Aaron Perlman would not protect Katrina from the ugly side of the business. And, besides, Katrina had much, much better places to go with her life than where Michelle had taken hers, and Aaron knew this.

They did not talk about *The Ballerina* for several reasons, all of which were Aaron's. Michelle could not say for certain if Katrina even knew about the project. She guessed not and did not mention it. Aaron did not discuss his film projects with his daughter, nor did he like for others to discuss pending plans with Katrina or even in her presence. "Never tell her you might do something," he would say. "Because then that's all you will hear about. If I tell Katrina that you might be coming to Los Angeles, then every day she will ask me when you are coming. If I tell her I am making a movie that has dancing in it, then she will want to choreograph the whole damn thing."

Aaron also did not like Michelle to talk about doing things with Katrina unless she was absolutely sure that those plans would not be broken. Michelle had promised Aaron that she would spend some time with Katrina and that she would talk to Katrina. So she had to do both.

They heard Aaron yell to them.

"You better hurry," Katrina said, abandoning her task of organizing Michelle's wardrobe, leaving Michelle to select her own clothes, a task that, now alone in her room, suddenly seemed impossible. *Why didn't I handle that better? Why didn't I say something?*

Michelle found Aaron and Katrina waiting for her in the kitchen.

"So, you really are coming after all," Aaron commented, pleased.

"Yes, but I don't have any skis or boots. I'll have to take care of that," Michelle replied.

"Consider it done." Aaron picked up the phone. "What size boot do you want?"

"Size seven," she replied.

"Any preference?"

"No," she replied. Aaron would select the best for her. Everyone always did. She only half listened to Aaron as he described what he wanted—skis, bindings, size seven ladies' boots. Top of the line. And poles. Ready in twenty minutes. He hung up the phone.

"Did you enjoy your time with Jason?" Aaron asked.

Michelle nodded. "We had a wonderful time." She looked at the pink bakery box of muffins on the counter.

"Help yourself," Aaron said.

Michelle wasn't interested in eating, but she suddenly felt pressured because both Aaron and Katrina were watching her, waiting to see what she would do. Feeling her throat tighten, she took a knife and cut a muffin in half. Of that half, she took two bites then abandoned it. She just couldn't eat. Aaron was watching her. He was looking for the telling signs. Michelle knew this. They were honest with each other in ways that did not always require words. Aaron knew and Michelle accepted that.

"Marc called this morning," Aaron said. "He wanted you to attend a luncheon with him today. I told him you couldn't. He didn't argue, but he did say that he was going to be making some changes and that you would have to meet with him. He didn't say when."

Michelle said nothing, but deep inside something dark and painful stirred.

"And those flowers are for you," Aaron said, indicating the large bouquet on the table.

Michelle turned her attention to them. "They're lovely," she said. "Who sent them?"

"I don't know," Aaron replied. "I thought they might be from Jason."

She frowned. "I don't think he would send me flowers." She took the card from the bouquet and opened it. "See, they're from the Garrisons." She read the card. "Welcome to Aspen, it was a joy meeting you. We look forward to introducing you to our musical society." She held up the invitation to the Christmas concert. The performance was Friday. Friday? She tried to think what day it was, but couldn't, and so she had to ask.

So like her, Aaron thought, telling her that today was only Monday.

11

Aaron pulled his SUV into the alley behind the ski shop. "If I get towed, that will solve my parking problem." He laughed.

Michelle's equipment was ready for her. The boots were new and fit well. Just walking around the ski shop in them made her legs ache. Her body had no physical strength. *How will I ever be able to ski?* She actually skied well. Her father had taught her when she was very small, and every winter they would go to St. Moritz to ski, just the two of them, sometimes every weekend. It seemed to be the only thing that made her father smile. Then the snow would melt and the house would be dark again. She still skied occasionally with people she worked with and once before with Aaron's family, which was very different than skiing with her father. It was fun and she never thought about falling.

Even in her ski clothes and glasses, people recognized her. They would look at her, then look quickly away, not wanting to be caught looking. It was an interesting phenomenon. Children had the habit of staring openly at strangers, but at what age did doing so cause self-consciousness? Michelle realized long ago that she could openly look at someone and make them visibly uncomfortable. Why, she did not know, but she had long ago adopted the habit of not looking at people around her until they became invisible. She saw no one. Aaron carried her skis across the street to the gondola. While they waited in line, people Aaron knew stopped to chat when they saw him, and Aaron would introduce her. She would smile and they would act like they knew her already. Had she forgotten? She didn't know.

They couldn't talk about *The Ballerina* because Katrina was with them. Katrina talked continuously, so much so that her constant voice rang in Michelle's ears. Michelle smiled and acknowledged her comments and answered her questions, but couldn't concentrate on Katrina. She couldn't concentrate on anything. She was just there, worrying about how she was going to ski, worrying about how she was going to be able to do anything and wishing she could sneak away long enough to get a dose of courage.

Michelle and Katrina sat together in the gondola, watching the town spread out below them as the car rose. Aaron was crowded into the car behind them.

"Where's your mother?" Michelle asked Katrina.

"She took my brothers to Buttermilk. She doesn't like this mountain," Katrina replied flatly.

Michelle got the impression that Aaron and Hannah weren't spending much time together, and she hoped there were no problems between them. They had been married a long time.

It was a brilliant, crisp December day, and the view that unfolded as they rose was breathtaking. Michelle pulled her turtleneck away from her throat. She was hot already.

"It's so beautiful here," Michelle said, thinking she never wanted to take something like this for granted. How could she? It was offered to her so rarely, and then stripped away so quickly.

"Prettier than Switzerland?" Katrina asked.

"Pretty like Switzerland," Michelle replied.

It seemed like a long, long time since she'd skied there, since she'd looked down on St. Moritz, the way she was looking down on Aspen now. She had skied in Switzerland since leaving her father's house, but she hadn't been back to St. Moritz in seven years. She missed it. There were so many details she'd let herself forget, details that being here now were bringing forth. She carried with her a child's memory of winters in St. Moritz, and those memories, although fragmented, were happy. She remembered walking down the snowy cobble streets, following her father, trying to trace his footsteps in the snow, trying to place her boots in his tracks. But, try as she did to keep up with him, his stride was too long for hers and she would slip, laughing. She remembered following him down the mountain, keeping her skis in his tracks. He would make large, slow, graceful turns down the slope and then pause, waiting for her. She remembered the thermos of hot chocolate he carried and how they would sip it from the tiny plastic cup while they rode up in the chair lift, just the two of them, to the top of the mountain. How many times had she actually skied with her father? She couldn't remember exactly, but those occasions had marked such an outburst of freedom in Michelle's life that her memory of them was inflated to something far greater than the actual event. *That hot chocolate would be so good now.*

She looked up at the dome ceiling of the gondola. She preferred the open chair lifts. She liked hearing the wind through the trees as the cable passed over them. She liked the feeling of being suspended in air, looking down at billows and billows of fresh snow. She liked the way the chair would rock and sway, making her heart jump. She liked the cold wind on her face and the sharp smell that cold air could have.

She gazed across the valley to Smuggler Mountain. Jason's house stood out clearly, clutching the jagged edge of the mountain. When she first noticed it, she did not realize it was his, but as the gondola continued to rise, the castle became more and more prominent. It was much larger than she realized, and she knew now that she had seen only a part of its interior. She could see sections of the narrow road leading up to it, long and winding, high above the rest. She didn't feel like she had just been there the night before. Like everything else that was good, it seemed as though last night was a long time ago.

"That's Jason Henrey's house," Katrina pointed out.

"Yes, I was there last night. He had a Christmas party."

Katrina frowned. "I wish I could have gone. Were they all there?"

"Who?" Michelle asked.

"All of them. The Henreys."

"No," Michelle replied, remembering the Henrey family photo.

"I wonder if they're coming this year," Katrina said.

"I don't think so," Michelle replied.

"I wish they were here. It's more fun when they are."

Michelle thought about the photograph again. Yes, it would be fun to have them here. It would be fun to be part of anything that large and that unified. *Family.* Michelle closed her eyes as the heavy feeling of loneliness overcame her, sinking down through her, taking what little bit of strength she had saved for thinking and breathing with it. She had no family left. Had she ever really had one?

Heroin. She looked back at Jason's house. *There is no heroin living in that house. Family gathers around the fireplace in winter and under the sun in summer. In that house, there is no kin in a plastic bag. There is no loneliness.* She thought back to her first night in Aspen, back to that moment in Keith's bathroom, and then tried counting the hours to the present. Forty hours. Forty drug-free, needle-free hours. And then she realized that it had been forty hours not because she had made any effort, but because nothing in the past forty hours had set her off. *When I get back, I am going to flush the rest of that crap down the toilet.* She scratched her arm subconsciously, because the thought made her skin itch. She would never flush it. She would never make it through the day. Just thinking about not doing it made her want it. And there would be no depriving herself of that. She sighed, resigning herself, as she always did. But today she was afraid of needles. That was good.

"So, what did you think of Jason?" Katrina asked.

"I really liked him," Michelle said. "I hope I see him again." It amused her that she would want to share such thoughts with a sixteen-year-old.

But she wanted to tell someone. She wanted to hear herself say it, listen to her voice. See how it felt. What she wanted to say to Katrina was that she found him very different from anyone she had ever met. Even though she might not see him again, he was on her mind, and it was good for him to be there.

Katrina frowned. "Well, don't like him too much; he's too old." She had taken Michelle's comment seriously and differently than Michelle had intended. "You'll just have to get over it. You're my only friend here this Christmas. If you go off with Jason, then I'll be stuck with my brothers."

Michelle sensed the possessiveness in Katrina's voice. *She's lonely, just like I am.* "I doubt I'll be going off with him," she said, looking back across the valley, which was falling farther and farther beneath them. *But I wish I could.* "I wish I lived here, Katrina. It would be so wonderful."

"That's what everyone says. But if you lived here, then you couldn't be a famous model."

Michelle looked over at Katrina, who adored her, and tried to smile. "But I don't want to be a famous model."

Katrina's expression turned to one of profound devastation. Then she turned away, as if she had just been betrayed. The silence lasted a few uncomfortable minutes, but Michelle waited it out. She was accustomed to uncomfortable silence—years of it.

"How can you say that?" Katrina finally said, exasperated. "You always talk like you hate what you do, but everybody envies you."

"I do hate it, and being envied is not a good thing," Michelle replied.

"Yeah, well, maybe if you didn't do so many other bad things, you would like it a little more," Katrina snapped at her.

"What other bad things?" Michelle asked, almost choking on her words, even though she already knew the answer.

Katrina only shrugged.

Michelle let it go. "Katrina, you seem very angry with me, and I'm sorry, for whatever reason."

"I'm not mad at you," she said, reluctantly. "I just wish I could trade places with you. I wish I could have what you don't want. I'd be happy. But I think if you quit modeling, you will regret it."

You don't want to trade places with me, Katrina. I wouldn't wish my life on anyone on earth. You think my life is about having my picture on the cover of a magazine. You can't imagine what my life is like. "Well, we can't trade places," Michelle replied. "But if we could, you would probably do a better job than I have," she said, only to pacify Katrina.

Skiing came back easily to Michelle, once she got past the fear of not finding her legs through the first few turns. After her fear eased, and she was able to enjoy herself. She was an able skier; it was her conscience that made things difficult for her. They lost Aaron almost immediately, but she and Katrina stayed together down the runs. Michelle did not know Katrina was having trouble keeping up with her. It never occurred to her.

They found Aaron again just before noon, and decided to stop at Bonnie's for lunch. Although it was crowded and people were waiting impatiently for a vacant table, Aaron managed to get them seated right away. Peeling off the top layer of ski clothes, Michelle slid into the booth between the wall and Katrina, her ski boots clanging against the table's pedestal.

Aaron smiled at her from across the table. "Are people bothering you?" he asked.

"Not at all," Michelle lied.

She was tired of being followed, but she said nothing to Aaron. And, thankfully, neither did Katrina, but only because Michelle had asked her not to. If either of them said anything, Aaron would assign someone to the duty of being her bodyguard, and she didn't want that.

The deck outside the window was crowded with skiers. The sun shone brilliantly, reflecting off their sunglasses, making everyone appear dazzling. She watched skiers come and go, struggling to get their skis on, struggling to get their skis off, juggling drinks and food and clothes and hats.

She looked over the top of Aaron's head, toward the door, and saw Jason. She didn't say anything, but watched him cross the crowded room. He was with friends. He was laughing. She watched every move he made—taking off his jacket, folding down his turtleneck and running his fingers through his hair. She watched the way he stood, how his knees bent to the angle of his boots, how he crossed his arms and how he laughed and talked at the same time.

As if he had known all along exactly where she was, he looked across the room at her, directly at her. Their eyes met and for one brief second, they were the only two in the room. Without hesitation, he approached them, and Michelle could feel her face flush. Aaron looked back over his shoulder and saw him, too, and waved. Michelle smiled brightly, which was rare, as he sat down beside Aaron.

"Where are the rest of the Perlmans?" Jason asked, reaching over to tap Katrina affectionately on the head, knocking the bill of her baseball cap down over her eyes.

"Who the hell knows?" Aaron replied, chuckling.

Katrina squeezed Michelle's arm, "Look, Michelle, here they come," she said of two young girls, maybe two years younger than Katrina, who were pushing each other toward the table. "I told you they'd be back. Dad, pay attention. This is so funny."

Michelle cringed, but she couldn't tell Katrina no. She adored her far too much to deny her anything.

"What are you two up to?" Aaron asked slyly.

"Michelle pretends she can't speak any English, and I get to be her interpreter. We've been doing it all morning."

Aaron frowned, but he was amused. "Yes, I know this trick."

The two girls approached the table and bashfully asked Michelle for her autograph, holding out a copy of a magazine with Michelle on the cover. Michelle took the magazine and looked at Katrina.

"Comment s'appelle-t'elle?"

"What is your name?" Katrina asked one of the girls.

"Samantha," she replied, not knowing whether to look at Katrina or Michelle, "and this is my friend Laura."

Katrina turned back to Michelle. *"Elle s'appelle* Samantha *et s'appelle l'amie* Laura.*"*

Michelle wrote a quick note on the cover of the magazine, then offered her hand. *"Enchanté."*

The two girls just looked at each other but then shook Michelle's hand.

Jason took the opportunity to reach across the table and retrieve the magazine. He looked back and forth between the cover and Michelle before setting it down again.

Michelle handed it back to one of the girls.

After they walked away, Katrina burst into laughter.

"You two are so bad!" Aaron said.

"I can't help it Aaron, Katrina makes me do it," Michelle said lightheartedly. "You know I can't tell her no."

"Try, Michelle. Please," Aaron replied.

"Jason, did you like Michelle's magazine cover?" Katrina asked.

"Very provocative," he replied, not saying whether or not he liked it.

A woman dressed in shocking pink ski pants and matching jacket interrupted their conversation. Her colors startled Michelle.

"Well, well! Good to see you, Jason!" the woman said, stopping in front of their table, then weaseling into a place for herself next to Jason, without waiting for an invitation.

Jason smiled politely. "Have a seat, Lisa," he said sarcastically after she had already taken one.

"I was wondering when you might get here," Lisa said. "When *did* you get here? I just saw Keith. You know who he's skiing with? Marc, you know, the designer, and his wife . . . Annalise . . ." The woman tried to recall Annalise's last name, but could not, so instead she bombarded Jason with a continuous train of chatter before even thinking to look around her at the others across the table.

"Hello, Aaron," she said, looking past Jason.

Aaron only nodded.

Everyone at the table remained mute.

Then she looked at Michelle. For a moment, she stopped talking and it was as if the room suddenly seemed very quiet. Then she held her hand out over the table, to Michelle. "Hi, I'm Lisa Cooke."

Michelle took Lisa's hand, quickly, yet delicately, but only smiled reluctantly. Instantly, she began to feel like the room was closing in on her. Marc. Annalise. Just the mention of them and she suddenly felt like she was suffocating.

"Lisa is a reporter for the *Aspen Times*," Aaron said. "She writes the society column, which means she's going to gossip about us." He gave Lisa a sarcastic smile. "Perhaps *reporter* isn't the correct term."

Michelle suddenly wanted desperately to get away. She couldn't breathe. She felt everyone's eyes on her, including Jason's. She whispered to Katrina to let her out, saying she wanted to wash her hands before lunch. At the same time, the waitress brought the lunch Aaron had ordered for them, so Michelle's desperate escape was not so obvious. Lisa watched her go, then, offering a quick goodbye, moved on to the next table.

"What was that all about?" Aaron asked. "Katrina, what's up with Michelle?"

Katrina only shrugged, pulling the sandwich plate toward her.

"Go and get her," Aaron said, pushing his daughter away.

Rolling her eyes, Katrina reluctantly obeyed, but then returned a few minutes later, sitting down again.

"Where's Michelle?" Aaron asked impatiently.

"She's said she not coming back. She said she's not hungry." Katrina bit into her sandwich.

"Well, where did she go?"

"Back outside."

Aaron threw his napkin down. "Let me out," he said to Jason. "She shouldn't go alone."

Jason rose from the booth. "I'll go," he offered.

Aaron let him go, grateful to be able to eat his lunch.

Jason walked out onto the deck, looking past the many skiers standing around, scanning the runs, which took off in different directions from the chalet. He spotted Michelle just past the corner of the deck, just as she stepped into her skis.

Michelle adjusted her glasses and pushed off down the hill. She took the left fork, not looking back.

Jason smiled. Gretl's Run. Gretl's led to Deer Park and nowhere else. He left the deck, knowing he could catch her.

Michelle made wide turns down the run as it meandered through islands of snow-covered pines. She took deep, easy breaths, now that she could breathe again. The runs were crowded, and so Jason had to keep his eyes on her and keep a lookout out for the other skiers at the same time. He didn't want to lose sight of her, but he didn't want to get into a wreck, either.

Ahead of him, Michelle worked her way down a run of moguls. She made her turns consciously and carefully, able to negotiate the tough terrain with skill even though she was not strong. What she lacked in strength to muscle her turns on the moguls, as many people did when they carved into them, she more than made up for with experience.

Jason hit the moguls with jarring speed, feeling the concussion in his legs with every leaping turn, but this was his opportunity to catch up to her. As she came to the bottom and took a gliding turn around a bend, she caught sight of him out of the corner of her eye. She had known she was being followed and that it was him, but she tried not to look back, not wanting him to know that she was aware of his presence. It was a game. He was trying to catch up to her, and she wanted him to have to work hard to do so.

Michelle did not see the two skiers bearing down above her, nor did they see her. Jason was closer now, but not close enough to do anything as the two runs merged together, and the skiers did, as well. They were already directly in her path when she saw them, and they left her no room to get out of their way. Heading for the side of the run, which was the side of the mountain, she needed to cut around, but there was nowhere for her to go. She was going too fast. Her skis chattered as she dug in, trying to slow herself. The two skiers missed her by inches, yelling at her, just as she ran out of slope and the mountain dropped out from beneath her. Her moment of flight was all too brief before she met with the steep bank of the plummeting mountainside. She forced her heels down with all her strength, digging the edges of her skis in, trying to stop herself, but the snow was too deep and too irregular, and she felt her skis catch and slip as she was pitched forward, down the embankment. Buried to her waist, her skies crossed and grabbed and she felt first one boot and then the other wrenched from her bindings, giving way to a sudden burst of momentum that toppled her forward, somersaulting her in a cloud of snow. With arms outstretched, she rolled, grasping, reaching for any grip on anything to slow her tumbling descent. She managed to slow herself considerably, but not before somersaulting again and colliding feet first with a tree. The silence came as instantly as her halt. Then a large limb above her released its load of snow onto her, as if to have the last word about her intrusion.

Not too shaken, she looked up. She hadn't fallen far, perhaps only thirty feet down the side of the crusty, deeply drifted, tree-laden snow bank, but the steepness of the slope was extreme, and she was now wedged against the tree, up to her chest in snow, her skis buried somewhere.

"Shit!" she swore, throwing down her only remaining pole.

Jason appeared at the top, clicking out of his bindings and jabbed his skis into the snow. "Are you all right?" he called down to her.

Michelle looked up, brushing some of the snow away from her face. "I imagine I am," she replied, barely loud enough for him to hear her.

Being careful not to knock any snow down on top of her, he carefully worked his way down the embankment toward her. He dug his heels in, making his descent look easy, uncovering her trail of equipment as he traced her turbulent path. She tried to push away from the tree, but the snow, which was fresh and deep, yielded, and she made no progress.

She looked up again and Jason was much closer to her. He seemed to know exactly what to do. Using the nylon strap on his poles, he hooked them together and handed them down to her. "Take this with both hands and don't let go," he said. "I'm going to pull you up."

Michelle grabbed the end of the pole with both hands then turned herself over so she was facing him and could get her feet underneath herself. Silently, she prayed that getting out would be easy.

Bracing himself, Jason backed against the embankment and pulled her up easily. When she was close enough that he could grab her wrist, he did. Michelle winced under the strength of his grasp. Reaching down, he got his other arm around her waist, pulling her up between his legs.

Suddenly, their faces were just inches apart.

"Are you okay?" he asked again.

She nodded, gasping.

Removing his glasses and gloves, Jason carefully pulled Michelle's snow-covered goggles from her face. Blinking, her snow-tipped lashes flicked droplets of water onto her cheeks. With great care, he wiped the snow from her face and neck. His hands were warm on her skin, although she expected them to be cold. He scooped the snow out from around her neck and out of the back of her jacket, and plucked several chunks of snow from the neckline of her turtleneck sweater.

Michelle tried to stand up to shake off some of the snow, but he stopped her. She looked at him, surprised, but his amused smile told her he didn't want her to move just yet, which confused her.

"That was a fabulous wreck," he said, smiling.

With one hand still on her neck, he kissed her. It was a soft kiss, full of curiosity and emotion, brief and warm. She looked up at him, blinking in absolute, complete surprise. She hadn't expected his kiss; in fact, he surprised her so completely she didn't know what to do.

He looked at her a moment, his smile warming into a laugh at her reaction. "You can't believe I did that, can you?"

No, she couldn't believe it. And she felt it to her very core. Her face flushed and she bowed her chin, averting her eyes, not knowing how to react. Her forehead brushed his cheek; he was that close. He touched her face again, raising it, and kissed her a second time.

She suddenly felt alive and she kissed him back, hesitantly, unsure of herself—not him—yet wanting to. She could feel his strength swallow her up, but it was his gentleness that overwhelmed her. Their eyes met and she searched his, wanting to know, suddenly needing to know what it was about him, so unlike anyone she knew or had ever met, that made her feel the way she suddenly did. It was not enough for him to kiss her like that; she had to know what it meant.

He rolled his eyes mockingly, and his smile, so casual and comfortable, put her at ease. "I guess I'm in trouble now," he said, laughing.

"Why are you in trouble?" she asked.

"Because you are so, so . . ." He hesitated.

Michelle flinched. Because of who she was? No, she hoped, not because of that.

He touched her chin. "Because you are so young."

Michelle laughed. Not at him, although that was what he thought, but because she was relieved. Being too young, she could accept; being Michelle Seko, she could not accept.

She looked back at him. "We have a saying in France," she said, "about testing the water. You can do it one toe at a time if you want to be careful about it, or you can just jump right in and perhaps be in for a big surprise. You know you surprised me, but perhaps I surprised you, too."

"You are right," he replied.

"You think I'm too young for you to be kissing, but you did it anyway. I'm glad you did." She looked at him then stood up.

She dug her boots into the steep bank to keep from falling again and brushed off the snow from her clothing. She looked up at the distance that remained of their climb, contemplating whether or not she could continue up without his help. She had a matter-of-fact way about doing so. She looked back down to the tree that had stopped her, then up to the ridge again. She was an equal distance between the two, and Jason was right there beside her, ready and willing to raise her up to the top. As much as he was there to help her, she wanted to get there herself, without his assistance. She took a deep breath. She felt good. Despite being covered with snow, having fallen—although not too far or too hard—she felt good. She looked at him again. *Let him help you. He wants to.* She smiled at him.

They looked at each other awhile, contemplating each other. Their question, though not spoken, was the same. *Who are you and how long will you be here?*

He laughed again. "What's your hurry? Do you have to be somewhere, or can you stay awhile?"

His question stopped her. He had a point.

"Well, Jason," she said, sitting down on the bank just above him, so he would have to turn around to look at her, "actually, I can stay awhile."

He laughed again. "So how long can you stay?"

"Two weeks. I can stay here, right here, for two weeks, and then I have to go back to doing whatever it is I do."

"That's good, and during that time you will age two weeks," he said, making her laugh.

"There are a lot of things about my life that I'd like to change, but my age is not one of those things," she said. "If you think I'm too young, I regret that. Maybe you are wishing I was ten years older, but I'm not." She looked at him in a way that overwhelmed him with respect for her. "I'm only twenty-two, but I am here."

He found her words profound. She was so young, yes, but for all the naïveté he assumed she possessed, she was actually very wise. What he did not know was that he was witnessing a rare phenomenon. The person he was seeing as so bright and so alive was just this moment blooming. She was just that minute emerging from beneath a dark cloak, under which she had been smothered for a long, long time. He didn't know how free she suddenly felt—only that she seemed free. To him, she was someone who had not yet outgrown the desire to take every day, every single day, and live and breathe it. What he did not know was that these days, if they were hers, were numbered. While he thought she was telling him to grab the chance while he had it, what she really was saying to him was, *Have me, help me, and continue to breathe the life into me that you have started to breathe into me. You started this and it doesn't have to stop. Not now, not here. Not if you don't want it to. In a few weeks, yes, then it will all come to an end and I will be gone, but I'm here now.*

He reached up to her, grabbing her boot, pulling it so she slid back down. He searched her eyes, touching her cheek again. One minute she was ageless, timeless, and more mature in mind and emotion than any woman he had ever met. The next minute she was a child, teasing, as children do. He kissed her again, then again and again. She was right. It suddenly seemed so obvious.

And yes, she thought, *I'm still here.*

12

They skied together for the rest of the afternoon, and Michelle enjoyed his company tremendously. They skied well together, even though her strength was failing on some of the more difficult runs. But she felt no need to prove her ability, and it was easy for her to say that a route was too difficult for her or that she wasn't strong enough to attempt a challenging drop-off. And Jason always obliged by choosing an alternate route. But on the smoother runs, her strength returned, and she was a fast, elegant skier. Like music, it came to her easily.

At the bottom of each run, they would pause to discuss their descent. At one point, they found themselves at the top of the run Michelle had taken just before her spill. Famous for its moguls, the run looked like a hillside of buried cars—hundreds of them.

"I can do this," she said, heading down with cautious intent. Her progress was slow yet precise. Jason waited until she was near the bottom before starting down. He hit the moguls hard, using his strength to shave his way around them.

Michelle was grimacing at him when he skied up to her. "You take those like a woodcutter takes to a pile of firewood. You hacked away at every bump."

Jason only laughed at her critique.

By the time they started back down to the base of the mountain, Michelle had agreed to have dinner with him. And when he offered to drive her back to Aaron's, she accepted.

The base of the mountain was crowded, and Jason took her skis for her. "I've got a locker here. We'll just put these in it so we don't have to haul them around."

"I need to let Aaron know that I'm riding back with you—otherwise, he will worry," she said.

Jason retrieved his phone from the depths of his jacket and fired off a brief text to Aaron. "Done. Would you like to go over to Andiamo for a drink?" he asked.

"If it's not too crowded." She followed him to the locker.

"Oh, it will be crowded, but I always get good service there."

Andiamo was indeed crowded, but Keith saw them coming and quickly made a place for them on the patio. "It's about time you came in," Keith said to her. "What can I get you?"

"Brandy would be nice," she replied, working her way out of the top layer of her ski clothes. "For you, Jason?"

"Oban on the rocks," he replied.

Michelle was down to her turtleneck and jumper, and Jason noticed that people around them were looking at her. She seemed not to notice. But Jason did. He noticed the room gradually transfer its center from one that was floating to one that was fixed on Michelle. As the recognition of her spread, more and more people looked her way. Some only glanced at her, either smiling or frowning. Others took a longer, more studied look at her. Jason noticed that it was the women more so than the men who studied Michelle, and that they did so with an odd look on their faces. It took him a moment to identify the look, but eventually he did. It was a look that combined envy, jealousy, and despair. To envy Michelle was understandable. She was young and she was beautiful. But her youth and beauty caused jealousy, and that jealousy caused despair, because there was nothing that these women could do that would give them the same youth and beauty that Michelle had. And so they hated her. *Interesting,* Jason thought. *Very interesting.*

The gas heater was close to them, and her face was flushed from its warmth. *Her composure is perfect. She's natural.* He thought about what had transpired the night before. *Any problems she has to deal with are her own. And, hey, don't we all have them? She doesn't seem to mind that she's got everyone in the room holding their breath. She doesn't play to it or against it.*

Keith joined them, throwing himself down into the chair with a grunt. "I'll tell you, this holiday season is going to kill me."

"You say that every year," Jason replied, laughing.

"Yeah, but this one is going to *hurt*."

"No, it won't. You just like to have something to complain about."

"Yeah, yeah, yeah," Keith said lightly, smiling. "So, Michelle, how did you like the skiing?"

"Marvelous," Michelle replied. "And I even had a terrific spill. It was quite spectacular."

"I'm sorry I missed it," Keith said.

Jason saw Aaron coming down the sidewalk and whistled to him. "I was just going to call you," Jason said to Aaron as he approached them, stepping with some effort over the railing that sectioned off the restaurant's patio. Jason moved over, making room for Aaron.

"Then I've saved you the trouble," Aaron said, dropping his heavy body into the chair.

"Hey! Don't you know you've got to wait in line for a table, just like everyone else?" Keith said. "The owner's not going to cut you any slack."

Aaron only laughed. "You finish out the day okay?" he asked Michelle.

"I certainly did," Michelle replied, smiling.

"That's my girl. Always running with the big boys."

"Where's Katrina?" Michelle asked.

"She ran into some girlfriends. I think they went over to the Aspen Club to swim." Aaron looked back and forth between Jason and Michelle. "You two got dinner plans?"

"We do, actually," replied Jason, without hesitation.

"Anything you want to break? I'd love to get a group together. Maybe go over to Pinons."

"Hey!" Keith protested. "What's wrong with my place?"

"Too crowded, too noisy, too expensive," Aaron replied.

"And since when do you ever have to pay?" Keith chided, getting up. "Back to the galley," he said, excusing himself.

"Life would be so dull without him, wouldn't it?" Aaron said to Jason.

"Definitely dull," Jason agreed.

They are all good friends, Michelle thought. *Old friends. Loyal friends.*

They talked for a while and, periodically, others would stop by their table and say hello to Aaron or Jason, or both. Keith returned with more drinks for them.

"Are we still on for tomorrow morning?" he asked Jason and Aaron. "Or are you two suddenly not up for it?"

"We're up for it," Jason replied, with a mocking challenge to his tone.

Aaron raised his glass. "Then nine o'clock at the airport."

"Sounds like perhaps you're going heli-skiing," Michelle said.

"Every year, we try to live like we're twenty again, just for one day." Aaron laughed.

Michelle was happy for them, but a little envious, too. *Yes, they are good friends.*

Jason looked at his watch. "We might want to think about going," he said to Michelle.

"If you're leaving, would you mind dropping me off at my house?" Keith asked. "I gave Marc my car, and I'd like to get out of here for about an hour."

"Sure." Jason turned to Aaron. "Dinner another time?"

"You name the time," Aaron said, then looked at Michelle. "I'll see you later?"

"A little later," Michelle replied.

The four of them left the restaurant together and a hundred pairs of eyes followed Michelle.

"See you back at the house," Aaron said, splitting off from the group.

Michelle wiped the steam from the passenger window of the Range Rover, only to fog it again. It was late afternoon and the streets of Aspen were crowded. Jason wound his way through town, taking marvelous little side streets when he could to avoid a majority of the après-ski congestion.

When Jason pulled into Keith's driveway, Marc and Annalise were just leaving the house. They came toward the car when they saw her. Michelle tensed.

"Thanks a lot," Keith said, getting out. "Why don't you come down to the restaurant later? I'll be back down there by about six."

"We'll see," Jason replied.

Michelle watched Keith walk away and then stop to talk to Marc. Annalise continued toward her. She came around to the passenger side of the vehicle, and Michelle reluctantly lowered the window.

"Have you talked to Rita?" Annalise asked, electing to speak to Michelle in English, rather than French.

"No," Michelle replied softly.

"Well, you should call her. I'm sure she's called Aaron's today. She's very concerned. She said that your father called her yesterday and several times today. He's looking for you. Don't you find that odd?" Annalise asked, knowing very well that it was more than odd for Michelle's father to be calling around for her.

Michelle could feel an instant panic circulate in her stomach, but she said nothing.

"You should call Rita," Annalise said again. She looked only briefly at Jason, then walked away.

Jason looked over at Michelle, who suddenly looked devastated. No, she looked frightened.

"You want to go?" he asked.

She nodded vaguely, distantly, and remained strangely silent as he backed out of the driveway and headed across town.

Aaron's SUV was gone, meaning that, unless Hannah was back, the house was empty. Michelle hoped that was the case.

"I can wait for you," Jason offered, stopping in Aaron's driveway.

Michelle let out her breath she had been holding. "I'm sure you'd rather go home and change," she replied tensely.

Something had rattled her. "Would you rather go another night?" he asked.

"No," she said, realizing she was not hiding her uneasiness.

"Then I'll be back at seven, okay?"

She smiled or, rather, tried to smile, then got out quickly and hurried into the house, leaving Jason to wonder what in the hell had just happened.

To her relief, no one was home. She closed her bedroom door quietly behind her, sinking back against it. She tried not to think about it, but failed. She snatched her cigarettes from the nightstand and closed herself in the bathroom. Her hands were shaking so violently she could barely light her cigarette. She hadn't smoked all day, and so the first deep drag she took hit her like lead, deadening her nerve endings but not the sickening feeling in her core. *I knew it would be just a matter of time before he'd start trying to track me down.*

Holding the cigarette in the corner of her mouth so that the smoke curled up into her eyes, making her squint, she looked at her reflection in the mirror. She tried to fight it, but her reasoning was lost somewhere far, far away. *This is Aaron's house. There will be no hiding it.* She took a deep breath. She wasn't too far gone yet to fight it. But, damn, it was hard. *If Aaron were home right now, I'd go talk to him. I'd tell him.*

And then there was Jason.

She coughed, spitting the burning cigarette into the sink, leaving it there. She was past thinking she could fool people. *My father!* She could feel the old familiar anxiety creeping up on her. *Don't think about it. Don't think about it. What can he do? What could he possibly want, other than to hide the truth?*

She wanted the same thing. To hide the truth.

Michelle looked at the window, then out the window, thinking about her mother, wondering what it must have been like. *How could she have done such a thing? What had driven her? What could have—would have—prevented her?*

Michelle turned away from the window, unable to look at it, closing her eyes to it, only to have the vision become more vivid. She tried to close her mind to it, but her mind would not let go. She sank down onto her knees. She heard shattering glass when no glass was shattering. She could hear and feel her heart beating in her throat, faster and faster and faster, until she could no longer breathe, and she thought it might explode. She squeezed her eyes shut tight and pressed her palms against her ears, begging, pleading, screaming to forget. She could not.

When the glass stopped shattering, she opened her eyes and met them in the mirror. The monster in the mirror was even more hideous than the monster in her head. She dug through her makeup bag for her lipstick case.

Just. One. Sniff. She sat absolutely still and stared at herself, staring, until her image in the mirror became another person, moving, making evil faces at her, hating and distrusting her. She stared and stared, letting the smoke of the cigarette in the sink curl up between them until she could face herself no longer. In her mind, she screamed again, then she cried, lying down on the floor, hiding from the eyes in the mirror, rolling onto her back, staring up at the ceiling, the beautiful ceiling. She could feel the anxiety crawling through her veins, the anxiety that made her want to do something, anything, to make it go away. It was once scratching at her from the outside, trying to get in. Now it was clawing desperately at her insides, trying to get out. She let it go.

Reaching up for the cigarette she took one last, deep drag, so deep it made her head spin heavily, then flipped it into the toilet, where it landed with a brief hiss. Lying back down on the floor, she crossed her arms over her face, exhaling, hooking the back of her heels on the vanity, feeling the blood pressure in her face increase.

She remained there, lying as she was, for a long, long time. Never could a moment pull her in so many different directions at once as it could when part of her desperately wanted to lose herself and another part of her just as desperately wanted not to.

There was a knock on her bedroom door. She expected to hear Katrina's voice, which she would have chosen not to respond to, but heard Aaron's voice instead and called him in. She was still lying on the bathroom floor when he walked in. She didn't bother to get up.

"Are you okay?" he asked, pushing the door open. It was a large bathroom, and he was able to step in and over her without her feeling cornered.

"I'm trying to be," she replied, looking up at him, distorted by her perspective.

He cocked his head, looking back down at her. "Anything you want to tell me about?"

Michelle didn't respond and only shrugged instead. She wanted to tell him, but she wasn't sure how much to tell him. She sat up slowly and leaned back against the bathroom counter. Her head spun.

"Have you talked to Rita?" he asked.

"No. You?" she replied.

Aaron nodded. "Well, don't worry about calling her. She's going to call back here in about an hour. You should talk to her. She's going to keep calling until you do." He didn't press her any further. Whatever was camped inside of Michelle at that moment would work its way out eventually. He had no reason to push too hard. He sat down on the edge of the bathtub, resting his elbows on his knees. He saw the lipstick case on the counter and picked it up, turning it over in his hand. He knew what it was.

"Is this the first time today you've done this?" he asked.

Michelle looked at him and nodded.

"Is this a good thing?" he asked.

Michelle nodded again.

Aaron sighed. "Michelle, you're killing yourself. You must know that."

She looked up at him. *How can you say that to me? You don't know, and you couldn't imagine. Killing myself? What an absurd notion. I do it to stay alive, not to die.* She looked away, having nothing to say.

Aaron leaned back, bracing himself and stretching out his knee, which ached from skiing. He looked at her thoughtfully. "Michelle, if you could do anything you wanted, what would it be?"

Michelle closed her eyes, because his question made her feel tired. Her blood was racing, and she could feel its heat coursing through her. Yet she didn't feel she could move. "Sleep. I would sleep."

Aaron sighed again, resigning the conversation. "When Rita asks me if you are doing this crap, I'm going to tell her no. And tomorrow morning I want to take you in to see a friend of mine. Maybe we can get a head start on getting you off this and on with your life."

Michelle closed her eyes and agreed, knowing that Aaron already had plans to ski tomorrow with Jason and Keith. And she agreed because it was the easy way out.

Aaron returned the lipstick case to the counter. He wondered, though, what Michelle would do if he were to just pitch it into the toilet. Would she react at all? He didn't know, nor did he find out. It just wouldn't be worth it to be cruel to her.

"So, you're having dinner with Jason?" he asked.

"I'm having dinner with Jason," she echoed.

"And what do you think of him?"

"I like him," she said. "He doesn't patronize me. I like that. And he seems so grounded."

"He's a good person."

"Yes, a good person," she replied, as if perhaps she wasn't.

She got up to get her cigarettes from the other room and Aaron followed her. "You and Jason are good friends?" she asked.

"For a long time." Aaron replied.

"So, what's his story?"

Aaron was quiet for a moment, thinking about how best to respond to her question. "Jason has lots of stories. What do you want to know?"

"Why does he seem so real, yet so unbelievable at the same time?"

"That's because you don't know him, Michelle. And don't get overwhelmed by someone you don't know. If you do get to know him, then he won't seem so unbelievable."

Michelle pursed her lips. "Sounds like a warning."

"It is. I'm just trying to protect you."

"From him? Why?"

Aaron laughed. "No, from yourself."

Michelle bit her lip. She didn't find that funny. "Would you do something for me?" she asked. "Would you not tell him about me?"

Aaron nodded, understanding. "If you'll do something for me. If you'll try to stop doing this death walk."

Michelle nodded, not so much in agreement, but in acknowledgment.

After he'd gone, Michelle poured herself a glass of vodka from the flask she kept in her bag. It was a beautiful flask of ornately carved sterling silver. It had been a gift from Sasha, a long time ago. She needed a few quiet minutes to regroup, so she sat on the corner of the bed, cigarette in one hand and vodka in the other. She sighed. Jason didn't know what he was getting himself into. It almost didn't seem fair. She didn't want him to find out things about her that would turn him away. She thought about the evening ahead. Dinner together. It was the one thing she had to look forward to. *Get yourself together.*

Rita was going to call. Michelle knew that she needed to prepare herself for that, but she didn't know how. She didn't know what to expect from her father. She wished she had someone on her side whom she could confide in. That could only be Aaron, and she had come very close to telling him why, after seven years of silence, her father was calling for her.

The hot shower helped. The vodka numbed her. Michelle sat in front of the mirror, combing out her wet hair. It fell straight to her waist. Looking at herself in the mirror, she thought about Jason, wondering what he saw when he looked at her. She sighed, wishing that she could be someone else, wishing she could just pick out a new life for herself. Her life was so off track that she wanted to just cut the tape and start a new reel. She smoothed her hair back and braided it. She selected a black cashmere knit dress that fell to her ankles, similar to the one she had worn the night before, without really thinking about it. She hated thinking about clothes. Clothes were work. The dress was warm, simple, elegant, and comfortable.

Jason was waiting patiently, alone, in Aaron's living room. She wondered where Aaron was, but didn't ask. She apologized for making him wait. She hoped it wasn't long. She tried as hard as she could to maintain her composure, which she had left scattered in pieces behind her.

She turned away briefly to gather her coat, and he could not take his eyes off of her. She ran like night and day at the same time. He could not deny that she possessed a simple sophistication unlike any woman he had ever found himself in the presence of. There was a natural elegance in everything she did—the way she carried herself, the way she talked, so soft-spoken, and the way she smiled. And yet, Jason strongly suspected that something very wrong was going on.

The house phone rang. Michelle froze. It rang again. Still, she did not move, did not breathe. It rang again. She just stared at it, the color draining from her face. Where was Aaron? Why didn't someone else answer it? She knew it was for her, that it was Rita calling. Michelle refused to carry a cell phone. This drove everyone around her crazy, but she relented. She had one, but rarely used it unless mandated to do so.

She thought about not answering, but, reluctantly, she picked up the receiver.

Jason elected to move out of earshot, disturbed by her behavior, not wanting to listen to her conversation.

Rita dedicated her usual thirty seconds to small talk, telling Michelle she was in New York, which Michelle already assumed because Rita was speaking to her in English. Rita had advised Michelle years ago "to speak the language of the country you are in—otherwise, you are being rude." This became second nature, even with phone calls. Then Rita got to her point. "Your father called me yesterday," she said. "He said he needs to speak to you. Said it was urgent."

Michelle choked on her words. "Did he say why?"

"No, but I promised him you'd call him, so please do," she said, as if the instructions were routine, as if Michelle could just pick up a phone, punch in a number, and talk to her father. "And Aaron called me this morning," Rita added.

"What did he say?" Michelle asked. She knew it was Rita who had called him.

"We had a long talk. We all want what's best for you; you know that."

"I know." Michelle looked over her shoulder at Jason, who had retreated farther away from her. She hoped he couldn't hear her. "I'll do what Aaron wants." She knew what Rita and Aaron had talked about. It would not have been the first time.

"That's my girl." Rita sounded genuinely encouraging. "You know I'm right there with you."

"I know," Michelle replied.

Rita detected the edgy tone in Michelle's voice. "Are things better?" she asked. "At Aaron's?"

Michelle sighed but said yes, they were. She didn't want to talk about Marc and Annalise.

Rita did not press. "I love you, Michelle. You have a good Christmas."

Michelle replaced the receiver, remaining where she was, staring at it for a while. She closed her eyes, taking a deep, trembling breath. She took another.

"I promised him you'd call." Sorry, Rita, that's a promise I can't keep. You made it, not me. And, besides, I'm good at breaking promises. She took another deep breath. She'd never call him.

"Michelle?"

She spun around as if she had forgotten Jason was there. She tried to quickly regain some fragment of composure, knowing she should provide some explanation. "I'm sorry," she said, forcing herself to display perfect composure. "I'm deathly afraid of the telephone," she said, then immediately regretted it, knowing she was setting him up to form a million reasons in his mind as to why someone such as herself might be afraid of the telephone. She didn't know she could not fool him. Not for one second. "That was my fairy godmother, my manager," she explained, somewhat sarcastically, trying not to look affected by the call. She would soon learn that there was no emotion she could hide from him.

He had overheard fragments of Michelle's conversation, enough to wonder, but he didn't let on.

"So, where are we going?" she asked, wanting to change the subject, wondering what type of place he would choose—a noisy, crowded place, like Andiamo, or someplace quiet. Michelle hoped for the latter.

"Well, I know of this really cool castle, way up on the hill," Jason replied, smiling. "If that's okay with you."

Michelle couldn't help looking surprised. "Dinner? At your house? Who's cooking?"

Jason laughed. "I am."

"Really? What are you cooking?" she asked.

"Well, what do you like?"

"Fish. I like fish. And pasta," she replied. She liked the concept of food and of eating; it was swallowing that she had trouble with.

"Then that's what I'm cooking," he replied.

"Would you mind if I brought my portfolio?" she asked.

Jason frowned, not understanding what she was referring to.

"My music portfolio," she clarified. "My *travaux en cours.* I travel with it, because I never know when I might encounter a beautiful piano such as yours. Perhaps I will have an opportunity to play something for you tonight."

It was well after dark, but when they left the house Michelle noticed the same man was again at the bottom of Aaron's driveway. He followed them with his camera, taking their picture. Jason noticed him, too.

"Does that bother you?" he asked.

Michelle only shrugged. "I'm accustomed to it." People were always trying to get her picture. It was part of her life.

"Well, it bothers me." He opened the passenger door for her, but then, instead of getting into the driver's seat, he walked down the driveway to where the man stood poised against his truck. A few minutes later, Jason returned. When they pulled out of the driveway, the man smiled and waved as they passed.

"We struck up a deal," Jason said, offering no further explanation.

As they approached Jason's house, still standing out in the darkness, Michelle looked up at it. "This place is so incredible. How could you not want to live here?"

"Thank you," he replied. "And who says I don't want to live here?"

He pulled into the garage behind the house and they entered into the kitchen through the back door. She loved his casualness. The smell of herbs and garlic was overwhelming. A fire crackled in the huge hearth in the sitting room off the kitchen. Everything was warm and inviting. Michelle felt like she had just walked into a cozy cabin, not the kitchen of Jason's enormous house. He took their coats and hung them near the door. Pouring them each a glass of wine, he then turned his attention to a sauté pan on the stove. Michelle couldn't help smiling at him. Spread across the counter was an array of fresh vegetables and herbs, which, with careful attention, he added to the pan. She took the same stool she had sat on the night before.

"You've really gone to a lot of trouble," she said.

"No trouble at all. I love to cook," he replied, setting a seasoned salmon into the pan of sauce and herbs to poach. "About ten minutes."

A flash of anxiety passed through Michelle. What if she couldn't eat? Food had a way of lodging in her throat and choking her. The reason she didn't eat was because sometimes she couldn't swallow. The half of a muffin that morning had been a lot for her. She had skipped lunch without missing it. An appetite was something she did not have. Often it was not until she was near fainting from lack of food that she would realize that she hadn't eaten for sometimes days.

But as she watched Jason at his counter, her anxiety gradually subsided. She was very hungry. It was not so much physical hunger, but rather something she wanted to participate in.

They ate and talked and laughed, and Michelle, reluctantly at first, then more bravely, asked him questions about himself. She asked him the kind of questions that a foreigner would ask, and he answered her questions and told her stories, which she listened to intently, hanging on his words, loving his voice and the way his eyes lit up and seemed to laugh when he talked.

He learned a lot about her by the questions she asked him. She wanted to know more about Montana. She wanted to know what it was like to ride broncos and rapids and to go to a public school. He realized that most of what she knew was from what she had read; so much of her knowledge was imbedded in lore, which, in many ways was inaccurate by today's standards. She had an idealistic view of places she had never been. They talked about things that were as far removed from her life and her world as anything could possibly be. Jason sensed a deep-seated significance in this. They talked about dancing and skiing and doing both again soon. And all through dinner, there would be brief lapses in their conversations when they would just look at each other.

She pushed her last few bites of fish around her plate, unable to finish it. The food had been wonderful and she'd eaten a lot, a lot for her. It left her feeling warm and sleepy, and she liked how it felt.

"You must think I'm so nosy," she said.

He laughed. "I don't mind." He speared the last piece of fish from her plate, eating it. "You must think I talk a lot."

She smiled. "Not at all. I like your stories."

While Jason rose to clear their dishes and clean up, Michelle wandered to the far window. Occasionally, he turned to look at her. She stood before the window, erect, her arms folded in front of her, as still as a statue, her eyes searching the darkness, her mind searching farther. He had noticed it during dinner; her thoughts seemed to drift of their own accord and settle somewhere far away. Then she would suddenly come back, startled that she had drifted away in the first place. What was taking her?

He refilled her wine glass, took a beer from the refrigerator for himself, and left the kitchen to sit on the couch by the fire.

"It's snowing," she said, turning to look at him, reclined back with his feet on the table in front of him, his beer bottle wedged between his knees and his hands crossed behind his head. She smiled at his casualness and went to sit beside him.

"I don't know about you," he said, smiling, "but I am very full."

Michelle nodded, agreeing. "That was wonderful. Thank you." She pulled her legs up, folding them under her. Her eyes fell to the hem of her dress, smoothing it with her hand, doing so nervously. She wanted to say something, but was finding it difficult to find the right words.

Jason sensed this and was quiet. Patient.

"I want to thank you," she finally said. "You've been very kind to me in a way that I've not found myself on the receiving end of . . ." Her voice drifted. "You've shown me a lot of courtesy." Her voice drifted again. "If I seem unappreciative, it's only because I've never met anyone like you. I feel like I don't quite know how to react."

"I don't find you unappreciative at all," he said. "You've been a marvelous guest. You're easily entertained," he said lightheartedly, having told her so many stories.

She looked up at him, smiling. "If it wasn't for this afternoon, I'd say you were quite the humanitarian."

Jason laughed. "You hardly seem like a charity case to me."

"Oh, but I am in a way," she replied. "Not economically speaking, but rather a case for kindness. You might think I live amidst constant flattery, but quite the opposite is true. You can't imagine what it's like being me."

"You are right. I can't imagine," he replied. *Come on, Michelle, let me in on yourself.*

Michelle smiled, a little reluctantly. "I know that you've been conscientious about not questioning me. You've been good about letting me question you all night long and you've left me alone about myself. You must wonder. I'm sure you've been warned about me."

"No one has said anything to me about you," Jason said, coming to her defense.

"They will," she said. "Aaron will."

"And what will Aaron say?"

Michelle tipped her head back, closing her eyes. "I don't know what he tells people about me. I do think he puts people through a debriefing about me, or I get that impression anyway. I can tell not so much by what they say, but by what they don't say."

Jason smiled. "The only thing Aaron said to me about you was that you love to play the piano." He looked at her, softly. "Do you want to know what I wonder about you?"

Michelle smiled, but was a little afraid. "I do, actually," she said.

"I wonder how long you will be here and if you have a boyfriend some-where who will be angry at us for spending time together." That was not all, not nearly, but that was all he chose to say. He wondered so many things that concerned him, such as why she never mentioned her family and what it was Aaron had on her. He had overheard her on the phone saying she would do what Aaron wanted. What did he want? If he did not know Aaron so well, he would wonder about Aaron and Michelle. He suspected she had other problems, as well; she certainly showed the signs. He mentioned none of these things that truly concerned him, only things that he thought she would answer.

Michelle laughed. "I didn't expect that."

I didn't expect you.

"I don't really know how long I will stay. At least through New Year's." Marc's show was New Year's Eve, but she didn't remind Jason of that. Nor did she mention what Aaron had planned, possibly as soon as the show was over. "As for my having a boyfriend . . ." Michelle laughed. "You are flattering me to ask something like that, but, no." She looked up at him. "Men don't much care for me. Not like that, anyway."

"What do you mean?" Jason asked.

"Men in Europe are very different, especially the men that I meet. I have a lot of fans, but they are terribly young and idealistic. And they are madly in love with me. But so are the young girls. They are probably more in love with me than the boys. But the men, they don't believe in love. There are no straightforward, heterosexual men in my life. They are all so complicated, so dramatic. I never have a boyfriend because I don't know anyone who could be such a person to me." She continued, "The men that I am closest to are gay." She thought of Sasha. "I have been told that I have the face of an angel and the body of a twelve-year-old boy. I can't help it, you know. Even Aaron teases me. He says I attract gay men and little girls. And I've heard it all—that I'm too thin, that my modeling career will last because I look like an adolescent, that I'll never have a real man because real men like real women."

Jason smiled, amused that she was able to laugh at herself. But, looking at her, he could understand how she could be so correct in her assessment. Besides, the homophobic, heterosexual American male would have no idea what to do with her. It was like the elephant and the mouse, except in this case, the mouse was more than capable of hurting the elephant, but it might not know that.

"I had a boyfriend once," she said, "when I first started modeling. I was sixteen. He was nineteen. A race car driver. He says to me, 'Ah, God, Michelle, you know nothing about sex. How can I be with someone so stupid?'" Michelle threw her hands up. "I am surrounded by men, hundreds of them, but most of them are in the business and so they are not interested in the models. I do get messages of love from men I don't know. They ask for all sorts of things. Sometimes they are very obscene. I get marriage proposals. I used to be flattered. I don't even read those anymore." She paused, sorting something out in her mind with an enlightened frown. "I used to confuse sex with affection. I used to not think there was a difference. When I learned that there most definitely was a difference, a lot of things changed for me."

"Changed for the good, I hope," Jason said.

Michelle did not reply. She couldn't say. She didn't know. She had no control over her life anymore.

He picked up her hand, which was tiny compared to his, but she was all woman to him. Yes, she was young, dangerously so for him, but the way she looked at him intrigued him. And it was not so much her physical appearance, although she was exquisite, but the way she carried herself. She didn't walk like a child, and her private thoughts—those that kept her quiet—were not a child's thoughts. She was different from most women, but she was no child. And what she lacked in volume, she more than gained back with her aura.

The phone beside him rang. It made Michelle flinch, and he felt it in her hand. He answered it. There was a long span of silence from Jason, who was listening intently, his eyes focused away from Michelle.

"I'm going to put you on hold a minute," he said to the person on the line, then turned to Michelle. "I need to take this call. It won't take long. Do you mind?"

"Not at all."

He squeezed her hand and left the room, leaving her alone. Michelle leaned her head back, watching the blinking light on the phone. When it stopped flashing and became a steady, glowing red light, she knew he had picked it up somewhere else in the house. She was drowsy from dinner, calmed by the wine, and content. She gazed at the red button for a long while. It had a mesmerizing effect on her. She felt herself drifting off, so she pushed herself up off of the couch and retrieved a cigarette from her coat pocket. She craved it, and so the first few drags rushed through her. Her gaze wandered around the room. She liked it here. It was a comfortable place to be. This house had nothing to do with her; there were none of her skeletons in its closets. She was glad of that. She glanced over at the phone and its still-illuminated red light. She didn't mind, because she sensed that the call had nothing to do with her. She thought about the piano in the main room. She wanted to play, and didn't think Jason would mind if she did.

The house was dark, except for the twinkling of the Christmas tree lights. She retrieved her portfolio and made her way to the main room by its light. The piano stood waiting for her. She sat before it, sitting in the dark, fingering the keys before turning on the small lamp that illuminated only the keys and nothing else. She played softly, a simple tune in her head. Pulling off her shoes, she pressed the pedal with her bare foot, loving the muted echo. Slowly, she began to lose herself in the music.

Jason stopped in the foyer by the Christmas tree. At first, he thought to join her, but instead chose to sit down on the stairs, as she had the night before. He listened to the music rise softly. He wanted to hear what she played when she played alone. He closed his eyes and listened. The music was solemn and classical. There was a sound of sadness, remorse, and loneliness that he sensed she was putting into it. Time passed. Then the music stopped and he heard nothing. He sat where he was, listening, but, for a moment, there was only silence. Then there was a muted shuffle, a knocking, and a soft clatter. He tried to place the sounds, but could not. A click. He listened more intently. Another click. A shuffling of paper.

Then it began. The draw of the bow across the strings. He closed his eyes. The violin. He held his breath as he listened to the scale she played. In his mind, he followed her hands back and forth between the piano and violin as she attempted to tune the long-neglected instrument. In his mind, he was right there beside her; he could see her clearly, her face, her eyes, her chin on the violin, her delicate hands, the way she stood beside the piano. He longed to be there beside her, closer than his mind could place him, but he stayed where he was, on the stairs, just outside the room. From the scale began an exercise, and from the exercise began a simple score. There was a skip, then a pause. He heard her set the violin down and, for a brief moment, he thought regretfully that she might stop. He heard a shuffling of paper. She picked up the violin and began again. Bach's "Violin Concerto in A minor." He knew this. He looked up at the ceiling, as if his eyes were following the notes as they floated upward.

She had noticed the violin on the shelf the night before. He remembered exactly how she had looked up at it, asking Jason who played. No one, he had said. He told her he had bought the violin at a Sotheby's auction, the same one he bought the piano from.

He didn't know that it had been a long, long time since Michelle had last played the violin. She could play other instruments as well, but, gradually, their presence had faded from her life. It was only the piano that she continued to pursue.

She abandoned the violin; too much of her ability had left her, and she was too tired to try to bring it back. Maybe another time. She returned to the piano, and her music flowed and grew stronger as she played the same piece so easily that she had only attempted on the violin. It quickly absorbed her.

He wondered what moved her to play like this, in the brief span of a few moments to herself, in the house of a man whom she did not know, where she had never been before and might never be again. He closed his eyes to that thought. Her talent astounded him. She astounded him. Yet he felt he was listening to something very private and personal.

Then the music stopped. He heard her replace the violin where she had found it. The small light from the piano that barely illuminated the foyer floor went dark. He expected her to come around the corner and find him on the stairs. He hoped, if that happened, he would not frighten her. But she did not. There was only silence. Then he heard a chair move—not the chair by the fire, but the one at the far end of the room, by the window. He remained where he was for a long time, listening. There was only silence.

Eventually, he rose and entered the vast, dark room. He would not have found her had she not rotated the chair so that it faced the window. From where he stood in the entry, he could barely make out her reflection in the glass. He came quietly to stand behind the chair, crossing his arms and leaning on the top of its winged back. They looked at each other through the reflection in the window, seeing each other clearly, even though the light was dim. Neither spoke.

She looked as though she had just returned from a long, difficult journey that had left her drained. She looked tired—tired from fighting some battle she could not win. He could see she had been crying, though she was not crying now. *What are you hiding, Michelle?*

The chair was easy to move; he just took it by its back and rotated it toward him. She faced him now and he sat down in the chair's mate so that they were facing each other. He took her feet, wrapping his hands around her ankles, bringing them to rest on his knees and covering each foot with his hand. Her bare feet were cold, ice cold. He pressed them between his jeans and his hands, pocketing them in warmth, wondering where her shoes were. They sat as they were, looking at each other solemnly, silently, and tiredly. His usual warm, lighthearted expression was now deeply concerned.

"Why am I finding you like this?" he asked.

"I am looking for something," she replied. She said it matter-of-factly, as if it was the obvious answer to his question.

Her reply was not above him. She was looking for an answer to something, although to what he did not know. The answer was not here, in him or in his house. He suspected he was merely providing her with a comfortable place with which to sort through a hurt-filled mind. Her eyes were clouded in painful preoccupation, a look she could not quickly and easily clear. He wondered what it was. Her eyes gave no hint as to what lay behind them, only the weight. He could see that it was heavy. He took her hands, clasping them in his. He smoothed them open, relaxing her fingers. There was something in Michelle that caused her much sadness and pain, and this worried him because he had seen it so many times already. It lived in her, showing itself from behind her beautiful face and sweet smile. What caused this, he wondered, although he could guess many things—her life, her job, the family she did or did not have.

He looked down, looking at her hands in his, looking at her skin against his, looking at the difference. Compared to hers, he saw his hands as aged. Since that first moment, when he had found her in his chair, by his fireplace, in his room, in his house, and then again and again, he had caught glimpses of something. She seemed to seek out quiet corners of solitude. Until now, he only noticed and wondered. Now, he knew. Michelle was living with something, and whatever it was, it was grave. It seemed to dig its way to her surface, and just when it was about to break through, she would isolate herself until it retreated. But it was more than she could hide. It was something that frightened her and consumed her from the inside out. It appeared behind her beautiful facade. It peered out through her sad eyes and pained, soft smile.

He closed his eyes. It was at that moment that he was convinced there was something terribly wrong. Michelle was not well, and she knew it. Whatever it was, she was trying desperately to deal with it. Jason did not have her answers, nor did he think she expected him to. No, she was battling something that had nothing to do with him. Whatever it was, it was not new, and she had come into his presence already in possession of it.

But what was happening between them was something else. He guessed she wanted nothing more than to separate the two. Jason could see this. Her face clearly reflected her feelings each time their eyes met. How could someone so young even attempt to hide such intense feelings?

Michelle smiled at him, but she also looked frightened, although not of him.

He looked at her, into her, searching for what he might possibly do to resurrect her. He found the clues. He stood and picked her up from the chair so he could sit down in it and cradle her in his lap. She didn't resist. The house was so quiet that every sound they made was amplified. It was the kind of silence that held its breath, waiting to see what would happen next. He kissed her, gently at first, questioning her, wanting to be sure it was what she wanted, then more passionately as she answered him. And when his hands found her bare legs, he caressed them; he was not afraid to. He wrapped his hands around her waist, thinking how tiny she was, pressing her against him. His chest rose with a deep breath, which he caught. Her eyes lit the darkness. This time there were no layers of ski clothes, no bright, icy snow to chill them. Being so close to her, stroking her body beneath her dress, was almost too much for him.

Michelle could feel the heat radiating from his body. She could feel his heart beating in his chest. His mouth on hers was gentle yet passionate, both giving to her and taking from her.

"Tell me you trust me," he said, wanting to hear her say she trusted him, and she did.

Jason rose and picked Michelle up with ease, carrying her upstairs to his bedroom.

He held her close. She was different, so different. He felt an overwhelming sense of protectiveness. He felt like he had to be careful not to hurt her, and this feeling aroused him.

She was unsure of herself, but excited. She wanted him, of that there was no doubt. And she needed him, because she did not know what she needed, and so she trusted him to show her. But above all, she was shameless.

He carefully pulled her dress up over her head. She raised her arms to help him. She wore nothing underneath it. He held her on his lap, on his bed, kissing her, taking his time. He unraveled her spiral of hair at the back of her neck, setting it free. He very lightly traced his finger down her neck until she giggled with delight. Never had he felt or seen anything as provocative as Michelle poised on his lap, fully naked, while he remained still fully clothed.

He told her about the first time he ever made love and about the woman who had seduced him in a Montana meadow when he was barely sixteen. She had been twenty-six. She had taught him things about woman's body that a man who took his time ought to know.

He made no effort to undress himself, choosing to wait patiently until she did. He wanted her to discover him. The light was soft and their bodies glowed under it. He caressed her, explored her, ever so gently pushing his fingers inside of her, making her tremble, reminding her she had promised to trust him, coaxing her to open herself up to him, blooming like a flower. She was sweet and he kissed her so she could taste herself, so she would believe how sweet she was. He held her above him, slowly, slowly, pushing himself into her, asking her to touch herself, and to touch him, wanting her to know him.

His passion overwhelmed her and she became lost in it, taking her far beyond what she had ever felt before. He filled her with an emotion she had never known. The love they made was hot and sweet, and he made Michelle love him. He could see it in her face and feel it in her body. It showed in her eyes, the way she touched him, and the way she gave herself to him. And he kept her with him, for the remainder of the night. Whatever had taken her away earlier, did not come to take her away again. She stayed with him.

13

She was dancing now—spinning, bowing, floating across the stage. She was leaping now, high into the air. Suddenly, her feet dangled limp and lifeless and she felt herself falling . . . falling . . . falling . . .

Michelle sat up abruptly. She looked around the dark room, momentarily overcome by a fearful panic, unable to recognize her surroundings. Gradually, as her mind focused and the room became familiar to her, her panic ebbed. Jason was beside her, asleep. She listened to the wind and his breathing. It was snowing heavily and, as her eyes became accustomed to the dark, she could see the billowing swirls against the pale gray windowpanes. She listened for sounds within the house, but there were none. She looked around the room. Its comfort made her heart ache.

Sitting up quietly, she looked over at Jason. She envied him for so many reasons. Although he showed her nothing but kindness and honest caring, there was so much more to him. He was the very core of the same reality she desperately longed for. She longed to touch him, just to feel his warmth, his breath, and his strength. Her hand hovered over his shoulder for a moment, contemplating. Then, clenching in a fist, she retracted her hand. She silently pounded her fist on her knee, clenching her teeth, but the tears came anyway.

His flannel shirt was draped over the arm of a chair. She got up quietly, not wanting to disturb him, and put it on. It swallowed her up, and she loved it for its smell, its warmth and its softness. She loved it because it was his.

She went to the window, staring out at the swirling, gray nothingness of the snowstorm. She pressed her palm to the windowpane. It was cold, ice cold, and touching it sent a chill through her. It was so thin, so clear, so fragile, yet it could hold back so much, she thought, looking out at the blizzard. She could feel the wind pushing the glass from the other side, wanting in. She pressed her forehead against the glass, closing her eyes. There were clouds in her mind, affecting her judgment, that she needed to be free of. What she longed for, more than anything, was peace of mind long enough to make the right decisions. And she was afraid. She was afraid because some things could cause such incredible pain, while other things caused only numbness, and she did not understand either. She hated the sleeplessness. She hated the dreams. She did not know what was happening to her, only that it was bad. She looked over at Jason, although she could not see that he was watching her.

The glass. She pulled away.

Quietly, she returned to the bed, and he reached out to touch her.

"I can't sleep," she said.

"If you are uncomfortable here, I can take you back."

"No." She didn't want to go back. She didn't want to go anywhere. She sank back against him, melting into his strength and warmth. Looking down at his arms around her, Michelle closed her eyes.

For a long time, neither spoke.

"I can be someone to talk to," he finally said.

Michelle sighed. "I wouldn't know where to start." She held up her hand in a desperate attempt to grasp something she could not. Her hand collapsed into her in failure. "I can't sleep . . . My heart aches . . . My head hurts." Images flashed before her that she tried to verbalize, but couldn't.

She withdrew again, and he did not press her. He held her, cradled against his chest, warmly and securely. There were no words, only silent, gentle comfort. Looking at her, he saw two things, both of which concerned him—despair and a desire to find a way out. This was much more than not being able to sleep. Michelle was troubled, deeply troubled.

"I remember the worst day of my life," he began softly, smiling at her. "I was six years old."

Michelle turned and looked up at him. "You were six?"

Jason only nodded, continuing his story. "My father decided that I was too old to be riding the ponies and I ready for a ranch horse of my own. Mind you, I was a pretty good little cowboy by then." He raised an eyebrow at Michelle. "So my dad picked out one of the ranch horses and gave him to me. Well, we went out for a ride and that old cow horse did a duck and turn and I hit home pretty hard."

"You mean you fell off?" Michelle asked.

Jason nodded. "And where I come from, it's a pretty serious crime to fall off your horse. That was my first mistake. My second mistake was that I started crying. My old man was furious. He picked me up out of the dirt by the back of my collar with one hand, took off his belt with the other hand, and gave me quite a tanning.

"A tanning?" Michelle asked. She didn't know what that was.

"A whipping," he replied. "And a good one. I can still hear his voice like it was yesterday. 'That's for fallin' off your horse, and that's for cryin'. Then he took me by the shoulders and shook me real hard. 'You're a Henrey, boy,' he said, 'and Henreys don't fall off their horses and they don't cry. And don't you ever forget it. Now get back up on your horse and stay there!'" Jason laughed. "Well, I never forgot it, that's for sure."

Michelle laughed, and then she realized he had told her the story for just that reason—to make her laugh. "Did you ever fall off again?"

Jason frowned, laughing. "All the time."

"But did you ever cry about it?"

Jason shook his head. "Never."

Michelle frowned. "Was he always so hard on you?"

Jason nodded. "He was on all of us. That's just the way he was. He ruled the roost with an iron fist. I used to think that he hated us, that he was just a mean slave driver, and me and my brothers were just free labor. As I got older, I realized that just because he wasn't affectionate toward us didn't mean he didn't love us. In fact, he loved us more than anything in the world."

"How did you know?"

"By getting to know him, and getting to understand the kind of man he was and why he was that way. I won't deny he's a cold, demanding person, but he always wanted the best for us. He didn't praise us much, but he would have put his life on the line for any one of us."

His story made her realize how little she really knew her own father. She looked up at him. "I wish I had a fraction of the understanding that you have."

Jason smiled. "It's something that comes with age."

"So, then I do have something to look forward to," she said earnestly.

"You have a lot of things to look forward to, Michelle."

Something about the way he said her name made her heart ache. *Maybe if I just knew what some of those things were . . .*

14

Morning, its light barely penetrating the persistent winter storm, came and turned the windows a cold, pale gray. Jason awoke alone. The bedroom door was ajar, and he heard the piano downstairs. He remained still, listening carefully, bringing the music closer to him. It was intense. What possessed her to play like that? He looked over at the clock. It was seven o'clock. How long had she been down there?

She was the picture of absolute concentration, yet her face was placid. Occasionally, she would stop and repeat a bar that to Jason sounded perfect the first time. She wore his flannel shirt, with its too-long sleeves flipped up over her elbows. Around her waist, she had wrapped one of the throws from the couch. When she saw him in the doorway, she stopped.

"I love this piano," she said softly.

He sat down on its bench beside her, brushing her hair away from her face. Could it be that simple? Did she play so intently just out of love for the instrument?

"Do you have a piano like this at home?"

Michelle nodded. "In my apartment in Paris, I have a 1914 Steinway B just like this one, but it's more precisely tuned. I have another Steinway in New York, but it is new, and I don't care for it as much. It's too perfect. But this one . . ." She touched a single key, swiping it. "I like this piano."

"You think it needs to be tuned?" he asked.

Michelle nodded. "Not urgently. It's very dry here, and so it's aging faster here than it would in a more moderate climate. Pianos go through cycles with the seasons. My father used to say that it is always better to tune a piano in the summer than in winter. If you tune a piano in the winter, when it's so dry, it stresses it more when the weather warms and the wood expands."

Jason nodded. "Then I will wait until summer."

Michelle subconsciously rubbed her hands together as if they were hurting her.

"Your hands hurt?" he asked, noticing.

She clenched and released her fists several times. "Yes, they ache sometimes." *They ache because my whole body aches. And when I stick them with needles they scream in pain.*

"You said the other night that your father taught you. Does he still?" he asked, although he already knew the answer.

He asked in hope she would open up to him.

"No, I stopped studying with him when I was fifteen, almost sixteen," she said. *Because I ran away.* "I haven't had a teacher since. Sometimes, I wish I did. Now I just teach myself. I practice as much as I can. It's hard, though, to travel with a piano." She laughed.

Jason smiled. "What about Aaron's piano?"

"I feel sorry for it. His children have banged on it so much that it's worn out. It's not right anymore."

"Well, you can't take this one with you, but you're welcome to come up every day and play it if that's how you want to spend your time."

"Thank you," she replied.

Jason touched her shoulder. "Why did you stop studying with your father? Did something happen to him?"

"No." *Something happened to me.* "I moved to Paris and he stayed in Switzerland."

"Is it that simple?" he asked, pressing her for the first time.

"Nothing is that simple," she replied.

Jason smiled at her and did not press her further. "Do you mind if I stay and listen?"

"Not at all," she said.

He moved to one of the chairs behind her. When she continued to play, it was as if she were alone again. Jason remained where he was, content to listen, and, as he did, he became aware of something in her for which he began to feel great admiration and respect, so much so he had to admit to himself he was surprised. It was the way in which she applied herself to the music; her practice was diligent and disciplined. She persisted methodically, her patience never shortening, never faltering. In what at first seemed to be the same scores repeated over and over, Jason began to decipher something else.

Michelle would not play each piece through repeatedly, but, rather, would isolate sections and exercise them independently of their whole. Through this method, her art became science and she mastered the music. Jason came to observe he was witnessing the difference between being trained in music and simply knowing how to play. Here, undisturbed, Michelle's practice was uninhibited. It was as if she had something inside her that she would only let out in private, making Jason feel as if he were imposing on her just by being present. Michelle possessed the rare ability to focus herself in such a way that every act was deliberate and significant to the whole. Jason took great interest in studying her, analyzing her, learning much about her, learning much from her. Her intelligence evoked in him feelings of great respect.

The music stirred something in Michelle that had been buried. She was, in her own way, confessing her deep appreciation for the music that she was playing. Her intentions were not to conquer the music—in this case Tchaikovsky—but to recite it in such a way as to prove she possessed the highest regard and utmost respect for the composer.

Occasionally, she would pause, close her eyes and tilt her head back. Jason continued to watch her, knowing she was hearing something he could not. What she was hearing was Tchaikovsky's voice, telling her she was playing his music as he intended it to be played. Michelle told Jason this, and it was then that he realized what Michelle was—gifted. There was one score that she seemed to devote much time to, although to Jason it did not seem to be because of its difficulty. He asked her why, and she confessed that it was because it did not feel right.

"There are two intentions written into music," she explained. "How it should sound and how it should feel. The written score explains how it should sound. This is its correctness. But in the knowledge of the music is the meaning of its feeling." She played a few bars again. "I can play this correctly, but I cannot play it knowingly. "My father . . ." She paused, closing her eyes. "My father is the only person I've ever heard play this the way I think Tchaikovsky truly meant it to be played. I've heard others play it brilliantly, but when I would hear my father play it, I think he must have been present when it was composed. He brings out what was put into it."

She continued playing, letting the music take her back to a time before so many things had separated them. Her memories quickly consumed her, flooding her with sadness and regret as she remembered, again, that there were so many things she could have learned from her father had her life unfolded differently than it had.

"Do you ever see your father?" Jason asked, trying again.

Michelle took a deep breath, and Jason could hear that it was uneasy. The topic of her father pained her. "I'm sorry, but I cannot talk about my father," she said. "I wish I could, but I don't know what I would say."

He did not question her further. He was a patient man. And he had learned that, given time, something that was buried could work its way back to the surface. And he did not want to upset her now. He went back to the bench and sat down next to her. He brushed her hair away from her face. Her hair spilled from her shoulders and fell all around them. He loved her hair, the way she had so reluctantly let it free and how it now ran wild around her. And he loved how she didn't care that it did.

"I should call Aaron. He's probably worried about me," she said.

"You can call him if you want, but he knows you're here. He won't be worried."

Michelle believed him.

"I'm going to make coffee. I'll call him for you. I've got to anyway. We are supposed to ski today," he said, looking out the window, "if the weather improves."

Michelle nodded, aware of his plans to ski with Aaron, and he left her alone at the piano. She watched him go, listening until she heard sounds far off in the house that told her he was in the kitchen. Then, gritting her teeth, she shook her hands as hard as she could, trying to shake some life back into them. They ached deep into her bones, and the pain shot lightning-hot flashes up her arms. She longed to plunge them into hot ash and burn the pain away. She clenched her eyes shut, because of why her hands hurt. Even though her entire body ached from skiing, so much so that she had barely made it down the stairs because her legs were so weak, it was a good ache. It was an ache that reminded her she had lived for a day. But the ache in her hands was the ache of death.

She sat for a while longer at the piano, until the pain subsided, then ventured into the kitchen.

Jason was there, reading. "Hungry?" he asked.

"Yes," she lied.

He offered her toast and eggs, which she tried to eat. "I'm sorry," she finally said, pushing her plate away.

He said nothing.

They sat together by the fire, Michelle bundled into his lap, Jason loving her there. Michelle wanted nothing more than to shower him with affection, to touch him and hear his voice, and to laugh at him and with him and because of him. She made this apparent. But he hadn't forgotten the other side of her, nor that every minute with her left him with more questions than answers. But for now, she seemed happy.

Michelle looked up at him, quoting a passage from a favorite poem. *"Vous pourriez penser que je suis un artiste de cirque, mais si je pouvais être libre de vous aimer, alors je serais un clown heureux."*

Jason frowned. "I have no idea what you just said."

Michelle smiled and repeated the passage in English. "You might think I'm a circus act, but if I could be free to love you, then I would be a happy clown."

Jason looked at her for a long while, studying her. Thinking about her words, he suspected that the key was not love but to be free.

"I wish it would never stop snowing," she said, looking out at the blue sky that was slowly breaking through the clouds.

"We would be snowed in," Jason replied.

"I'd be glad to be snowed in." *If we can't get out, then no one can get in.*

She returned to the piano, after Jason reassured her several times that he didn't mind. He took the opportunity to see to things he had put off—such as clearing his road—for her.

She sat down on the bench and fanned her fingers out across the keys, hovering just above them, her slender fingers as alabaster as the keys themselves. Her fingers felt rigid, like the ivory. She fluttered them, then tapped several keys. The individual, random notes suddenly reminded her of her young self, wide-eyed, intelligent, and eager to discover the world through music and through her father's eyes. He was, for a while, the all-knowing, guiding light that would show her the way.

She stopped. She placed her hands, palms up, on the edge of the keys and watched her fingers curl inward into themselves, recoiling like a shriveling flower drying in the sun. She watched her hands age before her eyes, and, as her childhood flashed backward through her mind, time sped forward through her body, until she was looking down at the decrepit hands of an old woman crippled with age. She tried opening them again, but they would not open. She closed her eyes. *Papa, you told me the buckets of hot water were to keep your hands supple. You said it was because you were old and the house was cold, which made your bones ache. I know why now. And I wish I had those buckets.*

She didn't know the difference between the anxiety caused by her memory and the anxiety caused by her addiction, because it crept up on her the same way. It was cold and clever and found her when she least expected it. It caught her too late in its thundershower. It pricked the back of her neck with its icy needles. It chilled her and robbed her of any passive thought. It made her shake and gasp for air. She sought out her cigarettes and lit one with shaking hands, still frozen, claw-like. She huddled so close to the fireplace that the heat made her skin itch uncontrollably, and she scratched it until it was crimson red. The cigarette burned quickly to its filter and she lit another. Her hands softened only when they wrapped around the lipstick case. They cooperated only to unscrew the cap. It was her bucket of hot water. Her little finger extended itself eagerly and disappeared into the cylinder, reappearing with the hot white cure dusting her fingernail. It moved steadily to her face. There were no mirrors in the room, so the demon left her alone. She stayed where she was, her skin prickling from the heat, her hands slowly unfolding themselves.

Another cigarette and she started to feel her pain and anxiety ease up and warmth return to her hands and body.

Jason reappeared. She must have looked dreadful, because seeing her stopped him abruptly.

"Michelle, are you okay?" he asked, alarmed.

"I don't know," she said, barely above a whisper, avoiding his gaze.

He came closer, and she recoiled, so much so that he stopped.

She didn't mean to, though, and this upset her. She didn't want to push him away. But she couldn't look at him, because she knew what she would see in his face. She didn't want to see how much he didn't understand. She didn't want to see how much he thought he had done something wrong.

"Michelle . . ." he said earnestly. "What's wrong?" He took another step closer to her.

This time she looked up at him. From the light of the fire he saw the vacant look in her now bloodshot eyes.

"I'm sorry," she managed to say.

He knelt down in front of her and took her hand, smoothing it open between his palms. "You don't have anything to be sorry for," he said. "And you certainly don't have to apologize to me for anything."

She tilted her head back and gave him a sad smile. *Yes, I do.*

He tenderly brushed her hair way from her face with his fingers. "I talked to Aaron. We are meeting at the airport in an hour, to ski." He paused. "He asked me to drop you off at his house. He said he didn't want you left alone here."

Michelle only nodded. "Perhaps you could drop me at the music school instead."

15

"Where's Michelle?" Aaron asked when Jason arrived at his house to pick him up.

"She wanted to go over to the music school to see Melissa. I dropped her off on the way here."

Aaron nodded. "That should probably be okay," he said as he got into the passenger seat of Jason's Rover.

Jason frowned. "What does that mean?" he asked Aaron.

"Michelle . . ." Aaron said, then paused.

"Uh-huh," Jason replied.

"How is she?" Aaron asked.

"I don't know. I was going to ask you," Jason replied. "What's her story, Aaron?"

"Her story?" Aaron replied. "You got a couple of days?"

"I imagine I've got as much time as it takes."

"So what do you think of her?" Aaron asked, evading the question.

"I think a lot of her," Jason replied. "But I suspect that something is not right."

"By not right, you mean something is wrong," Aaron said.

"I mean something's not right."

"Did she tell you anything about herself?" Aaron asked.

"Very little. She is pretty closed-mouthed on that topic," Jason replied.

"Any mention of her father?

"Closed-mouth on that topic, too."

"He's a big problem," Aaron said. "It's complicated and I don't quite know the whole story, but I will tell you what I do know. Michelle has some serious issues buried as deeply in her subconscious as she can possibly bury them. And it's not only that she doesn't want to talk about it—it's that there aren't the words."

Jason nodded. "Yes, she more or less said that. But *it*? What's *it*?"

"Her relationship with her father," Aaron replied. "Michelle was a child prodigy. You've probably figured that out. But she had a very unconventional upbringing. She was raised by her father. Alexander Sekovich, you know who he is?"

"No, but I get the general idea."

"World renowned, but an incredibly eccentric and private individual," Aaron said. "And he's not a young man. He must be in his late seventies now. Her father educated her; she never went to a school until I think she was about twelve years old. Yet, by that time, she could speak four languages fluently, had read more classical literature than most graduate students, and had completely mastered the piano, as well as a few other instruments, but her talent on the piano was remarkable."

"And still is," Jason added.

"Yes. She is truly remarkable," Aaron said in agreement. "Michelle's mother left them when Michelle was about four or five—and that's another story I won't get into right now. But it was a very reclusive period for Alexander Sekovich, and, therefore, for Michelle. I honestly think that Michelle spent maybe ten years of her life mostly confined to her father's house."

"He didn't do anything weird to her, did he?" Jason asked.

"I don't know," Aaron replied. "I'd like to think he just pushed and pushed her until she couldn't take it anymore. She wanted to go to school and have friends her age, and eventually he acquiesced. But since Michelle had never been exposed to that kind of environment, she had a hard time. At one point she discovered ballet, and she realized that having both feet off the ground was a good feeling. Mind you, we're talking about a twelve- or thirteen-year-old girl here. These desires were completely normal."

"So what happened?" Jason asked.

"I'm not sure exactly what happened. I don't know that anyone does for certain, except, of course, for Michelle and her father. But Michelle ran away from her father's house when she was fifteen, and never went back."

"So?" Jason asked, wondering if he was missing something.

"So, she hasn't spoken to him in seven years, and now he's calling for her. I talked to him last night, while Michelle was with you. He was frantic. But he wouldn't tell me why. But he *will* call back, and so I need to talk to her about it."

"You think something's going on?" Jason said.

"Something's definitely going on," Aaron replied. "And since Michelle is what she is, I'm going to have to referee in case it's something too weird . . . so she doesn't go off the deep end."

"What do you mean, *is what she is?*" Jason asked.

Aaron sighed. He had promised her. He chose his words carefully. "Jason . . . Michelle can be extremely self-destructive, especially when something upsets her or she is faced with a situation she cannot cope with."

"Self-destructive how?" Jason asked.

Aaron did not respond.

Jason, too, was silent. He rewound his thoughts back through their time together. She was a swinging pendulum. Self-destructive? He had explored every inch of her body last night and not a mark on her. She was perfect. He remembered Aaron's words . . . *Just don't let her drink too much . . . I don't want her left alone . . .*

16

Melissa Garrison found Michelle's behavior odd, yet intriguing. Her request was not that unusual—a practice room for part of the day—and Melissa was happy to oblige. She showed Michelle to one of the school's private practice rooms. Michelle followed her quietly.

The room was small, with one glass window looking out into the hall of the school and the other looking outside, offering a view of the icy, bubbling Roaring Fork River. The piano was a new Steinway, similar to Michelle's in New York, but since it was here, Michelle did not associate her dislike of her own piano with this one. Melissa understood when Michelle explained that the Perlman's piano was beyond being good for much more than playing "Chopsticks" and the theme from *The Sting*, since both tunes had been played on it to such an extent that the twang of the notes stayed, regardless of what was played. And there were too many distractions in the Perlman house.

Melissa had students waiting, and so she was not able to talk at any length with Michelle. She left her alone in the room, apologizing for having to do so, promising to come back in a few hours to see if Michelle needed anything.

Later, with a tea service in hand, she started down the corridor of practice rooms. The music coming from the last one met her with such force that it stopped her in the hall. Liszt. No? Yes? Yes. It was Liszt she was hearing. She thought she was listening to a recording, but no. It was no recording. She continued on, carrying the tray steadily, so as to not make the saucers rattle. She stopped outside the door, waiting. She knew the score and knew that it would conclude soon, so she would wait until its end. She resisted the urge to move down and look through the window.

The notes closed and Melissa knocked on the door. There was no answer, but she opened it anyway. Michelle looked up at her from over the top of the piano, folding her hands quietly in her lap. They were trembling, but Melissa did not see this.

Melissa set the tea down on a side table. "I've brought tea and muffins." She turned toward Michelle, noticing immediately that she looked exhausted, and tears were streaming down her face. "My dear! Are you all right?" Melissa asked, alarmed.

Michelle only nodded, wiping her face on her sleeve, but said nothing. She took a deep breath and finally gave a sad but visible smile.

"You look very tired. Are you sure?"

Michelle nodded. "I am tired. But I'm fine." She accepted the tea that Melissa offered, sliding to one side of the bench, the only indication she gave that she wanted Melissa to stay awhile.

Melissa took a cup of tea and sat down beside her. When she looked up at the sheet music propped up in front of her, Liszt revealed himself with striking reality. "It's hard for me to believe," she said, her voice trailing off. She looked over at Michelle, who sat less than a foot away from her. "Not many can play this. No wonder you look so exhausted."

Michelle offered another smile. "I've been working on this piece for only a few hours, but I feel like I've been wandering around for days, lost in the middle of a giant city that I've never known. Liszt makes me feel like that."

"He does have a way of digging up the most remorseful of emotions, doesn't he?" Melissa said.

"Yes," Michelle agreed. "But I love him."

Melissa sipped her tea. *Who is this person next to me? This is not normal. This is almost not acceptable.* She looked over at the small stack of sheet music that Michelle had placed on the windowsill. She picked it up, wanting to look through it, wanting to see what this person chose to play.

"Do you mind?" she asked.

Michelle said no, she did not mind.

Melissa paged through Liszt's "Hungarian Rhapsodies," piano concertos by Tchaikovsky and Rachmaninoff, and a handwritten piece entitled "Ballade für Michelle." Melissa singled it out, curious. The composer's name was not legible. She looked questioningly at Michelle.

"Alexander Sekovich," Michelle said, taking the music and placing it on the stand so that it covered the Liszt score she had been playing.

"Sekovich, really? An original?" Melissa asked.

Michelle nodded. "It's not published. It's not really an exceptional piece, not even a ballad per se, and not particularly challenging to play, but it's very personal." She played the opening bars for Melissa without looking at the sheet music.

Melissa nodded to the flow of the notes. "It's very nice. How is it that you have this?"

Michelle looked over at her. "He's my father. You didn't know that?"

Melissa put her hand to her mouth. "Oh, heavens, no! I didn't, and I'm sorry."

"You don't have to apologize," Michelle said, easing Melissa's reaction.

"Well, that explains so much, and leaves so much more to question," Melissa said.

"Not too much," Michelle replied. "Questions about him are hard for me to answer."

Melissa accepted that she did not want to talk about her father. "But you'll tell me about this piece?"

"He wrote it for me when I was two years old. It was my birthday present." She played it in its entirety, not needing the sheet music to guide her.

Melissa listened silently, without moving, her eyes fixed on Michelle's hands as they moved across the keys. It was clearly music written out of love. It was the musical expression of the love of a father for his daughter. It was simple, beautiful, and moving. When Michelle finished, the music left both of them with a feeling for which there were no words, and so both remained silent, as if they had been sedated. When Melissa looked over at Michelle, seeing tears again in her eyes, she still had nothing to say. So, with a kind hand on her shoulder, she left Michelle alone in the room.

Aaron arrived at five o'clock, and Melissa was relieved to see him.

"I'm so glad you're here," she said, her voice sounding a little strained.

"Why? Is everything all right?" Aaron asked, a little alarmed.

"Well, yes, but . . ." Melissa took his arm, guiding him out of earshot from the students who were lounging in the main room of the school. "Aaron, it's just so odd. I mean, she's been playing for hours. I've looked in on her several times, and she just looks so sad. And the way she plays, what she plays—it's just so odd." She lowered her voice to barely a whisper. "It's like she's exorcising herself or something."

That's exactly what she's doing. That's why she wanted to come here. Melissa, of all people, should understand that. Aaron crossed his arms.

"Oh, Aaron, I'm sorry. I didn't mean it like that. I meant no disrespect. I'm honored to have her here. I was just a little . . . concerned."

Aaron gave Melissa a reassuring smile, but went down the corridor alone to get Michelle. The two did not emerge until almost an hour later. And when they did, Michelle looked as though she'd lost a battle. She smiled cordially and thanked Melissa for allowing her the time. Melissa said she was welcome back any time, but wondered if she'd ever return.

17

It was another crowded night at Andiamo and Keith, although exhausted from the day's skiing, was moving around the room with elastic and authoritative energy. From his seat at the bar, Jason watched him, amused, and occasionally harassed him about having to work when everyone else was vacationing. Tony Grant, one of Jason's friends from his early Aspen days, contributed lightheartedly to the bantering with Keith.

Keith went around behind the bar, shaking his head at his friends. He saw to it that they had full drinks. "You just remember that I am not your servant; you are my guests." Then Keith leaned into Jason. "Catherine called. She's on her way down. She wanted to know if you were here. And the fashion brigade is coming in, too. Michelle included."

"Oh? You sound irritated," Jason said.

"Nah," Keith replied. "Not much. It's just that Marc . . ." He paused, trying to redefine his friend. "Hell, I don't know. People change, I suppose." He said nothing more about Marc.

Catherine entered the restaurant with several friends, including Jayne Brikelle. Keith went to meet them, kissing Catherine. Jason watched this. They were good friends. Always had been. It was a good thing, because Catherine would talk to Keith about Jason, and Keith would say all of the things that Jason was tired of saying himself. Catherine looked over her shoulder at Jason and gave a reluctant smile. He smiled back, watching her as Keith showed them to a table at the far end of the restaurant.

Not a minute later, *they* walked through the door, and the restaurant grew quiet. Even Jason turned to look, and felt what others felt when he saw her. Michelle Seko, the five-foot six-inch French phenomenon, was indeed a star. She carried with her an aura that hushed people around her. Diners stopped their conversations mid-sentence and looked up from their plates. They collected in the entryway—Michelle, Marc, Annalise, Aaron, Hannah, and George and Julie Peters. They were a powerful group and tiny Michelle was their center.

Keith offered to take their heavy winter coats and then showed them to a large table. All eyes followed.

Tony elbowed Jason. "There she is. I heard she was in town."

Jason only nodded. He glanced causally around the room. *Amazing. People are so interested in her, and it's not like the place isn't crawling with celebrities.* His gaze caught Catherine's. He suddenly felt sorry for her. He smiled reluctantly, but had to look away.

He looked back at Michelle. She radiated, and her voice and laughter, although soft, seemed to float up and find him. He watched her lean over to Aaron and say something then smile. He wondered if he could actually hear her voice, or if it was his memory he was hearing. He was torn between wanting to go over to her and wanting to leave, so he chose to do nothing but turn away from her. He didn't want to sit there watching her like everyone else was.

Keith returned to their table with a bottle of wine under his arm. "On the house," he said, standing over Aaron, opening the bottle quickly and skillfully. He made his comments to each of his friends as he went around the table, including Michelle. She looked up at him, smiling.

Damn, she looks good, Keith thought. *Certainly not like an addict, or at least the addicts I've seen.* Marc had been going on about what a mess she was, but Keith wondered if she was really as bad off as Marc said she was, or if his complaints about Michelle weren't just a ploy, just as this dinner together was.

"Let's get into town and smooth out some bumpy roads," Keith had overheard Marc say to Annalise earlier that evening.

Keith made his living by assessing situations and groups of people. He could read this group clearly. Fortunately, Aaron was present, which kept Marc on a tight leash. It also kept Marc from thinking that he was the center of the universe, something that Keith had quickly picked up as being Marc's primary assessment of himself. *Well, Michelle is the center of this universe and Aaron is the armed weapon orbiting her, and if you jump out of line, he's going to blow you to bits.*

Keith hastily poured Marc a glass of wine. They certainly weren't the friends they used to be.

Aaron, too, knew Marc's motive for inviting them out to dinner, as it had been Marc's invitation that had brought them all together. It was Aaron who had added George and Julie to the group. Marc thought he was sly, but his own self-interests prevented him from seeing himself as others saw him. And Aaron, always holding the alpha position, went along with Marc. *Let him make amends. Let him do it in front of everyone.* To further the cause, Aaron carried the conversation, casually asking Marc about the rest of his holiday plans and the plans for the upcoming show. He even went as far as to patronize Marc, letting Marc think that the ringleader's hat was his. Aaron, the mastermind of plots, carried the evening and kept the group engaged without ever mentioning *The Ballerina* or Michelle's well-being.

When Marc had called about getting together, Michelle had been reluctant, but Aaron had convinced her it would be a good thing to do. "The public light on the two of you has been bad lately," he said. "Marc knows that, and he wants to get out under better circumstances and change that. The public has been watching all of us. He wants to feed them something positive."

So Michelle had agreed. And now, sitting with them, she was not regretting it. It could even almost be something other than the false situation that it was—if she let herself pretend. Except for Annalise. Michelle looked across the table at her often. Annalise had little to say to her, but she was smiling and courteous toward her. She was this way because she had been told to be, although Michelle did not know this. The camaraderie was gone and Michelle missed it. She blamed herself, and if anyone were to try to tell her she was not to blame, Michelle would never believe it. But they ate and talked and laughed, and no one would have said that it was not a good evening together.

Catherine stopped by the table to say hello to Aaron, who, in turn, intro-duced her to the group. She expressed being a big fan of Marc's, who took the compliment with a smirking smile. She said she was honored to meet Annalise. She said nothing to Michelle, which made Michelle think about Jason. *Jason.* He had been on her mind all afternoon. She wondered where he was now.

As if summoned, his laughter caught her attention. Michelle followed the laugh that was now so familiar to her. She saw him at the bar across the room. And, just like the day at Bonnie's, he looked right at her, as if he'd known all along where she was. She smiled, raising her hand in a discreet wave, not wanting to draw attention to herself. He smiled back, then pointed in the direction of the back of the restaurant. She followed his gesture, seeing the long hall lined with coats, and nodded to him.

Michelle leaned over to Aaron. "I'll be back," she whispered. "I want to talk to Jason." Aaron pulled her chair back for her as she stood, and everyone else at the table looked up at her. She knew what they were wondering. Suspecting.

She worked her way to the back of the restaurant. Across the room, she could see that Jason, too, was moving in the same direction. They converged in the hall, with Jason falling in behind her. She continued walking a few strides toward the short flight of stairs that led up to the restrooms. On the first step, he caught her and turned her to face him. For a moment, they just looked at each other, eye-to-eye. Jason wanted to kiss her, but he refrained, and not doing so just made him want her more.

He took her hand. "Let's get out of here," he said.

Michelle smiled. No, she radiated. "All right. Let's do."

"But let's not be brave about it," he said, nodding toward the back door.

"I have to tell Aaron," she said.

"I'll tell him. You wait here."

She agreed, and he left her in the hall.

When Jason reached Aaron, he bent over him and whispered his intentions so no one else could hear. Aaron gave his approval with a slight gesture and Jason left. Aaron said nothing to the rest of the group, taking great satisfac-tion in knowing that Marc would wonder why Michelle never returned. It was none of his damn business. He'd offer an explanation eventually, a vague but satisfactory one that implied Michelle had an acquaintance in town that had nothing to do with him.

Michelle was waiting with her coat by the back door.

"We're free!" Jason said, grabbing his own coat off the rack.

He pushed open the heavy door that emptied out into the alley behind the restaurant. Michelle glanced quickly over her shoulder. The hallway, other than the row of coats hanging along the wall, was empty, and no one was taking note of their departure. She followed him out into the alley.

When the door closed behind them, closing out the trailing sounds of the restaurant, the world became different. Silent. Winter. In the last hour, it had started to snow again, and the giant white flakes that fell had already dusted everything, giving even the garbage dumpster a touch of charm.

The alley was lit by high, overhead street lamps that cast their light down in yellow cylinders. The snow seemed thicker, heavier, and more defined as it passed through the cones of light. To try to see past the light was impossible. There was only darkness, as if the snow were falling from the lights themselves and not the sky above. Michelle looked around, holding her face up, marveling at the snow. It clung lightly to edges of the brick buildings surrounding them. The air was heavy and still. If it was a windy night, the wind was not reaching them. Only faraway sounds of the town barely reached them, yet still sounded distant. What was immediately around them was hushed, and so every sound they made was sharpened and seemed to intensify, yet could not drift.

Michelle followed Jason as he started down the alley. He walked casually, with his hands buried in the deep pockets of his overcoat. He would pause every few steps to wait for her as she walked, or rather shuffled, so as not to slip. He put his arm around her to help her along.

"Is there night skiing here?" she asked.

"No, not in Aspen. But there is at Snowmass."

"Snowmass? Is that far?"

"About twenty minutes down valley."

"Could we go?"

"Tonight?" He looked at her. "By the time we get our gear and get there, it will be too late."

"Oh," Michelle replied. "Maybe tomorrow then."

"Tomorrow will be daytime. We can ski here." He smiled.

"Tomorrow night, then," she said, laughing. She blew into the air, watching her breath mix with the snow. "This is marvelous!" she said, holding her arms out, wanting to take in as much of the new snow and the stillness as possible. She spun around, executing a perfect pirouette, her toe turning on the ice beneath the new snow, coming to a stop in front of Jason.

"Well?" she said inquisitively. "You said we are free, so what do free people do?"

"Whatever we want," he replied. "How about we go up in the gondola? It's operating until midnight."

Michelle smiled. "I'd like that."

It was a short walk through town to get to the base of the Silver Queen Gondola. There were others waiting, but it was late enough that families with children had already gone in for the night, and most others, like Jason and Michelle, wanted a car to themselves, which they got. They climbed in as it rotated around, so that they would be facing the town as the car ascended.

"Too bad it's snowing. We won't have much of a view." Jason said.

"I don't mind," she replied, looking anxiously out the window as the car cleared the base house and started to rise. She could still see the lights of Aspen through the snow.

Jason smiled at her and touched her face, brushing her hair away from it.

"What kind of people live here?" she asked. "Is anyone actually born here?"

Jason leaned back in his seat, propping his foot against the Plexiglas window. The gondola was rising quickly and the view of town was fading to nothing more than a yellow glow behind the falling snow. "There are basically four types of people here," he said. "There are the people who were actually born and raised here, which are very few, and most of them are down valley. There are people like me; there are the people from LA, like Aaron; and there are the people who come here to hide, because it's a great place to hide if you can afford it."

"Hide from what?"

"Lots of things. A shady past, a bad marriage, you name it."

Michelle laughed.

"What? You don't believe me?" he asked.

"Oh, on the contrary. It sounds so typical. Sounds like Monte Carlo. Only colder." She paused. "People like you . . . ?"

Jason smiled. "People who capitalize on opportunities here," he said. "My father has always been into real estate. Land acquisitions he calls it. We used to come here every year to ski. My folks still own a house in town. Cute house. And another one up Castle Creek. It wasn't until after college that I decided to live here full time, on my own. That's when I met Keith. He basically did the same thing. He used to be a ski bum, getting jobs in ski towns, making just enough money to get by and to ski. Eventually, he figured he'd gained enough experience working in restaurants that he could run his own."

The gondola continued to rise, and so did the wind, which rocked the car. Michelle sat back, closer to Jason, but neither was bothered by the turbulence. Jason looked out as the last evidence of town faded behind the snow.

"I was just out of college when I actually moved here." He laughed, remembering. "The motto back then was all that glitters is either gold or cocaine. This used to be the cocaine capital of the world, back in the day. At least that's what we called it. When we'd pay our dinner tab, we'd add a hundred bucks to the bill and the waiter would come back with our change and a gram of cocaine."

Michelle looked at him suspiciously. Was he baiting her? "You don't do that anymore, do you?" she asked.

"No. That was a long time ago. I'm a lot older and wiser now."

"I hate cocaine," she said flatly. "I hate all drugs, but coke in particular. It makes me paranoid." She did not clarify to him whether she did them or not, only that she hated them.

He wanted to ask her about it, but she seemed to grow distant. *There's that thing again, pulling her away.* He said nothing, waiting for her to come back.

Michelle did drift away, back to her early days in Paris. Then, drugs—speed, cocaine, barbiturates, heroin, and a host of others—were a routine part of every model's life, including Michelle's. Back then, she rarely binged, but she did small amounts of whatever she had—or whatever she could get—on a nearly daily basis, and on the days when she didn't do any, she wished she had. The other models depended on their drugs to keep them thin and to keep themselves going. For Michelle, it was the only way she could keep up. With it, she found there were endless hours of work she could do. It was the typical lifestyle of the modeling world. It was something that everyone did, even the photographers. Michelle would never forget one particular incident. A coked-out photographer lost his temper with her. He began screaming violently and threw his camera at her. He missed hitting her in the face by a matter of inches, but that was close enough for Michelle. She refused to work with that photographer ever again. Despite everything else, she never touched coke after that. Just the thought made her paranoid and made her heart race and her lungs fill with concrete until she thought she would suffocate.

She pushed the thought away, which was difficult, and looked at Jason. "I'm sorry," she said. "I was just thinking about the good old days that weren't so good."

"Want to tell me about it?"

"No," she said.

The gondola was close to reaching the top. "I don't think we should get out," Jason said. "It's snowing pretty hard up here. It will be very cold."

"That's fine," she said, still enjoying the ride.

The gondola made its turn around the top carrousel, and they switched to the seats on the other side so that they would be facing town again on the descent.

"So why did you leave Montana?" Michelle asked.

"I left Montana because I had to," he replied. "Mind you, I grew up with three older brothers. We were all fiercely competitive. Darn near killed each other at least once a day. My oldest brother would take over running the ranch. That was something between him and my dad. As for the rest of us, my father fully expected us to go out into the world and make a life for ourselves, not sit around the ranch waiting for him to die so we could collect an inheritance."

Michelle laughed.

"We all left and went off to college," Jason continued. "I went to USC to study architecture and structural engineering. Ever since I was a kid, I was always designing and building things. I had a knack for it. Believe me, I came up with some pretty grand designs. So, off I went. I kept coming here with my family for the holidays while I was in school. I always loved it here. I had the idea to build spec homes here while I was still in college and my dad backed me. I got my general contractor's license when I was twenty. He bought the property and I designed and built the homes—twenty of them by the time I graduated. It was an incredibly successful venture. I moved here after that. I was well on my way by then."

"Is that when you met Catherine?"

Jason nodded.

"Aaron told me a little about her," Michelle said. "I saw her tonight at the restaurant. She looked sad." Michelle looked up at him, knowing that he was the reason. "Will you tell me about her?"

Jason didn't really want to talk about Catherine, but he obliged Michelle. "I met Catherine at a party. I thought she was incredible—strong, beautiful, intelligent, and outspoken. She's two years older than I am. I thought she was the most dynamic woman I had ever met. She was always challenging me, always proving that she was my equal. I thought she was the woman I would marry someday."

"How old were you when you met her?"

"Twenty-four."

"So what happened?"

"A couple of things," he replied. "I realized that all of the virtues I so admired in her were not the same virtues I wanted to live with. Catherine was always competing with me. She fully expected me to marry her. She saw us as some sort of corporate merger between two strong, independent companies. I realized, gradually, that wasn't what I wanted. Also, I was young, and I had a long list of things I wanted to do before I settled down. Then I started on Mountain House. It took me a year just to get the property, then another ten to get all the permits and to build it. All that time, Catherine assumed I was building it for us. I wasn't. It was an entirely selfish endeavor. I wanted to create something, no limitations, just to see if I could do it. And I wanted to do it for myself. No clients telling me that they wanted this, then telling me, no, they wanted that instead. She became that client. The client I never wanted. She couldn't leave me alone with my project. She had to stand over me and dictate—

Jason stopped himself, sensing that his irritability was seeping into his tone. "Her input into the project—into all my work—eventually drove us apart. She was devastated, but she should have seen it coming. I gave her plenty of warning. She was pretty angry with me, saying that I had led her on all of those years. Maybe I did, but I don't think so. I stayed here for a few more years because I had projects I was working on. It was really difficult, being such a small town, and we shared the same friends. But, by then, my projects were getting bigger and bigger—a resort in the Caymans, two in Florida, Cabo. Then the project in Hawaii came up. That's why I moved there for a while. Leaving Aspen helped a lot. Catherine and I were able to talk about things. She knows she pushed me. I always came back for Christmas, because my family was still coming here, and a few other times during the year, mostly because of business. She and I would spend the holidays together." He paused and looked over at Michelle, smiling at her open interest, thinking how different she was from Catherine.

"Catherine is an incredible person," he continued, "as long as she is not trying to grasp onto something. She knows there is nothing between us but a past relationship and a long friendship. I think that, every year, when the holidays approach, she lets herself believe that this is the year that things will change, but I've never given her any reason to think that. I have a great deal of respect for her, but I don't love her, and I haven't for a very long time."

"That must be hard," Michelle said.

"For her, yes," he replied.

They were midway down the mountain now, and the wind was subsiding.

Jason let out a laugh that hinted at regret. "Now I look back at the last ten years of my life, thinking what in the hell happened to all that time?" he said. "It went by so fast. I've done nothing but work, good work, but just work. I watched all my brothers get married and raise families. In a way, I envied them, not necessarily because they had what I wanted, but still I envied them. But I kept on working. It wasn't until this Thanksgiving that I realized I was barreling down the highway, when what I really wanted was a quiet country road."

"What happened?"

"My dad got shot."

Michelle gasped. "But he's all right now?"

"So-so," Jason replied. "He was in pretty bad shape for a while. He's better now, but that's why they're not here this Christmas. The thing is, he got shot in an argument. He had to settle it the old-fashioned way. He actually started it, old bastard. The whole thing is just so stupid. He's still mad as hell about it." Jason laughed, but it was a dry laugh, not his usual, warm laugh. "The whole incident made me take stock in my own life."

Then he sighed and changed the subject. "You know, I've never really lived in my house here. Not like I wanted to. Not like I had intended to." He looked down at Michelle. "I'm going to, though. Starting now, I think. I don't have anything going on to keep me away. And I'm not going to start anything that will, either."

Michelle smiled, but inside she hurt, because she envied him.

The gondola was approaching the base of the mountain, and Jason and Michelle fell silent, taking in the view of town as they approached. It was snowing heavily now, making the view almost surreal.

"I bet they close the gondola early," Jason said. "It's supposed to snow through tomorrow afternoon."

"I would love it if it did," she replied. "I'd love to be snowed in somewhere."

Jason looked over at her, "Oh, yeah? Well, I know of this really cool castle, way up on the hill," he said, exactly as he did the night before.

Michelle smiled. "You already said once that we were snowed in up there, and we weren't."

He laughed again. "Yes, but you know, it never seems to stop snowing here."

18

With every room in the house available to them, it was unusual they would pick the foyer. But it was where the Christmas tree was, and Michelle wanted to be near it, so they sat on the wide, carpeted stairs beside it, with no lights on but those that decorated the tree. It illuminated the foyer, reflecting off the windows on either side of the door. The music playing softly throughout the house was the soundtrack to *The Nutcracker*. Occasionally, Michelle reached out to grab one of the tree's branches and crush it lightly, releasing its aroma.

She bent toward it with her eyes closed, taking in the scent. "I just love that smell," she said.

Jason just sat back against the stairs, leaning on his elbow, casually watching her, as that had become his pastime. She was fascinating to watch and he was content to do so.

She came and sat down beside him.

"I have a surprise for you," he said, showing her the ornate, black crystal bottle sitting on the stairs beside him. "This is my favorite holiday spirit. I was saving this particular bottle for a special occasion, and *this* is the special occasion."

She inspected the neck label. *Louis XIII de Remy Martin Rare Cask Grande.* "I know this cognac," she said. "It is very special."

Jason nodded. "It is. This is called 43.8. It was released in 2010. I bought it at a wine auction a few years ago. And we are going to drink it." He smiled at her, opened the bottle, and poured them each a glass. "Not the whole bottle, though. It would give us one hell of a hangover if we did." He smiled at her, thinking about what Aaron had said: *Just don't let her drink too much.*

Michelle took a sip. It was delicious.

"How many bedrooms does this house have?" she asked him.

"Nine bedrooms, fourteen bathrooms," he replied. "I still need to give you the full tour. Tomorrow? It's a better tour during the day."

"Okay." She paused. "Have you ever had your whole family here for Christmas . . . a full house?"

"Oh, yeah." He laughed. "This is the first year it's been just me."

She closed her eyes, focusing on the music that wafted through the foyer. She felt an ache in her chest. *Memories.*

"Have you seen *The Nutcracker*?" she asked.

Jason nodded. "More times than I can count."

"It's my favorite ballet," she said. "I have seen it a thousand times. For the last five years in a row, I've gone to every performance at the *Palais des Congrès de Paris* . . . except for this year. I will miss it this year." She paused, listening to the music. "I could play the 'Dance of the Sugar Plum Fairy' by the time I was three years old, but I wanted to *be* the sugar plum fairy."

"So, this year, I am without my crazy family and you are without your beloved *Nutcracker*," Jason said as he set his glass down and stood up. "Here, sugar plum fairy," he said, taking her hand, asking her to follow him. He led her to the center of the foyer and turned her around so she stood in front of him with her back to him. "You said you trusted me. I want to see if you really do."

"Okay," she replied, with only a hint of uncertainty in her voice.

He placed his hands on either side of her waist. "Are you ready?"

"I don't know. What are you going to do?"

"I can't tell you. You have to trust me."

"I do." She placed her hands over his.

"Okay, now give me a little hop."

She did and with great ease he lifted her over his head. She could feel her body rise effortlessly, arching over the top of him like a diver, then stop, suspended, cantilevered over him. She raised her hands over her head, creating a continuous arc with her arms, through her body, and to her toes. She closed her eyes, letting him find her center of gravity. She felt his hands move from her waist to the center of her back, then one moved away, so she remained balanced, perfectly still, on the palm of his one hand. She never moved, never flinched, and he never faltered in supporting her. With the same ease, he brought her back to the ground.

"You're steady as a rock, sugar plum fairy," he said.

Michelle turned to look at him. Her face was flushed from the blood rushing to it. She laughed from the exhilaration. Then she went quiet. She searched his face. She felt her chest tighten, and tears welled in her eyes. The feeling that was coursing through her body at that moment was something new to her. She had felt it last night for the first time. She let it absorb her. She gave him a faint, quivering smile.

"Thank you," she whispered to him. "You are making me feel very happy. It's not a feeling I am accustomed to."

Jason wiped a tear from her cheek. "Well, that makes me happy to hear you say that," he replied.

For a moment, she just stood in front of him, looking at him. He watched the look in her eyes change from gratitude to desire, even though it was showing itself unlike it had before. Before it had been a need. Now she wanted him, and she would have him, there on the stairs, because he wanted to give himself to her. She pulled her clothes away, letting them fall to the floor, letting her hair and her body fall on him. There was a difference in her laughter, in the way she kissed him and the way she touched him. Her curious hands were now knowing hands. The places on him that she had once touched with a joy of discovery she now knew—and found. From deep within her, a strength emerged, and he marveled at this, because he suspected it had always been there, somewhere deep within her, and he said so. But she said no, that the strength she showed was not from within, but from him.

He carried her upstairs and laid her down beside him, pulling her back against him. They laid quietly, neither moving, neither speaking. Strange, sexual emotions rose to his surface. He almost felt guilty, as if, gazing at her back, he was spying on her. He traced her spine. He loved lying naked next to her. Her skin was absolutely alabaster, like porcelain. He traced the outline of her ribs. She was so thin, too thin, but he was getting used to how thin she was, and so it was not so apparent to him. If she were to gain a little, even a pound or two, it would make a difference. Her skin seemed to flush wherever he touched her, and he marveled at this. He traced the outline of her hip, then the line between her legs. Again, he felt a slight pang of guilt. What was it about her that made him feel that in exploring her he might be exploiting her? He certainly wasn't. He turned her over and she became all woman again.

19

Michelle awoke, blinking her eyes. The great plush bed had swallowed her up and she had no desire to leave it right away. She lay there for a moment, listening to the wind howl across the mountaintop. Morning light spilled through the window. She couldn't believe she had slept through the night. Her gaze traveled around the room, and she noticed things she had not noticed before—the craftsmanship of the deep mahogany wood, the detail of the fixtures, and the richness of the furniture. This room was Jason. She could feel him. Her gaze caught the photograph on the mantle. For the first time, she felt like she might be able to actually participate—even if only for a moment—in the sense of reality that the photograph evoked.

There was a black cashmere sweater on the chair by the bed. Michelle knew it was there for her. She pulled the sweater over her head. It was so large on her that the neckline hung off one shoulder and the sleeves swallowed her hands. The cashmere felt good on her skin. It smelled like Jason and she loved it. Pulling on a pair of socks also left out for her, she made her way down the stairs.

The phone rang in the kitchen and Jason answered it. It was Aaron.

"You're there," Aaron said, sounding surprised. "I thought you might have lost your mind and gone skiing today."

"No," Jason replied lightheartedly, looking out the window at the remnants of the storm. "Today would not have been the day to be up on that mountain." There was a momentary pause, and Jason waited patiently for Aaron to fill it.

"Michelle is still there, I hope," Aaron said.

"She's here," Jason replied. "She's fine, if you were worried."

"I'd like to talk to her," Aaron said.

"She's asleep."

There was another span of silence from Aaron. "Why don't you come down? We can talk."

"What about Michelle?" Jason asked, not sure if Aaron's suggestion included Michelle, or if Aaron wanted to talk to him alone. From his tone, Jason could not tell.

"Yes, what about Michelle?" Aaron replied. "I really think we should talk. There are things about Michelle—"

"Michelle is fine," Jason repeated, a little angry, defending her.

"No, Jason. Michelle is not fine. And if you think she is, then we certainly should talk."

Jason considered it, remembering what Aaron had already said about her.

"Bring her down for dinner," Aaron said.

"Okay, I'll ask her," Jason replied.

"You don't have to ask her, Jason. Just tell her you're coming to dinner tonight," Aaron said.

Jason closed his eyes. *So, this is how it is.*

"Come down about five," Aaron pressed, then said goodbye.

Jason hung up the phone, not sure if he was angry, not sure if he should be angry. Aaron knew Michelle and Jason could not dismiss that.

"Ask me what?" Michelle said from the doorway where she had been standing. Listening. She stood with her arms crossed, looking both defensive and defeated. She had heard enough to suspect that it had been Aaron on the phone.

Jason turned around, surprised. "I'm sorry. I didn't know you were up. That was Aaron. He wants us to come down for dinner tonight." There was no change in his voice, no indication that he knew about the eggshells he was walking on.

She stayed where she was, in the kitchen doorway, studying him. She didn't want him to know anything about her. If she didn't care about him, then she might not care if he knew, but everything about him stirred her heart. He held his hand out to her, motioning her to him. Michelle came and leaned against him, and was enveloped in his security. She closed her eyes. She didn't want Aaron to be a part of this. Just this once, she wanted Aaron to leave her alone. *Don't bring my past into this, Aaron. Don't do anything that you think might be for my own good.* She didn't want to think about what Aaron might have said, or might say.

Jason wrapped his arms around her, pressing his cheek into her hair. "You are precious," he whispered to her.

Michelle smiled. His words made her feel beautiful inside. Made her feel loved. He picked her up, sitting her on the counter in front of him. Running his hands up her bare legs under the sweater, he kissed her gently. For a long time, they just looked at each other, their faces close, smiling happily, curiously. So much passed between them during the few moments of silence. So much was said without words.

Michelle blushed, looking away.

"What?" Jason asked, lifting her chin.

"The way you look at me. It's like you're looking into me, looking for something." She paused, smiling. "I was just wondering if you are finding whatever it is you are looking for."

Jason smiled. "You are very perceptive."

"Oh no!" Michelle jumped to correct him, laughing. "I'm not at all. It's my biggest fault. If I'm perceptive, then this is new insight I've acquired—since yesterday."

"You are very perceptive," he repeated. "And yes, I am finding what I am looking for." He kissed her softly. "So, Aaron wants us over at five," Jason finally said.

Michelle closed her eyes. *So much for the fairy tale.*

It was almost five o'clock. Jason found her in his room, sitting on the edge of the bed. She had showered and pulled her hair back. She had put her clothes from the night before back on and she looked exactly as she did then. He paused in the doorway, looking at her, and when she did not look up at him, he suspected she did not know he was there. She sat quietly with her head bowed. In her lap she held his flannel shirt. She stroked it, then pressed it to her face, closing her eyes to its softness. He walked toward her and knelt in front of her, and she looked at him for the first time. Quietness had settled over her, and there was a sadness to that quietness. The effects of the last twenty-four hours had faded—her laugh, her smile, and the color in her cheeks. The pain that hid behind her eyes he could now see. He took her hand, touched her cheek, and kissed her.

"Why the sad face?" he asked, trying to keep his question as light as possible, although he was genuinely concerned.

Michelle only shrugged. Her gaze remained on the shirt. "Today went by so fast . . ." Her voice faded away.

"We don't have to go if you don't want," he suggested, knowing that staying was not really an option. When she didn't respond, he lifted her chin. "We can come right back after dinner, if you like."

She smiled. "Do you mean that?"

"Of course," he replied, although suspecting that leaving Aaron's might not be so easy. "Do you want to tell me why you suddenly seem so reluctant to go to Aaron's?"

Michelle only shrugged again and did not answer him.

"You're not afraid of Aaron, are you?"

"No, not at all," Michelle replied, a little surprised at his question.

"Well, you seem afraid of something. That leaves me to think you're afraid of something he might say or do."

Michelle closed her eyes.

"Michelle." He wanted to be gentle, but he also wanted her attention. He wanted to know—something at least. "Does Aaron have something on you?" He squeezed her hand. "Come on, Michelle. If you're afraid Aaron is going to tell me something you don't want me to know, then maybe I should hear it from you."

She pressed her palms to her eyes. "I don't want Aaron to tell you and I don't want to tell you. It's a bad thing and I don't ever want to talk about it. I just want to forget about it."

Jason took her hand again. "How bad can it be?"

Michelle laughed sarcastically, but she was hurting.

"Are you sleeping with Aaron?"

Michelle looked at him, not expecting his question, not thinking he might consider that. "No," she said.

"Have you ever?"

"No."

"Well, that would have been the worst thing you could have told me." He squeezed her hand. "I'm sorry. You don't have to tell me anything." He did not press her further, because he wanted her to come back with him.

Michelle looked at him for a long time. Aaron would tell him, without a doubt. One way or the other, he was going to find out.

Jason just looked at her, patiently, waiting, wanting her to open up, knowing there was much, much more. *It's okay, Michelle, you can tell me.* But she said nothing.

He sighed. "Sometimes, it's better to air things out than it is to bury them. I promise you I'm a good person to talk to. There's probably nothing you could tell me that I haven't heard before."

Oh yes, there is, Michelle thought.

Jason moved closer to her, wanting to comfort her. He kissed her cheek, taking her hands in his.

She looked up at him. "I'm not so wonderful, Jason, and you're going to hear a lot of ugly stories about me from a lot of people."

He stopped her. "I know why you're doing this. I know why you're telling me this, but I can separate the hype from the human. And I appreciate you seeing something in me to not want me to see a facade of you." He clasped her hand in his. "You said the other day that you are here to make some changes." He kissed her hand. "I want to help."

She smiled up at him. She believed him. "If you really mean that, then please understand that there are some things I want to change and some things that I cannot change. You can help me by not regretting those things I cannot change."

"Okay, I can do that." He smiled and took the shirt from her lap and set it on the bed. "Come on," he said. "It will still be here when we get back."

Michelle stood inside the entryway, looking out at the courtyard. While the wind blew the snow off of the roof, sending it swirling above her, the courtyard was peaceful and protected. Even though it had just snowed, the walkways and driveway were clear. It had melted, Michelle realized. Heat. She glanced around at the balconies and walkways, all clear of snow. Like the heated sidewalks in town, all of the walkways and driveways were also heated, on this side of the tunnel, at least. All part of the master plan. Jason had thought long and carefully about the layout of the courtyard, about everything. And everything was exactly as he had planned it. She looked up at the stonework over her head. Every brick, every block, every corner, every light, window, step, was exactly so, because Jason had planned it that way. Michelle smiled. He was deliberate to the most intimate detail. He created things. He built things. He made things happen.

She heard a deep, vibrating rumble from somewhere on the other side of the tunnel. She waited curiously. Jason appeared from the tunnel, walking toward her, whisking the snow from his shoulders. There was something about the way he walked that she loved. He carried himself casually, yet with strength.

"Ready?" he asked.

Michelle nodded. "Are we really going down in a snowcat, or are you just kidding me?"

Jason smiled. "Your chariot awaits." He motioned her out into the courtyard.

They walked together toward the tunnel. The rumble grew louder and seemed to echo inside the tunnel. Emerging at the other end was like emerging into another world. This was the world where the blizzard had hit. There was nothing but the vast whiteness and the fading sunset. The road had vanished, and Michelle could see down the entire mountainside, which was covered in pristine snow. It was both breathtaking and frightening.

She was completely unprepared for the snowcat. It was nothing like the one she had once ridden in as a child in St. Moritz. Idling in front of her and towering above her was a state-of-the-art piece of machinery. Michelle stopped, staring.

Jason laughed at her reaction. "Pretty pricey way to shovel the driveway," he said, "but it's fun." He took her hand, leading her past the curved blade that arced across the front of the snowcat, shining brilliantly, reflecting the last rays of sunlight before they dipped behind the mountain. The blade alone was taller than Michelle. Carefully, he helped her up the step, pushing her above him, up into the shiny red cab. She looked out the opposite side, not believing how high up she was. As soon as Jason sat down, she did the same, wanting to be as secure as possible. He reached over and buckled her harness, then buckled his.

"Just remember, I trust you," she said. She looked behind her and could see the section of road already been cut into the snow. "Where do you keep this?" she asked, thinking that it certainly would not fit in the garage.

Jason smiled slyly at her. "I've got things hidden all over this mountain."

She watched silently as Jason expertly positioned the blade. With a lurch that forced a gasp out of Michelle, the snowcat moved forward. As soon as it hit the steep incline of the mountain, where there seemed to be nothing before them, Michelle tightened her grip on her seat.

"How do you know where you are going?" she asked, worried, remembering how treacherous the road was when it was cleared of snow.

Jason reached over, placing a reassuring, comforting hand on her. "See those markers?" he asked, pointing to a shaft of pipe sticking up out of the snow. "That's the edge of the mountain. As long as I keep the blade about four feet inside of them, I know I'm on the road. I tried this once without the markers. I came damn close to taking the shortcut down." He pointed to the edge. "Don't look, though. It's scary."

Michelle looked anyway, and wished she hadn't, because the edge did indeed drop away with frightening perspective. She sat back quickly, looking out ahead at the spectacular view down the mountain, watching the blade cut into the perfect blanket of snow, casting it aside in great chunks. She was less afraid of the ride down in the snowcat than she was of what might transpire at Aaron's.

20

s soon as they walked into the Perlman house, Michelle felt everyone's eyes on her—Aaron, judging the past twenty-four hours according to how she looked at that moment; Hannah, who would only look at Michelle with a fleeting gaze, constantly looking for a diversion; Katrina, who pouted, clearly showing that she felt rejected and betrayed by Michelle's change in attention; and even Jason behaved courteously, like nothing was wrong, knowing full well that there was.

She couldn't take it. Excusing herself, she went up to her room and locked the door. Locking the inner door of the bathroom as well, she lit a cigarette and sat down on the floor, using the toilet for an ashtray. The cigarette calmed her, and she was relieved to have the moment alone with it. She felt both defeated and deflated. Why, when she wanted so much to put the past behind her, was it so firmly attached to her? She sighed, taking another drag from her cigarette. What was the point of trying? What was the point of anything anymore?

She heard a knock on the bedroom door and Katrina's voice. Michelle put her hands over her ears, hating herself for ignoring Katrina. When the knocking—and Katrina—went away, Michelle went for what she really wanted.

Katrina returned to the dining room, sullen-faced. "She's not answering."

"Leave her be then," Aaron said, the tone of his voice dismissing Michelle's absence without further discussion.

Dinner was served without Michelle. The conversation was friendly and family-like. It was as if only Jason noticed Michelle's absence. Aaron pressed Jason into a deep discussion about a real estate venture.

Eventually, Aaron rose from the table. "If you would excuse us," he said to Hannah, "Jason and I have some business to discuss." It was Jason's cue to follow him, a cue given without opportunity to decline. Aaron left the room, giving Jason no choice but to follow.

They went to Aaron's study, closing the door behind themselves. Aaron took his time pouring them each a drink, and Jason took a seat on the couch, waiting patiently. He'd spent many hours in this room with Aaron, for many different reasons. Michelle was just another reason. Aaron sat down in a deep chaise opposite Jason, rolling the tip of his cigar between his lips while Jason absent-mindedly balanced the glass of whisky on his knee, letting it rock between his fingers. He knew it wasn't real estate that Aaron wanted to talk about. He took the cigar Aaron offered him, and they sat quietly for a moment, smoking.

"It seems that we suddenly have something in common besides real estate," Aaron finally said, as if he had read Jason's mind. His tone was different than it had been on the phone that afternoon. But there was a reason for that. "I have a tremendous amount of respect for you, Jason. You know that. And I would never interfere with or even inquire about your personal life. I know you are a very private person." He paused. "But since Michelle has been your guest these past few days, I'm compelled to intervene. I don't know what has transpired between you two, and I'm not going to ask, but I must remind you that Michelle is one of the most publicly watched individuals in the world. You know that, don't you?"

Jason only nodded.

"Anything she does is front-page fodder," Aaron continued. "Anything she says or does is scrutinized and anyone she is with is exposed, as well. She's a media meal ticket. There are people who do nothing but try to follow her around. I can't imagine you wanting to read about yourself all the time, and it can be very cruel."

Jason was solemn. Aaron's point was clear.

Aaron turned his attention to his cigar for a moment then his voice became serious. "If you are getting yourself into something with her, do you know what you are getting yourself into?"

Jason bristled.

Aaron leaned back. He had made his second point. "You've seen *The Islanders*."

Jason nodded.

"And what did you think?"

"It was very good."

"Good? Fuck you, Jason," Aaron said with dry sarcasm that did not offend Jason. "It was fucking brilliant. *She* was fucking brilliant. Best film I ever made."

"So what about it?" Jason asked, sensing Aaron had yet to arrive at the third point he wanted to make.

"Michelle was trashed the entire time," Aaron replied flatly, matter-of-factly. "Completely wacked out on heroin. Sometimes she was so bad we had to film around her. And not just that shit. She did everything she could get her hands on. She drank and popped pills until her body couldn't take it anymore. She was a mess."

Aaron paused for a moment then said what he had promised Michelle he wouldn't say to Jason. "She ODed on the set. Right in front of my entire crew, she had a drug-induced seizure. She almost died." Aaron paused, reflecting on that particular day. "It blew me away. She was so unbelievably brilliant, and she almost died right there in my arms. She made that film. And she almost killed herself doing it."

Jason remained silent, not sure why Aaron was telling him this, but knowing he would soon have his answer. It was time for him to listen, and listen carefully. He knew that.

"I'm not telling you this to slander Michelle. I have no reason to do that to her. I care about her. I'm telling you this so you can understand the seriousness of her situation."

"And just what exactly is her situation?" Jason asked.

"She's getting worse, Jason. This didn't start with my picture, and it certainly didn't end with it either. She's been using for years. But it's getting out of hand. She can't hide it anymore. She can't function when she's doped up, and she can't cope when she isn't."

"So why hasn't someone done something about this?" Jason asked. "I can't believe that there isn't someone close to her that hasn't stepped in to intervene."

Aaron worked his cigar. Jason had a point. But there was a reason. Would he understand that reason? Aaron went to his desk and sifted through some papers. He held up a photograph of Michelle.

"What do you think she's worth?" Aaron asked.

Jason shrugged. He hadn't really thought about Michelle's net worth. She mentioned an apartment in New York and one in Paris. "I don't know." He knew nothing about the modeling industry or what Aaron had paid her.

"Cash, assets, real estate, investments, somewhere in the neighborhood of a hundred million. Half that's in contractual agreements, including her agreement with Marc. Assuming she inherits her father's estate, then her net worth will double, maybe triple." He put the photograph down. "Surprising, isn't it?"

Jason was more than surprised. "How does she deal with that?"

"She doesn't."

Jason just shook his head. "She's quite a ticket."

Aaron leaned back. Yes, she was, and he knew that as well as anyone. "Michelle is an extremely talented young lady," he said. "She possesses talents unlike anyone I've ever seen—on screen and off. She's brilliant. But Michelle has a serious drug problem, among many other problems, and she is dangerously close to destroying herself. She's a mess." Aaron paused. "Do you think she's fine right now? What do you think she's doing, locked in her room?"

Jason had no reply.

"Did she tell you about my next picture, *The Ballerina*?" Aaron asked.

"No. She hasn't told me anything," Jason replied.

"Michelle is the lead in my next picture. We have a deal. She gets the film if she goes to rehab."

Jason nodded, thinking about overhearing her on the phone, saying she would do what Aaron wanted.

"What Michelle doesn't entirely know is that she's going straight from here to The Oaks, right after Marc's show, which . . . " Aaron rolled his eyes. "Is another, entirely different fucking mess, but nonetheless the reason why she's even here in the first place."

"What do you mean she doesn't *entirely* know?" Jason asked, now suspicious.

"She's kind of, sort of agreed to go to rehab in that she hasn't said she won't go, but I've not discussed any details with her as to when or where. It's basically been decided for her. And not just by me. Unfortunately, there are other people involved in her life who want her patched together without taking her out of circulation."

"Isn't that a little harsh?" Jason asked.

"No, not when we're talking about someone's life," Aaron replied.

"I'm not talking about your tactic, I'm talking about treating her like a public bus or something," Jason said. "You make it sound like no one wants to give her any time off because they're not making a buck unless she's working."

"That's exactly the situation," Aaron replied flatly.

Jason rubbed his hands across his eyes. He thought about what had transpired between him and Michelle. "I don't get it," he said. "Of course, I believe what you are telling me, but I've been around people on all sorts of drugs and people trying to kick heroin, and she's just not showing the signs."

Aaron only shrugged. "Because she's making no effort to kick it. She's a very high-functioning addict. You don't think she's been doing it the past few days?"

Jason thought for a moment, recounting in his mind how she had recoiled from him the previous morning. "I don't know," he said.

"Trust me, she is," Aaron said. "That's why she plays the piano for hours on end. The higher she is, the better she plays. And she doesn't want to give that up. She's so talented already; this shit she does escalates her to genius status. And it enables her to cope with the really ugly aspects of her fame, for lack of a better term."

"If you say so," Jason said, not knowing what else to say.

"The reason I'm telling you all of this is because I don't want you to interfere. I'm not asking you to stay away from her, because I think you are good for her, but I do want you to remind yourself whenever you are with her that she is *not* okay. You could have a profound influence on her, and you need to be careful with that kind of power. It's going to be hard enough to get her in there if she won't consent."

"Hard enough to get her there if she won't consent? Jesus, Aaron, what are you going to do? Commit her involuntarily?" Jason asked, exasperated.

Aaron nodded. "If that's the only way."

"Does she really need such drastic action?"

"If I ask her to go voluntarily, and she says no, not now, or for whatever reason, and she suspects that I might force her to go, then she will just disappear." Aaron snapped his fingers. "Case in point. Twelve days ago, she disappeared from a Paris couture show. Five nights later, she turned up on the bathroom floor of a fetish club in New York City. Her little network of underground friends found her. She should have been taken to a hospital, but they took her home to avoid any bad press. She's lucky to have made it through the night. This has happened so many times that the odds are against her now."

Jason rubbed his eyes. He felt sick. "How in the hell did she wind up at my house?"

"It was Keith who brought her to your house that night," Aaron replied. "I think he just asked her. I never would have taken her that night. She had just arrived here and I didn't yet have a handle on what kind of condition she was in. But once she was there, I changed my mind. She seemed to come around quickly. I didn't think leaving her there that evening would have any lasting repercussions." Aaron crossed his arms. "You are one of the most rational people I know, so I won't ask you what's going on between you and Michelle. Just don't disillusion her, Jason. She can't take it."

"I won't lead her on, I won't get involved, and I won't interfere." Jason leaned back. "You have my word."

"Whatever you do, be careful how you go about it. She doesn't handle rejection well."

Jason was quiet, but then he burst out laughing. "Christ, she's got a lot of money, Aaron."

"But not more than you," Aaron replied.

"Oh, I see. I get to spend time with her because I don't need her money." Jason's voice hinted at sarcasm.

"A man who is kind to her and who is interested in her money is a dangerous combination. She needs to be protected from those people."

"I agree," Jason said, but he didn't agree. It sounded to him like the people who wanted to make money from her were far more dangerous than someone who might want to take money from her.

"And this, my friend, is only a fraction of it all," Aaron said. "There's also Marc, Annalise, and her agent. And then there's her mother and father."

Aaron moved closer to Jason, taking up his cigar again. The rich, heavy smoke curled up between them. "You want to hear an interesting story?" Aaron asked. "A classic tragedy? A story I'd like to make into a film someday?"

Jason only nodded.

Aaron leaned back, rolling his cigar thoughtfully. "She was born into this life of hers, the result of an unlikely marriage between two very eccentric people." Aaron paused, as if tasting his own words, listening to them as if to judge whether or not they translated into something cinematic. He contemplated Michelle's parents.

When he spoke again, it wasn't about them. "I never really understood what Michelle's life was like until, one day, I took my kids to the zoo in San Diego. Here was this incredible collection of exotic animals. And it was noisy and crowded and everyone was pushing everyone else to get the best view of the animals. But then there were the pandas, and, if you wanted to see the pandas, you had to obey the rules. In the middle of all the chaos and crowds, we were ushered into this climate-controlled environment. Everything was so subdued that it reduced everyone around to whispers. We came around the corner, after waiting in line forever, and there they were, living in this little world created just for them, being provided with anything and everything they needed to sustain life and to make them as comfortable as possible. We just stood there, awestruck. Unless you've seen them, you've never seen anything like them. They are so magnificent, so big yet so delicate. And then when I walked away, I felt so sorry for those pandas, because they seemed so far away from home. Later, when I heard they were sick, I thought of Michelle. She's just like one of those pandas. She's lived this incredibly sheltered life, even at the height of her career. Her environment is totally controlled. And she is dying. Slowly."

Aaron paused, his thoughts scanning over the many complexities of Michelle's life. Finally, he spoke again. "I told you her father has been calling for her. It's odd."

"Why? You keep saying that."

"They are estranged," Aaron said. "I don't know the man personally, but I've known of him for many years. I once looked into having him write the score to one of my earlier films. I found out there was a five-year wait to get anything commissioned by him. That was probably twenty-five years ago. He was at the height of his career then. A number of years later, I saw Michelle and her father together in Geneva. I didn't know who this man and small child were, but it was brought to my attention. Michelle must have been, I don't know, about seven years old. She was so tiny and so beautiful, like a little deer. Hannah and I were at a café, and they were sitting at the table next to us. I listened in on their conversation, and I was astounded. They were talking about music on a technical level that was way, way beyond me. I remember watching her. She looked up at me. I can't describe what I saw in her eyes, but I'll never forget it. It was profound."

Aaron's thoughts diverged again, but he shrugged it off. "But I don't want to get into her family now," he said. "There is a woman in Michelle's life named Rita Herron. She's Michelle's agent and business manager. She's the one that discovered Michelle and the one who is most responsible for Michelle's success. Rita Herron is a smart, shrewd woman. She is the grand creator of images and a marketing genius. She knew exactly how to market Michelle. It was as if Rita kept Michelle her secret treasure and just brought her out once in a while. And when she did, my God, people went crazy for her. Rita was very smart about the way she went about building Michelle's career. She eased her into the business and kept her separated from the masses. Rita marketed Michelle as something rare and elusive, which she is, and the fashion industry went nuts over her. Rita could have booked Michelle seven days a week, but instead she was very selective. She booked her for only the best jobs, strictly print work at first, very classy, very sophisticated, and she did a lot of covers right off. Two years into the business, Michelle had done, I don't know, a couple hundred magazine covers worldwide and was earning probably $50,000 a day. Rita negotiated several exclusive contracts for her. Fragrances, cosmetics, jewelry. Big bucks. She tailored Michelle's editorial work and pared down her runway work so that she was only working with a handful of the best people. Rita built her up to the number-one position by allowing the demand for her to be so great. Because of this, every time Michelle came out, it was a big deal. Like getting a glimpse of a princess. You can bet that major marketing firms around the world are using Michelle's career as a stellar example of product marketing." Aaron thought about Marc. *Except for Marc. Rita had really fucked up with that deal.*

Jason emptied his glass then got up to refill it. "So, how do these people at Keith's house fit into this? They seem out of place here, and Keith seems to have mixed feelings about having them here."

"Marc and Annalise are a dangerous pair," Aaron replied. "But Annalise and Michelle go back a long way. Rita is also Annalise's agent. That's how they met. I don't know what Annalise's attraction to Michelle was, but they used to spend a lot of time together. It was Annalise who showed Michelle the kind of life she could have because of who she was. They were part of a small, elite circle of people on the Paris fashion scene. Who knows what went on with these people; it was insiders only. Michelle never talks about her early Paris days. No one does. But you can bet that Annalise and Michelle know things, and have probably done things, that would shock us. It was when Marc came into the picture that Michelle started taking some bad turns. The three of them were working together in New York. Marc's shows are very conceptual. He once did an entire season of shows using just the two of them. It was very theatrical and very popular. Marc had carved himself out a big chunk of the fashion industry with them, and he's been very successful. The timing of everything had more to do with Michelle's demise than anything else. It was obvious that there was something developing between Annalise and Marc, which, I am sure, left Michelle feeling very cast-off. At the same time, Marc decided to do a season of shows with just Michelle. People wondered how in the hell he was going to put on runway shows with just one model, but he did it and it was spectacular. It was based entirely on theatrics. He set up the top of the runway like a bedroom with a giant closet, with all his designs for that season hanging in it. Michelle did this thing where she tried on all of these different outfits like she couldn't decide what to wear. She changed into every garment right up on the stage and then would walk down the runway by herself. The fashion aficionados went mad. Marc started coming up with all of these new ideas for his shows, and Michelle would pull them off. They went through three seasons like this, and his business exploded. While it went over unbelievably well, it caused tension between Annalise and Michelle. And at the same time, Annalise and Marc got married. And then Marc started treating Michelle poorly. I don't really know why. Granted, he's a harsh man anyway, but he wasn't that bad at first. It got progressively worse until it came to be pretty well known throughout the fashion industry here in the US that what went on behind the scenes of Marc's shows and his photo shoots wasn't too pretty. It was a weird situation all the way around. I think that Rita didn't really know how bad it was, or she would have done something. But, then again, she was bringing in a hell of a lot of money with it. Michelle was forced to spend more and more time in New York, which isn't a good place for her to be. It's such a harsh city, and she *is* a foreigner. The people in New York are different. They're harsher, too. That's when she got into the underground scene there. That's when she started doing some really scary things."

Aaron paused, thinking, then continued. "So, this New Year's Eve show with Marc is their last one together—so to speak. Her contract expires with this show, and it's been real hush-hush about whether or not it will be renewed. Under the circumstances, I can't imagine it will be. I think they've all had enough of each other. This whole season has been exceptionally hard on Michelle. Rita wanted to just ride it out and be done with it, only it became obvious that Michelle might not make it. Michelle always does the Paris and Milan couture shows, which might have been a nice break from Marc for her. Even though she would still be working, at least she would be in Europe and away from Marc for a little while. So then Marc decided to show in Paris. It was a disaster—for about a hundred reasons."

Aaron paused, because he really didn't know what had happened in Paris, or why Michelle suddenly disappeared. "But this particular show here is Marc's grand finale," Aaron said. "And doing it in Aspen instead of New York only adds to the whole scheme. The whole thing is highly conceptualized. Marc's got six models in this one, including Annalise and Michelle. It's part runway, part theater, and part fantasy. It's about these women who fantasize that they have been invited to all of the greatest parties in history. They transform themselves with some of the most elaborate costumes you've ever seen. It's genius."

Aaron leaned back, scratching his head. "I have to admit, I'm sitting back watching all of this happen, with one phenomenal yet disastrous film with Michelle behind me, thinking that she is going to be the next Audrey Hepburn if I can get some control, and wondering if there will be anything left of her when I do."

He looked at Jason. "You know, every day I think about that day that I saw her with her father, and I think about how she looked at me, that look in her eyes," Aaron said. "All these years, I've followed her modeling career. In every photograph of her, that look is there. When she looks into the camera, it's there. It's just lately that it's starting to change. And I don't want to lose it. So, what can I do?" Aaron continued, asking himself more than Jason. "Michelle's drug problem is critical; she's starting to have blackouts and disappear for days at a time. Now everyone is starting to rein her in at the same time, which only makes it worse. She's got this show to do for Marc, she's got contracts she obligated to fulfill, and I want her to do another picture. It's a tug-of-war. No one wants to let go of their part of her and give her a break. Me included. So here we are, deciding her fate without even bothering to ask her what she wants. Why? Because she doesn't know what she wants or which way to turn. That's one of the reasons why it's so easy for everyone to dictate to her what she does. And she doesn't defend herself. I've never heard her complain about anything. And she is in a position that she could be downright difficult if she wanted to be, and people would bend to her. She's been on photo shoots where she's been so cold she's nearly gotten hypothermia, and she doesn't say anything. And she takes Marc's crap like she's obligated to."

Jason rubbed his eyes tiredly. "In a way, I wish you hadn't told me all of this. It makes me sick. And it pisses me off."

"It's a sick situation. Entirely at Michelle's expense. But I can tell you this: I'm going to be the last one to cave in. I've gotten Rita to collaborate on a rehab plan for her. But you can bet that no one is forgetting what's at stake."

There was a knock on the door. Aaron acknowledged it and Michelle opened the door. Instantly, she knew. She could sense the tension in the room, which stopped her in the doorway. Her eyes darted from Aaron to Jason, who did not look up at her right away, no doubt affected. She looked back at Aaron, and the silence lingered forever.

"You told him, didn't you?" she asked, sounding defeated.

"Michelle, please," Aaron said, taking on a patient voice.

She threw her shaking hands up in despair, in surrender. "Why, Aaron? Why can't you just let it go? Why is it that every time you are rolling for something that has to come up? Why this time?" She looked at Aaron, not really expecting him to answer her, because she already knew the answer. "You know what I feel like?" she cried out. "I feel like a lab rat in a cage with a group of scientists hovering over me, waiting to see what I'll do next." She started to back away, but her eyes never left Aaron. "Damn you! How could you do this to me? You promised me you wouldn't tell him." She was both angry and pleading at the same time. "You've just got to have everything out on the table, don't you?"

Jason closed his eyes, feeling caught in the middle. But she was right.

"Michelle, I'm sorry." Aaron sounded sincere. "It was not my intention to hurt you."

"Hurt me?" Michelle choked. "You've humiliated me!" She retreated farther, through the doorway. Then she stopped. "You know, Aaron, I woke up this morning feeling happy, and actually feeling like I might make it through the day. Do you know how long it's been since I felt like that?" Her gaze darted once more between the two of them, and then she was gone.

She hurried back up to her room, locking the door behind her. Aaron would be on her heels, she knew that. He would be too goddamned worried that she would do something—just like the last time. *To hell with you, Aaron.*

She didn't care about leaving her clothes, nor was she even selective about what she left and what she took; she just filled a single bag in a frenzy. In the bathroom, she scooped her toiletries into her makeup bag. The lipstick case stopped her. This time, there was no hesitation, no regret, no denying wanting it. She wanted it. She needed it. The effect was instant and amplified. She could feel it explode throughout her body, like electricity, but better than electricity. She turned away from the mirror, for fear of catching the glare from the monster in it and having it catch her.

The knock on the door came, as she knew it would. She went to the door, but did not open it.

"Michelle?" Aaron tried the knob.

"Aaron, please, just leave me alone," she said, concentrating on absolute coherence.

"Michelle, I'm sorry. Please open the door."

"I'm fine, Aaron. I'm used to it. Just leave me alone."

"Okay, I'm going to give you a few minutes, and then we're going to talk. And Jason is still here."

"Okay," she replied flatly.

She heard his footsteps fade away. She organized her flee. She dug her cell phone out of the bottom of her bag and turned it on. *Rita, you are always nagging me to carry it, in case of an emergency. This is an emergency.* She put her coat on, dropping the lipstick case into the inside pocket. She fingered it one last time through the lining, then grabbed her bag and her music folder, lit a cigarette, and unlocked the French door.

The night was bitter cold. Carefully, she navigated her way down the dark, icy steps that took her down the back of the house. She could hear laughter within the house, which made her hurry. Light from the kitchen flooded her path and she ducked beneath it, catching a glimpse of Hannah as she passed through the room.

Michelle stopped at the edge of the driveway. Jason's snowcat loomed ahead of her. She glanced quickly back up at the house, imagining for a second that the entire Perlman family was chasing after her, then hurried down the steep, icy road, afraid of slipping, but more afraid of being caught. She could feel her heart slamming against the inside of her rib cage. If she could just make it to the bottom of the hill so she could call a taxi . . .

The ticket agent at the airport counter said the next flight, the last flight of the night, did not leave until eight forty-five. Michelle could feel the panic rise in her throat. That meant an hour of waiting. That was enough time for Aaron to stop her. She bit her lip frantically, looking back over her shoulder, not that she expected anyone to be there; it was just an instinctive response. She thought about renting a car and driving to Denver. No. She could hire a lift to Denver. Take a taxi—a four-hour taxi ride.

The agent's recognizing yet impatient gaze made Michelle uncomfortable, so she stepped away from the counter. She had a little time to decide. The plane was barely booked. People were coming to Aspen, not leaving. She retreated to a corner, out from under the bright lights, away from the center of the room. She could feel the agent's eyes in her back, watching her go. Would the agent call security? She should buy the ticket whether she used it or not.

Instead, she ducked into the restroom. She used the tip of a nail file to scoop the white powder out of the lipstick case. Her hands were shaking. In the stall next to her, the toilet flushed. She sniffed at the same time, returned the case to her coat pocket and hurried out, hating that, although the terminal was nearly empty, those who saw her stared, recognizing her. She hated that everyone knew who she was. She flipped the hood of her coat up over her head.

She bought the ticket. The agent looked back and forth between Michelle and her credit card. Michelle knew why; because the name on the credit card was *Alaina M. Sekovich*. She showed the agent her passport.

Michelle returned to the shadows and lit another cigarette. She closed her eyes and sniffed.

The automatic doors parted and Jason passed through them, coming directly toward her. He never faltered, never changed his pace, as if he knew all along exactly where she was. Michelle saw him and froze, questioning the reality of the image coming at her, frightened yet not believing, not expecting. It wasn't until he was closer that she could see the concern on his face. He reached her without hesitation, took the cigarette from her hand, tossed it on the tile floor, and pulled her against him. He wrapped his open coat around her. For a moment, neither moved. Then someone else inside of Michelle started to cry.

"Michelle," he whispered, a little choked, "you don't know how sorry I am that this happened."

She didn't want him to see her. He'd seen too much already. When she tried to free herself from him, he held onto her. People were watching them now, but he had no intention of letting her go. He held her, like a helpless, panicked rabbit in a snare.

"Shhh," he said quietly, trying to calm her. "It's okay."

But it wasn't okay. Nothing was okay.

"You have every reason to be angry," he finally said. "But you know it wasn't Aaron's intention to hurt you." His words made her fight him, but he didn't let go. "Michelle, it doesn't matter to me." He held her as close as he possibly could have, doing what he could to comfort her. "I'm still here. I'm still here and I won't leave unless you want me to."

She finally looked up at him on her own. For a long time, she just looked at him. She found it hard to believe what she was hearing, but she wanted to believe him.

"You promised to trust me, remember?" he asked.

She did remember.

"I don't want you to ever feel like you can't talk to me," Jason said. "I know you're angry with Aaron, and you have a right to be, but Aaron cares about you. He just wants me to be careful so you don't get hurt, and that's exactly what I'm going to do. Come on," he said, coaxing her out of the airport.

Michelle balked. "I don't want to go back to Aaron's."

"Then we won't." He offered his hand, picking up her bag with the other.

Jason helped Michelle into the passenger seat of Aaron's SUV then got into the driver's seat. He sat quietly behind the steering wheel, thinking. He tipped his head back, closing his eyes. He didn't tell Michelle what he really thought, that, although Aaron did care about her, he cared about his picture more. Of course, Aaron didn't want Jason to distract her or for Michelle to hurt herself. He wanted her held together and committed to a hospital long enough so she could get through the production of his film in one piece. Aaron was pulling every string he had, including Jason's.

He looked over at Michelle. She was far, far away. Long gone were the bright eyes, the laughter, the joy of discovery, the sugar plum fairy. Gone. Her skin had taken on a ghostly tint and her lips were bluish. She stared vacantly out the window. He picked up her wrist, but she didn't seem to notice that he was touching her or that he was even there at all. He felt her pulse. It was shallow and rapid. Now he had another problem on his hands.

He drove back up the mountain to his house. She followed him silently, but she was edgy and wanted to smoke. He let her, although he hated it. He set her bag aside, so she would have to ask for it if she wanted it. He took her coat and went through its pockets as he hung it in the closet. He found the airline ticket and looked at the name. *Alaina M. Sekovich.* And he found the lipstick case. She noticed none of this. He called Aaron to tell him that she was with him, that she was all right, and that he would bring his car back and pick up the snowcat as soon as he could.

When he set the phone down, she looked directly at him and, although her gaze was expressionless, it was lucid. She wasn't that far gone. "Am I?" she asked.

"Are you what?" Jason asked.

"All right. You told Aaron I was all right."

"I meant that you were accounted for and that you weren't out on any ledges," he said.

She took a deep, deliberate breath. Her body was warming up and the chemical in her system was doing its job—it pacified her. She felt no anguish, no anger, no fear, nothing.

"You can take me back to Aaron's if you want. My father should be there soon to get me." Her voice was calm, and it seemed to flow out of her as if it was someone else's voice and not her own.

Jason frowned. She had curled herself into the corner of the couch, and he sat down beside her. He watched her closely, wanting to note every single, minute detail, and to memorize everything. She wasn't behaving normally, although he couldn't really say what her normal behavior was. But she wasn't distressed. He touched her hand, which was warm. She was breathing normally. He put out her cigarette, which was burning untouched in the ashtray he'd set down for her. Where were all the signs he expected to see?

"What do you mean your father's coming?" he asked.

"He's coming," she said again. "You'll see."

Jason said nothing. She wasn't making sense to him, and he wasn't sure how to reply.

"The window was like the one upstairs," she said, her gaze drifting for a moment, but then she looked at him, and the steadiness of her gaze gave Jason an eerie feeling. "Do you think it would be hard to jump through stained glass, with it all welded together like it is?" Michelle tipped her head back against the couch, closing her eyes. "It must have hurt her badly."

"Hurt who?" Jason asked, growing alarmed, yet trying to decipher her at the same time.

"Alaina," she replied.

Alaina. He thought about the name on the ticket. *Alaina.* Sirens went off in his head. Was she talking about killing herself? Or had she tried already? Or was she reminiscing about something? It could be anything, but, regardless, it was disturbing, very disturbing.

"I wonder if anyone knows what happened." Michelle sighed again and then she was quiet.

"What are you talking about?" he asked.

Michelle didn't respond.

Jason, too, was quiet. He offered her something to eat, which she accepted, but then didn't touch. He stayed with her, but neither said much. She passed an hour by sitting blank-faced, with downcast eyes. Finally, she sat back, letting out a defeated sigh, as if all this time she had been thinking carefully, concentrating, on a problem that she just couldn't solve.

"I just don't get it, so maybe I'm not supposed to," she finally said. She asked for her bag, and he gave it to her, saying nothing, but watching her. She sorted through a small makeup case, pulling out a medicine bottle.

"What is that?" he asked.

"Valium." She never looked at him as she quickly swallowed one tiny pill, absent-mindedly tossing the bottle back in her bag. She just wanted to sleep off what she could not resolve, and he didn't try to stop her from taking it. It took some time, but, slowly, he could see the look in her eyes change, until she closed them.

When her breathing steadied, he covered her with a blanket and settled into one of the overstuffed chairs beside her, propping his feet up. He was tired, but he stayed awake for a while, watching her, thinking about everything that Aaron had said and everything that had transpired in so short a time. He thought also about the pandas.

The sound of the piano woke him. It was still dark, and it took his eyes a moment to adjust before he could read the clock. It was three in the morning. The sound that echoed from the main room was the same sound that had echoed through his house the day before. The same music, the same tone, the same style, the same precision.

He followed the sound to the other room. She was there, just as she had been the day before, and the day before that, with her eyes on the keys and her expression one of absolute concentration. Her music was as perfect and as fluid as it always had been. He sat down in one of the chairs by the dark fireplace. Listening to her, he realized that he could draw no borders around her. He could not define where reality began and ended with her. In that sense, she was far beyond him. He was a strong individual, but he could deal best with what was concrete and tangible. She was beyond definition.

She stopped playing and turned to face him. "If you want to take me back to Aaron's, I'd understand." She pulled one of her knees to her chest, resting her heel on the edge of the bench. "I'm sure that after last night . . ." She closed her eyes and took a deep, trembling breath. "I can't change my past; I just wish I didn't have to keep paying for it." Tears rolled down her cheek, and she quickly wiped them away. She had no control over her tears. They seemed to just come on their own.

He couldn't call it crying, because she was not, nor was her voice emotional. They simply came. He came and sat down beside her. "Michelle, that couldn't be farther from the truth. If you left, I would be heartbroken," he said earnestly.

She gave him a faint—very faint—but grateful smile.

"You want to know what I think?" he asked.

"I do," she responded, reluctantly.

"I think that everyone says they are trying to help you, but no one has really done anything." He pressed his face to her hair. "Come on. I have a surprise for you."

He led her through the house, to a lower level that Michelle had not seen before. They passed through a door that opened into a large gym. There was a faint smell of chlorine. They passed through another set of doors and suddenly everything was white marble, and Michelle found herself looking at the perfectly still water of a swimming pool. Their footsteps echoed, but everything else was silent. Steam rose from the pool.

Michelle's eyes brightened, which was what Jason wanted. She went to the edge of the pool. "Can I swim?" She looked back at him.

"Of course," he replied.

With the renewed excitement of a child, she began pulling off her clothes. She stepped into the water without hesitating and stopped on the steps of the pool with the warm water lapping at her waist.

Jason was painfully aware of her nudity, but it was the most natural thing in the world to Michelle. He knelt at the edge of the pool. At what point, he wondered, did a woman become self-conscious? When did a woman lose her inhibition and become aware of her age and that she was aging? He closed his eyes. For all her complexities, he loved her for being the way she was. She submerged herself and glided through the water. Jason stayed on the edge of the pool. This wasn't about them; this was about *her*.

The water felt wonderful on Michelle's skin. It was neither hot, nor cold, so she could not feel it as water, but she could feel it passing over her body and she could feel herself moving through it, washing away the very last of her anxiety. It both aroused her and soothed her at the same time. She tried to think of the last time that she had swum, just for the pleasure of it. She couldn't remember. But she was now. She looked back at Jason, who was still sitting at the edge of the pool. She wondered why.

He watched her move across the water in a way that was both childlike and exquisite. She kicked, and her foot broke the surface with a small splash that echoed like her music, and the water rippled, and the ripples drew rings round her, radiating out from her. She was their center.

As he watched her swim, he tried carefully to separate all the different, mixed emotions that her presence left him flooded with. In the forefront of his mind was how different they were from each other. They were from two vastly different worlds, and all that that implied. Then there was their difference in age, which thinking of made him wince, because he was so painfully aware of it. She made him feel both old and young again at the same time. He sighed. Those were his insecurities and, compared to hers, they were insignificant. There was something about her. She was so beautiful, but did she know how beautiful she was? Could she comprehend what it was like for someone to be standing back and looking at her? Could she comprehend the experience of experiencing her? He didn't think so. He was convinced already that she had her own, different concept of what beauty was and what being beautiful meant. He wanted to know what she thought of herself, because knowing that would add many pieces to the puzzle he was trying to solve. He was sure she had no idea the effect she had on others. On the outside, she seemed so naïve, which made others want to protect her. He wondered if that was really the case.

What Aaron had said—and done—made Jason angry, yet he understood Aaron's intentions clearly. Aaron had taken it upon himself to propel her through the world in which she existed and also to protect her from the ugly effects of that propulsion. He wanted to exploit her, but protect her from being hurt by that exploitation. Aaron's intentions were so obvious to Jason, but were they to Michelle? He didn't know. But he did know that Aaron did not want her involved with or exposed to anyone or anything that did not directly relate to those intentions. And, as angry as that made Jason, he could see Aaron's point. Michelle's life, and the circumstances surrounding it, was precarious. She was this way now, probably because she had been this way most of her life, and Aaron knew her life. And it wasn't just about drugs; it was about money and talent, and all the things that could be gained from her. Everything Aaron had said was true and Jason could understand that. To let her go would only mean that someone else would get a bigger piece of her. And everyone wanted a piece of Michelle. The problem was, there wasn't that much of her to go around. Aaron was determined to have the controlling interest in her, which he tactfully referred to as protecting her. Jason was pretty sure there were many others who wanted to *protect* Michelle, each wanting to pull her in and do so in their own way, to their own advantage. Who was he to say what Aaron had intended for her was not the best sheltered life she could lead? It probably was.

Jason sighed again. He could not get involved in this tug-of-war over her. Aaron had made some valid points. She didn't seem like she would be capable of self-sufficiency, but had she ever been given the opportunity? She certainly didn't seem to have any difficulty getting around. Who was to say that, if left alone, she couldn't live a normal self-managed life? He had an overwhelming desire to liberate her, but as overwhelming as his desire was to try and free her, the freedom he idealized for her only made him another person wanting to pull her in another direction, offering her another form of shelter.

Thinking this through eased his anger at Aaron. Aaron wasn't preoccupied with making her a celebrity; she already was one. His intentions were to help her return to some degree of emotional stability, taking into consideration who she was. He was talking about drug therapy, which she obviously needed. And Michelle's options seemed limited. Perhaps what Aaron was offering was, in fact, Michelle's best option. Jason told himself he wouldn't interfere with Aaron's plans, but she was here now, and he was free to offer her his companionship if she wanted it.

She swam back to him. "Will you swim with me?"

Jason shook his head no, smiling at her.

"Please?"

With a little laugh, he agreed, and Michelle swam away again, across the pool. When she turned around again, Jason was gone. He had dived into the pool and was gliding across the bottom with incredible strength and speed. He surfaced at the far end of the pool from her, then disappeared again, surfacing closer and closer, until he was beside her. She wrapped her arms around his neck. Floating on his back, with Michelle on his chest, he moved slowly, gracefully through the water. He made her feel like she could exist on his strength alone.

He stopped, rolling her over on her back, floating her, barely supporting her. "Close your eyes," he said.

There was no sound. He moved her just slowly enough through the water to feel it. Michelle was smiling. That was what he wanted.

With his cheek near her ear, he whispered to her. "You are far too beautiful on the inside not to be at peace with yourself. I know that people hurt you, and that you hurt yourself. But it doesn't have to be like that." He moved her through the water ever so slightly.

Michelle turned in the water and looked up at him, her eyes were troubled again. He was speaking the truth about her and the truth hurt. He was talking about achieving what he had achieved, what she wanted, but didn't know where to begin. The pain showed in her eyes, but when she reached out to him, he was there, holding her close. She didn't have to ask for him to show her how. He would.

21

The sun was rising again, but they were both tired, so she followed him through the house and up to his room. He held her close against him, but there was no sex between them. Long after her breathing steadied enough for him to be assured she was sleeping, he remained awake, watching the sky lighten, trying to sort out the recent events. The gaps—and he found many—he tried to fill in using his best judgment. He tried to come to a conclusion—any conclusion—about how he felt, which was harder than trying to fit the fragmented pieces together. He had been so suddenly exposed to so much about her. There were things he wanted to know about her, but they had to come from her, not from Aaron. He wanted to know more about her life and what she wanted to do with it, not what others wanted her to do. He wanted to know about the simple things that made her happy, if there were any. He wanted to know what she thought about herself and what she thought about him. Could she define herself? Could she be defined? He wanted to ask her about her father, and about Alaina, because what she had said earlier made no sense to him, yet it had to have come from somewhere.

Later, when she awoke, they went back to the kitchen and Jason made them breakfast. Michelle was quiet—they both were—but the silence was not uncomfortable. She committed herself to a corner of the couch and there she stayed. At one point, she reached for Jason's photo album, which was on the table.

"May I have this picture?" she asked, turning to the photograph of Jason rock climbing, suspended in riggings against the sheer granite wall.

Jason nodded, removing it from the album for her.

Michelle looked at the photograph for a long time. "Who is this man," she asked aloud, both to herself and to Jason, "who makes me think I may never see Paris again?"

Jason only smiled when she looked up at him. It wasn't a question that he necessarily needed to answer.

"This picture says so much about you," she said.

"What does it say?" Jason asked, amused.

"It says that you are patient, yet determined, strong, stable. That you know who you are. You know how tall the mountain is and that you will reach the summit because that is your goal." She looked at him, admiring and envying him at the same time. "And you will reach it, without hesitation. I envy this person." She shook the photograph. "He is confident and he is comfortable with who he is."

Her expressiveness and observations surprised him, and he found himself offering her a silent apology, because occasionally she would say something that indicated she was much smarter and far more insightful than he gave her credit for.

"And what about you?" he asked.

Michelle retorted, "It's different with me. Pictures of me are not like this. The stories they tell are made up. There is nothing real about them. In a photograph, I can be anyone I want to be. I could be a rock climber in a photograph just like this, but I would be without goals. I wouldn't be trying to reach the top. Someone else would be lowering me down into the frame, and then someone would hoist me up again. I wouldn't have to do anything except look like I was doing something." Michelle sighed. "That seems to be the story of my life," she said, both reluctantly and sarcastically. "For all I seem to be, never have I made anything happen. I don't make things happen for me; they just do. I just stand in one place and everything revolves around me. It's a very helpless feeling.

She paused. "You know that old Elton John song?" she asked, singing the chorus, "Someone saved my life tonight . . ."

Jason smiled. "I love that song."

"That's how I feel, like you are saving my life."

This was going to be one hell of a tug-of-war.

"I want to show you something," she said, pulling away from him, but wanting him to follow her back up to his room.

From her bag, she retrieved an envelope and a thick magazine she had taken from Aaron's house. Jason thought it was a catalog. She sat down on the bed. From the envelope, she took a dozen photographs of herself and arranged them across the bed. At one end, she placed the magazine, which Jason could now see was an issue of *Italian Vogue*. The photograph on the cover was of Michelle, and he found it unsettling. It was harsh. At the other end, she placed a Polaroid that Katrina had taken of herself and Michelle at the Perlman house, just a few days ago. Jason realized that Michelle had arranged a spectrum of herself across the bed, with the photographs going from one extreme to the other.

She picked up the magazine. "Shocking, isn't it?" she asked.

Jason nodded. It bothered him. It wasn't Michelle, or at least the Michelle he knew.

She flipped through the magazine, opening it to more photographs of herself, some harsh and dramatic, with death-white, heavy makeup and ice-hard, glaring eyes.

"These pictures," she explained, "this is what my life is like most of the time. This is what my life feels like. Like I'm dead, but I'm alive."

She returned the magazine to its place and pointed to the next three photographs. "This is the Paris runway. Haute couture. This is my life in Paris. The catwalk. High fashion, chic, sophisticated. In. Rich. Glamorous." She laughed, because it was a joke and she knew it. "You would think so, anyway, but Paris is a dangerous place. Life in Paris is very dangerous. People are very beautiful and very rich. It's competitive, and the models are insanely jealous of each other. There is a lot of jealousy in Paris." She pointed to the next few pictures, of herself and friends, famous friends, at a nightclub in New York. "This is my life in New York. People in New York think they are invincible. They never sleep. Like vampires."

Each picture was drastically different. Jason found it disturbing to accept that they were all of Michelle.

"This is my life," she explained, waving her hand over all of the photographs, except for the last two. "I can be any one of these at any time. I switch back and forth like that." She snapped her fingers. "Sometimes I wake up in Italy in the morning, go to Paris in the afternoon, and then to New York, and it's still the same day, because of the time change. I feel like I am sometimes two entirely different people in two different places at the same time." She laughed. "It's insane."

From her wallet in her bag, she retrieved a small photo of herself when she was fourteen. She was dressed in a dancer's leotard, with her hands outstretched and her toes pointed in a ballerina's pose. She was smiling. She looked at the photo for a long time, and it saddened her.

"This is the person I've always wanted to be. And this is the last time I can remember really wanting to be something. Seems like so long ago." She sighed, shrugging off the regret that consumed her. "It's hard to explain, but I remember wanting to be in the ballet so badly, and it was because it gave me this idea that I would be free. And I wanted freedom." She sighed again.

How could she make someone else understand what she herself barely understood?

She picked up the Polaroid of her and Katrina, looking at it sadly. In the photo, she looked very plain and very tired. "I don't know what to think of this. Is this the person I really am? I don't know who this person is." She replaced the picture. "This is my life. I bounce back and forth so much that it's too much. This person"—she pointed again to the photo of her and Katrina—"could maybe be the same as this person"—she pointed to the ballerina—"but this person . . ." She pointed to the *Italian Vogue* cover and her voice faded. She looked up at Jason. "All these different lives. It's so complicated. I am all of these people, yet none of them at the same time."

Jason nodded. *Yes. Complicated. Very.*

"I don't even know why I carry these around with me," she confessed. "Sometimes I think just to torture myself. I took the magazine from Aaron's house because I didn't want Katrina to have it."

She paused then looked at him. "You're the only one who hasn't invested in any of these," she said.

"But that's not true," he replied, picking up the Polaroid. "I've invested in this person here. It's an emotional investment, but an investment nonetheless."

"Ah," she replied. "So then you cannot be objective after all."

No, Jason thought. *I thought I could at first, but now I know that I can't.* Jason bowed his head and pressed his fist against his lips in deep thought. All of the things that had happened over the past few days flashed through his mind. That evening flashed through his mind. The pictures of Michelle flashed through his mind.

Suddenly, he understood. And never, in his entire life, had he understood another person as he understood Michelle at that moment. He looked at her. She was so sweet, so delicate, and so feminine. So beautiful. So right. He found her hand. On his own shoulders, he felt the weight she carried on hers. He knew what she was asking him—for the unconditional support to help her make a decision she knew she must make. And she was asking him because she trusted his judgment more than her own. She was asking him to help her choose what was best for her, even if it meant putting his own feelings aside.

She looked at him, waiting patiently for him to respond. He had saved her life, she had said. That was a big responsibility. He glanced at the pictures again then looked back at her. He knew that at this moment he could crush her if he wanted to, kill her if he wanted to, or send her back to the pages of *Italian Vogue* to kill herself. But he wouldn't. Again, she had surprised him. Not only had she opened herself up to him, but she had done so with an uncanny self-perspective. While she put forth questions for which she had no answers, she was not ignorant. Her life was unbelievably complicated. No wonder she was confused about her identity. But was confusion what it really was?

Michelle sighed. "Then there is the money. People don't say it to me, but I know what they're thinking. I have no right to question my life. I have everything."

Jason nodded, understanding. "I feel sorry for you, Michelle. I don't mean that to sound how it does, but I do."

Michelle closed her eyes. "When I first looked out over this town from your balcony, I felt so out of place, so lost." Her voice trailed off.

Jason remembered that moment vividly. He remembered wondering what compelled her to seek out such solitude. He remembered wondering what she was thinking.

"I'm not sure where I should be," she said. "Where's my picture of this place?" She picked up the Polaroid. "Is this me? Is this the person who feels what I am feeling right now? And, if so, how is it that I can look so tired and feel so sad? And if this isn't me, then where's my photo? Don't you see? If there is no photo, then there is no proof of life."

Unbelievable, was all he could think. And say? He didn't know what to say.

She looked up at him earnestly. "Is there something wrong with me because I don't understand what's happening? I feel so detached from myself."

"There is nothing wrong that you can't change," he replied.

Michelle started to think back. Her mind drifted for a moment, until her thoughts found a starting point.

"When I first went to Paris, I only saw the good things, but there were not-so-good things going on all around me," she said. "Now, I can think of so many bad things that I was unaware of at the time." Her voice trailed off. "The one thing that is so hard for me to do is to look at myself in the mirror. But I do it all the time. I have to. Seems like I spend half my life sitting in a makeup chair. I have to sit and stare at myself for hours, watching the transformation, and I think, 'Who is this person?' I see a monster that hates me, but then who am I? I have a stylist, Sasha, he loves to turn my back to the mirror, make up my face, and then turn me around so I can see. It freaks me out. Sometimes, when I have to do my own makeup, I can do it in two minutes, only because that's as long as I can stand looking at myself in the mirror. Somewhere out there, there is this big star named Michelle Seko. She's everywhere." Michelle looked at Jason. "I don't know who that person is. I don't see that person in the mirror, but I don't see myself, either." Michelle frowned, getting frustrated with herself. "Am I making sense?"

Jason nodded. *Sense* might not be the word he would use, but yes, he understood.

Her expression became solemn as her thoughts drifted. Her voice sounded sad. She looked at the photos again then closed her eyes. "I just don't want to go back."

"Michelle, you can stay here for as long as you want," he said.

"But, I can't expect—"

Jason touched her lips, silencing her. "I care about you. I want to help you. If this is how I can help you, then it's the least I can do. I don't want to see you hurt." He pressed his lips against her temple, taking up her hands in his. "Tell me what it is you are afraid to go back to."

Michelle closed her eyes. "Going back means going back to work, and I just can't bear what I do anymore. It's hard for me to explain, but I feel like I've sold my soul. And there's so much hate and jealousy. I just can't take it."

She looked up at him and his expression told her he understood.

Jason was quiet. He had been wrong about her. She knew exactly what was going on. She was on this course, not because of ignorance, but because she had allowed it to happen.

"What about Aaron's film project?" he asked, referring to *The Ballerina*.

"I don't know what to do about that or if I even want to do it," she replied.

"Why not? I thought you did?"

Michelle sighed. "I have a lot of reasons, I suppose. It's hard for me to talk about it."

"Try?" he asked.

Michelle sat up, pulling her knees to her chest. "Ever since I was a little girl, I wanted to be a ballerina. I can't tell you how many scores for original ballets my father has written, but I think I have seen every production of every ballet produced by every major company in the world. I begged and begged my father to let me take ballet. And whenever he would play, I would dance around him, pretending I was a ballerina. It would make him crazy. He would get so angry with me. But I didn't give up until he finally let me. When I started taking dance lessons, I loved it. I loved being with other girls my age. It was a good time for me. But my father always seemed to be there to drag me away before I wanted to go. He said it was taking too much time away from my studies. But I was so tired of studying music, and I wanted to dance. And I wanted to go to a regular school, where I could have friends. I learned that if I asked enough times and never gave up, eventually he would, and so I begged and begged him to let me go to the summer ballet school in Geneva. He finally said that I could audition for the school but, if I didn't get in, then that would be the end of it. I was so excited. But it was short-lived. My father had made sure in advance that I didn't get accepted. He just wanted me to think that I didn't get in because I wasn't good enough."

Michelle looked at Jason seriously. "Well, he got his way." Her voice drifted and became vacant. "But I've never gotten over that. Every time I step out onto the catwalk, I'm fifteen again and back up on that audition stage. All the faces looking up at me are still my father's. I finally stopped looking at them."

Jason was solemn. Already, he could see a pattern to Michelle's life, a never-ending roller-coaster ride of searching for herself, companionship, and acceptance; gaining it, losing it, being rejected; and then searching again. It was sad, he thought.

"About six months ago, Aaron mentioned *The Ballerina* project to me. He asked me if I would be interested in a part. He knew I loved ballet. I couldn't believe it, especially after what had happened on the set of *The Islanders*. Then he sent me the script, but he didn't mention which part he wanted me for. He just wanted me to read it. So I did. Anna Pavlova had always been my idol, even though her life was so tragic. I wanted a part in the film, no matter how small it was. It was a chance for me to be a ballerina again. My first night here, Aaron told me he wanted to cast me as Anna Pavlova." Michelle looked up at Jason. "You know the rest." She sighed. "But, deep down, I still feel like this is my last chance to be the dancer I always wanted to be. When I was a little girl, I dreamed about Anna Pavlova. Now I have a chance to be her, even if it is only a movie. It's something I can relate to. And I want to do it because I want to do something. This isn't something that can just happen; I have to make it happen. But I just don't think I can do it." Her voice turned to despair.

"Why not?"

"I just don't think I can do it."

Jason studied her. He wouldn't tell her that he thought making a movie was the last thing in the world he'd like to see her doing. He understood her wanting to pursue something that had a purpose, but he couldn't see her fulfilling that purpose by stepping into the character of a dead ballerina. After listening to her, he concluded she had no idea who she was outside of the roles she was placed in. She had no sense of self and so she drifted in and out of other roles, other lives, trying to make them her own.

"I know that Aaron cares about you," he said, "and I don't think he will pressure you into doing this film if he doesn't think you are up to it, especially if you have a therapist who doesn't think you are up to it."

Michelle grimaced. "You think I need to go, don't you?"

"I have a lot of friends who have benefited from going to rehab. It's not something you should be afraid of."

She nodded, in submission. *Yes, but you are wrong about Aaron.*

❧

Aaron called for her. "Marc wants you for a fitting this afternoon. Are you all right with that?"

"When?" she asked reluctantly.

"At two, at Keith's."

Michelle closed her eyes, fighting the outward signs of dread that was filling her up inside.

"I'll go," she said.

"Have Jason take you," Aaron said.

She told Jason about the fitting.

"How long will it take?" he asked.

Michelle shrugged. "It's hard to say. It's mostly a lot of waiting around."

"Is it really necessary?"

"It's best if I do."

"Why?"

Michelle sighed. "Because it will cause the least amount of problems."

"I understand," he replied. And he did understand. They owned her. This made him angry.

"Do you think we could go into town for a while first?" She didn't want to talk about Marc or think about the fitting.

"Of course we can," he replied, surprised she asked, thinking it was an unusual request.

But it wasn't. Since arriving in Aspen, she had wanted to browse around town. It reminded her of St. Moritz, and she wanted to walk around and take it in. She wanted to do more than just look down on it from afar or take it in from through a passenger window of a moving vehicle. She wanted to be a part of it.

The snow-lined brick and cobblestone streets and sidewalks were bustling with skiers coming to and from the mountain, some of them scrambling to manage their skis as they walked heel to toe in their plastic boots, zigzagging across the dusty white, icy streets. The shops lining Gant and Cooper streets were busy, as well. Michelle was content to window-shop, and was far more interested in the art and furnishings than she was in any of the clothing boutiques.

When they passed the Wheeler Opera House, situated in the center of town, Michelle stopped, looking up at the historic brick and granite-block building.

"What a marvelous old building," she said.

"One of Aspen's most famous," Jason explained. "This and the Jerome Hotel." He loved Aspen's historical architecture. The old buildings, like the Wheeler, had been a great influence on him when he was younger.

The door was open and music from inside floated out to them. Michelle recognized the music and looked questioningly at Jason.

"They're getting ready for the concert tonight," he said.

Michelle frowned. Then she remembered.

Jason smiled at her, somewhat amused. Had she actually forgotten about it? He recalled hearing Melissa invite Michelle that first night at his house. Since then, he had thought to ask her about it, but in light of the events of the past few days, decided not to bring it up.

"Do you still want to go?" he asked.

Michelle thought about Aaron. She couldn't avoid him. "Yes," she replied.

"Why don't we go together?" he asked.

Michelle smiled, looking relieved.

They stepped into the dimly lit opera house. Michelle's gaze followed the wall, following the series of photographs that depicted the theater's history. The auditorium door was ajar, and, as the chorus rose from the darkness beyond it, Michelle was drawn in. Stepping inside the dark theater, she walked down the aisle, following the lights along the floor until her eyes adjusted to the dimness, and then tucked into a seat, not wanting to interrupt the rehearsal. Jason followed and sat down beside her. The choir stood on the stage, an odd ensemble in their street clothes and heavy coats. A few wore gloves; a few held sheet music.

Michelle saw Melissa Garrison sitting in the front row. John Garrison was poised in front of the group, clapping his hands. As soon as their voices rose in unison to the music of Handel, Michelle could feel her emotions rise with them. She sang along softly, knowing every word of "For Unto Us a Child Is Born." Mesmerized, she moved closer to the front of the theater. Jason let her go, choosing to hang back in the shadows. She slipped into a seat a dozen rows from the front. No one noticed her. The chorus rose and filled the empty auditorium with a rich, ringing echo that found its way into the inner depths of Michelle's heart, filling its painful voids. As they sang, the music carried her away from the events of the past few days to a place and time far away, and tears formed freely in her eyes. She both rejoiced in the music and felt an almost unbearable anguish at the same time. The music brought her both sadness and joy. It enveloped her and she was grateful for it. It brought a hint of something she could not quite grasp, a hint of something that had to do with her life, or, at least, the part of her life that was her past. That something just about to break through her surface when John tapped his podium and the voices stopped abruptly. The feeling died with the scuffle of feet on the wooden stage and the shuffle of sheet music.

Quietly, Michelle rose and, sinking her hands deep into the pockets of her overcoat, retreated to the back of the theater.

Jason followed her out without a word.

Emerging from the dark interior to the bright, busy town, Michelle lingered on the stone steps of the theater. She seemed to be watching what was going on around her, yet her gaze was glazed-over and vacant, which concerned Jason. She again seemed silently, deeply disturbed by something.

Jason stopped Aaron's SUV halfway up the driveway to Keith's house. He looked at Michelle apprehensively. "Catherine is here," he said, recognizing her car in the driveway. "Are you okay with that?"

Michelle only shrugged. "I don't know. I guess I'll find out."

They walked into the house to find Keith, Annalise, and Catherine in the living room. Keith greeted them, but his reception was falsely charming and smug. Jason and Michelle sensed it immediately. Catherine and Annalise looked at Michelle, then at each other, making Michelle uncomfortable. They had been talking. It was obvious.

Annalise looked back at Michelle coldly. "We were wondering if you were ever coming," she said. "Marc's downstairs. He's been waiting for you all morning. People have been calling for you. Did it ever occur to you to at least check in?"

Michelle could feel the heat rise in her face. She did not need to check in, and Aaron had told her two o'clock. She was on time. She walked past them all, without looking at anyone, and hurried down the hall. She felt sick.

Jason looked back and forth between Catherine and Keith. Catherine glared back at him, but said nothing. He nodded to Keith to follow him into the kitchen, leaving Catherine. It was rude, but so was Catherine, he thought.

"I may have to go home for a few days," Jason said to his friend. "No one around here but you needs to know that."

Keith nodded, understanding that Jason was referring to Montana and Catherine. "Are you taking Michelle with you?" he asked dryly.

"Hadn't planned to, but I would, if she wanted to go."

Keith looked at Jason, shaking his head. "I'm sorry, Jason, but you're my best friend and I absolutely do not approve of you getting involved with her. I know it's none of my business, but I love you like a brother and people are already starting to talk."

"I'll be sure and keep that in mind," Jason replied, a little sarcastically. He clapped Keith on the back as he walked past him, leaving the kitchen. He went back into the living room to find Catherine sitting alone on the couch, but she would not look at him. He heard angry voices, including Michelle's, which sounded more defensive than angry, rising from down the hall. He chose to investigate the argument, rather than linger in the living room with Catherine.

"I can't believe the nerve you have!" Annalise snarled at Michelle. "Why do you have to create a scandal where ever you go?"

"It's not like that," Michelle replied.

"Bullshit, Michelle! You don't even know who he is."

"Why are you saying this?" Michelle asked. "What do you care?"

"Michelle, I don't care," Annalise snapped. "And I bet he doesn't either. Do you really think that anybody could care about you like you were a real person? You're so wrapped up in your goddamned name and fame. Do you think anyone could ever get past that?"

Michelle just stared at Annalise, not believing what she was hearing. She couldn't respond. She walked out of the room, wanting to get away from Annalise, but Annalise followed her.

They met Jason in the hall. "Maybe we should just leave," he suggested, having heard Annalise.

"If you leave, you are in deep shit." Annalise sneered at Michelle, her tone icy and threatening.

Michelle looked stricken. She felt cornered, with everyone breathing down on her.

Catherine appeared in the hall, coming to stand between Michelle and Jason, making Michelle feel even more cornered.

"You know, Jason and I have spent the holidays together every year for almost twenty years now. I'm sure if you have no place else to go . . ." Catherine did not finish her sentence. She did not need to, having inflicted the damage she intended.

Michelle could feel the heat rising in her face and the pain rising in her throat. "Just leave me alone," was all she could manage to say. Her voice gave away her secret. She ducked between them and went back to the room that had been hers for a very brief time her first night in Aspen.

Jason wanted to turn and somehow hurt Catherine the way he knew she had just hurt Michelle, but he said nothing, did nothing. Instead, he followed after Michelle.

Catherine grabbed his arm. "You're not really going to fall for that, are you?" she asked bitterly.

Jason pulled free from her. "Yes, Catherine, I am." He wanted to tell Catherine how cruel he thought she was, but didn't, because Catherine would never let him have the last word. It was easier to say nothing, because then she could not respond.

He found Michelle outside on the deck.

"What, am I supposed to be made of stone or something?" she cried. This wasn't about explaining herself or defending herself, or even being weak or insecure. This was about reaching her breaking point.

She lit a cigarette. He noticed her hands were trembling.

"Annalise says that wherever I go, whatever I do, I manage to disrupt the lives of those around me. She seems to think that I've set some sort of record."

"Ouch. That's a pretty sharp ax." He looked at Michelle.

He certainly didn't blame her for crying. He took the cigarette away from her, tossed it over the railing into the snow, and pulled her against him, letting her cry. He felt so badly for her. Jason held her quietly, listening to her uneasy breathing. In his arms, her body, her whole being, felt like she had just given up, as though she had been fighting with something more than just Annalise, and whatever it was had won.

She sighed, wiping her eyes. "She also said that Keith is not too happy about my being with you."

"What Keith thinks, or anyone else for that matter, is no concern of mine," he replied.

She pushed away from him, not knowing if she believed him or not. She left the deck and went back into the room. Jason followed, closing the doors behind her. She paced the length of the bathroom, lighting another cigarette and occasionally flicking the ash of her cigarette carelessly in the sink. Her anxiety mounted. She threw the cigarette in the toilet and reached for the glass bottle of mouthwash. Her trembling hands unscrewed the cap, but the bottle slipped, smashing in the marble basin. The sound of shattering glass was so loud in Michelle's mind that it made her jump in fright and press her hands to her ears, trying in vain to force the sound away. The breaking glass seemed to also break Michelle, and she collapsed on the rim of the bathtub.

Jason moved forward, pulling her up. "I'm sorry. I'm sorry she said those things to you. She was very cruel. I would be hurt if someone talked to me like that." He turned Michelle to face him.

She looked up at him. "It's just so hard for me to be here."

"I want you here."

Michelle tried to smile. "Then you're the only one."

"How long will this fitting take?" He asked.

"I don't know. Marc's making some changes. It's only two dresses. Shouldn't take long."

"Do you have to? Can't he do it another time?"

"No."

"Why not? What could he do if you left?"

Michelle closed her eyes. *Send me to hell; that's what Marc would do.*

From the hallway, they heard Marc's assistant, Marta, who had flown in that morning from New York, yell impatiently for Michelle. She wiped her eyes and got up quickly to leave, seeming very concerned that she not keep Marc waiting.

Jason made his way to the lower level of the house, where Marc had set up shop. The large game room was crammed with trunks, garment racks, and dress forms, on which hung some of Marc's designs for the show. Marta scampered around the room, a tape measure dangling from her neck. Jason stepped into the room, trying to stay out of the way.

In the center of the room was Michelle, standing on a dressmaker's pedestal, wearing a glimmering Edwardian wedding gown. He moved closer to her. The pedestal put her eye level with him.

"This is beautiful," he commented. It was the most exquisite dress he'd ever seen.

Michelle's eyes darted nervously. Marc was kneeling on the floor in front of Michelle. He looked up a Jason.

"Yes, it is," Marc replied. "Too bad it's on Frankenstein's bride."

Jason winced. How could he say that? *I wish I were Frankenstein.* He winked at her. *Hang in there, Michelle.* He touched the sleeve. The beading on the dress was glass.

"This must be heavy," he commented.

"It is," Michelle replied softly, swaying slightly under the weight of the gown.

"Damn it, Michelle, hold still!" Marc snapped at her. "And stand up straight."

Michelle did not move. Marc's words seemed to bounce off her.

Jason squeezed her hand and then moved out of the way, watching Marc.

"Damn it!" Marc threw his pins down in frustration. "I cannot shorten this! She is too short for this dress, and I cannot fix it for her, for one show!" He talked as if Michelle were not there. "And it's too heavy. How will she turn around? The walk is not wide enough!" He ran his hand through his dark hair, angrily. The dress was so long on her that even with very high-heeled shoes, Michelle would step on it when she walked. He was unwilling to shorten it, which would take a great deal of time, because of the beading. "I can't believe I even thought about putting it in this show. This will never work!" He hit the hem in frustration, nearly knocking Michelle off the pedestal.

Marta seemed to shrink away from him as he got to his feet and furiously paced the floor. She had worked with Marc for as long as Michelle had and knew better than anyone when to be invisible.

Michelle remained where she was, perched in the center of the room like a target. It amazed Jason that Michelle seemed to be absorbing Marc's verbal attacks, when earlier, Catherine and Annalise had hurt her so. *This is her job. This is what she is subjected to on a daily basis.* She was paid to face such insults with a beautiful smile. No wonder she wanted out.

"Get it off her," Marc barked, waving his hand at Michelle.

Marta hurried over to her and unfastened the dress from its back. It seemed to crash to the ground from its weight, leaving Michelle still standing on the box, wearing only black panties. She lifted her shoulders, having been relieved of the weight of the dress. Jason was unprepared for the starkness of her nudity, but he seemed to be the only one to notice. He tried to remind himself that this was typical, that only he was unaccustomed to what was going on around him. But he wished she would put something on, because her nudity in the presence of these people made him uncomfortable. She did not, so he quietly left.

Catherine met him in the hall. Hurt and angry, she faced him, confronting him about Michelle, blocking his way so that he had no choice but to answer her.

"How could you do this to me?" she shrieked. "And in front of all our friends? The whole town knows about the two of you!" She threw her hands up, spilling the glass of red wine she held in her hand, wishing there was something she could do to hurt him.

"Catherine," he spoke calmly, but when he placed his hands on her shoulders, she slapped them away violently.

"Don't you touch me!" she hissed. "Not if you've been touching her, don't you dare!"

He crossed his arms, remaining calm. He wanted to tell her he didn't care what people said, about him anyway, and that she shouldn't either, but that had always been Catherine's biggest worry—what people thought and what they said. He remained quiet, deciding it was the best way to deal with her. He'd done nothing wrong. She was angry and jealous and she would just have to get over it.

Michelle floated around the fitting room in the canary-yellow crepe empire dress, turning for Marc on command so he could see how she carried herself in the dress, and how the fabric flowed. It was a spectacular dress.

"Can I show it to Jason?" she asked.

Marc only half-nodded, already preoccupied with something else.

She hurried out of the room. Trotting around the corner, she came up behind Jason and Catherine and stopped. Jason's back was to her, but Catherine saw her.

"You bitch!" Catherine shrieked at Michelle, startling her. "You little bitch!" Pushing past Jason, she flung her glass of wine at Michelle before Jason could stop her, hitting Michelle in the chest with the glass. The red wine splattered over Michelle's face and Marc's dress.

Michelle looked down at the dress in horror, and everything seemed to stop. Jason turned away from Michelle for just one second, taking Catherine by the arm and pulling her away from Michelle. He took Catherine by both shoulders and shook her, just once, but sternly. When Catherine looked up at him, it was not his grip on her that was hard, but the look in his eyes. She knew at that point that she had gone too far. He told her to leave and she did. When he turned back around, Michelle was gone.

A thunder rose from the fitting room, sending Marta spilling out into the hallway. As soon as Marc saw the dress, with the grotesque burgundy stain splattered down the front, he came at Michelle like a raging bull and struck her closed-fisted across the face, catching her full force and sending her sprawling across the floor. She stayed where she had fallen, half-sitting, half-lying across the carpet, afraid to move, afraid to look at Marc. Marc moved over her and grabbed her by the arm, lifting her from the floor. Michelle tried to pull herself free, but Marc gripped her tighter, shaking her violently. Then he slapped her. Hard.

Jason reappeared in the doorway. "Let go of her," he said calmly.

Marc turned, surprised. "Get out!" he barked at Jason.

Marc let go of Michelle's arm and she crumpled to the floor.

"Marc, I apologize," Jason said, not wanting the situation to escalate. "This is my fault. I will pay for the dress."

Marc whirled back around, glaring at Jason. "Oh no, I want Michelle to pay for the dress." He turned back toward Michelle, yelling at her. "She is always ruining things, always causing trouble, and no one is going to buy her out of this!"

Jason grew angrier, but he did not raise his voice. "This is not her fault. I will pay for the dress."

Marc ignored Jason. He threw his hands up, shouting obscenely at Michelle, making her flinch as he picked her up with one arm and wrenched the dress from her with the other. The fabric tore easily, but not before gouging her in the neck. Jason grabbed the heavy wooden door and slammed it with a force that splintered the doorjamb.

Marc jumped, startled.

Jason had his attention. "Stop yelling at her, damn it! I said this wasn't her fault and I will pay for the dress!" Jason picked up a robe from the back of a chair and held it open for her. She took it, putting it on without looking at him, without looking at anyone.

Marc glared back and forth between Michelle and Jason. "Get out of my sight, you fucking junkie, and take your boyfriend with you!" Marc turned his back on them.

Michelle tucked herself deeper into the robe and hurried out of the room, fleeing past Jason. But when she turned, he saw the crimson red mark across her cheek and the blood running down her nose.

"Did you hit her?" Jason asked, his anger no longer controllable.

"Get the hell out of here!" Marc yelled, keeping his back to Jason.

It took Jason three strides to get to Marc. He grabbed Marc by the back of the neck, spinning him around, and slammed him against the wall, holding him there by his throat. "If you ever lay a hand on her again, or so much as raise your voice to her, I'll kill you, you son of a bitch." Jason pulled Marc away from the wall and slammed his fist into Marc's stomach. Marc doubled over with a loud groan. Jason let him go, and Marc, like Michelle earlier, fell in a heap on the floor. Jason turned away and rushed out.

He caught Michelle in the hallway, and hurried her forward, back up to the bedroom, where he locked the door behind them. He turned her around to look at her face, but Michelle pushed herself away from him and went into the bathroom, where she sank feebly down onto the floor, falling back against the wall. He could only stand and watch as she lit a cigarette, taking a long, deep, unsteady drag from it, then, tilting her head back, letting the smoke leak out of her bloodied nose.

Jason sat down on the floor beside her. "I'm sorry," he said.

"You shouldn't have said anything," Michelle said, softly. There was no anger in her voice.

"Why not? I was only trying to defend you."

"I know," Michelle replied. "But it wasn't necessary."

"Wasn't necessary?" Jason asked in disbelief. "How could you just stand there and take that man's abuse? What happened wasn't your fault."

Michelle only shrugged. "It doesn't matter whose fault it was. It doesn't matter who threw the wine, only that it landed on me. Your offering to pay for the dress only made him angrier. He hates people thinking that he can be bought." She took another drag from the cigarette.

He turned her cheek toward him, which was already dark red and beginning to swell. "We should get some ice on that." He paused. "You should file a complaint against him."

Michelle closed her eyes. "I can't do that."

"Why not? The man assaulted you. What are you afraid he'll do?"

Michelle wouldn't answer him.

Jason threw up his hands. "This is so ridiculous. Michelle, this is wrong. You've got to stand up for yourself. He's doing this to you because you're letting him." He made her look up at him. "Michelle, please, trust me. The best thing you can do is file a complaint against him. I'll stand behind you, I promise. He doesn't have any legal grounds to defend himself."

Again, Michelle did not reply.

He looked at her, brushing the hair away from her face. "This shouldn't be happening. You don't deserve to be treated this way."

Tossing her cigarette into the toilet, she moved to get up. "Maybe I should just go back. I think if I stay here with you, you are just going to find out all these things about me that you don't like."

She moved to step over him, but Jason put his hand up against her leg, stopping her. "That's absurd, Michelle," he said. "You just said yourself this morning that you never wanted to go back to, wherever, I don't know. And besides, I've already found out a lot of things about you that I don't like." He took her hand, pulling her down onto his lap. "I don't like how you let people treat you. I don't like that you don't take care of yourself, and I don't like what you do for a living, because I don't think that you like it." He touched her cheek. "Why are you really doing this?"

Michelle looked down. "You don't understand."

"You're right. I don't understand. But I want to. And there is one thing I do know. I can understand your wanting to find something in your life worth doing, but you have to find yourself first."

Michelle closed her eyes. It was so easy for him to say that. He was past that point. She knew what he was saying was true, but she was quickly losing hope of achieving what he made sound so easy to do.

"Come on," he said, getting up. "Let's go. You're through with these people."

"But my clothes are downstairs," she said.

"Forget about them," he said. "I'll get your clothes back for you later."

The living room was empty. Michelle pulled her coat on over the robe and tucked her bare feet into her boots. As they walked to Aaron's SUV, Jason picked up a handful of snow and held it to her cheek.

Once in the car, Michelle fell into a solemn, vacant mood that seemed to take her away. Jason did not want to press her, and so they drove back up to his house in silence. There, she curled up on the couch, still wearing the same robe, burying herself under a thick blanket. Jason made her some tea, which she accepted, but did not drink. He gave her a cold towel for her cheek.

"Will you be okay here if I go back down into town? I won't be long. I need to get the snowcat."

Michelle nodded vaguely.

"If you want to stay here for a while, I can get the rest of your things from Aaron's. I'm sure he won't mind."

She didn't reply. She didn't care about what she had or didn't have.

"Can I bring you anything back?"

"No," she replied.

Okay," he said reluctantly. "I'm going to call you when I get to Aaron's."

Aaron met him at the door. "Come in," he said, looking past Jason. "Where's Michelle?"

"She's up at my house."

"You left her alone there?" Aaron asked, concerned.

"She said she was okay," Jason replied.

"What happened at Keith's?" Aaron asked. "I've been getting some very irate phone calls. I understand you doubled Marc over."

"I did and I regret it, but he did a worse job on Michelle."

"He hit her?" Aaron asked, surprised.

"He did."

"I'm surprised he would do something like that. He can be awful, but it's not like him to do something he can't explain his way out of."

"Well, he sure as hell isn't going to explain his way out of this one," Jason said.

Aaron nodded, thinking. "I hope you're not forgetting what we talked about."

"I'm not forgetting anything, Aaron," Jason replied. "Michelle wants to stay here. She doesn't want to go back to work, back to New York or Paris, or wherever. I think she just wants to be left alone for a while."

Aaron nodded in acknowledgment, but said nothing.

Jason thought for a moment. "This show or whatever it is . . . You know I could probably get the plug pulled on it," Jason said.

"But don't," Aaron replied. "It's too big of a deal to a lot of people. Don't do it. There are other ways."

"What if she just refused to do it?"

"Don't encourage her to walk out, Jason," Aaron warned. "Marc could create a lot of problems for her if she canceled on him, and Rita won't like it, either."

"I'll take any legal flak that results. She needs to be done with those people. She said she can't take it anymore," Jason said.

"You said you wouldn't get involved, Jason, so let it go. Just let it blow over."

Jason looked at Aaron in disbelief. How could he say that?

"Has she said anything about my film?"

Jason clenched his teeth, realizing the film was Aaron's number one concern.

"She says she's looking forward to it," Jason lied, only to pacify Aaron. "She's even beginning to see therapy as something she might benefit from, as opposed to just a trade-off. I talked to her about it. You might want to reconsider an outpatient program."

"And until then?" Aaron asked.

"I think she just needs to be left alone."

Aaron was quiet for a moment, thinking. "Okay, if she wants to stay up with you for a while, that's fine, just don't leave her alone again."

The phone rang and Aaron answered it. He was quiet for a long while then finally spoke. "Send it here now." He hung up the phone. "Amazing. The man is fucking unbelievable."

"Who?" Jason asked.

Aaron turned to him. "That was Marc. He's sending over a dress for Michelle. He said to tell her that if she goes to the concert tonight and if she knows what's good for her, she'll be wearing his dress."

Jason said nothing. He was beyond being able to verbalize his anger. He called his house, but Michelle did not answer.

Jason returned to his house with two suitcases and the large box for Michelle. She hadn't moved from her spot on the couch, but seemed to shrink away from the box when she saw it, as if she already knew what it was. He opened the box. Inside was a red velvet evening dress, a pair of matching shoes, a black cashmere coat, a small clutch, and a jewelry case.

Aaron called. He wanted Jason and Michelle to come to his house early so that they could all attend the concert together. "We'll meet here for cocktails," Aaron said, giving Jason the impression that others would be meeting at Aaron's as well. "I have a limo arranged," he added.

Jason frowned. Who needed a limo in Aspen? Still, he did not object. He was still in a state of disbelief over how everyone could so quickly dismiss what had happened less than a few hours ago.

It was decided. Anything and everything that had to do with Michelle was carefully orchestrated in advance. Everything, right down to her shoes. And if Jason wanted to go with her, then it had been decided for him, too. He could only shake off his mounting frustration. So much for a nice evening together at the theater.

22

The bathroom door was closed, and Jason heard the water running in the sink. He looked down at the red velvet dress, which was neatly laid out across the bed in the room below his own. For some reason, a reason Jason did not ask for, Michelle seemed to avoid the bathroom in his bedroom, choosing instead to shower in another.

The dress was beautiful. He touched the rich fabric, picturing Michelle in the dress. From the box beside the dress, he lifted out a red satin and velvet shoe. He returned the shoe to the box. He opened the jewelry box and fingered the diamond and ruby necklace inside. Try as he might to do otherwise, Jason could only look to the evening ahead with great reluctance. He heard Michelle turn off the water.

Picking up his tuxedo jacket, he left the room. He made his way down the stairs, taking each step slowly, subconsciously, being preoccupied with his thoughts. The foyer was dark, except for the lights on the Christmas tree. He could smell its aroma as he passed it. His descent slowed, until finally, reaching the bottom stair, he sat down. His jacket, hanging off his finger, dangled between his legs.

Seeing the dress on the bed disturbed him. He sighed, trying to shake what he could not. All he could think about was that dress and what it meant. He had this overwhelming feeling he was being sucked into this fight over Michelle, and fighting over her was something he wanted no part of, yet could not seem to avoid. What was going on around him seemed so absurd. He wanted no part of it, yet, by wanting Michelle and wanting to help her, he was finding himself in the middle. The whole situation made Michelle seem like property he had wrongfully taken, and the rightful owners were demanding her return. And the red velvet dress was the package in which she should be returned.

Hanging his jacket on the end of the banister, he looked up at the dome ceiling of the entryway. Every aspect of this house brought back memories of its conception. He could remember exactly what he was thinking, what he was wearing, even what he ate the day he had designed the ceiling. Most of all, he could remember his excitement and anticipation. The process of building this house, his ideas, his dreams, his work, seeing it rise out of the mountaintop as a result of his own mind and his own hands, was a feeling that would never again in his life be matched. This was a once-in-a-lifetime endeavor. It was the ultimate selfish act.

What he seemed to have lost, however, were the ten years between finishing the house and meeting Michelle. The last ten years had been filled with nothing more than work—great work, but work nonetheless.

Jason rubbed his eyes, envisioning the red dress again, thinking that at that very moment, Michelle was slipping into it, and tonight, he would meet Michelle Seko. Maybe then he would be able to fully understand what the fervor was all about. But whom would he see? He didn't know, and he didn't really want to find out for fear of wanting her more than he already did. He laughed at himself. Why her? When he could have anyone, why her?

He had the sinking feeling that soon there would be nothing more, could be nothing more, between them. Did he really care that much? Maybe. But, nonetheless, he had the overwhelming sense that it was coming to an end. This group of people who in the most literal sense defined Michelle's life, would never, Jason knew, let him walk away with her. And Michelle seemed to have neither the strength nor the desire to fight for what Jason thought she should be fighting for. And, he had to admit, he really did not know her well enough to judge what she should do or what she should change. There were so many, many unanswered questions.

Pulling himself to his feet, he put his jacket on and crossed the foyer to the window. He studied his reflection in the glass and adjusted his tie. Looking through the window, through his reflection, he could see the twinkling lights of the town far below. It had started to snow. He looked back at his reflection.

A movement in the window caught his attention. It was Michelle's reflection. Jason turned and looked up at the landing. What he saw took his breath away. At the top of the stairs, coming down toward him, was Michelle Seko. It was not the troubled young woman who had occupied his time and thoughts for the past few days, but the woman whose presence took the world's breath away. It was her in every sense.

Descending his staircase was the most stunning woman in the world. He looked up at her and felt his heart split in two. She smiled as she came toward him, and her smile radiated. She looked exquisite in the red dress. With each step, her slender legs were exposed, looking long and elegant in the red shoes. Her blonde hair was neatly twisted at the back of her head. Her eyes were darkened by her makeup; her lips were painted a deep, rich red to match the dress; and the bruise on her cheek was invisible.

Jason watched every step she took, taking her in as she drew nearer. And when she was close enough to touch, he could feel the warmth radiating from her without touching her.

"Well?" she asked. "What do you think?"

He could only smile at her, and, when he realized his smile was a sad one, he knew he loved her. Regretfully, it was true.

She touched his cheek and he took her hand and pressed it to his lips.

23

Michelle looked anxiously out of the window as the limousine pulled to the curb. A half-dozen photographers stepped forward in anticipation, as did the group of people gathered on the sidewalk. The concert was a celebrity event, partially due to Marc Montori's much-anticipated fashion show. Still almost two weeks away, the town was gearing up—more people, more celebrities, more celebrations. The concert was one more stop on the road to New Year's Eve. Aspen was like this. Every year, from Thanksgiving Day to New Year's Day, it reaffirmed its decadence.

Michelle gave Jason a tense smile, not for her sake, but for his. She was accustomed to this, although, on several occasions, she had learned the hard way that the paparazzi could be dangerous. But she was not sure how Jason would react. She felt guilty, as if she were subjecting him to something she knew he would want no part of, if given the choice. She felt like a child playing a mean trick on a friend, feeling guilty about it and sorry for her friend, but doing it anyway.

Aaron patted Jason on the back. It was a not a reassuring gesture, but rather, a cue for Jason to get out of the car. He did.

It would not have mattered if it were one camera or one hundred; Jason was unprepared for the explosion of light in his eyes. The momentary blinding effect sent a flash of panic through him, and he instinctively raised his arm so he could see. He turned his back on the pressing crowd and helped Michelle out of the car. The cameras pressed closer, so the security men at the entrance had to move forward to make room for their group to pass.

Michelle maintained her smile, keeping her head up. The flashbulbs exploding frantically in her face seemed not to faze her. She never faltered, not a single step did she take hesitantly. But she had them all fooled, everyone except Jason, because it was he who was holding her hand. This link was her lifeline. He could feel it in her grasp. Her fingers, holding on to his desperately, sent him the message: *No matter what happens, don't let go of me!*

They made it to the door. "I'm sorry," she said, softly, so that no one else would hear her. She said it as if it were her fault.

Did he look that shaken? He smiled at her, trying not to look reluctant, and offered to take her coat to the coatroom.

Aaron, undaunted, was laughing. "Good thing this is Aspen and not LA." He took Hannah's coat and gave it, along with his own, to Jason. Suddenly, the Peters, too, were giving their coats to him. Burdened with an armful of coats and no choice but to check them all, he looked back over his shoulder. Aaron was whisking Michelle away into the crowd.

After taking care of the coats, he smoothed his tuxedo jacket and joined the reception. It was packed, and it was only by the advantage of his height was he was able to navigate through the crowd. Every few steps, someone would say hello, and he would be caught in a conversation he didn't want to be a part of. It was the same conversation over and over again. "So good to see you again. Been skiing? What have you been doing?" Jason would mention his Maui project, which, of course, they had either seen or heard of. Occasionally, out of the corner of his eye, Jason would catch a glimpse of red.

Somehow, he made it to the bar. It was jammed four deep with men in tuxedos, but the bartender, a local friend, saw him and passed him a double cognac over the heads in front of him. Double, for the sake of convenience. Jason appreciated that.

He turned around and saw Michelle. There she was, across the room. Her presence seemed to light the area around her. She radiated, and the glow that emanated from her seemed to fall like a magical aura all around her. It seemed to draw people to her. She was a shining light that everyone wanted to be close to. She was the center—the center of attention, the center of the room, the center of the universe. Jason felt like an insignificant satellite in her outer orbit.

Keith came up and clapped his friend on the back. Jason offered a dry greeting, looking over Keith's shoulder toward where Michelle had been, but he was no longer able to see her.

Keith caught his averted glance and looked behind him. "Too late. She's gone," he said, openly mocking Jason and pushing him to react. "Maybe you need to take a number."

Jason looked at Keith, shaking his head. "Is this the part where I'm supposed to ask what's eating you? You're starting to sound like Catherine."

"Well, maybe that's because the same thing is eating both of us," Keith replied.

"That wouldn't be Michelle, would it?"

Keith let out a dry laugh. "Damn right it is." Keith leaned closer to Jason. "Catherine's problem is that she's jealous. But my problem with Michelle is a little different. My problem is that I know you very well." He pressed his finger into Jason's chest. "You must be really going against your grain to be with her. You'd have to be. I know you, and I know that everything she is is everything you hate. And she's half your age on top that."

Keith took Jason's arm and escorted him away from the bar and into a somewhat quieter corner. "Man, I'm so pissed at you, I can't even see straight," Keith continued. "What are you doing with her? She's only going to fuck you up. She's going to fly out of here without you—you have to know that." Keith shook his head. "And Catherine—"

"I don't want to hear about Catherine," Jason interrupted.

"Yeah, well, lucky you, because I'm the one that has had to listen to her and Annalise and Marc do nothing but bitch about Michelle Seko," Keith said.

Contempt silenced them, until Keith, shaking his head, turned from Jason and walked away without saying another word. Jason watched him go. He knew what Keith's problem was. He was jealous, too. Jason returned to the bar, surprised, but relieved, to find a vacancy at the far end.

The doors to the main theater had opened and people were starting to file toward the auditorium, even though the concert would not start for another half an hour. He didn't care. He turned his attention to his cognac, although it seemed inappropriate, because cognac was his favorite festive drink and he wasn't feeling very festive at the moment.

"You look like you've lost something in the crowd," the familiar voice said.

He looked at Catherine.

"Mind if I join you?" she asked.

Jason moved over, giving her room. He wondered if she would mention the incident at Keith's. He doubted it and was right. Catherine looked stunning and he told her so.

"Thank you for noticing," she said.

"I always notice," he replied.

"You just don't always say so."

Jason made no reply. He cared for Catherine and had never wanted to hurt her, but always seemed to anyway. All because she loved him. He looked at her in his kind, quiet way that always made her heart ache. She was stunning, with her sleek black hair pulled back tightly, her olive skin and dark, bold eyes. She was beautiful, slender, and agile. How many times had they skied together in the winter and biked in the summer? How many summer nights had they walked in the woods together? How many times had they made love? Catherine saw herself as his equal and as the woman who should be his partner in life. Although he had once loved her deeply and always would feel something for her, he could never find it in himself to fall in love with her the way she wanted him to. God knew he tried. But the truth was, he didn't want a partner. He didn't need one. He probably owed her an explanation he honestly didn't have, at least not the one she wanted to hear.

And now there was Michelle. This was going to be a painful, perhaps even ugly, conversation, he could tell already. Somehow, Catherine would figure age into the equation. Jason looked down at his glass, swirling the cognac around in it.

"I have to be honest with you, Jason," she said, "at your house that night, when I saw her coming down your stairs, I was devastated."

Jason did not reply.

"So, what's she like?" Catherine asked.

Jason looked at Catherine. He felt compassion for her and did not want to hurt her. "You don't want to know what she's like," he replied quietly.

Catherine sighed. "You're right. I don't. I've made up all these horrible things about her in my mind. I feel better thinking it's all true. I've built up this incredibly negative impression of what a spoiled, rich little diva bitch she must be. I don't think I could stand to listen to you tell me how sweet and wonderful she is. I'm sorry, but I just hate the thought of her being with you. She is so young and so beautiful, and I hate her."

Jason looked at Catherine. "It's okay to hate her, Catherine." He was truly starting to understand what Michelle was up against, what she meant when she said she couldn't take the hate and jealousy anymore.

"You know what hurts the most?" Catherine's voice broke slightly. "Listening to all of our friends talk about you like you're some love-sick fool, reliving your youth by getting your brains fucked out by someone half your age."

Jason closed his eyes. Her comment stung. Although he denied it, even to Keith, he cared what his friends thought, and not one person from his tight Aspen circle, except Aaron, who formed opinions so strategically, approved—not that he was necessarily seeking their approval. It wasn't like that at all, or was it? He chose not to defend himself, knowing it was best to say nothing at all. But he suddenly felt like *he* was the unsuspecting victim. He was here by means of circumstance, a whole chain of circumstances, in fact. He knew what the real problem was. Everyone else wanted her. It didn't have anything to do with him.

"So, are you in love with her?" Catherine asked, choosing her words carefully, knowing the difference between loving and being in love was the gap that Jason had never bridged with her.

Jason did not reply. In love with Michelle? He couldn't say aloud that he loved her, wouldn't say he loved her.

"Keith told me to leave it alone," Catherine said, not waiting for an answer. "He said she'll blow over. It that true?"

Again, Jason stayed quiet. Catherine wasn't really looking for answers. She never wanted answers to her questions. She merely posed them to reflect what she was thinking—the answers she had already formulated for herself. He couldn't look at her now, but he wondered what things would be like today if, ten years ago, he had married her. He didn't know. He had to laugh to himself. Catherine was always convinced she could read his mind. She was always sure she knew what he was thinking. Did she know now that he wasn't thinking about Michelle, but about her, and what his life would be like now if he had married her? He didn't think so.

"Jason . . ." She put her hand on his arm. "You have friends here who really care about you—I, for one."

"I know that," he replied sarcastically, not believing her.

It was out of jealousy that his friends—Catherine in particular—said the things they did, and not because they cared about him. He knew damn well that Catherine would love to see him hurt by Michelle, devastated by her, left alone with a broken heart while she flew off back to Europe to resume her bigger-than-life life. Jason knew that might very well happen.

"You look sad, Jason," she said. "Don't get lost in the crowd." She walked away.

Jason flinched. He knew exactly what she meant. He swallowed his cognac, ordering another, thinking about what she had said. One thing about Catherine, she always let him know exactly how she felt. He thought about Michelle. God, was he really a fool? If he was, then why did he feel so sorry for her?

Aaron worked his way across the crowded room toward Jason. He had an uncanny way, Jason thought, of creating coincidence. Aaron slapped him on the back, nodding to the bartender to bring two more drinks.

Why was everyone going for his back tonight, Jason thought, then wondered where Michelle was.

Aaron seemed to read his mind. "She's backstage with the choir. John wanted to introduce her." Aaron leaned into the bar.

Aaron's behavior so far that evening bothered Jason. Hell, everyone's behavior was bothering him.

Aaron pursed his lips. "It's important that everything go smoothly, Jason."

Jason clenched his teeth. He was already tired of Aaron reminding him not to make waves. Not to interfere. Jason just shook his head in disbelief and disgust.

"I can't believe after what happened this afternoon—" Jason said.

Aaron cut him off. "Nothing happened this afternoon." He clapped Jason on the back again. "You keep that in mind." Aaron picked up his glass and turned away into the crowd.

Jason watched him walk away. What had happened to cause Aaron to so completely change his attitude since the other night? Jason suddenly had the suspicion that Aaron's agenda was entirely different than what it outwardly appeared to be. Jason suspected that perhaps Aaron was setting him up—or maybe setting Michelle up.

The lights flickered, cueing people to take their seats. More than anything, Jason wanted to just get up and leave. But fighting it, he finished his drink and started toward the theater doors. He hated sitting so close to the front. He felt like the eyes of the entire town were drilling into the back of his head. He took his seat behind Melissa Garrison.

"Oh, Jason! Hello!" She turned around in her seat, touching his knee.

Hannah and the Peterses took their seats behind Jason just as the lights went dark. The seat beside Jason remained vacant, as was the seat next to Hannah.

The first half of the concert seemed endless to Jason. He sat with his eyes transfixed on the glowing red exit sign to the far left of the theater, wishing he could just get up and walk out. But he stayed where he was. He heard nothing of the concert, only an imaginary clock ticking in his head.

The chorus came to a close. Applause. Lights. Intermission. Jason sighed, relieved. The audience began filing out of the theater. He felt a hand on his shoulder. It was Hannah.

"Do you know where they are?" she asked.

Hannah's question caught him off guard. He hadn't for one second considered that Hannah might not know where her husband was, or Michelle.

She squeezed his shoulder. Her face said it all. *I don't know what's going on, but I'm going to save face. You should do the same.*

Jason wanted to leave, but suddenly he couldn't. He didn't feel like he could walk away from Hannah, couldn't leave her sitting there by herself.

"Hannah, do you want to go get a drink with me?" he asked.

Hannah smiled, obviously relieved. They followed the stream of people out of the theater's auditorium. Jason got their coats and they left together, walking slowly, stride for stride, down the street, where just that afternoon, he and Michelle had walked. He offered her his arm, and she wove her own through it. Hannah, although quiet for the moment, wanted to talk. Jason could see this. And he wanted to hear what she had to say.

She looked at her watch. "Let's go to the Smuggler," she suggested. "The concert will go for at least another hour, and I don't really feel like going back in there yet, do you?"

"No," Jason replied.

"They won't miss us," she said, as if reading his mind. "We can go back before it's over."

They were quiet for another moment, each listening to the other's shoes on the icy sidewalk.

"He's obsessed with her, Jason," Hannah finally said. "You know that, don't you?"

Jason looked at her. "No, I didn't, actually."

"Well, trust me, he is. It's all he thinks about. Being in control of her. And he'll never stop until he is."

"And how do you feel about that?" Jason asked.

Hannah sighed. "We've been married a long time, Jason. Aaron's had his share of affairs over the years. Some of them I knew about—too much about. More than I certainly cared to know. I've pretty much gone through the last ten years assuming that my husband was sleeping with at least one other woman at any given time. I went numb to it after a while, and now I really don't care. But this . . ." She paused. "This is different. I don't think he has affairs anymore because of her."

Jason stopped. "What are you saying? Please don't tell me he's sleeping with her."

Hannah shook her head. "He's not, and I don't think he ever has. But she consumes him. It's worse than if he was sleeping with her."

They continued walking. Hannah put her arm on his, stopping him. "Jason, would you do something for me?" Her voice sounded both tired and desperate.

"Of course," he replied.

"Could you get her out of here for a while?"

"We have a surprise for you this evening," John Garrison said to his audience as the final applause died down. "I've recently had the opportunity to meet a remarkably talented young lady. Many of you know her by her name, and certainly by her face, but she is also a gifted pianist. My students have talked her into closing this evening's performance, and so I'd like you to welcome Miss Michelle Seko."

Michelle stood just beyond the curtain, at the wing of the stage. She stood calmly, her hands crossed at her waist, holding one delicate wrist over the other. She looked out at all the people who could not see her. She took a deep breath. People hovered around her. They would stop close to her, as close as they could get, just to be near her.

She stepped out onto the stage and into the light. She absolutely radiated. Walking past the piano, she went to a single microphone on a stand at the center of the stage, close to the edge, close to the audience. Once again, she crossed her wrists below her waist. She smiled. The theater was absolutely quiet, waiting, and they would wait all night, for her to speak. She thanked them all for coming. She said she hoped they had a nice time and hoped they had enjoyed the presentation. They clapped because they had. She explained she had been asked to close the evening by playing a piano sonata of her choice. She said that, while she had been playing quite a bit over the past few days, she had not really prepared herself to play for an audience, and would they please be gentle in their judgment.

She looked so tiny up on the stage, under the lights, alone, and yet she radiated with the light of the brightest star. Michelle went to the piano. There was a brief pause of absolute silence. Then, when her hands touched the keys and she started to play Mozart's "Piano Sonata no. 11," it was Jason who was the most astounded, because she was playing something that he had never heard her play before. All the hours at his house, at his piano, and never had he heard these notes before.

The last notes rang and faded and there was a brief silence in the theater, and then the approval rose and continued to rise. Michelle nodded and thanked the audience, said good night, wished them a merry Christmas, thanked them again, and walked off the stage.

Long after she was gone, the applause continued. Behind the curtain, heads bowed to her courteously, approvingly. Again, people surrounded her and followed her, just to be close to her.

Jason worked his way down the corridor to the backstage area. The large room was still bustling with people, mostly families of the choir members. He made his way through the crowd, nodding to those he either knew or recognized, not sure where he might find Michelle.

Jason found John Garrison, who greeted him enthusiastically.

"Do you know where Michelle is?" Jason asked.

John looked around. "She was just here. She played wonderfully, didn't she?"

Jason offered a strained smile.

From the corner of his eyes, he saw a glimpse of brilliant red. She was sitting down, out of the way of the many moving bodies. Although people floated in and out of her immediate space, exchanging comments with her that he was still too far away to hear, he could see the look on her face. She was a million miles away. He approached slowly, taking in as much as he could before she saw him. People kept approaching her, stopping to talk to her. She would return to them, respond, then, as they moved on, she faded away again.

She blinked nervously when she saw him. She looked up at him, only briefly, smiling nervously, shakily. Her eyes darted away. Jason noticed everything. Her averted eyes, her hands shaking ever so slightly. The trembling way she breathed. She could hide nothing from him but her reasons.

He sat down beside her, all too aware that people were watching them.

"Wasn't the choir wonderful?" she asked, her voice edgy.

The anxiety in her voice, although soft, convinced Jason something was very wrong. He glanced around, apprehensive that Aaron would appear and pounce on them at any moment. Jason was not sure how to respond to her question. Honestly, he had hated the concert. Now, seeing her like this, he hated it even more. He realized how little about her and her life he actually knew. When she went up on that stage and played something that he, even after all the time she had spent at his house, had never heard before, she became a stranger to him. Up on that stage, she was someone else to him. Someone he did not know.

John Garrison approached, thanking her again. She smiled at him as he left. It was a smile Jason had seen before—the painted eggshell. So beautiful, so colorful, so perfect. But on the inside—nothing.

"I've been looking for you everywhere," she said, trying to sound cheerful, but her voice sounded strained and her eyes looked tired. Her smile faded. "I asked Aaron to find you before the concert. He said he thought you might have left."

Jason clenched his teeth. He had been talking with Aaron right before the concert.

"Is something wrong?" she asked, sounding worried.

He was so fed up with everyone that it was hard not to be irritated with her, as well.

His mood was foul, and he couldn't hide it. "If you don't mind, I would like to leave," he said to her.

His words caught her off guard.

"But why?" she asked, alarmed.

"Because, Michelle, this isn't for me. This whole charade makes me sick." He pushed his chair back and stood up.

Reason begged him not to be so harsh, but he was angry and that made it hard for him to care about what effect his words might have on her.

"Are you leaving right now?" she asked, trying to make sense of what was happening. "What about the Garrisons?"

"Why should I be thinking about them?" he snapped, then immediately wished he hadn't. He stopped himself and apologized to her. "I'm sorry, Michelle, I didn't mean to sound so harsh," he said.

He stood there for a moment just looking at her. He was sick of all the people. He touched her cheek, the one Marc had hit. She had done a good job of covering it up. Like everything else, she was able to put on an amazing front.

"I'm sorry for sounding so angry, but I just can't participate in this."

Michelle's head dropped and she closed her eyes. He realized he had no idea what she was thinking, and the gap grew wider.

She looked up at him again. "Please, can I come with you?" she asked.

"Of course," he replied. "Would be the best thing to happen all night if you did."

Jason got their coats and summoned a cab.

"Why don't you wait and ride back with us," Aaron suggested when he learned they were leaving. "We'll be leaving shortly."

"I've already got a cab waiting," Jason replied coldly. He turned to Michelle, offering her coat. As he helped her put it on, he leaned close to her, whispering so no one would hear. "I'm walking out of here right now. Aaron is not going to stop me. If you let him stop you, I will keep going." He took her hand and started for the door, working his way through the people standing around it. He heard Aaron's voice behind him, calling for Michelle. He never looked back. She never let go of his hand.

Jason ignored the many photographers as he opened the door of the waiting cab for her then eased in next to her. He asked the driver to take him to his house. "What about your car?" Michelle asked.

"I'll get it later," he replied. He had more than one vehicle. "I really don't feel like going back to Aaron's. I've had enough of Aaron."

They rode the rest of the way in silence, watching the heavy snowfall. Another storm. Jason silently hoped the taxi would make it to the top of the mountain.

Michelle followed him into the house and up the stairs to his bedroom, practically running to keep up with him. He started a fire in the fireplace, focusing on fanning the growing flames.

"Jason, are you angry with me?" she finally asked, the desperation in her voice evident to him.

"I'm not angry with you," he replied flatly.

"Then what?"

Jason was silent for a moment. The silence grew heavy and Michelle grew more agitated as she waited for an answer.

"I talked to Aaron tonight," he finally replied. "I didn't like what he was telling me."

"What did he say?"

"He told me to just forget about what happened this afternoon. I didn't like hearing that too much, and I can't help thinking about how I'm going to feel when you're gone."

"But, I never said . . ."

"No, Michelle, I believe you didn't," Jason snapped. "But that's just it. That's what I can't tolerate. You don't make your own decisions. Everyone else makes your decisions for you. You've got all these people telling you where to go and what to do. Aaron could call right now and tell you to be on a plane, and you'd be gone. Just like that." He snapped his fingers in her face then turned his back on her.

Michelle started to back away from him, stepping out of her shoes. As soon as he moved away from the fireplace and away from her, she picked up the red shoes and threw them into the flames then she whirled around to face him.

Her breath came in sharp gasps and her whole body trembled as she shrieked at him. "I'm still here! I'm still here, and you're talking about me like I'm already gone. If you want me to leave, then say so, but I'm here. And nobody told me to be here. I'm here because I want to be. I made my own decision . . . I asked to come with you . . ." She gasped and let out a wail that was pure anguish. "I'm here . . ." She choked on her words. She was sobbing uncontrollably now and couldn't talk.

The shoes began to sputter in the fire, and the smell of burning plastic rose from the flames. Michelle retreated toward the door and ran down the stairs.

Jason leapt forward to rake the smoldering, stinking shoes from the fire. A few seconds later, he heard a door slam far off in the house.

Michelle streaked out into the blizzard and ran barefooted across the courtyard toward the tunnel, her stockings shredding instantly in the icy snow.

Jason raced down through the house and reached the door just as Michelle disappeared into the tunnel. He yelled, but she didn't stop. Grabbing a coat, he raced after her.

In a span of time that represented the culmination of her life, but in reality lasted less than a minute, Michelle ran through three worlds: the present, the one protected by the cobblestone courtyard, where the wind howled overhead but could not reach her and the walls rose high around her, giving the illusion she was being protected when, in fact, she was being held prisoner; the tunnel, where neither life nor light could live, like the underground world she craved, where the only sounds were the moan of the wind at the other end, the beat of her heartbeat in her throat, the short gasps of her breathing, and the faint echo of her flailing footsteps on its walls; and the world beyond the tunnel—a world of unbearable elements and instant death.

Into the blinding black and white world on the other side of the tunnel Michelle ran, as hard and as fast as she could. She ran, fighting the restraints of the wind and snow against her body. The red dress, which was not meant to be worn for running, because no one could run in a dress made by Marc, bound around her legs as if it were Marc himself, shortening her stride until it tore enough to set her legs free. Her bare feet fought with every step to push her out of the snow. She saw only blinding whiteness that was not the snow but her own mind screaming to be free of its darkness.

She followed what was left of the taxi's tire tracks, now barely visible. She ran down the hill with the wind lashing her in the face, into the darkness and the blinding white light. But she didn't feel the vicious whip of the wind, or the ice below the snow that was cutting her feet. She didn't feel that if she stopped for one second she would die, because she never thought of stopping. She wanted only to run through every world, until she had run through them all and left each and every one far behind. She no longer wanted to be a part of this world now, or any in which she had lived before, and so she would run until she reached the next. She would run until she ran out of worlds before she would stop and let one of them kill her.

The taxi's tire tracks were no longer visible, and the swirling billows of snow made it impossible to make out the width of the road. She veered into a drift and the snow filled the folds of the dress that wrapped across her legs, pulling her down. The snowdrift swallowed her up, stopping both time and her travel through it. She tried to pull herself up but the weight of the dress and the wind knocked her down. She tried to breathe but the howling, vicious mountain knocked it back out of her. She didn't know that the high-pitched wail that rang in her ears was her own voice. She pushed through the snow and found solid ground. Staggering under the weight of dress, she was able to stand up out of the drift.

Turning her back to the wind, she saw the large, looming figure coming at her from out of the white darkness. Michelle backed away, but she could no longer run. She didn't know that it was because her feet were frozen and that her body temperature was dropping quickly. She only knew that she couldn't run.

"I'm still here! I'm still here!" she shrieked at him, her voice rising above the sound of the wind.

Jason moved cautiously toward her. Behind her, jutting up out of the snow bank, he could barely see one of his markers. He knew that beyond it was nothing.

"Michelle, please stop!" He held out his arm, yelling above the sound of the wind that could kill them both. He had to get her back in the house. "I'm sorry. That's not what I meant at all, but you have to come back in the house. You'll die out here." He reached out to her and she backed away from him.

Just as she stepped past the marker, Jason leapt forward and grabbed her. Using the heavy coat as a snare, he swallowed her up. She didn't fight him because she had nothing in her to fight with. When he picked her up, he thought instantly that she weighed nothing more than the icy snow that clung to her.

Fighting the storm, he pushed his way back up the hill, backtracking though the worlds she had almost escaped from.

He slammed the door so hard that the house seemed to shake—a house that seemed could never shake. He put her down, but did not let go of her. He held her facing him, holding her by her shoulders, and shook her so hard she could feel the icy snow falling from her hair. He was angry beyond any anger he had ever felt before, and he fully realized it was fueled by fear.

When he yelled at her, his anger seemed to shatter the ice that encased her. "Don't you ever, ever do that again!" He shook her again, his face hard and cold.

She tried to free herself from his grip. "Let go of me!" She felt like she was screaming, but she could barely speak. Her voice trembled because her whole body was trembling violently. "Let go of me. You're hurting me."

Her words cut into him like he never thought he could be cut into. He had promised her he would never hurt her. He let her go. He never thought he'd let her go.

Michelle was freezing. Her lips and hands were deathly blue, her skin ashen. The red dress was soaked and icy, as was her now-matted hair that had come loose from its twist. Her dark eye makeup was streaked down her face. He looked down at her feet, at the stockings that were shredded and icy around her ankles. What he thought at first was water running between her bare toes he quickly realized was mixed with blood.

"Jesus," he muttered, picking her up again. "We've got to get you out of this dress. You're going to freeze to death on me."

"Let go of me," she pleaded. She was crying now, her tears mixing with the melting ice that ran from her hair down her face. "Let go of me," she pleaded again, barely above a whisper.

When she began to shake uncontrollably, Jason's anger quickly faded. With one hand, he was able to pull the dress away from her back, pulling it away from her body so it fell in a slogged heap on the floor. He pulled a blanket off the back of the couch because it was within reach and wrapped it around her. Now even lighter than she was before, he carried her upstairs to his bedroom.

"Michelle, I am never, ever going to let you go."

She looked up at him. He was crying. He said he never cried.

It would take a while for the large Roman bathtub to fill enough to submerge her. While he was waiting for it, he kept her bundled, toweled her hair and massaged her hands, hoping to bring back their color. He pressed a towel to her feet, trying to stop the bleeding from several jagged cuts. The cuts weren't bad and the bleeding eventually stopped.

When the water was about a foot deep and the steam from it filled the bathroom, he coaxed her into it. She reluctantly stepped down into the tub, but then resigned herself and sat down in the very middle. Pulling her knees to her chest, she huddled into a ball, with the water slowly rising up her back. She sat with her back to him, with her head tucked down, her forehead resting on her knees.

He could see every vertebra and every rib in her back, and it sickened him because this, like so many other things, reminded him how vulnerable she was. The water continued to rise, making her appear smaller and smaller, until he shut it off for fear she would disappear. She never moved. He didn't know it was because she couldn't. He wanted to take his clothes off and join her in the water, wanting to hold her close and nurture her back with his strength. But something about the way she sat huddled, motionless, with her back to him, prevented him from doing so.

He went downstairs to the bedroom below his and gathered together her clothes and toiletries she had left lying about when she had dressed earlier that evening. He picked up her small bag and went back upstairs. She hadn't moved. He placed her clothes and belongings on the vanity. He looked at her carefully. Some of her color had returned, most likely because the water was so warm.

"I'm going to go downstairs just for a minute and get you something hot to drink."

She nodded faintly.

He left her again, this time closing the door behind him. As soon as she heard the door click closed, her head popped up and she let out the breath she had been holding. *Please, please don't close the door. Please don't close me in here. Alone.* She arched her neck back, stretching it, but kept her eyes closed so that she would not see the stained glass overhead. She couldn't look at it. It was too close and too real and too much like death. She pushed herself backwards, inch by inch, to the step, then up the step until she was on the edge of the tub. Jason had left a towel on the edge, and she pulled it toward her.

She was warmer now, and the circulation had returned to her hands and feet, which tingled painfully. The cuts on her feet were bleeding again from soaking in the warm water. She pressed the towel to them, until she saw blood on her hands. And when she wiped her hands with the towel, she saw the blood spread on her legs, dripping down them as she tried frantically to rub them clean with the towel, rubbing furiously until she saw herself covered in blood, and the towel covered in blood and the bath from which she emerged filled with blood. She tried to back away from the water, but the oxygen dropped out of her head and the stained-glass dome began spinning wildly above her.

The bronze eagle, cantilevered over the bath, its great wings spanning across it, came alive and came at her, its talons outstretched and reaching for her. She forced herself not to look as she crawled across the carpet, forcing herself toward the vanity. On it she saw her makeup bag and its presence urged her on. She reached up and pulled it to the floor next to her, spilling its contents. Huddling naked over it, she found what she needed, everything she needed, carefully tucked into a pocket in the lining.

She worked quickly and methodically, keeping her head low for fear that raising it would make her dizzy again and draw the attention of the bird that was preying upon her. The needle bit into her skin as she pushed it into the back of her hand. But the rush became ice as she pushed the plunger and expelled life into her dead body. Time stopped. Then, as if the very room was holding its breath, waiting in intense anticipation for the coming storm, her stomach contracted in one violent heave. She pulled herself forward to the toilet, letting it come until her head spun so wildly that her eyesight disappeared into the inner black deaths of her cranium. Her body continued to heave in mechanical repetition, long after there was anything in it to expel. She collapsed back onto the floor, too weak to try to stand.

How long she remained lying on the floor, for minutes or days, she didn't know. Her eyes rolled up toward the stained-glass dome that arched over her head, and it became an inferno crashing down upon her. She groped frantically at the edge of the toilet, trying to pull herself up, to get out before it fell on her. She pulled herself up to the edge of the vanity.

Then her eyes met those in the mirror, and the monster looking back at her leapt forward, lunging at her, letting out a piercing, wailing shriek as it came at her, grimacing and frightening with its matted mass of hair and swollen, welted face. It terrified Michelle, and she fell back, screaming. But it had her and would not let her go. She tried to get away, flailing her arms, fighting its weblike stare. She backed away from the mirror onto the edge of the Roman tub and lost her balance. She fell backward into the clutches of the eagle as it descended upon her, its huge, razor-sharp talons catching her by the back of her head, entangling itself in her hair and digging into her back. She screamed again, struggling frantically to get away from the giant bird that was screaming back at her. With what little strength she had, she pushed at the bird's beating chest and it rocked back on its pedestal.

It happened in a motion so slow that all of time seemed to pass. Absolute silence fell. Then the broad, bronze sculpture teetered backward on its base, like a giant bird lifting itself into a free fall on a wind current, and it rocked back on the edge of the tub, releasing Michelle. It crashed through time and light and sound as it fell backwards into the stained-glass window, exploding in a brilliant, deafening shower of color and glass. As the glass dome became its cage, the eagle wrapped itself in the girders that held the glass in place and took flight down into the depths of darkness.

The force of nature that so delicate a glass could hold back could only have been imagined, until it was gone and the full rage of the storm consumed the now blown-out turret, attacking it with a viciousness that could carve away the mountain top. Michelle stood frozen and naked, just inches from a jagged edge that could take her down into a thousand feet of blackness. One step and her body could pass through the opening and into emptiness, through which her mind had already passed. Her fingertips twitched, splattering blood from the shards of glass that had showered her. She stood on the edge, with only the wind holding her back, looking out into eternity for the eagle, which was gone.

Jason started back up the stairs just as the powerful draft pushed itself through the house, powerful enough to slam doors and blow ashes up from the fireplaces, carrying with it a moan and clatter of the great house giving in to it, a moan so deep it sounded as if it had been gutted. The draft was so strong, so cold, and so eerie Jason knew it could only be one thing. He threw down the cup of hot tea he was carrying and bolted up the two flights of stairs as fast as he could, taking the steps three and four at a time. At his bedroom door, he had to use his shoulder to force it open. He was barely able to push his way through before the wind sucked it closed again with a force so hard the hinges were wrenched loose. He leaned against the bathroom door and could feel the storm fighting to get in from the other side. He took a deep breath, turned the knob and forced his weight against the door. The gale whipped past the crack he created, blowing the drapes in his bedroom with enough force to rip them from their rods. He managed to get himself through the door, and when it slammed behind him, what was left of the stained-glass dome fell around him like a deadly hailstorm. He ducked, falling back against the door, covering his head with his arms.

She stood on the edge. Her bare feet were covered with blood and glass. The full force of the storm whipped at her, pushing her back away from the edge and pulling her to it at the same time. She turned to face him, and her presence seemed more ghostlike than real. She started to waver and her hands floated up, like the hands of a marionette being pulled by their strings.

The swirling wind around her became a thousand icy faces of her father and the blowing glass continued to shatter in her mind. She was dancing now, floating across the stage, leaping into the air, into nothingness. She was falling now, falling, falling, falling . . .

In one giant, lunging step, Jason catapulted himself forward and caught her tiny, bloodied wrist.

24

Deep, droning voices hovered overhead, buzzing in her mind. She could feel her body rolling on a wave of swirling whiteness. She tried to focus her mind on something tangible, but couldn't. She tried to open her eyes, but her lids were weighted. She could not differentiate between her eyesight and her mind's eye, the fading flatness of the bare white walls, the equally flat white light, and the colorless curtains all blended into nothing.

Jason held her wrist, thin and frail in his hand. She did not stir, even when he pressed her hand to his mouth. He looked at her hand in his. How could this hand, so delicate, master Tchaikovsky? It did not seem possible. He turned her palm down, pressing his lips against the many scratches, some deeper than others, that now marred her once flawless skin. He traced them up her arms to her elbows. In time, they would heal. Time healed most things.

Her only movement was her breathing, and, for hours now, through the night and into the next day, he remained at the side of her bed, watching every breath she took. Never in his life had he looked at someone and prayed, prayed to God, prayed to whomever would listen, for someone to breathe forever. He was frightened for her. He had never known a human being could be so fragile. The faint rise and fall of her chest beneath the sheet consumed him. He found himself holding his own breath until, reassuringly, she took another. Never had life been so clearly defined as now. Never, until now, had he known just how vital to life a breath was. He could hold his own breath, even skip one or two, but not Michelle. Not a single one. He traced his finger down her side, following the outline of her body under the blankets. She was so small. Would he ever get used to that? No, never. She would always seem so small to him. He rested her hand at her side, touching her cheek for the hundredth time. He loved the way her lashes fell on her cheeks, which now were colorless and scratched. He wished they would heal before she woke up, and that she would remember nothing.

He closed his eyes, pressing his fingers to them. He was exhausted, but he couldn't sleep—wouldn't sleep—until he was sure she was going to live. He hated the uncertainty. He hated the waiting. It was like cowering in a cellar, in dark, damp echoing silence, waiting for the storm to come, knowing it would be bad, but wondering just how bad it would be, and then waiting for it to pass. He had had enough of storms.

He hated that he had allowed this to happen to her. He hated her shallow, irregular breathing. He had been warned. Michelle had a history. He should have let that warning bear more weight than he had. The signs were there, only, at the time, he hadn't looked closely enough. The night on the balcony, the exchanges with Annalise, the deep hurt that periodically peeked through from behind her beautiful smile, the sickening submissiveness to Marc, the resignation toward Aaron, the fear of her father. He should have grasped all of these things, pulled them out and uncovered the source. He hadn't and that had been his biggest mistake. He had taken it all too lightly. He could have prevented this.

Aaron's words echoed in his head. "Michelle can be extremely self-destructive, especially when something upsets her or she is faced with a situation she cannot cope with." He could feel it in the pit of his stomach.

And what had he done? Not enough. Not nearly enough. Aaron knew Michelle's situation was delicate and complicated. So why in the hell had he allowed it to continue? This was something that had happened repeatedly; Aaron had said so himself. This was something that should have ended with the first incident, or better, never been allowed to happen in the first place. Why they never took her to the hospital, why she had evaded intervention—it seemed almost cruel that Michelle had been allowed to exist on this level for so long. It made Jason sick.

He thought about the first time he saw her, sitting in his room. She had taken a hold of his heart from that very moment. He thought of the love they made and the talks they had. Rationality fought for space in his head. Logic told him that these few days were not enough time to justify his feelings for Michelle. But they were strong, so strong. What was it about her? Her age? Her beauty? Her celebrity? No. It was none of those things, because he had been able to see past each one. It was that moment when he looked over his balcony and saw her standing below, alone, where someone should not be alone. In that one moment, she had revealed to him that she was a person so tormented by her public life that she sought out private moments to face that torment. Yet there were still so many more unanswered questions.

He did not know how long he had been asleep, perhaps only minutes, but the slight flutter of her hand under his woke him quickly. When he looked at her, she was looking back at him with glassy, vacant eyes.

Her gaze shifted around the room, taking it in in fragments. She thought she was in her own bedroom in New York, but she could not recognize anything. The room's unfamiliarity and the dullness in her head confused her. She looked back at Jason and tried to focus on him, trying to find Sasha in his face. Slowly, her conscious cleared and so, too, did other fragments, and with them, the fear that she had done something terribly wrong. Her fingers twitched. They felt strange. She lifted her hand awkwardly, trying to comprehend the white gauze bandages. Her dull, heavy drowsiness was pierced by fragments of recollection, like a film with frames missing.

Through her hazy memory, she ran. She saw herself running from her father's house, with the sound of shattering glass still falling behind her. She saw herself running through the airport. She saw Sasha leaning over her, speaking in a deep, computerized voice. She saw Rita and Aaron and Annalise, and felt Marc's hand roughly grabbing her thigh, then his fist exploding against her face. She saw glass crashing around her. She saw her mother. Then, like a blowtorch across the bed, the image of her mother became her own.

Jason quickly covered her mouth with his hand, stifling the scream he could see rising from within her. He put his other fingers to his lips, coaxing her to be quiet. Slowly, he removed his hand from her mouth.

She instantly recoiled.

"Michelle." His voice brought her back. "You're in the hospital."

Her eyes darted, panicking.

"Shhh, it's okay. No one knows you're here." That was true. He had brought her in himself, driving her down in the snowcat, in the height of the blizzard. It was the most dangerous thing he had ever done in his life, but he had had no other choice. He had brought her in, bundled in blankets, demanding absolute privacy and confidentiality. Behind closed doors, she had been treated, and behind closed doors, she remained. No one knew she was there.

She tried to talk, but he quieted her. He told her that everything was okay, that she was okay and to rest.

She closed her eyes, but not her mind, which cleared gradually, bringing her more fragmented images—strange, swirling images of ice and glass.

The door opened, and the white-coated doctor entered and took Jason's place by her bed. He introduced himself as Dr. Bernard. He surveyed the array of monitors over her head. Then the doctor's coat quickly blended into the background.

When she opened her eyes again, the room was dark. The fear of being alone instantly grabbed her, and she struggled to sit up. She felt a hand on her shoulder. She heard Jason's voice. She wasn't alone.

The lights came on and Dr. Bernard reappeared. "Michelle, do you know why you are here?" he asked. "Do you remember what you did?"

She was instantly terrified. "No," she whispered.

He told her everything that Jason had been able to recount to him. "Do you remember trying to jump?" he asked.

"No," she whispered again.

The doctor told her how long she had been there. Four days. What day it was, she didn't know. Another gap had opened in her life, another that was dark and deep, another that she had fallen into.

"Who's here?" she asked.

"Just Jason," he replied. Michelle looked past the doctor. Jason was gone.

"Aaron," she muttered.

"Aaron Perlman?" the doctor asked. "Would you like me to call him?"

"No, please don't call him. Don't call anyone," she replied.

"What are you afraid of, Michelle?"

She didn't have an answer for him.

"You know, I'm not inclined to let you leave anytime soon," he said. "I know it's Christmas, but you have pneumonia, Michelle, and your condition warrants that you stay here until I am satisfied that you are out of danger."

Christmas. His words floated heavily through her mind.

The doctor sat down beside her. He looked back and forth between her, the monitors that surrounded her, and the chart in his hand. "It's not just pneumonia that I'm worried about. Actually, compared to the effects of what is obviously long-term drug abuse, your pneumonia isn't bad. Overall, your health is very poor. Your immune system is weak. Your red blood cell count is dangerously low. You have a critical iron deficiency. You're anemic, malnourished, and dangerously underweight, and your blood work shows the beginning signs of liver poisoning. Your nasal cavity is damaged, also from long-term drug use." He looked at her from over the top of his glasses.

Michelle didn't bother to reply.

"I'm not going to discharge you and let you walk out of here as if this never happened," he said. "I understand the need to keep this confidential, but I don't think that is the primary issue here."

"What are you going to do?" she asked.

"The question is, what are *you* going to do?"

Michelle's gaze left the doctor and floated around the room until it found something to fix on—the growing white slit between the beige curtains. *What am I going to do? Anemic . . . malnourished . . . poisoned.* She hated the sound of the words that were used to describe her. They were the slowly accumulating by-products of the life she led, a life she no longer wanted any part of.

"I understand that some things may be beyond your control," the doctor continued, "but your health is your responsibility."

His words activated her. She pushed herself upright. She was sick and tired of things being beyond her control. "What if they come for me?" she asked.

He didn't ask who they were. Based on his conversations with Jason, he assumed he already knew. "Michelle, you are an adult. You don't have to see anyone you don't want to. No one can force their way in here. I don't care who they are. If you are afraid of something or someone, this is a safe place for you to spend some time, and I can promise you privacy and confidentiality."

The word *safe* rang in her ears.

"Michelle, I won't discharge you until your health improves," he said. "And I say that for your own good. Believe me, I have your own best interests in mind."

My own best interests in mind. Michelle silently repeated the phrase.

"I could try to keep you here involuntarily, but I would much prefer that you cooperate," the doctor said. "I think it's the best thing that you could do your yourself."

"What day is today?" she asked.

"December twentieth."

Michelle closed her eyes. The image of Jason's Christmas tree in his foyer came to mind.

"I realize that you don't want to spend Christmas here," he said.

"No, I don't." She looked down at her bandaged hand. "Jason. Where is he?"

"He's in the hall. Would you like me to get him?"

"Please."

The doctor left the room, and Jason reappeared. He sat down next to her, taking her hands.

As soon as their eyes met and she could see the exhaust and concern in his face, she started to cry. "I'm sorry," she said. It was all she could say.

"I know," Jason replied.

"I don't remember wanting to jump. I wouldn't do that." Her voice faltered. "I never meant to . . ." She couldn't talk. Agony filled her, along with a heavy, humiliating guilt.

"I'm not angry with you," Jason said calmly. "But I am angry. None of this should have happened. I don't care about anything that can be replaced, but I do care about you. You cannot be replaced. And because of that, this can never, ever happen again." He touched her face. "You can't take this, and I can't take this."

Michelle closed her eyes. Jason wasn't willing to do what Sasha and everyone else did. Cover for her, pull her through, and then pretend like it never happened. Again and again and again.

"This is hard for me, Michelle," Jason confessed. "I feel like I might be letting you down, but I've realized that I'm not as strong as I thought I was." He closed his eyes, finding it hard to say what he had to say. "I'm sorry, too, but there are things about you that I just cannot accept."

She closed her eyes, hating his words, knowing he was right and hating that, too. And hating the thought of being alone. She looked back up at him. Jason's face was solemn. He looked very, very tired.

"You need to decide what you want to do so that this never happens again," he continued. "I'll do everything I can to help you, but I can't deal with wondering if this might happen again. I cannot tolerate what you do to yourself, and what you allow others to do to you. I love you, Michelle, but I cannot compromise." He pressed her hand to his lips. "I'll do anything in the world for you. Please do this."

Michelle took a deep breath. She knew she would not be leaving the hospital. "They'll come . . ."

"Don't worry about that," he said. "No one can come in here and take you out. It's all taken care of."

She closed her eyes, wanting to sleep. "Just don't let anyone in," she whispered.

When she awoke, she found herself alone in the colorless room, where everything, even the air, seemed muffled. She lay awake, listening only to silence. Loneliness crept in and found her. She started to cry.

25

J ason left the hospital and started across the parking lot. The snowcat was an ominous sight. Even covered in snow as it was, it stood out starkly against the few cars buried under the snow. He contemplated just moving it to the parking lot across the road and getting a lift back to Aaron's to retrieve his Rover. But the cat was obviously his and obvious wherever he left it. It would be better to move it across town and back up to his house now, rather than have to answer questions later. The storm, having moved in the night of the concert, had finally cleared out just before sunrise that morning. After forty-eight hours of heavy snowfall, the town had yet to even begin digging itself out.

Fortunately, the same storm that was partially to blame for Michelle's hospitalization had also bought her a little time. But how much longer would it be before her entourage began demanding to know her whereabouts? More than likely, they were already.

Jason tracked his way across the snow-covered parking lot. Only the driveway from the main road to the emergency room entrance had been cleared of snow so far that morning. The least he could do was clear the rest of the lot before he left. He kicked the snow off the step and pulled himself up into the cab. The engine was cold, but it started with a deep rumble that shattered the surrounding silence. The vibration of the heavy machine shook most of the fresh snow off the body. Relieved to have something deafening ringing in his ears after the endless hours of silence, he pressed it into gear. Working the blade back and forth across the length of the parking lot did Jason some good. He needed to clear his head, and concentrating on the job at hand helped. As he made a last pass around the front of the hospital, he saw Michelle's doctor standing in the lobby window. He waved.

Pulling out onto the main road that would take him across town and up to his house, he again dropped the cat's blade, angling it to take another layer of ice and snow off the road and churning it into the bank of snow along the side. There was a science to clearing snow in this town: the main arteries first, along with the airport, then the residential streets, then the public parking areas. It was amazing how quickly the town's drivers could work. They would have every foot of pavement in Aspen cleared by noon.

He contemplated what to do about Aaron. He had to be told, and the longer Jason waited, the greater the confrontation would be. And, really, there was no reason not to tell him. What he should have done was call him from the hospital, except that doing so would have been like handing the keys to the whole situation over to him. Michelle didn't want any visitors. Aaron would fight that.

He thought about what Hannah had said the night of the concert. *Could you get her out of here for a while?* In a way, he had. But the more he thought about it, the more he resigned to the fact that it would be better to go to Aaron than to have Aaron come looking for her—if he hadn't already. He didn't want a conflict with Aaron. But, also, he didn't want to go home, home to the big, cold, empty castle with its smashed-out turret and kiss of death.

Aaron heard the snowcat and came out of the house to meet him. Jason stopped the cat and watched Aaron move down the driveway through the deep snow toward him. That he knew was Jason's first impression.

Aaron stopped at the end of the driveway as Jason stepped down out of the Snowcat and approached him.

"How long did you think you could keep this from me?" Aaron asked.

Jason stopped. He didn't want a confrontation with Aaron. He did not reply, remaining calmly quiet, as was his way. He looked past Aaron at the two people who had appeared in the front doorway of Aaron's home—a dark-haired woman and an older man. Jason did not recognize them. They remained where they were, studying Jason intently. Jason could feel the tension of a fight over a single, helpless little mouse about to start. He had the feeling that if Michelle were to present herself at that moment, they would attack her out of their own greediness, and a vicious tug-of-war would ensue.

Aaron crossed his arms impatiently. Jason was his friend—a well-respected friend—but friendship was secondary to someone as valuable as Michelle.

"I've not tried to keep anything from you," Jason replied.

"Where's Michelle?" Aaron asked.

Jason looked at him hesitantly. Maybe he didn't know. "Michelle is where she's been for the last four days," Jason replied cautiously.

"Don't play games with me, Jason. Keith said you were talking about going to Montana with her, and I've been trying to reach you ever since the concert."

In his panic to get Michelle to the hospital, Jason had left his cell phone behind. He hadn't realized it until much later, and was silently glad he did. "I never went to Montana," he said.

"Then where? You went somewhere."

"To the hospital," Jason replied with conviction. "That's where I've been, and that's where Michelle is. I just came by to tell you. Figured you would want to know."

"Fuck," Aaron muttered. "What did she do?"

"She didn't do anything," he lied. "She has pneumonia."

"And what brought that on?" Aaron asked.

Jason didn't reply.

"There's a lot you aren't telling me," Aaron said.

"Yes," Jason replied, then nodded up toward the duo standing in Aaron's doorway.

Aaron looked back, suddenly reminded of their presence. "That's another issue," he said.

"Michelle is fine," Jason said. "She just needs to rest for a while." What he really wanted to say was that they were pushing her to her death and that Jason would do anything to keep them away from her.

Aaron grasped Jason's arm. "Look, Jason, I don't know what Michelle has done, but I can certainly give an accurate guess. But I am not the enemy, and so there is no reason why you or she should have any animosity toward me."

Jason's eyes narrowed suspiciously. Aaron had a canny way of turning things around.

Aaron looked back toward the house. "There's been an accident. Michelle needs to see us."

"What kind of accident?" Jason asked.

"Her mother's been killed in an auto accident. She needs to be told."

Jason shook his head. "That's the last thing Michelle needs to hear right now."

"Is she in that bad of shape?"

Jason didn't answer the question. "She just wants to be left alone."

The dark-haired woman approached them. "I'm Rita Herron," she said. "I'm Michelle's manager. I don't know what you are trying to do with her, but this is not the girl next door you're dealing with. Michelle is very important to us, and I don't know who you are to think that you can hide her away. Michelle is a very important person."

"You make it sound like I'm harboring stolen property," Jason replied.

Rita stiffened. "You can't just go traveling around the country with her," Rita snapped back.

"Hold on," Aaron said. "Jason just came here to tell us that she's in the hospital with pneumonia."

"Well, that's just great!" Rita threw her hands up. She spun and started back up to the house. "I'll get my purse and we'll go get her."

"I don't think so," Jason said.

Rita turned around slowly and gave Jason a look that clearly indicated he had no right whatsoever to tell her what she could or could not do.

"Let me tell you something," Jason said calmly, although he was angry. "Between this show"—he pointed a finger at Rita—"and Marc Montori's abusiveness, which I've witnessed firsthand, and your expectations," he said to Aaron, "you are driving Michelle to her grave. You can't just go get her. She's at the hospital because she needs to be there right now, not when all of you are through with her, if there is anything left of her by then." Jason took a step away. "If you do anything, why don't you talk to her doctor? He's going to tell you the same thing."

Jason turned his back on them, heading back to the snowcat. He had no reason to stay, and he wanted to get back to the hospital and make sure they couldn't talk their way into seeing Michelle.

He climbed up into the cab and looked back at the house. Aaron and Rita had disappeared inside, more than likely planning their own race to the hospital. Jason thought about pushing a bank of snow up against Aaron's garage so he couldn't get out. His own Range Rover was still in the driveway, buried in snow.

The old man who had hung back was now coming toward him. He looked cold.

"Mr. Henrey?" He stopped beside the snowcat and looked up at Jason.

Jason opened the cab door and stepped down in front of the man.

"I'm Alexander Sekovich, Michelle's father. Could I have a word with you?" He offered his hand out to Jason.

It was hard for Jason to hide his surprise. The person this man introduced himself as was the last person Jason expected. When their eyes met, Jason felt instantly judged, but Jason took his hand anyway, thinking of Michelle's own talented hands when he did. There was something about the man that told Jason to be careful, but not defensive. Alexander Sekovich was soft-spoken, yet intense. He wore an air of extreme intelligence. Jason found himself facing a man who was revered as the greatest living composer, a man who was as intense as his daughter, and, perhaps, Jason wondered, just as disturbed, because he instantly saw so many similarities between the man in front of him and Michelle.

Alexander rubbed his chin thoughtfully, looking for a starting point.

He looked steadily at Jason. "Does Michelle talk about me?" he asked.

It was the most unlikely question Jason would have expected. It surprised him.

"No, not really," Jason replied.

"Aaron says you spend a lot of time with her. I've been trying to get in touch with her. Has she told you why she won't contact me?"

"No," Jason replied, not knowing what else to say. The old man's questions seemed odd to him.

"I just want to see my daughter. It's been a long time. I will be here for a while. Maybe if you talked to her . . ." He stopped himself, as if his words pained him. He looked around, trying to divert himself for a moment. "This is my first trip to Aspen. I am sure there are things about this place that remind Michelle of her home, our home," he paused, "not that that would be a reason for her to want to be here."

Jason remained quiet, but he was puzzled by Alexander's last comment. The old man said goodbye and walked away quietly.

Jason returned to the hospital and gave his name to the nurse behind the glass window. She looked up at him then paged Dr. Bernard. Michelle's doctor appeared and opened the double doors to the wing, which were kept locked. He motioned Jason in.

"I've had Michelle moved to another room. She's doing much better. Her fever is down. She seems to be responding well to treatment. Mostly, she's been very quiet." The doctor walked silently down the hall, and Jason followed. "Aaron Perlman called wanting to know more about her condition. He wants me to convince her to see him. And I spoke to a woman by the name of Rita Herron. She seems to think that you've got Michelle here in order to keep her out of some sort of a contractual agreement that she has. I assured her that Michelle's condition justified hospitalization."

Jason grunted in disgust. "They're going to fight their way in here, you know."

Dr. Bernard was undaunted. "She is not the only celebrity here. We're accustomed to maintaining confidentiality. Michelle is what we call an unofficial. It's not uncommon."

The doctor opened the door to Michelle's room. She was sleeping and did not stir. Jason sat down beside her and took her hand. She looked a little better. He hoped she wouldn't wake up, so he wouldn't have to tell her he had seen her father, and so he wouldn't have to keep it from her.

Thinking about his brief encounter with Alexander Sekovich unsettled him. What in the hell was that all about, anyway? It seemed so odd. Experience had taught him to trust his instincts and to be suspicious, and both were telling him that something highly unusual was going on.

Jason shook his head. How in the hell had he wound up in the middle of it? He looked at Michelle. How was it that she was growing physically smaller by the day, yet, at the same time, consuming more and more of him? But he couldn't let her consume all of him. He had other things going on, things he needed to give his attention to. He stayed with her a few more minutes, then left. She never stirred.

26

Michelle looked back and forth between the two doctors, the one in the white coat and the one in the suit. The psychiatrist did everything he could to make Michelle feel comfortable with his presence. He went as far as to take off his jacket and loosen his tie. It didn't occur to her she might be making him nervous. Dr. Bernard introduced him as Dr. Terashima. Michelle wanted to ask him about Japan. She'd been there. Endless possibilities of questions floated through her mind, wafting lightly in her thoughts. But she couldn't concentrate on any one question long enough to ask it, so she remained quiet. She still felt the heavy effects of the sedatives, but, occasionally, her anxiety would punch through.

They had questions, too. The first one? Was she willing to talk about her drug use?

An interesting question, Michelle thought. It was so simple. Could the answer be that simple? "Yes," she said.

"Michelle, do *you* think you have a drug problem?" Dr. Terashima asked.

Michelle smiled at his emphasis on *you*, because it implied that others already thought she did. It was a rhetorical question. "Yes," she replied, thinking she had never actually posed the question to herself.

"And are you interested in solving this problem?"

She sighed. Yes, of course she was interested in solving the problem, but drugs weren't the real problem. Her life was the problem. How could she solve something so overbearing and intangible at the same time? She didn't verbalize this to the doctor, assuming he wouldn't understand. She made it easy on him by just giving him a simple nod. *Who knew where this would lead?*

Another question. Was she interested in committing herself to their program, something her friends felt strongly about?

Michelle looked at Dr. Terashima. "You've been talking to Aaron."

She thought about her conversation with him that first night in Aspen. She wouldn't be surprised if Aaron had called the doctor and told him to expect her.

Dr. Terashima said yes.

Michelle did not resent this. "Okay, yes," she finally said, answering all three questions. "I will commit myself to accepting whatever treatment you think I need, but I will not commit to time here."

"Why is that, Michelle?" Dr. Terashima asked.

Because I am already serving several sentences for other things. Because I cannot stay in a room where the door has no window. I have to be able to see who is coming, and I have to feel like I can leave at any time. I cannot have doors locked behind me.

She wanted a cigarette. Would they let her smoke in here? She doubted it. She thought Dr. Terashima would ask her to clarify herself. He didn't, so she regarded him more carefully. She welcomed the opportunity to talk to someone without having to explain herself. Would he be the person who could understand things she did not entirely understand herself? She watched him make some notes on a yellow legal pad.

"When did you start using heroin?" he asked, changing the subject.

Michelle eyed him carefully. *That was a trick question. When did I start using heroin, or shooting heroin? Those were two distinct questions with very different answers. The first she would never answer. When did I start shooting heroin?* Michelle had to think back, think hard. She remembered the first time vividly. It was recalling the date that was difficult, but it was an important date. "Six months ago," she replied.

"Six months? Is that all?" He made some more notes.

Michelle nodded.

"Who turned you on to it?"

"A friend." She thought about naming Sasha, but decided against it.

"And what did you think the first time you did it?"

Michelle thought back to that day, in her apartment in Paris. Annalise's wedding day. She hadn't been invited. Sasha had. She would not have even known about it had Sasha not mentioned it. And he did so thinking she hadn't wanted to go, not that she didn't know about it. She remembered how hurt she had felt, and how cold and lonely she had felt. She remembered Sasha offering her something to take the pain away. She remembered feeling both frightened of the needle and anxious to have it at the same time. She let Sasha give it to her because she trusted him. She remembered thinking about her father.

"I felt like I had found the answer to life I had been searching for," she said.

More notes, but no questions about her life as Michelle Seko. Maybe he already knew what it was like.

"Do you binge, Michelle?" he asked. "Do you ever close yourself up alone someplace for an extended period of time and do it because that's all you want?"

She hated being alone. "I've only done that once," she replied.

"When was that?"

She tried to think back to the black hole. "I think about a week ago."

"You mean to tell me that you binged for the first time a week ago?"

"No," Michelle said, but not defensively. "That's not what you asked me."

He nodded. "But you've been using regularly for the past six months?" he asked.

Another trick question. Using or shooting? "I use it to get me through any day that I don't think I can get through otherwise. Is that so bad?"

"It is when you almost die," the doctor replied.

Michelle's gaze shifted nervously between the two. She didn't want to die. It wasn't the outcome she sought.

Dr. Terashima contemplated which direction would be the best to work in. He decided that it might be better to start as far back as possible and work to the present.

"So, six months ago—what about before that?"

Michelle shrugged. "Nothing that everyone else wasn't doing," she replied.

Scapegoat.

"But not heroin?"

"No, that, too."

Dr. Terashima took his glasses off and frowned. "But you just said you used for the first time six months ago."

"No, I shot up for the first time six months ago." Michelle crossed her arms. She no longer felt like cooperating.

"Okay, Michelle. You are right. Please tell me the first time."

Michelle just looked at him. Her face remained expressionless. She never let on what her answer would be if she were to answer. Did she dare tell him that she had been snorting it since she was fifteen? Did she dare tell the doctor that it was her father who had got her started, indirectly?

What would the doctor say if she told him that she had been watching her father use heroin since she was a very small child? That, as a small child, she would ask her father what the white powder was, and he would say it was the soul of his creativity? That it was the artist in him? That he told her, under no circumstances, should she ever, ever touch it. And that one day, when she couldn't please him, no matter how hard she tried, even though she practiced and practiced *Pathétique Symphony* until her fingers were numb, she went to his soul of creativity, hoping it would help her?

What if she told him that it did? It helped her find the courage to understand there was a world outside the walls of her existence? It helped her find the courage to seek it. What if she told him that she had been born into it? That she had grown up around it, and when it became not just around her but in her, it simply gave her another perspective on the same life? And when she chose to leave that life and start another, it gave her the courage to do that, as well? It helped her find her way to Paris and back to her mother. And it gave her the ability to move on when her mother no longer wanted her. It moved her through days she could not move herself through.

She sighed. *This doctor wants me to stand up and say, I am a heroin addict. So what if I am? I am also Michelle Seko. I once was Alaina Michelle Sekovich. I was a heroin addict before I was Michelle Seko. They would not believe it was not the other way around. But it is the one thing that has always been with me.*

Michelle closed her eyes. Life without heroin. Why? Without it, she would no longer have the one thing that moved her through life—no matter how many turns she took.

"Michelle?"

Michelle brought herself back to the doctor. "I don't know," she replied. "It's been a long time."

The doctor nodded, suspecting correctly, that there was much more to it than that. But he didn't push her to be more specific.

Michelle picked at a snag on her fingernail. She resisted the urge to tear it, but the urge was stronger and she tore it, wishing immediately that she hadn't.

She looked at the doctor. "So, what happens now that I'm here?" she asked. "Do I sit in this room and take medication every day? Do you stop in and talk to me every day? Ask me how I'm feeling, what I've thought about? Do I sit around and wait passively for the next day? What gets accomplished?"

Dr. Terashima closed his notebook. "What we do is help you understand that what you are doing is hurting you, then we help you realize that you don't need it, and then we help you realize that you are, in fact, better off without it."

Michelle just shook her head. "You don't know what hurts me."

"Then help me understand," he said. "Michelle, you don't have to stay here. You can stay anywhere you want, if that's what it's going to take to get your cooperation. All I ask is that you commit to being open-minded about changing your habits. Freeing yourself from drug addiction means freeing yourself from the reasons you do it. It's nothing more than a substance. It's not bigger than you. All I want to do is help you change what motivates you to do it and what makes you think you need it."

"You're wrong," she said. "It is bigger than me. You think you can separate the source from the substance? You can't. You're talking about unraveling my entire life. Facing tomorrow is hard enough. But going back to yesterday is the one place I never want to go."

"I have a hard time understanding that, Michelle," the psychiatrist said.

"Then I cannot explain my life away," she replied.

Michelle slept most of the day, and it was dark when she finally awoke. She wondered what time it was—something she never did—but was afraid to look for fear that it was some awful hour of the night. She looked at the clock anyway. It was eight o'clock. This upset her, because she still had a long, lonely night ahead of her. She felt like she was going to sink right through the mattress and crash through the floor. Crash. She hated crashing. She felt heavy and sedated. She stared at the ceiling, listening. The room was so quiet it made her ears ring, and she could hear nothing but the ringing in her ears. Her lungs ached when she breathed.

The phone by her bed rang. It startled Michelle so much so that her heart lurched, and when it beat again, it was louder than the second ring; and then it beat so furiously that it was pounding wildly against her chest by the third ring. She was so afraid of the fourth ring that she picked it up, hoping it would be Jason.

"Michelle, it's Alexander." Her father's voice clutched at Michelle's throat like talons. "Michelle, I've been trying to reach you for days. There's been an accident." His voice faltered, but it was still cold and pragmatic. "Your mother. She's been in an accident—an automobile accident."

Michelle closed her eyes, listening to him.

"We need to talk, Michelle," he said. "I'm concerned about you."

Michelle found her voice and interrupted him. "I know about the accident, Papa," she said.

"What do you mean?"

"I mean I was there."

"No, Michelle. You are mistaken. You could not have been there. It was an accident. We need to talk, Michelle . . . please . . ."

Michelle set the receiver down and stared at the phone for a moment, thinking certainly that it would ring again. It didn't. She picked up the receiver and listened for the dial tone, then set it down on the table. She left her bed and went to the window, pulling the drapes back.

Light from the other rooms cast a faint glow out onto the snow, but its reach was not far, so the blackness of the landscape beyond the ring of light was close, and seemed to grow closer as Michelle stared out into it. She gazed both at the window and through it at the same time, imagining the intricate, weblike pattern that breaking glass made when it shattered. She hit the glass lightly with her knuckle, then a little harder, wondering how hard she would have to hit it to make it break, wondering what breaking it with her fist would do to her arm.

She spread her palm against it, then put her face close, steaming it. *Here, Papa, listen to this.* She held an imaginary receiver to her ear so he could hear the shattering glass she heard in her mind. She licked her lip, which was bleeding. *Here, Papa, tell me this is my imagination.*

"Michelle was very distressed last night," Dr. Bernard said, filling Jason in on Michelle's condition when he arrived. "About nine o' clock she came out of her room like it was on fire. She was very agitated. Told the nurse on duty that she wanted to leave right away. It took two nurses to catch her and to calm her down."

"Were you here?" Jason asked.

"No, but I came as soon as I got the call. By the time I got here, she was back in her room, but she was very, very upset." He shook his head. "She's been so quiet and compliant up until now, perhaps because of the fever. Her fever is down now, which could explain her behavior."

"Withdrawal symptoms?" Jason asked.

"I don't think that's what it was." The doctor stopped and turned to Jason. "I know we promised her absolute confidentiality, but she got a phone call last night. The nurse put it through to her room. She had just come on at eight. She hadn't been thoroughly briefed yet on Michelle's circumstances. She put the call through."

"Who was it?" Jason asked.

"The man said he was her father."

"Did she say anything about the phone call?"

"Not anything coherent. I gave her a sedative. She went out pretty fast. She doesn't seem as agitated this morning, but we've still got her on a sedative."

Jason said nothing, but wondered why he wasn't called.

Michelle was, in fact, unusually calm when he entered her room. She even smiled at him.

"You like this room better?" he asked her, sitting down in the chair beside her bed.

"I didn't think it would be like this," she replied. "I pictured myself being locked away in some psycho ward with row after row of little narrow beds and loud linoleum floors and nurses asking lots of questions but not bothering with the answers." She even laughed.

Jason watched her closely, suspiciously. She was jovial. Too jovial. "This place is meant to be comfortable, just for people like you." Jason stopped himself, not meaning to say that, but it was too late.

"People like me." She echoed him, suddenly remorseful, sounding more like herself. "I don't think there is anyone like me, and if there is, I feel sorry for them." She let out a small, sarcastic laugh. "But why do I have to be so different? Why am I always singled out?"

She looked up at the ceiling at the row of identical, repetitive wood slats that stretched across it, then she started rambling. "At the agency in Paris, there is this big poster, it's called the roster. It has pictures of all the girls who are with the agency. Hundreds of faces listed in alphabetical order. Some of the girls change their names so they can be at the top of the roster. My picture isn't even on it, because Rita says I'm different. I don't need to be on the roster. Everyone knows who I am. There is a special conference room at the agency that Rita calls Michelle's room. It has my pictures all over the wall. When clients want to meet me, that's where they go. When clients want to meet any of the other models, she sends them out to their office. I hate going into the agency because the lobby is just packed with girls hoping to get in. They're everywhere, sitting on the floor. Sometimes they sit and wait all day. I never had to go through that. Sometimes I wish I had, and I wish someone had said to me that I was too small to be a model, to go back to wherever I came from, not that that was a place I wanted to be, either . . ." Michelle's voice faded.

Jason took her hand. Her scratches were healing, but slowly. "I understand you got a phone call last night that upset you," he said, hoping to prompt her to talk about it.

Michelle became more distressed at the mention of the phone call.

"Do you want to tell me what it was that upset you?" he asked.

Michelle didn't reply.

It seemed to Jason that she was unable to. "I saw your father yesterday," he said, hoping to elicit a response from her.

But Michelle showed no surprise. She had known all along that it was just a matter of time. She had come to Aspen knowing that it would catch up with her, even here.

She looked at Jason. "So, then you must know about the *accident*," she finally said.

"Yes," he replied cautiously. "And obviously so do you."

"He called me last night," she said flatly.

"And?" Jason asked, not sure now how to read her mood, which was changing from second to second. She again seemed far too passive.

"And nothing," she said.

Jason sighed. *And nothing, hell. And something.* "I wish," he began, a little reluctantly, "that you would tell me this secret you've been carrying around with you."

The heavy silence returned. Jason waited it out.

"What makes you think I have a secret?" she asked, although she already knew the answer, which was obvious.

"I know you're carrying something around with you. I can see it in your face. I also think you'd like to talk about it, and maybe you're not sure how," he said.

"You're right," she replied. "You know you are about everything." She paused then looked at him. "I'll tell you my secret if you'll tell me yours."

Jason laughed. "What makes you think I have a secret?"

Michelle shrugged. "I don't know. Sometimes things don't make sense to me because I don't understand them, but sometimes things don't make sense to me because they just don't seem to add up. I just wonder why you always talk about Montana but it doesn't seem like you've actually spent much time there. You talk as if you miss it, but you never talk about going back. And I wonder why you live alone in places like Hawaii, where I can't picture you being there."

This time, Jason was quiet. Was she serious, or was this just a good effort to get off the subject of herself? Jason almost felt offended, because she was suddenly questioning the many, many stories he had told her. Until now, he thought she had simply taken his stories as just that—stories. She never questioned the more realistic aspects of his life. He had always kept things light, thinking she was not interested in anything else. Whether or not she actually wanted an explanation, he did not know. Until now, he simply thought the deeper details of his life were something she wasn't interested in.

"Those aren't secrets I'm keeping," he finally replied. "I've not kept anything from you. You've just never asked."

More silence.

"Well?" he asked.

Her gaze was so far gone she seemed to forget he was there. There was just that hurt in her eyes; the one that crept out from within and took her breath, the glow of her skin, and her smile away. This concerned Jason.

He took her by her shoulders and made her look at him. "If I said I'd do anything for you, do anything to help you, would you tell me?"

Michelle cleared her throat. "Then can we go for a drive?" she asked.

"Where do you want to go?"

Her gaze drifted out the window, to the view of the mountains.

"There," she said, pointing to them. "I'd like to see those mountains."

"The Maroon Bells," Jason replied, following her gaze to the striking, bell-shaped mountains.

"Can we go there?" She asked.

Jason thought for a moment. Why not? What was keeping them from driving what was no more than ten miles up the road, which would take them right to the base of the Bells.

"All right," he said, "let's go see the Bells."

It took Jason a few minutes to round up enough clothing for her to keep her warm, and he had to borrow a coat from one of the nurses, who objected to Michelle leaving and insisted on calling her doctor.

Dr. Bernard appeared quickly.

"We're going out for a drive," Jason said. "Is there a back way out so we don't have to walk through the lobby? Michelle wants to see the Maroon Bells."

"I don't think that's a good idea," Dr. Bernard said.

"We're just going for a drive," Jason replied.

Dr. Bernard indicated the back way out of the building. Jason wondered why he was actually allowed to just walk out with her without much protest. *Because she's Michelle Seko.*

Michelle stepped outside into the brisk mountain air, taking in as deep a breath as her lungs could hold, even though doing so made them ache. She lifted her arms over her head.

"It feels so good just to be outside," she said, smiling.

The canyon parted before them and the Maroon Bells rose majestically like rough-cut diamonds, the dark, purple-black striated rock contrasting with the whiteness of the snow and the blue sky beyond. It was a short but winding drive up Castle Creek, with the Bells always in view ahead of them. When they reached the top of the canyon, Jason turned into the cul-de-sac.

"This is the end of the road," he said.

The road did, in fact, go right to their base, and the Bells loomed overhead now, the distance separated only by the frozen Maroon Lake.

"The snow never melts on the Bells," Jason said as they got out of the Range Rover. "Even in summer, when everything is green, there is still snow on them."

Jason cleared some of the snow from one of the boulders edging the frozen lake and they sat together on it, looking up at the mountains. The canyon was quiet and they were alone. Michelle sat quietly, bundled between his legs with her knees pulled to her chest, gazing up at the mountain.

"I remember reading something about Yosemite once, in an airline magazine, about what a precious pocket of earth it was," she said. "Have you been there?"

"I have," he replied. "But this is better because it's undisturbed." Jason nudged Michelle. "Okay. We came here for a reason," he said.

Michelle accepted that. "My mother," she began, having difficulty finding a beginning, "never misses a couture show. In the six years that I've been doing the shows in Paris, she's never missed one. Sometimes we don't talk, but she is always there. It was the last show of the year. It's actually a preview show of the upcoming season. All of the top designers were showing, even Marc Montori."

Her voice drifted away, then came back. "Usually, it is a fun show. There are so many people, and I just race from one show to the next, but this show was hard." Michelle had to pause.

She did not say what it was that had made this particular show so difficult, but it was because of Marc's presence in Paris—the one place she went to get away from him.

"My mother—she wasn't there." Her voice faltered, becoming as silent and distant as her thoughts, but then returned. "I thought it was odd. I hadn't seen her all week." Her voice wavered again. "The night before the closing day, she called me. She said she was in Geneva with my father, and that he was very sick and she wanted me there. I told her that tomorrow was the last day of the show, and I could come after that. She got very upset and said I had to come right away."

Michelle looked up at Jason. "It's about three hours from Paris to Geneva by TGV, but it was early, and I told her I could probably catch the ten o'clock train to Geneva and then get a taxi to the house. She told me not to get a taxi. She said to rent a car." Michelle shook her head. "It was so weird. I don't drive. I mean, I *can* drive, I have a driver's license, but I rarely drive. I don't even own a car. So, I did what she said. But I had a bad feeling about it. It was frightening to drive out to my father's house in the dark, and the entire time I'm thinking Mother doesn't go to Geneva anymore."

Michelle stopped talking, and it took her a while to regain her thoughts enough to continue. "I finally got to my father's house, about two o'clock in the morning. It's a big house, and it was very dark and cold outside, but all of the lights were on inside—in the middle of the night. I got out of the car. Something made me look up. I don't know what or why, but, just as I did, my mother crashed through the window on the third floor. She just came crashing through it . . ."

Michelle closed her eyes. She had said it. For days and days, it had eaten her up. Now she had said it.

It took Jason a long, long time to comprehend what she had just said, then to accept it, then to compare it to the fragmented incidents of the past week.

He suddenly realized how much of what she just said made sense, and how it suddenly made other things make sense.

"Where was your father?" he asked.

"He was there," she responded, her voice vacant.

"Where?"

"Looking out the window."

"Which window?"

Michelle's expression went blank. It was at this point that her mind and reality mixed together to form something beyond her control, until she did not know what was real and what was not.

"All the windows," she said faintly, from some faraway place. "He just stood there staring at me. For the longest time, he just stared at me. I'll never forget that look on his face." Her voice faded.

The face Michelle was remembering was the same face, the same look, that had occupied every seat of every theater at every piano recital she had ever performed as a child, and it was the same face that was every face at every show, down every runway she'd ever walked. Not for one single day had she ever been able to totally escape him. It didn't matter that she hadn't spoken to him in seven years.

"So, then what happened?"

Michelle closed her eyes, shaking away the image of her mother's bloodied body falling into an unnatural heap on the cobblestone. "I just got in my car and drove away. I just left. I went back to Geneva and checked into a hotel. I don't really know why; I just did. I didn't want to go back to Paris. I didn't really want to go anywhere. I just stayed in the hotel room for two days, trying to feel something. I didn't feel anything. But every time I closed my eyes, I saw my father's face. I waited for a knock on the door or the phone to ring, thinking I would never be left alone. But no one came looking for me."

Michelle started shivering, and Jason pulled her closer against him, tucking her into his own coat to keep her warm.

"And you never went back to Paris?" he asked.

"No," she said regretfully. "I had already missed the last day of the show. And worse, I missed Marc's second show." Michelle sighed. "Marc was so awful during the first show. There was a big scene. It was so bad that I think everyone assumed I left because of that."

"But at your father's house, did your father actually see you?"

Michelle closed her eyes tightly. "I don't know. I thought he had. I mean . . . he had to have seen the car. Now, I just don't know."

"Michelle, this is serious," Jason said. "You know that. Why is he saying that your mother was killed in an automobile accident? Why would he come here?"

Michelle couldn't breathe. "I don't know!" she shouted, frustrated. "My mother left my father seventeen years ago, and she hadn't been back to that house since."

"When exactly did this happen?"

Michelle tried to think, trying to count the days backwards, but couldn't. There were too many gaps. "I don't know," she said again.

"Aaron told me you disappeared for four days before you came to Aspen. Was it then?" Jason asked.

"Yes."

"And no one knew where you were for those four days, from the time you left the show until when?"

Michelle sighed, trying hard to remember. "I drove to Zurich and got a flight to New York."

"What did your father say to you when he called?" Jason asked.

"He said that there had been accident. That my mother had been killed in an automobile accident."

"And what did you say to him?"

Michelle looked at him. "I told him I knew it wasn't an auto accident."

"What did he say?"

"Nothing. I hung up." Michelle took a deep breath. "I shouldn't have said anything, but I just couldn't stand listening to him lie like that. My mother didn't die in a car accident. I don't know if she jumped or if he pushed her. I don't know, but she didn't die in a car."

Jason tried to put the pieces together. They were fragmented, but they fit. "I suspect that maybe no one knows you were there."

Michelle only nodded.

"Do you think if that were the case that your father would want to keep it that way?"

"I don't know."

"But why would he come all the way to Colorado with this fabricated story?" Jason asked.

Michelle didn't have an answer for him.

"Michelle, we are going to get to the bottom of this." he said, reassuringly.

"Maybe," she replied, but the bottom was something very deep—deeper than no one but she could imagine.

"I can't go back," she suddenly said, more to the mountains than to Jason.

"Back where?" he asked.

She turned to look at him. "I can't go back to the hospital."

This surprised Jason. Not once had she shown any resistance or reluctance to be there. She seemed to have passively accepted being in a place where she was safe and not bothered.

"Why? I thought you didn't mind it there?"

"Because I feel dead there. I sleep and I take their pills that make me feel like nothing."

"Michelle, you've been very ill."

"I met the psychiatrist, Dr. Terashima. He asked me questions that I cannot answer. That I don't want to answer. And I cannot stay there and not answer his questions. He is going to want me to talk about everything that I only want to forget. I cannot go back in time. I cannot go there."

Jason rubbed his face. That wasn't what he wanted to hear. "But I think that you should stay."

"I know you do," she replied. "But when that phone rang and it was my father . . . I can't stay there wondering when the phone is going to ring and who it might be. Or wonder every time the door opens who might come through it."

Jason understood. She had been promised confidentiality, and that was the one thing that had kept her there for this long. But he still thought she needed to be hospitalized.

"Tell me, what you are most afraid of?" he asked.

Michelle looked up at him. "When this comes out, it's just going to turn on me. It will never get better, only worse. And it's just a matter of time. I've known this all along, and it's the waiting for something to happen that I just can't take. And when something does happen, everyone will be waiting in white coats for me to do something." She paused. "And when Aaron and Rita find out the truth, I just want to be as far away as possible."

"Find out about what? You mean about your mother?"

"Yes, if they don't know already."

"What makes you think they will?"

"I don't know. I just do. How can you keep something like that a secret?"

It's easier than you think, Michelle.

He rubbed her shoulders. "Would you just stay at the hospital for a few more days? You won't have to talk to the psychiatrist. Just stay until your health improves."

Regretfully, Michelle agreed to stay a few more days. "What day is today?"

"December twenty-third," he replied.

"So. I'll miss Christmas," she said reluctantly.

"No. I'll stay with you," he said.

Michelle shrugged, but then agreed. "I always miss Christmas." Her voice faded away.

27

When the taxi stopped in the courtyard, Alexander Sekovich wiped the steam from the window and looked up at the massive stone house. How ironic, he thought. So much like his own home. So like Michelle. He paid the driver, who quickly left, leaving him standing alone in the dimly lit courtyard with the bitter mountain wind whistling overhead, bringing billowing mists of snow down into the faint light. He buried his hands deeply in his pockets, remaining where he was because he was not sure where to go. The towering door opened, spilling a yellow light out into the courtyard. Jason appeared and summoned the old man into the house.

Jason escorted Alexander Sekovich into the main room. He offered to take the old man's coat and to make him a drink, but said little else to ease his visitor's apprehensions about being summoned to the big house so late at night.

Alexander had a small wrapped gift in his hand, which he set down on an end table. "Perhaps you could give this to her," he said.

Something about the small package made Jason feel sorry for him. Jason took a seat in one of the chairs by the fire, and motioned Alexander to the chair opposite him. But Alexander chose to remain standing where he was, some distance from Jason, his gaze working its way around the room, taking in the art and artifacts that decorated it.

"I asked you here to talk about Michelle's mother," Jason said.

Alexander nodded in acknowledgment. "Yes, I assumed that."

"Why did you come so far to deliver this news?" Jason asked.

"Because I had no other way to reach her. I tried. I couldn't get through to her."

"I see," Jason replied. That was true.

"Michelle has told me that her mother did not die in an auto accident, as you say she did, but that she either fell or was pushed from a window at your house in Geneva." Jason searched for a reaction from the man, but there was none, only the same elusive gaze that existed permanently on Alexander Sekovich's face.

The old man said nothing.

"The problem," Jason continued, trying to elicit a response from the man, "is that, with Michelle's life being what it is, if a discrepancy of this magnitude were to come out, the publicity and pressure could devastate her." Jason stopped himself, aware of how much he suddenly sounded like Aaron Perlman.

He looked back at Michelle's father, who had worked his way farther across the room from him.

"I'm sure it's no secret to you that Michelle's well-being is a serious issue right now. Something like this could put her over the edge. Michelle says she saw her mother crash through your window. You say she died in a car accident. I'd like to know what really happened."

Alexander Sekovich slowly moved back across the room and finally took the chair opposite Jason. He looked quietly yet intently at Jason for some time, and Jason knew he was being judged. He knew that Alexander was deciding if and why he should answer Jason's inquiry.

"Who else has she said that to?" Alexander asked.

Jason crossed his arms. "Just me."

"That's good," he replied. Then he sat back in the chair and actually seemed to relax. "You must think I do not know my daughter very well," he said.

Jason did not reply, but the old man was correct.

"Has she shown you a picture of her mother?"

"No. She doesn't talk about her mother."

Alexander nodded thoughtfully. "Michelle looks like her mother. Alaina. Michelle was named after her. I was almost fifty when I met Michelle's mother. She was only twenty. Younger than Michelle is now. But's that where any similarity stopped. Alaina always had to be the center of attention, always had to be showered with praise, always wanted to hear how beautiful she was. She was working as a model when I met her, and she thrived on being part of Paris society. I took her away from Paris and her friends. At first, we thought we could be happy living a quiet life in Geneva. But Michelle was born and that changed Alaina. Alaina was too young and too immature to have a child. We had done something she was not yet ready for. And she was jealous of Michelle and my attention toward her. I can honestly say that I loved Michelle more than Alaina as time went on. In fact, I grew to tolerate Alaina for the sake of Michelle. But Alaina could not tolerate that she was no longer the center of my attention. She finally left us. She went back to Paris, back to her place in society that she so missed. But we never divorced, and I continued to support her in the manner to which she had become accustomed. She got whatever she wanted from me, and I got Michelle."

Alexander paused, thinking for a moment, then continued. "As a child, Michelle wanted only to know that she was wanted and loved. She did not need to hear how beautiful she was or how talented or charming she was. She wanted to hear that she was loved. I should have thought more carefully about this, but I was busy with my work, and I dismissed Michelle's anxieties as shyness that she would overcome. I look back on that as being a time when I made some of the gravest mistakes of my life. Michelle was by far the most gifted student I ever had. By the time she was ten, she was playing as well someone who had studied composition for many, many years. I so reveled in her abilities that I forgot that she was just a child and that she was just my child. When I look back now on how hard I pushed her and how much she tried to keep up with my demands, it makes me sick. When she would tell me that she wanted to do things that other little girls did, like go to school and paint and study ballet, all I could feel toward her was disappointment. I look back now and think, how could I have done that to her?"

Another pause. Alexander looked down and smoothed the crease in his trousers, then continued. "I don't think Michelle realizes this, but exactly ten years to the day after Alaina left me, Michelle did the same thing. I'll never forget that day." His voice trailed off. "All she wanted to do was be a ballerina. All I wanted her to do was play the piano. I did some horrible things to her. I actually pushed her so hard that she became physically incapable of playing anymore. I realized that the day she left. I also realized how incredibly strong my frail little girl was to have been able to survive beneath me for so long and then to leave me when she couldn't take it anymore. Shortly after she left, she wrote me a story about her life. It was one of the most profound essays I have ever read."

Jason said nothing, but he wondered what horrible things Alexander Sekovich was talking about. And he wondered what Michelle had written about herself. Jason quickly came to the conclusion that Michelle was far, far from ignorant. She was well aware of the complexities of her life. While she appeared weak and failing, she had actually been able to survive under pressure for far longer than what would be expected of any other individual. It was quickly becoming apparent that Michelle was quite the contrary of what she outwardly appeared to be. Yes, she had reached a threshold, but what she had thus far endured was almost incomprehensible. Her father was making it clear that this had been going on her entire life.

"She went to Paris," Alexander continued. "My little girl, who had never traveled anywhere on her own, got herself all the way to Paris. She went to her mother, because she didn't know anyone else. Alaina called me to tell me that Michelle was there."

He paused because his words pained him. "I never did anything to try to get her to come home. I was so guilt-ridden over the way I had raised her that I was never able to speak to her. And Alaina made sure of that. She also made sure to keep me posted on details of my daughter's life, more out of spite than anything else, I think. I don't know if Michelle ever missed me. If she did, Alaina would never have told me. In a lot of ways, living with her mother had been a good thing for Michelle. She was able to live in a woman's world for the first time in her life. Alaina took her in and showered her with the kind of attention that she herself thrived on. For a while, Michelle seemed to boost Alaina's self-esteem, which, at that time, was starting to falter. She is the one who got Michelle into modeling. She's the one who introduced Michelle to Rita Herron. But then, Michelle started meeting friends of her own," he continued. "She started going to appointments and jobs without her mother. She started traveling without

Alaina. I know all this because Rita Herron called me one day, about a year after Michelle left. She called me because she was frantic about Michelle's safety. She said that Alaina had come into her office and threatened her and threatened to hurt Michelle, all because Rita had told her that Michelle was capable of traveling on her own and didn't need her mother as a chaperone. Rita thought she was doing Alaina a favor, when, in fact, she had actually slammed a door smartly in Alaina's face. They fought over Michelle for a while."

Alexander paused. "Sound familiar to you?" he finally said. "Since the day she was born, people have been fighting over her. And the only person who ever loses is Michelle."

Yes, Jason thought. *It sounds familiar.* Right up to that very moment.

The old man continued. "I had never seriously considered it but, after that, I wondered if Alaina wasn't abusive to Michelle, which is certainly not something I wanted to be right about. Alaina threw Michelle out of her home one day, and Michelle was on her own after that. Rita helped her and has been with Michelle all this time. If it wasn't for Rita, I'd have no knowledge whatsoever about my daughter. Ever since that day she called me, Rita has kept in touch with me over the years."

He paused again. "I don't know what's happened to the years. I have completely lost my Michelle. Yet this media monster Michelle Seko has invaded every corner of the planet. I hate the degree to which she is exploited. I know it's not her; it is something that has happened to her. And Rita has orchestrated the whole thing. I'm not on the same side as Rita and Aaron. I don't want you to think I am."

No. You've got your very own corner in the boxing ring.

"Michelle's mother was a deeply disturbed woman," Alexander said. "Her life was falling apart and she wanted to come back to me. But she wanted things from me that I couldn't give her. I told her no, and she got very upset. I finally told her that I wanted to divorce her and that, in my will, I was leaving everything to Michelle. It was a mistake to tell her that. She called Michelle and convinced her to come to Geneva. She said that if I didn't help her, she would hurt Michelle. She was crazy, but I didn't believe her. I should have." The old man paused.

"I saw Michelle come up the driveway that night. Alaina saw her, too. She was threatening to hurt Michelle just to hurt me. I tried to stop her. I was trying to stop her . . . I didn't push her. She just turned and ran through the window like it wasn't even there."

Alexander left his chair and went to the far side of the room, to the window, touching it as Michelle had so many times. "Everything I did to cover this up, I did to protect Michelle. I tried for days to get in touch with her, and I either couldn't find her or she wouldn't return my calls. Rita did what she could to help me, because she knew something was going on. It was all very difficult for me."

He turned back and returned to Jason. "The only reason I came here was to let her know that no one would ever know the truth. No one but Michelle and I would ever know what really happened at my house that night, and no one would ever know Michelle had been there." He sat down again.

"I'm a lonely old man who lost his only child a long, long time ago. My life ended the day she left. I never would have gotten to know Rita Herron had she not called me that day about her fight with Alaina. All these years, I kept in touch with Rita just to get news about my daughter. Michelle never knew. All these years, Rita played the concerned surrogate parent. It wasn't until I got here that I figured out Rita, even though she took it upon herself to keep me informed about Michelle, would have never done a single thing to help me get my daughter back, because it would mean losing her biggest asset."

Jason nodded in agreement. How alike Rita and Aaron were, even though they stood at opposing ends of Michelle. On the outside, they seemed genuinely concerned for Michelle, and in reality, they were, but the greed that was at the root of their motivation was beyond definition.

"There is nothing about my life that I need to protect," Alexander said. "The only reason I staged the auto accident was to protect Michelle. It's a closed case. The police never questioned the incident. By the time it hit the newspapers, I had already buried her. Only the French publications raised any questions, because Michelle had disappeared at the exact same time. I made some statements to the press, assuring them that Michelle had not been involved in the accident. Rita confirmed that Michelle was fine and vacationing in Colorado before the next big Marc Montori show. Only you, Michelle, and myself know the truth.

If it stays that way, then that will be the end of it. But that isn't up to you or me. It's up to Michelle."

Jason closed his eyes. Michelle was going to have to make a decision—one that involved her life—not just whether or not to keep a secret. Did Alexander realize how difficult that was going to be for her?

Alexander went to Jason's piano, where the small lamp arched over the keys, illuminating them. He fingered the sheet music. He stared at it for a long, long time. Jason watched the color drain from his face. He saw his hand tremble as he picked up a loose page. Tchaikovsky's *Pathétique Symphony* for solo piano.

"She's been playing this?" He turned to Jason, holding out the sheet, where it fluttered in his shaking hand.

"She plays every day she can," Jason replied, not realizing the effect his words would have on the old man. "She's been working particularly hard on that piece. I say she's perfected it, but she says she never will."

The old man collapsed on the piano's bench. The life seemed to drain from him as he crossed his arms on the top of the piano, as Michelle once had. He looked up at the music, fingering the page again.

"This piece was the reason she left me," he said, barely above a whisper.

28

nnalise shifted her weight impatiently, waiting for Dr. Bernard to appear. She caught her reflection in the glass and ran her fingers through her hair. She paced the length of the small lobby while the nurse behind the counter watched her from over the top of her bifocals.

Fuck off, you old bag. Stop staring at me.

Dr. Bernard eventually appeared and introduced himself.

"I'd really like to see Michelle," Annalise said.

"I'm sorry, but she's not accepting visitors."

Annalise let out an impatient breath. She wasn't accustomed to being denied anything, but she tried to remain somewhat cordial. "Please, if you could just tell her I'm here and ask her if she will see me. I just want to talk to her. If she says no, then fine, I'll leave. But if you would just ask her."

"Do you understand that she is not in any condition to be upset by anything or anyone?"

Annalise let out another impatient breath. "Dr. Bernard, I've known Michelle for six years. She's always been that way. Please, if you would just ask her to see me."

"I will ask her, but I don't think she will agree." He turned his back on Annalise and disappeared through the double doors. The nurse at the counter continued to study Annalise.

A few minutes later, Dr. Bernard reappeared. He held the door open, indicating that Annalise should follow him. They walked silently down the hall, having nothing to say to one another.

He stopped in front of Michelle's door. "If you say anything to upset her, I'll have you immediately escorted from the premises." He opened the door and Annalise stepped past him and into the room. Dr. Bernard pushed the stopper under the door so that it would stay open.

Michelle was sitting up in her bed, with her pillows propped against her back and her blankets pulled up around her. She had been reading a book, but marked the page and set it aside when Annalise entered. Michelle looked up at the woman who was once her best friend, but now was someone she no longer knew.

Annalise stopped mid-stride when she saw the battered, frail Michelle in the bed, with the many lacerations that, although healing, were still apparent. She retreated a step, and her hand went first to her chest, then to her mouth.

"Michelle . . . I had no idea." She gasped. "I was told you had pneumonia."

"I did have pneumonia," Michelle replied. "I am better now."

Annalise took her coat off and laid it across the foot of the bed. She sat down in the chair beside Michelle and tried not to look too hard at the cuts and scratches on Michelle's face and arms, but Michelle noticed anyway.

"I know they're quite bad," Michelle said.

"I hope they don't scar you," Annalise replied.

"They will."

Annalise sighed and ran her hands through her hair again. She pulled a pack of cigarettes from her coat pocket. She offered one to Michelle, who declined.

"Can't smoke in here," Michelle said. "Can't smoke anywhere around here. It's impossible, so I quit."

Annalise regarded her carefully. "*You* . . . quit?" she said suspiciously.

Michelle nodded. "I didn't have much of a choice."

"Are they giving you good drugs?"

Michelle smiled. "They are giving me lots of drugs," she replied. "Can't necessarily say they are very exciting, though."

Annalise regarded her for a moment then spoke. Her tone was earnest. "Michelle, I came to tell you I was sorry to hear about your mother. I know you had a hard time with her, but . . ."

"She was still my mother," Michelle said.

"Yes, she was still your mother." Annalise looked at Michelle. "If I had known, I would have gone to her funeral."

"I don't think she had a funeral," Michelle replied.

"She should have had a big funeral," Annalise said. "She would have wanted a big funeral."

Michelle smiled, but it was a sad smile. "Yes, she would have."

Annalise also smiled, just as sadly, because they were thinking the same thing. "I loved your mother. She was so glamorous. Crazy, but so glamorous."

Michelle laughed. "She was both, you are right."

"I thought about what her funeral should have been like," Annalise said. "It should have been a spectacular event, with all of Paris turning out for it, all wearing fancy black dresses and heavy veils and dark sunglasses. It would have been so terribly sad and so terribly fashionable at the same time. It would have been on the cover of *Paris Match*."

"She would have liked that," Michelle said quietly.

"Yes, I am sorry about your mother, and I am sorry about other things," Annalise said, then touched one of the many scratches on Michelle's hand. "Most of all, I am sorry about Marc. He's been horrible to you, and I was so angry with you that I was glad someone was hurting you."

"But why?" Michelle asked.

Annalise looked at Michelle. She looked closely, carefully, for a long, long time. She looked until Michelle had to look away.

"You really don't know, do you?" Annalise asked.

Michelle didn't understand.

"Don't you see? Michelle, it was all a game. I was so sick of you being the little princess, of being everyone's little darling. I was jealous. Yes, we were friends, but every time something hurt you, I was glad for it. I wanted to see you hurt. But you always took it. You never complained about anything. You were always so good about everything. I could see you suffering on the inside, but you never let it out. I always thought to myself . . . eventually, she is going to break down. And I waited for that day. And I waited and I waited and I waited. But it never came. And then Marc came along. And I really loved Marc. I loved him because he loved me and hated you. And I reveled at how cruel he could be."

She paused, this time closing her eyes. "Michelle, I honestly just wanted to see you crack." She shook her head. "It went so, so far." She looked up at Michelle again. "But when I heard about your mother, I was afraid that her death would be the thing that would finally do you in. And that frightened me." Annalise bowed her head. "I never wanted it to be like this."

Michelle remained quiet. She was stunned, but didn't show it.

"This whole trip has been awful," Annalise continued. "I didn't realize how cruel Marc could be." She didn't tell Michelle that Marc had laughed when he heard the news of Michelle's mother, that he seemed genuinely happy about the tragedy.

"Michelle, I'm leaving Marc. I'm going back to Paris. When I heard about your mother, it made me really miss Paris." She touched Michelle's hand again. "I don't know how you tolerated him for so long. I don't know how you did it. I don't understand what it is in you that makes you hang on the way you do, but if you think it's because you have to, you are wrong."

Michelle just looked at Annalise. What could she say? It *was* because she thought she had to. And because she never saw a way out.

"When are you leaving?" Michelle asked.

"I'm leaving now. I came by hoping to be able to say goodbye to you."

Annalise's words suddenly made Michelle feel very lonely. "What about the show?" Michelle asked.

Annalise let out an exasperated laugh. "Michelle, I don't care about Marc's show. I'm walking out on him and his show, and I don't care about either one. And you shouldn't either. You need to stop feeling this incredible sense of obligation, because, trust me, Marc does not care about you. He doesn't care about me. The only thing he cares about is his himself."

"What about Rita?" Michelle asked.

"She's in a difficult position. She's running around trying to repair all the damage that has been done, and some things just can't be repaired." Annalise shrugged. "What can she say? I'm leaving my husband. It's really none of her business, even though she tries to make it her business."

Annalise stood up and went to the window. "Could I smoke in here if I opened the window?"

"It doesn't open," Michelle replied.

"You tried?"

Michelle nodded.

"Michelle, I just want to go back to Paris." She looked back at Michelle. "What about you?"

"I'm staying here for a while."

"Here in the hospital?"

Michelle nodded again.

"That's good. And after that?"

"I honestly don't know."

"And what about this man you've been staying with?"

Michelle didn't answer. She couldn't say anything about Jason.

Annalise was quiet for a moment. She stood gazing out the window, then returned to Michelle's bed, this time sitting on the bed beside her. "Has anyone seen you like this?" she asked.

"No."

"That's good," Annalise replied. She picked up Michelle's hand. "I've known you a long time, but I realize now that I never really knew you. I think there is a lot inside you that nobody knows. For the past few days I've thought about nothing but you. I've had to sit and listen to Marc and Rita argue about you, and all I could think was, my God, your mother just died and they don't even care."

Annalise picked up Michelle's other hand and held them together in hers. "Michelle, I know there's a lot I don't understand, and I know I've been really awful to you, and for that I am truly, truly sorry. I don't know what's going on inside you, but, for what it's worth, considering it's coming from me, I want to tell you it's okay to say you've had enough. They're all fighting over you, but they don't care about you. Don't let them make you feel obligated." Annalise sighed. "I'm going back to Paris. I'm walking away from it all. I've had enough, and it's okay to say you've had enough."

Annalise closed her eyes. She wasn't one to cry. "I'm worried about how you are going to deal with your mother," she said. "I am so sorry for every cruel thing I ever said to you. I honestly don't want to see this break you."

She stood up and took her coat. "I've got to go. If you decide to come back to Paris, please come see me, okay?" She bent forward and kissed Michelle's cheek. "Trust me, it really feels good to let go of the bad things."

As Michelle watched her leave, she wondered if she would ever see Annalise again. The emotion rose in her throat and she started to cry uncontrollably.

Dr. Bernard came into her room. "Michelle, is everything okay?"

Michelle tried to wave him away. She just wanted to be alone.

He did leave, but only for a moment then came back with a small syringe in his hand.

"This will make you feel better," he said, taking her hand.

Michelle pulled her hand away. "I don't want to feel better. Please, just leave me alone." She turned away from him, curling herself up in the farthest corner of her bed from him, hoping, if she was quiet enough, that he would just go away.

"Okay, Michelle," he said. "But I'm coming back in a few minutes to check on you."

29

As the Rover made the last turn at the top of the mountain, the house came into view. Michelle immediately noticed the scaffolding erected around one of the third-story turrets. Where the glass dome had been was now a shroud of heavy, black plastic.

A wave of humiliation washed over her. "Please at least let me pay for the repairs," she said.

Jason looked at her. "Now, you know I won't let you do that." He stopped the car for a moment. "Besides, I'm not going to repair it; I plan to completely rebuild it. I've already got it designed in my head. I hope it's going to be something you like. And if there is anything in any room of this house that frightens you, I want you to tell me so I can fix it."

Michelle smiled back at him gratefully. She remembered what he had said about Catherine.

He escorted her into the kitchen and emptied her bag of medications out onto the counter, reading each label and then lining them up.

Michelle was about to sit down on the couch.

"Hold on a second," he said. He walked over to her, wrapped his arms around her, picked her up and buried his face in her hair. He took a deep breath, as if he was trying to breath her entire being into his own body. She could feel him trembling. She heard him sniff and knew he was crying, or trying not to. At that moment, she fully understood how close she had come to dying and how it had affected him.

He took another, steadier breath. "Okay." He sat down on the couch and pulled her onto his lap. "We have to talk about a few things, about how this is going to work. I'm a planner, and I don't like things to go unsaid." He took another deep breath. "Michelle, I will never tell you what to do. I will never try to dictate what you should or shouldn't do. If I do that, then I'm no different than Aaron, or your manager, or your father. But I do want to give you something to think about. I want you to think about today as being the first day of the rest of your life. You're not out of the woods yet, but you are off to a great start. If you ever, ever feel yourself slipping or struggling, I want you to tell me. I want you to be as open and honest as you can. I don't think you can hide anything from me, so I don't want you to even try."

Michelle nodded.

"And I want to give you some advice about life, advice based on how I have chosen to live my life," he said. "I don't think you fully realize that you are in a position to be able to do whatever you want. No one can tell you what to do or force you to do something. You have every form of freedom that you could possibly want. You don't have to work another day for someone else for the rest of your life if you don't want to. There isn't a person on this planet that has any say so on the matter of your personal happiness."

Jason sighed then continued. He put his hand on her chest. "You have this big, beautiful, fragile heart, and you should follow it. Listen to your heart and focus on what feels good to you, what will make you happy. Discover yourself and that will open up to a whole new world for you. You are so young and you have your whole life ahead of you. Let it unfold. It won't happen overnight. It will take weeks, months, years, decades, but if you can learn to live in the moment, you will find your happiness. You can't go back and change the past, so let it go. Make new friends and build new relationships with people who will enrich your life, not the other way around. You don't owe anyone anything. You don't have to fully understand what I am saying right now. Just keep an open mind and listen to your heart."

He kissed her gently on her forehead. "Choose joy, even if you don't know what that is yet, and whether that includes me or not."

Aaron called Jason as soon as he learned that Michelle was no longer at the hospital.

"Do you realize this entire town is holding its breath?" Aaron asked. "The show is five days away, and, right now, it's not even certain if there is going to be any show. Rita Herron is not going to rest until she sees Michelle. I've had the press camped out in front of my house for days now. Hannah got so fed up with the whole thing that she took the kids and went back to Los Angeles. Jason, she can't keep quiet forever. No one but you and Michelle's doctors have seen her in almost two weeks. She's *got* to talk to Rita."

"I'll talk to her," Jason replied. Jason felt a hand on his arm. "Just a minute," he said to Aaron, covering the receiver.

"Talk to me about what?" Michelle asked.

"About the show."

"Is that Rita?"

"No, it's Aaron."

Michelle took the phone. "Hello, Aaron," she said quietly.

Her voice surprised Aaron. "Michelle, are you all right?"

"Yes, yes, I'm fine," she replied softly.

"Michelle, I wish you would speak to Rita. She's so worried about you."

"Perhaps you could all come here," Michelle said.

They filed through the massive wooden door that Jason held open for them, standing back to let them pass. Rita and Alexander followed quietly behind Aaron. They stood gathered in the entryway, waiting nervously for some direction. Only Aaron felt comfortable in the big house, and Jason allowed small gaps in time to fill with uncomfortable silence. The group followed him into the main room. Rita made a preprogrammed comment about the artwork. Jason allowed her to think he had not heard her.

Michelle sat curled into one of the wingback chairs by the fireplace. A heavy quilt was tucked around her, and in her lap she held a large book that Jason had given her to read, *The Art of Architecture*. On the table beside her was a cup of tea and several other books. There were no other chairs near her, which prevented the others from positioning themselves close to her. Only her eyes rose to meet theirs when they came in, but she said nothing.

They offered greetings, but only Rita approached her with the air of a mother who had been wrongly separated from her child and was finally being reunited. She bent over Michelle, embracing her, awkwardly, because Michelle did not return the embrace.

"I've been so worried about you," Rita said.

When she stepped back, she saw the marks on Michelle's face for the first time. Some of the scratches had already healed and the deeper cuts were healing, but were still apparent. When Michelle reached forward to set the book down, Rita noticed the deep gash on her arm that disappeared under her sleeve. Shocked, Rita reached out to take Michelle's wrist, but Michelle eluded her.

"Michelle!" Rita wailed. "What has happened to you?" Rita took a compulsive step backward, just as Annalise had done when she first saw Michelle's injuries.

Michelle remained quiet. Nothing that Rita or Aaron could say would erase the marks on her body. Michelle felt protected by them, because these people would not be so anxious to have her if she were damaged, as she was now. In time, most would heal, as she would. But for now, they shielded her from them. Still, Michelle could see Rita's mind reeling, as it always did, trying to devise a way around this, trying to find a way to keep her on track. Clearly, she was unable to come up with an instant solution, because she asked Michelle for one.

"Michelle, you need to come to some decision about the show. It's too close to have all these uncertainties. You can't hold everyone up like this."

Michelle looked up at her. "I can't do the show," she said softly.

"What do you mean, you can't?" Rita asked in disbelief.

"I mean I won't," Michelle replied.

Rita moved closer to Michelle, nearly bending over her. "Michelle, please don't do this. Please, I can understand you not wanting to do it, but there are so many people who want to see you. We could change the program for you. Whatever you want, just don't cancel. Please don't let us down like this."

Us? Michelle could feel Rita breathing on her. She couldn't move away from Rita, so she simply closed her eyes.

"But you don't understand," Michelle replied. "I just can't do it anymore. There's nothing more to say," she said quietly.

Another wail rose from Rita. Michelle had obligations to meet and contracts to fulfill. When Michelle did not respond, Rita turned to Aaron, looking for an ally. But Aaron remained quiet, thinking that Michelle's decision would be to his advantage.

"I can't believe you would just throw everything away like this," Rita cried. "And I'm not going to let you do it. You have too much to lose."

Michelle only gazed at her calmly. *I have nothing to lose.*

Jason watched them, not so intently that they would notice, but he was keenly tuned in to what was transpiring. They all wanted something from her and had placed themselves in the room according to how great and immediate their stake was in her. Rita had the most at stake and, therefore, remained closest to Michelle. Aaron was patiently quiet. Michelle's obligations to Rita posed a conflict with his plans. He was content to hang back for now.

Jason caught Aaron looking at him. He gave Jason a knowing smile. There was really no pressing reason for Aaron to be there, except that Rita needed him. She needed him to get to Jason, because Jason had become the lifeline to Michelle. It seemed so absurd to both of them. Aaron and Jason were friends in the sense that wealthy, powerful people did not like to fall out of favor with one another. Jason, for all his reserve, was a powerful man. While his connections were not as strong as Aaron's, he had his foot in the door, and if he intended to keep it there, he could. What Michelle decided to do now, with Rita, would most certainly affect what Aaron could do with her in the future. If Rita lost her, then Marc Montori loses her, and that meant two players were out of the game. *Three left*, Jason thought.

Jason looked back over at Michelle, only briefly. He had already spoken his mind to her. He had told her what her father had said. He told her he loved her and would support her, whatever decision she made, but she needed to speak for herself and put an end to this vicious circle. He also told her that he was not a follower. If she elected to continue down this path, he would not follow her.

Jason looked over at the ghost in the corner of the room that was Alexander Sekovich. He was barely present, yet he seemed to cast an eerie shadow that was slowly spreading. He had yet to say anything to Michelle, or she to him. Jason quickly realized that this was not a reuniting of father and daughter. Alexander seemed to have nothing to say to her, and there was nothing on his face that indicated he wanted his moment with his daughter, at least in front of everyone.

Michelle looked around the room at the people who represented everything she had in her life. *Was this it? Was there no one else?* No. She looked at these four people: her father, a man she no longer knew; Aaron, who was genuinely good to her as long as she met his demands; Rita, who saw no difference between life and livelihood; and Jason, whose presence in her life was the newest and the strongest.

Michelle looked back at her father. He sat motionless and stone-faced, his gaze fixed on nothing yet set far away, as she so often did. Seeing him brought back so many dark memories, so many memories that chilled her just with their recollection. She thought about his house in Geneva, with its perpetually dark rooms, vast halls, and cold floors.

She remembered always being barefoot in that house. She rarely went out, so she had little need for shoes. She remembered wanting tap shoes so that she could dance on the stone floors. Her father said no, because the sound would disturb him. She remembered knowing that it was better not to disturb him, that cold feet on the cold floor was better, because he could not hear her walking around. She remembered that he was always playing, through the night, and then through the day and into and through the next night. He played with such intensity and viciousness that he frightened Michelle. She would crouch in the hall, under the stairs, like one of the little sparrows that often got trapped inside the big house. She would stay there, outside his studio, and listen to the echo of the piano in the vast room. She remembered wanting to fly away, but sparrows had no courage. Sometimes, she waited for days, wondering if he would ever stop, knowing that when he did, he would either retreat to his room for several more days or he would call for her and demand that she practiced. Sometimes he would drag her from her bed in the middle of the night and insist that it was time for her literature lesson, and he would make her read to him, sometimes in English, sometimes in French, or Italian, or German, sometimes through the night and into the next morning. Sometimes, he would make her read an entire book to him, and sometimes he would make her read the same passage over and over and over. She remembered how tired she would be, and how she couldn't read fast enough for him. Her entire childhood was spent trying to maintain the pace he demanded.

You kept me prisoner in that house for fifteen years. You never took me out except when you wanted to go out. You drained my entire childhood from me with your insanity and your intensity. You were brilliant. I was brilliant, too. Now you are old and tired, and you've had enough of life. I can see that in your face. You didn't stage the accident to protect me. You've never done anything to protect me. You did it because you cannot tolerate any distractions. You would have staged the accident whether I had been there or not. But whatever happened that night drained you. I can see it in your face. You have no more life left. You have no music left in you.

Annalise's words echoed in her mind. *Michelle, it's okay to say you've had enough.* Jason's words also echoed in her mind. *Choose joy, even if you don't know what that is yet.*

Looking at her father, she realized she wasn't afraid of him anymore. She was afraid of the dark cave full of memories that was her childhood and the equally dark, desperate ache they solicited, but she was not afraid of him. She knew why he was here—because he wanted to make sure *his* secret was safe, not hers. *Well, Papa, I have a lifetime of secrets. What's one more? Is that what you are thinking? Well, I don't agree with you. I don't know that living with this secret won't be harder than facing the consequences of the truth. That's just it—I don't know.*

Michelle looked over at Jason. He had turned away from Aaron and Rita and was standing at the window, looking out at something far away, deep in thought. She watched him, knowing he had never intended to be involved in this. Michelle watched him as he ran his fingers through his hair and then turned away from the group. Without looking at Aaron or Rita or Alexander, he walked out. He had had enough, and had no problem walking away from them.

Michelle closed her eyes. Rita's voice continued to ring in her ears. Rita would never give up or give in. But Annalise's voice was louder. *Michelle, it's okay to say you've had enough.*

The blanket on her lap fell to her feet when she rose. She picked it up and wrapped it around herself. She floated across the room on the silent, bare feet of her childhood, past Rita, past Aaron, past her father, and past the vacant spot where Jason had stood moments ago. She opened the door and went out onto the balcony.

The lamps were lit to ward off the cold. There was no wind. The sun was setting on the snow-covered mountains. Far off, the pinks and oranges of the sky washed the rugged peaks with their colors. She had never seen colors so brilliant and overwhelming yet calming at the same time. The time of day made the town below look far, far away. It was barely visible in its pocket of space and time between the still light of sunset and the not-yet-dark of dusk.

Michelle, it's okay to say you've had enough. Choose joy, even if you don't know what that is yet.

She looked down over the heavy stone railing to the sheer, snow-covered mountainside. It was dark enough now that the mountain seemed to disappear down into the darkness. Its depth was such that there was no end to it. She looked up at the sky, now clinging to the very last wisps of color, fading to black. Should she face the truth and try to live with the consequences, or would the ugly secrets of her life remain secret and die with her? *Where is the truth? In the future?* But how could she have a future without a past? She didn't know, yet. She might never have a future that was entirely free of her past. Maybe, in time, she would learn to live with that.

Michelle, it's okay to say you've had enough.

She heard a noise overhead her and looked up. Jason appeared on the balcony above her, just as he had that first night she met him. He noticed her below him, smiled softly at her, and brushed a bit of snow off the railing down onto her. She smiled back as the light dusting of snow fell on her face.

Choose joy, even if you don't know that that means yet.

She thought about the people in the room behind her.

Papa, you never asked what I wanted. I was a good girl and I did everything you asked. Rita, I became the person you wanted me to be. Aaron, you have no idea how out-of-reach your demands seem to me. Your first film almost killed me. I know that, because it was the first time I ever felt so close to death. I don't know how I ever did it, but I will never be able to find the courage or the energy to do it again, especially to become a woman who is already dead. Jason, you had pity for me, and I think that is what finally broke through to me. You shared your life with me, and now I love this place the way I loved the picture books I looked through when I was young and the way I loved the view of a quaint town from the window of a train as it passed by. You have given me the answer to "what if" and helped me arrive at "someday." Papa, all I ever wanted was to be like other little girls. I wanted my feet in the air and the sun on my face and I wanted to fly. Yes, I wanted to fly.

ACKNOWLEDGMENT:
My Story and My Story

When I read the acknowledgements of other writers whom I admire, I am envious. Most thank with words of sincere gratitude a long list of individuals who participated in one way or another in the process of writing, researching and publishing their books. I don't have such a list. Writing, for me, is a solitary endeavor and a form of escape. I rarely admitted I was writing a novel for fear of having to answer the question, "Really? What's it about?" I've never been comfortable answering that question. Sometimes, I couldn't answer the question because I didn't yet know where a story was taking me.

I started writing *Lifeline to Marionette* while I was going through a difficult and often contentious time in my life. The writing was on the wall for me. My free-spirited, hard-partying days were over. I needed to get my act together and get serious about life. It was time to go back and finish college, get a career, get it together. I did it, but the process was a bit of a shock to my system. I needed an escape, and writing this book was my escape.

The original version of this book was a dark story with an interpretive ending. I was successful in acquiring an agent who believed in the book, but after more than a year of pedaling the manuscript to publishers, *Lifeline to Marionette* went into a drawer. I was *so* close. After that, I moved on. My life took a series of interesting turns, and I no longer sought out the form of escape that writing fiction provided.

Then, in 2018, I suffered a near-death experience that took me more than a year to recover from. I referred to the experience as the "Grand Derailment." Fortunately, it served as an opportunity to hit the reset button. I looked at my life from a different perspective and with much more respect for it. I took stock of all the things I had wanted to do and vowed to do them. I learned to say no in order to stay focused on my own path. At the top of the list was getting back to writing fiction. Despite my long and successful career as a journalist and nonfiction writer, I've always wanted to write novels. So, I resurrected *Lifeline to Marionette* and rewrote it, mainly giving it a more hopeful ending.

I have three new novels in progress: *The Fifth Language*, which is the sequel to *Lifeline to Marionette*, *Two Legacies*, and *Marigold: A ~~Love~~ Ghost Story*.

I do have some people to thank for bringing me and my writing back to life. At the top of the list is my wonderful husband, Barry, and a close circle of friends who were there for me and him when we needed them. You are my family.

This story is set in Aspen, Colorado. I lived there for a short period of time when I was in my twenties, and it made a lifelong, indelible impression on me. It is a truly magical place. In this story, it serves as a safe haven for my character, which she needs.

There are two characters in *Lifeline to Marionette* who were inspired by actual people in my life. I won't call them out here. They know who they are. The character Michelle Seko was actually inspired by the song "Avalon" by Roxy Music. You can read more about this by visiting my blog page on my website.

JENNIFER WAITTE is an award-winning journalist, editor, and author. She is a graduate of California Polytechnic University–San Luis Obispo and holds a bachelor's degree in journalism.

For fifteen years, Waitte worked as a writer and editor for numerous lifestyle, equine, and equestrian sporting magazines. She has won many awards for her writing, editing, and editorial direction.

Waitte is an avid equestrian. She competes in the sport of long-distance horse racing and dressage. She lives in Napa, California, with her husband, Barry. They own Tamber Bey Vineyards, a boutique winery located in Napa Valley.

CPSIA information can be obtained
at www.ICGtesting.com
Printed in the USA
LVHW080416220920
666764LV00017B/1112

9 781734 932201